I0574995

Sanctuary

Book 3 of the Living Myth Saga

Gabriella Creighton

GABRIELLA CREIGHTON

Copyright © 2025 by Gabriella Creighton

https://gabriellacreighton.com

All rights reserved.

No portion of this book may be reproduced in any form without written permission from the publisher or author, except as permitted by U.S. copyright law.

ISBN Information

Print: 979-8-9931454-7-1
eBook: 979-8-9931454-6-4

You can find more books by this author at:

GabriellaCreighton.com

About the Author

Gabriella Creighton is a life long lover of the Fantasy and Science Fiction Genres. She has been fascinated by Dragons and other mythical creatures from a young age and grew up dreaming of being a writer. Inspired by great authors like Jane Yolen, Anne McCaffrey, JRR Tolkien and Phillip Pullman, she loves to take an alternative view of myth and weave her own versions.

Growing up in Rural New York and around many of the real life versions of the locations in this book, as well as having been thrown all over the United States, Gabriella has learned she has only three desires. To write until the nail her coffin shut, to never answer the phone and for a cool glass of Salted Caramel Crowne Royal mixed with Cream Soda and Dr Pepper, which she calls a magic elixir. It helps get the writing done.

You can find more of her works at:
GabriellaCreighton.com

Contents

To Ness,

You helped me see a value in myself.

You helped me find myself again when I got lost.

Eternally thankful.

Mirror of Thorns

CROWLEY

CROWLEY DISLIKED THE WAY silence pretended to be empty. In the Dream it never was. It had seams and pulleys hidden in the hush, little weights that tugged a thought until it drifted where the place wanted. He knew the tricks and he admired them. He admired any stage with good rigging.

He stood in a clearing that wore its wounds like jewelry. Frosted branches formed an open ring, their tips glassy with a light that did not belong to sun or moon. The ground inside that ring was a dish of ash and pale, skeletal roots. At the dish's center, a single green curl had pushed up through the soot, thin as a new vein, color bright enough to insult the ruin around it. The Dream remembered a tree here. It remembered worship and fear, and it remembered the way a girl had changed the ending.

He adjusted his cuff and watched the green. Patience cost nothing to the eyes. It cost more to the hand. His hands stayed in his pockets.

The surface at his feet looked wet, but it was only shadow that had learned to act like water. His reflection swam there with a half second delay, as if the Dream wanted to make sure it agreed with the man before it gave him back. He tilted his head. The reflection tilted slower, then caught up. The place was testing him, or entertaining itself. He allowed it the pleasure.

"Still alive," he said. The words did not echo. The Dream did not waste echoes on statements it already knew were true.

He walked the perimeter, slow, counting the breath between each step. Under the ash he could feel the ghost of old roots. They were not dead so much as sleeping with their eyes open. He skimmed a shoe through the gray and revealed a stain like spilled light, a memory of where a larger root had traveled. The stain was not bright. It was memory bright, the way a closed eye sees sun through skin.

Far beyond the frosted branches, the false sky strained like painted silk pulled over a frame. He could smell the suggestion of old fruit, sweetness turned thin by distance. Silence here had a flavor. It tasted like a promise held between teeth.

A hare watched him from the shadow of a black stump. Its ears had grown into thin white leaves, and its eyes were the flat brass of pocket watch faces. When it breathed, the leaves turned. When it blinked, a minute passed. Crowley gave it the kind of nod one gives to stagehands who keep a show from falling apart.

It hopped once and was gone without moving at all.

He crouched and with one bare fingertip traced a circle in the ash. The ash shifted and a ring of eye shapes rolled outward, laughing without sound. Each pupil held a tiny barb, a serif that hooked inward rather than out. The eyes rode the ash like fish under ice and sank again. The circle remained, faint but present, like a pencil line under watercolor.

"The tide will come," he said to the circle. "It always does. A cliff is only costly if you want it fast."

A small wind decided to exist, wandered through the ring of branches, and then forgot itself. The frost did not melt. It never did. It only remembered melting. The Dream loved to wear old events the way actors wear costumes long after a play closes.

He stood and listened. Beneath the clearing, beneath the ash and the roots that were not roots anymore, there came a faint sound, like someone drawing a long nail across glass from a very great distance. It was the sound of a habit trying to return to its path. He smiled without teeth. Habits were loyal creatures. They could be coaxed back to heel with patience and a little sugar.

A second presence joined him. The Dream did not announce her, yet every small hinge in the world turned subtly toward her. Lilith crossed the ash as if the ground had asked her to. She wore night without stars and a braid that should have held them anyway. Bare feet. The ash did not dirty them. Her eyes were the kind that did not blink until you remembered you should.

"You lost the garden," she said. Her voice had the temper of a blade kept oiled for centuries. Not cruel. Not soft. Ready.

"I misplaced it," Crowley said. He did not look up yet. He looked at the ash where the wind, or something like it, had drawn faint whorls. "Doors are very fashionable this season. The Dreamer opened one where I preferred a wall."

"The sapling is not a door." Lilith's gaze went to the green curl. "It is a refusal to be finished. That changes more than you want to admit."

He drew a second circle, smaller and inside the first, then a third. When he touched the center, the ash rose in a tiny spit of sparks that were not fire. They were attention, condensed and then loosened again. "Tides change," he said. "They also measure cliffs. I am good with measurements." He rose, dusted a sleeve that had taken no dust, and finally met her eyes. "I will put a cliff where I need one."

"You want stone," she said. "But your tools are promises."

"Stone is reliable. Promises are obedient." He smiled without showing teeth. "I prefer obedient."

She walked the ring. The frosted branches seemed to bend closer without bending at all. "The Courts are restless," she said. "Summer polishes their manners. Winter sharpens its knives. Dragons hum in old metal. A girl with a voice like a lit match is learning to sing. Do you mean to host a dinner while a war leans on your windows?"

"A good dinner is always held while something outside wants in," Crowley said. "That is part of the charm."

"The old vows will be tested," she said. "Hospitals, temples, hearths. Houses with rules stitched into their beams."

"Rules are not walls," he said. "They are doors that enjoy being asked nicely."

Lilith knelt and pressed two fingers to the ash. When she lifted them, the pads were clean. The ash had refused her. Respect, not fear. "You call it charm. Others call it arrogance."

"Arrogance is what people call accuracy when they dislike the subject," he said. "I am accurate."

He straightened, and the clearing rippled into a corridor of mirrored air. The mirrors did not show him. They showed impressions. A smear of lemon oil on old wood. Chalk lines on a museum floor. A radiator that clicked as it warmed after a long night. Paper dust, the cheap kind that left a film on the tongue. A bell that did not ring so much as learn its pitch and keep it.

"A house that has taught itself to keep its hands clean," he said. "A vow stitched into its bones. No harm within these walls. No violence that keeps its name. Questions on every threshold." The corners of his smile sharpened. "Questions are invitations if you listen closely."

"You want to bend hospitality," Lilith said. Not a question.

"I want to be invited."

"The house invites those who belong."

"Belonging is the easiest story to counterfeit," he said. "I tell stories for a living."

They walked together without moving, the way distance behaves in the Dream. Around them the clearing became a theater in the round. The frost glittered like quiet applause. He spoke with the patient cadence of a man explaining a trick he would never perform for an audience that did not pay in full.

"Hospitality is old because fear is old," Crowley said. "Once upon a time, a traveler knocked and a door opened. The host said, eat, drink, sleep. You are safe while my fire is yours. It was a covenant against the dark. Later, the dark learned to shave and practice its smile. The covenant did not change. It only started to feel proud of itself."

"Pride is not a sin to you," Lilith said.

"Pride is soft," he said. "It bruises. When a house is proud of its peace, it assumes the guests will behave. That is when a host misses the hands that move under the table. I do not need to strike anyone at the table. I only need to ask for the salt at the right time."

"Speak plainly."

"I will dress well. I will speak gently. I will answer every question the doors ask. I will keep every rule they think to mention. Inside the rules, there are gaps. Gaps are where bargains live. I can work in a gap."

"The house is not a fool," Lilith said.

"I never said it was. I said it was proud. Pride looks away when it should check the hinges. Pride assumes its own story is the only one being told."

The sapling shivered. No wind moved. He did not touch it. He was not that sort of villain. He preferred long levers, not broken stems. He let the quiet prolong the moment until the Dream itself grew impatient and delivered a sound: a low, hollow note like a thumb on a drumhead in another room.

"You have always favored levers," Lilith said.

"Levers save effort," he said. "And time is a better currency than blood if you plan to dine long."

"The Courts will not like your dinner."

"The Courts love to be offended," he said. "It gives them something to do with their clothes."

She almost smiled. "You are not the only guest who knows that house. A fox has already found the door and bowed to it. The dog has learned the sound of the bells. A curator who is more than a curator keeps the ledger. You will not be given the good seat."

"I bring my own chair," he said.

He swept a hand through the ash. The circles he had drawn rose in a brief lace and collapsed again. From the gray, a small sigil lifted, an eye with a barbed serif that pointed inward. It looked up at him and down again in the same motion, then slid into the ground as if the earth had swallowed a coin.

"You are laying hooks," she said.

"I am offering hinges," he said. "Hooks are for amateurs."

"Your hinges lock from the wrong side."

"Only if you try to open them without asking," he said, and he meant it. He respected rules. He loved rules. He wrote his own and wore other people's like a borrowed coat, neat and well fitted until the moment he needed to shrug it off.

He tested the air. The museum taste grew closer. Lemon oil. Cold iron. Cloth that had been scrubbed by a careful hand

and dried in a room without sun. He pictured the front steps, shallow and kind to tired feet. He pictured brass that took and kept warmth. He had never been sentimental. He was efficient. He preferred places with routines and people who loved them.

"You are thinking of their routines," Lilith said, reading him as if he were a margin note.

"Routines are songs," he said. "I can harmonize."

"Until the chorus stops and asks who you are."

"I will tell the truth," he said. "I am a guest."

"What do you feed them?"

"Hope," he said. "In small portions. Seasoned well."

She glanced at the sapling again. "The girl who planted that will not starve on hope."

"She will not be asked to," he said. "Others will." He considered the sky, the false blue stretched over the clearing. It gathered itself like a held breath. He had always been good at waiting for breaths to end. "The house is a stage. I do not need to own it. I need only to direct a scene at the right hour."

"The hour when hospitality is tested," she said.

"The hour when it is most proud," he said. "Pride is soft. It bruises."

He took a slow step toward the sapling and stopped before his shadow could reach it. The green was not much yet. It was enough. He imagined hands that were not his, setting soil back in place, pressing gently. He imagined a girl who had learned how to make new paths through old stories. He disliked improvisers. They made good shows costly.

"Choose a side you can live with," Lilith said quietly. "The world is moving again. Do not pretend the motion is yours alone."

"I have chosen my side," he said. "I always do. I am very faithful to me."

He felt the Dream tighten, as if a stage manager had lifted a finger in the wings. Time here did not pass. It cued. A doorway gathered near the edge of the clearing, where the branches framed a rectangle of almost light. The smell of the museum strengthened. Lemon oil. Cold iron. Paper that had lived in boxes long enough to forget its tree.

"Shall we tour your cliff?" Lilith asked. There was humor in it, thin as a drawn wire.

"Not yet," he said. "First, I go to choose the shoreline."

The doorway of almost light peeled itself open. Beyond it waited a corridor that smelled like history handled often and with care. Crowley stepped toward it and paused. He glanced back at the green curl in the ash, the ridiculous insistence of living things.

Lilith watched him. "Grow," she said to the green, as if she were answering a thought he had not voiced. "He hates patience."

He did not rise to that. He only inclined his head, a gesture that could be read as courtesy by anyone who needed to believe it. Then he passed through the light and was gone.

Lilith remained.

The clearing's poise broke a fraction, the way a dancer's smile softens after the final note. She went to one knee beside the sapling. When she breathed on it, the green trembled and held. Roots whispered beneath the ash. She smiled, small and terrible, a kindness that had taken a very long journey to reach her mouth.

"The board remains," she said. "Pieces move. We will see which hand belongs to which."

She stood and walked out through the branches. Her footprints were there and then they were not, as if the ground had chosen not to remember the exact shape of her leaving.

The clearing listened to itself. The silence adjusted its costume, less empty now, more like a room after guests have left and the host stands alone, counting plates. The frost shed a single bead that did not melt and did not fall. Somewhere below, something turned over in its sleep and decided to keep sleeping. A thin thread of sound rose from the ash, not quite a bell. It curled once, settled, and waited, patient in the way seeds are patient.

CHAPTER 1

Door Beneath the Museum

Sia

"The library is my safe harbor since I dare not go into the cafeteria alone, a whale surrounded by starving sharks."

Lisa Fipps, Starfish

THEY LEFT THE FARM at first light because Mariah said mornings make healing easier. Gravel spat under the van's tires and a sheet of mist lay low over the fields. The farmhouse behind them didn't wave. It had already done enough.

Mia sat with her shoulder against Sia's on the back bench,

hood up, eyes on the window. When she tugged at her sleeve, the dog-eared edge of a hymn sheet peeked out and slipped back. Truth sprawled on the floor between their shoes with her chin on Sia's boot, riding each turn with the steady balance of a dog who had decided to keep people upright.

Eric drove like a kid who knows he can be reckless and is choosing not to be. Mariah had a paper map open on her knees even though the dashboard voice knew the route. She ran a finger along the highway line like she was keeping it honest. Marcus took the middle row, knees set to leave the aisle clear, watching mirrors and hedgerows and the angles of barns the way some people track plot twists.

"Remind me," Eric said after a few quiet miles. "How did we get a museum to let us stay there?"

"We didn't talk anyone into anything," Mariah said. "Charles offered. We accepted. It's hospitality."

"Feels like a hack," Eric said.

"It's a promise," she said. "You keep it or you're not who you say you are."

Mia kept her eyes on the glass. "Why would a museum want us?"

"Because we're people," Mariah said, then added, "and because we'll respect the place."

Marcus rolled his right shoulder, like shaking off a memory. "Blackstone's got a decent rep. Helps without a bill tucked under it."

"So a normal person," Eric said.

"In our world," Marcus said, "rare."

Ella pulled one earbud out in the back corner by the window. Sia hadn't realized she'd been listening through music. Ella's eyes were jumpy-tired but tracking everything. "What's the rule on phones inside?" she asked. "Airplane mode or off-off?"

"Off unless staff says otherwise," Mariah said.

"Got it," Ella said, and tucked the earbud away.

Tobias flipped a small notebook closed on the middle-row aisle. The notebook looked inexpensive; the habits didn't. "Check-ins on the hour until we're settled?" he asked.

"Half hour today," Marcus said. "New place."

Truth's tail thumped twice. The second thump landed as the road crested and the highway opened. Two lanes. A ditch. Maples just starting to go yellow. Signs for towns Sia knew only from weather reports and football scores.

She tried to let her body register that they weren't running. They were going toward. Different kind of movement. Cool air slid through the cracked window, smelling like wet leaves and gas and a hint of woodsmoke from somewhere they didn't pass.

"Rules," Marcus said, mostly for himself. "Don't fight in a house that promises safety. Don't lie to a building that listens. Ask before you shape."

"Hold consent like a key," Sia said. The words fit.

Mariah nodded once. "Keep that."

Eric checked the heavy cream card Charles had mailed to the Farm. "American Museum of Magic," he read. "Temporary residence offered. Training space provided. Sanctuary rules apply."

He tucked it back in the dash like the van might steal it.

By the time the city pulled in around them, the sun was higher and the mist had dropped into ditches. They passed a bakery with its door propped open, a barbershop with a striped pole pretending it had never stopped spinning, a thrift store window crowded with lamps arguing about shades. The brakes squeaked at a light and then remembered how to behave.

"Last chance to bail," Eric said to the windshield.

"No one's bailing," Mariah said. Not a pep talk. Just true.

Marcus pointed with two fingers. "There."

The museum sat one block off Main. Square-shouldered brick cleaned without being scrubbed into forgetfulness. A banner for a 1930s stage-magic exhibit hung straight. Ginkgo trees flanked the sidewalk, leaves at the hinge between green and gold. A metal sign by the steps said AMERICAN MUSEUM OF MAGIC in letters that didn't try too hard.

Eric eased to the curb and killed the engine. Quiet slid in and made space for them. Even the traffic down the block sounded like it knew better.

"Ready?" Mariah asked.

Mia pushed her hood back. "Ready." The word beat her hands to it. Brave.

Marcus had already unbuckled. "On you," he told Mariah. Lower, to Sia, "Eyes up. Breathe."

Truth jumped down first when the door slid open. Nails on concrete. Head up. Ears forward. She looked at the steps, then at the group, and wagged once like a nod.

The steps were shallow and kind to tired legs. The brass handles were warm for October. When the door swung in, the museum breathed out lemon oil, paper dust, and a thread of old candle smoke. The entry kept that scent the way a choir keeps a note between songs.

Charles Blackstone stood just inside, one hand on a cane topped with a small compass rose. He wasn't statue tall. He was exactly eye level in a way that made people feel seen, not measured. Charcoal suit with a quiet pattern, white linen cuffs, a pocket square folded simple like habit. His hair was the gray you get when you give time permission. His eyes were clear and steady, lake-water near the shore. Nothing showy about him, which made him the most interesting thing in the room.

"Welcome home," he said. No fluff. The words were solid enough that the tight place behind Sia's ribs loosened one click.

Truth pressed her shoulder into Sia's leg and leaned a little harder than needed, testing the floor under Sia. Three tail wags, then she sat with a soft drum of paws on polished wood.

The lobby was wider than the outside should allow. Tall windows poured pale light into bright and shadow lanes on the floor. Cases held a collapsible silk top hat with tired ribs, brass cups polished by palms that believed in misdirection, a cracked wand signed in purple ink by a vaudeville smile that promised laughs and secrets. Overhead, a mobile of tin charms and small bells turned slowly with no visible help, making small music that never became a full tune.

Charles tapped his cane once, not impatient, more like calling a room to attention. "House rules are simple," he said. "They're also not negotiable. Hospitality is enforced here. Inside the museum, violence doesn't work. We redirect. We escort. We ask before we act." He met each of their eyes. "Say you understand."

"I understand," Sia said. It felt like air after a long dive.

"Yeah," Eric said. "Got it."

Mariah put a hand on Mia's shoulder. "We understand." Mia's shoulders eased half an inch, which for her was a lot.

Ella edged left for a better angle on the exits and the cases. "Which way's the service hall?" she asked.

"This way," Kaelan said from near the fox masks.

Tobias nodded toward Charles's cane, not rude, just checking. "You want us on either side when we move, or you're fine?"

"Fine," Charles said. "You'll have plenty to do."

Only then did Sia really see the woman by the fox masks.

Kaelan Kuzunoha had the kind of presence that made a space look intentional. Red hair fell in loose waves to her shoulders, copper catching the window light. Freckles across her cheeks. Moss-green eyes that read a room without eating it. Small hoop earrings, bracelets that clicked a quiet beat on her wrist. Cream blouse, dark skirt that knew how to move. A small cloth pouch tied with white cord at her belt.

She gave Charles a quick nod that felt like long practice, then nodded to the group. "Welcome," she said, voice warm and clean. "If you need a minute, I've got you."

Eric half-smiled. "Do you take payment plans?"

"For you," she said, "sure."

"Later," Mariah said, and somehow the one word managed to be thanks and a boundary.

They passed photos of county fair tents and velvet parlor tables. In one, a woman in a white dress lifted a mirror, but the glass showed a field of sunflowers where the photographer would have been. Something inside Sia lifted like a bird.

"The public floors are above," Charles said. "The living floors are below. They talk to each other. They don't argue." He stopped at a door painted the same cream as the wall, a small brass placard beside the knob: STAFF. "This door is a door when the house says you belong." His eyes rested on Sia. "You do."

The paint around the knob had the soft shine of lots of hands. Before Sia touched it, the question inside the door found her. Ask before shaping. Hold consent like a key. Do no harm here. If harm shows up, take it outside or change it into something else. The rules had weight, like water when you're swimming under it. Not crushing. Just there.

"May we see the living floors?" she asked the door. It felt strange. It felt right.

The knob warmed under her palm. The seam deepened. Paint turned into the memory of paint. The frame softened into stone and a stairwell appeared like it had always been there and they'd finally remembered where to look. Orbs the size of apples woke along the wall, shining bell-metal blue. Sia could taste the color at the edges of her teeth.

"Okay," Eric said, quiet.

Marcus's mouth moved a few millimeters. His version of a smile. Truth sat at the landing and wagged once, like the house had told her a joke in a language for old buildings and good dogs.

They followed Charles down. The air cooled and picked up clean stone. The lights chimed in patterns that weren't a melody. Signals. Sia listened and the rules came back as harmonics, the same truths from a different angle.

At the first landing, a mural covered the stone. A road ran into a lake that held a still sun at noon. The brushwork caught the instant before glare broke. Kaelan paused, touched the frame with two fingers, and nodded like greeting a neighbor.

"Summer likes people who keep their word," she said. The stairwell seemed to hear her.

The hallway below did not fit inside any normal building. It ran straight, then curved, then admitted straight had just been a story. Doors in different woods faced each other across patient floorboards. Some carried carvings that almost moved if stared at. Some had plain brass numbers. Some drank light and gave it back as a feeling instead of a color. Somewhere distant, a kettle hit the exact note for ready and then stopped.

A cart rolled by, pushed by a woman with sleeves to her elbows and a pencil behind her ear. Stacks of linens. Wrapped soap. A small bowl of hard candy. A ring of keys like a skirt made of tiny doors. She smiled like she had seen every kind of guest. "Welcome," she said. "Keep right until your rooms find you."

"Rooms find us?" Eric murmured.

"Rooms listen," Charles said. "So do halls. Staring at a door makes it shy."

They walked, the floor wearing the faint polish of years of footsteps. A door with deep oak grain opened for Mariah and Mia. The air that slipped out smelled like cedar and ironed sheets. Another door carved with a flowing hymn in a language that tugged the back of Sia's teeth opened for Marcus and Eric. Truth trotted in with them, turned a circle, and found a rectangle of sun a basement had no business having. She sighed into it like she had been saving that breath.

"Don't name the sun," Kaelan told Sia, catching the look. "It likes being a surprise here."

Tobias's door opened on a simple room near the stair turn. He pressed a hinge once and listened. "Good," he said to the air, like it was normal. "Thanks."

Ella reached for a door that stayed shut. She stopped, took a breath. "May I?" The latch warmed, then clicked. "Okay," she said, a little impressed with herself, and slipped inside.

They stopped at a door marked with a small mirror set in brass. Sia's face didn't look back. The glass showed paper grain and an ink line curling like a fern. The line trembled once. Her sketchbook was zipped inside her backpack. The tiny movement still felt like hello, a thread running from the mirror into her palm and up her wrist.

"This one is yours," Charles said, voice softer without being hushed. "Quiet, not empty."

"Thank you," Sia said. Her fingers shook on the strap. She was more tired than she'd admitted.

Inside, the room smelled like cedar and paper. An old oak desk carried a circular candle scar. Bare shelves that read like invitation. A narrow window showed a small square of lawn that shouldn't be there, neat as a painting in the wrong gallery. A ceramic bowl held smooth gray stones. When Sia set her backpack down, the sketchbook thumped and then settled like a small animal changing positions.

She cracked the window. Air slid in with the sound of leaves. Under it, a bell rang once. The tone didn't fade. It sat down somewhere in the desk wood like a patient librarian.

A breath came from the floor vent. If she hadn't been listening, she would have missed it. The breath tried to be a child's laugh. It came out almost right and completely wrong, like audio played backward. The hairs on her arms lifted. The house's rules pressed the wrongness flat.

"Noted," Sia said. She drew a small square with a dot in a corner of a fresh page. Listen. The ink quivered. She told herself it was her hand. A tiny ripple moved across the paper. She set her palm on the cover anyway and felt a faint tap. Not a knock. More like a heartbeat. Just a hint.

Kaelan leaned on the doorframe, relaxed without assuming. "Towels and water are in the bath at the end of the hall," she said. "Tea in ten minutes, or whenever you want if you know where to look. If you hear bells away from the lobby, the house wants your attention."

"I'll learn the bell language," Sia said.

"You already started," Kaelan said, quick smile, then stepped aside.

Charles appeared with the easy quiet of someone who knows which boards squeak. "When you're settled," he said, "downstairs parlor. First-week plan. Rest first. Then learn the house. Training fits around those."

"Is that written down somewhere?" Eric called from the hall.

"It's written into the place," Charles said. "I'll also hand you paper."

The parlor looked like a room built for conversations. Two long sofas near a real-wood fireplace. Bookcases of books meant to be used, not worshipped. Photos of stairwells, corner windows, and a small courtyard with a bench under a ginkgo that wore its leaves like coins.

Tea steamed on a low table. Mismatched cups. Lemon slices and sugar cubes. A jar labeled in neat pen: honey, Michigan, spring.

Eric reached for the jar, caught Charles's eye, and backed off. "Asking first," he said. "Growth."

Kaelan poured and handed out cups with both hands. "Schedules stay light for two days," she said. "The house is safe, but new safe can feel weird."

Marcus chose the chair by the door without making a thing of it. Truth stretched into a bar of sunlight and sighed like yes. Mariah watched Mia watch the light. A quiet exchange passed between them. Mia ended up on the rug with her back to the sofa, knees up, fingers worrying her sleeves until Mariah touched her wrist.

Ella took a seat where she could see the hallway and the window at once. Tobias stood for a second, scanning, then sat where he could watch the door without blocking anyone else.

Charles set a notebook on the table. "Hospitality isn't decoration," he said. "It's the spine of this building. We keep it because it's right, and because something in the world needs to decide what it won't be." He let that land. "Training happens in rooms where raised voices drop and sharp thoughts get softer at the edges. If you want a fight today, you'll be annoyed. Later, you'll be glad."

"You'll learn the doors," he added. "You'll learn the bells. You'll practice the difference between asking a room and telling it. Don't sign anything you didn't read. Don't take what didn't offer itself. Listen before you shape." His eyes found Sia's. "Hold consent like a key."

Ella raised a hand a little. "If we get the long bell, are we shelter-in-place or meet-up?"

"Shelter," Charles said. "Staff will come to you."

Tobias tapped his pen once and nodded. "I'll write a quiet rotation. No boots in the lobby, no noise. Just eyes."

The sketchbook in Sia's bag felt like a small presence trying to match her breathing. Air moved by the vent. The house pressed it smooth. Four notes hummed, never in the same order.

"Questions?" Charles asked.

Eric raised a hand halfway, then zipped his lips like a joke he knew better than to tell. Marcus's six-millimeter smile appeared and vanished. Mariah shook her head. Sia felt Mia's stillness set a small root into the rug. Her question was there and would cut if she let it out. Sia spoke instead.

"What do we do if something inside the rules starts tugging the edges?" she asked.

"Ask for help," Charles said.

"From the house?"

"From each other," he said. "And from the house."

He opened the notebook. Cream paper. Faint lines. Handwriting that would have looked the same fifty years ago. They laid out the week. Mornings for rest and food that actually helps. Afternoons learning the halls and letting the doors learn them. Evenings for quiet skills that won't rattle glass. Kaelan would guide the house side. Charles would teach the etiquette no one admits is etiquette. Mariah would start Mia's voice work. Eric would help and get redirected by a look when needed. Marcus would run physical checks in a courtyard that borrowed daylight from wherever the house kept it. Tobias would draft the quiet rotations and post them where the house approved. Ella would handle tech hygiene and phone rules with Charles's sign-off. Sia would map routes and rules in a notebook that seemed to have chosen her first.

After tea, Kaelan gave them a quick orientation that felt more like the building introducing favorite corners. A brass bell in a wall niche. "Single light chime means the house is thinking," she said. "Two quick chimes means pay attention. One long chime means stay put. Someone's coming. Don't ignore bells."

The kitchen smelled like bread and onions in a pan. Butcher-block counters with grain worn into a map. A chalkboard menu. Someone had drawn a tiny fox and written, wash your cup and the house will thank you. Truth sat by the back door like she had always known this room.

A reading room waited with green-shaded lamps and tables scarred with initials the house didn't mind. Kaelan tapped a shelf. "Reference," she said. "Ask nicely and the house will bring what you need. Ask badly and it brings dictionaries."

Eric reached for a spine that read Stagecraft of the Fairgrounds. The book leaned into his hand. He tried again, slower. It met him halfway. He didn't hide his grin.

They finished in a small chapel with no altar. Just a low window and a strip of sky in a brick frame. Benches facing each other so people would be the view. Mariah traced the wood and sat. Mia sat beside her and rested her head on her mom's shoulder for one breath. The quiet wasn't empty. It felt like the pause musicians respect.

"Thanks," Mariah said to Kaelan.

"That's what it's for," Kaelan said. "Prayer rugs are in the cabinet. Water bowl on the shelf. The room doesn't pick a name. You can."

On the way back, Charles walked beside Sia. He didn't ask if she was okay. He pointed with his cane at a black-and-white photo of a man in a vest standing in front of this same building a long time ago. "Alastair Blackstone," he said. "My great-grandfather. First curator who wrote the hospitality rule in a way the building kept."

"How do you write a rule a house will keep?" Sia asked.

"Slowly," he said. "After you listen long enough to repeat what it already believes. Treat a house like an object and it becomes one. Treat it like a partner and sometimes it agrees."

"Ever disagree?"

"Often," he said, with a real smile. "That's why we're still here."

Dinner was thick soup and bread that cracked softly when you broke it. It tasted like someone decided salt should be kind. Charles ate like a man who respects food. Kaelan ate like someone who knows what fuel she needs. Eric talked less once he realized the house heard everything, and when he did talk he asked useful questions. Marcus took a seat that let him watch the door and the window without moving. Mariah gave Mia an extra ladle and left the crusts on because that's how Mia liked it when she forgot to say. Tobias ate neatly and kept an eye on the hallway. Ella sat where she could see the clock and the exit and didn't touch her phone. Truth rested her head on Mariah's knee and pretended not to count crumbs.

After dinner, Mariah caught Sia as the group drifted. "Walk with me," she said. They went as far as the lake mural and back. Mariah didn't fill the air. She waited.

"When I say rest, I mean it," she said finally. "Your magic has edges today. Sleep rounds edges. Food helps. Real laughter helps."

"I keep thinking about the Farm," Sia said. "About leaving. About what I did to make the door."

"You did what you had to and you did it with care. That's why you're standing here. Care is the difference." She nodded toward the mural. "Don't mirror everything around you. Hold your center. Let the house help."

"I hear the rules," Sia said. "Like a song I almost know."

"Hum along," Mariah said, squeezing her shoulder.

Back in her room, Sia drew a quiet map. Lobby. Staff door. Stairs that turned right and right again. Mural landing. Long hall. Her door with the small mirror. She left blank spaces where corridors had curved away. The blank felt honest.

The paper lifted its grain under her pencil, like attention. She drew a second, smaller map. Not rooms. Rules. Ask before shaping. Hold consent like a key. Do no harm here. If harm shows up, take it outside or change it. Listen before you name. The last one felt new. She couldn't tell if she'd made it up or if the house had handed it to her.

Two soft taps and a third sounded at the door. Marcus. "We're walking the courtyard," he said when she opened. "Eric wants a look at the roof. You coming?"

She almost said yes. Almost said no. "Tomorrow," she decided.

Marcus nodded like he believed her.

From farther down the hall, Eric called, "If it looks cool, send me a pic."

"Sleep," Charles said from nowhere in particular.

"Copy," Eric said, and shut up.

Sia set the sketchbook on the desk. The cover rose a hair and settled, like breath under a blanket. The vent tried a laugh again and almost got it. The house laid a soft hand over the sound and hushed it. The bell tone in the desk wood shifted up a little, like it had tuned itself closer to the room.

Through the narrow window, the small square of lawn darkened into a green she couldn't name. A radiator ticked a story about heat in pipes. Somewhere far off, a door asked a question and someone answered with please.

She lay on the bed and listened. For the first time in a long time, she didn't dream of running. She dreamed of doors that asked, bells that agreed, and a museum that might teach a language where asking was the strongest spell she knew.

CHAPTER 2

Keys & Rules

MARCUS

"Learn the rules like a pro, so you can break them like an artist."

Pablo Picasso

THE PARLOR SETTLED INTO a steady kind of quiet, not library stuffy, just the tone people use when they want to hear themselves think. Steam curled from the teapot. Mismatched cups sat ready on the low table. Truth took the strip of sun along the rug and made it hers, chin on paws, ears up.

Mariah set a small metronome app on her phone and placed the phone faceup on the table. "Four-count inhale, six-count exhale," she said. "Soft volume, no strain." She looked at Mia.

"You can leave if any part of this hurts."

Mia nodded. The nod was small, but it happened.

Eric dropped onto the arm of the sofa with a lanyard stopwatch and the kind of focus he usually saved for experiments. "I'm on timing," he said. "No pushing. If you see my hand, that means drop the volume."

Marcus took the chair near the doorway where he could see the hall, the front threshold line, and the window reflection at the same time. He set his notebook on his knee and wrote the time. He did not write anything about feelings. Feelings were not his job. Keeping space so other people could have them was.

Sia slid into the corner armchair with her sketchbook. The way she held the pencil said she was not doodling. Mapping, probably. She kept glancing at the ceiling corner where the light shifted. Listening before naming. He respected that even if he did not plan to ask what the sketchbook was up to.

Kaelan drifted in and leaned on the end of the bookcase. She had a pen behind her ear and a small stack of cards in her hand that said please ask before you move furniture. She did not post them yet. She watched the room decide what it was going to do with itself.

Ella arrived with a roll of tape and two laminated phone-rule sheets. She did a quick wave that took in the whole group and headed for the wall by the clock. "Phones off unless a staffer flips green," she read, checking for typos out loud. "Charging baskets in the parlor and kitchen. If you need a call, ask the desk." She taped the sheet low enough that shorter eyes would actually see it. Then she stepped back and checked for glare. "Looks fine."

Tobias followed with a corkboard, a handful of pushpins, and a marker. "Rotations are live," he said. He posted the schedule by the clock and a second copy inside the staff door. The blocks were simple, one-hour pieces with names slotted into "parlor," "hall," "reading," "courtyard." He had drawn a small dog icon next to any hour Truth was on duty with a person.

"Thank you," Marcus said. He meant both of them. A room that knew what to do did not go looking for drama.

Eric looked over in dread at the supplies the Loris had brought, "It's a terrible thing, organizational responsibility. Look what it's doing to our little Paladins."

He stepped into the hall and listened. The museum's normal morning sound was present, a light building hum, pipes working, distant footfalls where Charles must have been. He looked up the stairwell and down toward the chapel. Then he checked his watch and keyed the radio.

"Charles, tap the bell for a single please," he said, and waited.

One clean chime traveled the air, light as a coin placed on a counter. In the parlor, Mia did not flinch. Good. In the chapel, the sound carried and softened at the same time. He timed how long it took to fall away and wrote ten seconds. Back in the parlor, Eric raised a thumb without speaking to show he had heard the chime over the metronome ticks.

"Two quick," Marcus said into the radio.

Two quick chimes rang, close together. Heads lifted in the hall and one staffer in the lobby turned an ear and nodded like she now remembered what that code meant. Time to attention was immediate. Good.

"Long hold," Marcus said last. He watched people and places more than he listened. Long chime filled the space, not loud, but present, the way a hand on a shoulder is present. In the parlor, Mia dropped her hands into her lap automatically, then looked to Mariah, who said, calm, "Stay put." Eric killed the metronome without commentary. Ella looked for the nearest door, saw Marcus in the doorway, and stayed still. Tobias stood but did not move his feet. Sia lifted her pencil off the page, then rested it there again, patient.

"End bell," Marcus said. The tone faded. He took the radio from his mouth. "That worked," he told the room. "Long means shelter. Staff comes to you."

"Copy," Eric said, back to his timing job.

Mariah tapped the metronome again. "Four and six," she told Mia. "Pretend there is a candle a foot from your face. Breath should never flicker it."

Mia focused on a spot just past Mariah's shoulder and matched the clicks. Inhale four. Exhale six. The sound that came out was quiet and direct, not pretty yet, just true. Mariah nodded and let her keep going.

From his chair, Marcus adjusted what he would call the room's noise ceiling. The parlor could absorb a certain amount of sound and still feel safe. He watched how the air responded to different voices. Eric's was quick but not sharp today. Mariah's was low and steady. Mia's stayed below conversation level. Sia said nothing, pencil moving. Kaelan put up two cards, one by the door, one by the fireplace, and stepped back. Ella taped the second phone rule by the staff door, checked the height, and moved it down two inches without being asked. Tobias added a small line under the rotation that read questions at the desk first.

Marcus went to the hallway and walked ten slow steps toward the chapel, then ten back. He wanted to know how far a visitor could drift before the metronome became a bother. Not far. That was fine. He would not let wandering visitors drift without a hello anyway.

He stuck his head into the chapel. The room had benches that faced each other, a low window, and a square of sky framed by brick. He counted the exit lines and checked the door swing. "Bells audible," he told Kaelan as she passed. "No echo weirdness."

"Good," she said. She slid a thin card into a brass holder beside the door, something in her own hand that said quiet room in two lines. It did not feel like an order. It felt like a label on a drawer.

Back in the parlor, Mia's breath stayed steady. Mariah changed the pattern to four and four for a minute, then five and seven. Eric kept time and did not rush it. When Mia coughed once, he hit pause, and Mariah let the silence sit until Mia nodded. Then they resumed. Marcus liked that they did not treat practice like a performance.

Sia flipped a page and drew a rectangle that looked like the parlor and set a small square where the bell tone seemed to sit in the wood. Marcus could not see details, only that she mapped sound like other people map furniture. He made a note. Not as a problem. As a reality he needed to remember when he assigned spaces.

Ella drifted over to the desk and asked the volunteer on duty, "If someone argues about phones, what do you want me to say first?"

"Start with museum policy," the volunteer said. "If they push, call me, then call Kaelan."

"Copy," Ella said. She wrote that on a sticky and put the sticky on the side of the desk where only staff would see it.

Tobias came to Marcus with a smaller card. "Rally protocol," he said. "If visitors show during training, desk greets, floats steer to exhibits A and B, parlor stays quiet, chapel stays closed unless staff opens it."

Marcus read, made one change, and handed it back. "Add reading room as overflow if lobby spikes. No more than five at a time."

"Done." Tobias rewrote that line and pinned a duplicate behind the desk.

Truth stood, shook once, and walked to Marcus's chair. He scratched her chest and checked her focus. Ears up, eyes soft, tail a slow pendulum. "Courtyard sweep in twenty," he said quietly to her. She sat, which meant she was listening and also that she wanted him to know it.

The museum's first couple of visitors filtered in, a father and a kid in a denim jacket with a patch that said Robotics. Charles took them at the desk with a simple welcome and a map, no fanfare. They looked toward the parlor and saw people already doing something real and chose the exhibit hall instead. Marcus liked that too. The building felt like it knew how to steer.

Two teens wandered in a little after, eyes on their phones, then on the cases, then on their phones again. Ella stepped to the edge of the parlor threshold before they crossed it. "Hey," she said, normal tone. "Phones off in the living spaces. You can charge in the parlor basket and the kitchen upstairs."

"Why," one of them asked, flat as only sixteen can manage.

"Because people are working," Ella said. "And because the house works better when it isn't pinged every five seconds."

"The house," the kid repeated.

"Building," Ella said, shrugging. "Try it for an hour. If you hate it, you can complain to the suggestion box, which is Charles."

The kid laughed despite himself and slid his phone into the basket. The other followed. Ella nodded thanks and stepped back. The moment moved on without getting sticky.

"Nice," Marcus said.

"Thanks," Ella said, then lowered her voice. "If someone tries to sneak video, I'm cutting that off."

"Good," he said. "Start with polite. End with staff. No confrontations in the parlor."

Kaelan passed behind them with a small tray of cups. "Water," she said, offering one to Mia without interrupting the count. Mia took it, sipped, and put it back, then returned to the breath work without missing the next timing mark. Eric flashed a quick thumb and reset the metronome.

Marcus picked up the radio again. "Charles, reading room check," he said. "I am sending the next curious to you. Keep the door at five bodies max."

"Understood," Charles said. Even his radio voice sounded like it wore a suit.

Marcus wrote a line at the top of his page: noise ceiling holds at training volume, bells audible, visitor flow workable. He underlined workable.

A family of four came in with stroller wheels that complained. Tobias intercepted with a smile and a map. "Elevator this way," he said. "Exhibit A has wider paths. If you hear a bell, just pause for a second. You're good." The family followed him like he had handed them a small, easy quest.

"Lunch in an hour," Kaelan said to Marcus and Charles both, as if lunch were part of security. "I will run a five-minute bell hold right before we eat."

"Do it," Marcus said. "Short briefing after."

Mariah let the metronome die and set her phone facedown. "That's enough for now," she told Mia. "You did well."

Mia nodded again, bigger this time. She looked past Marcus to the window and the thin square of sky and did not flinch when someone out in the lobby laughed. Progress.

"Break," Eric said, stretching his shoulders. He mouthed to Marcus, good? Marcus gave him a simple yes and Eric sat back down instead of rushing off, which counted as growth.

Sia closed her sketchbook with a hand on the cover like she was answering a question it had just asked. She stood and crossed to the reading room, not in a hurry, just ready. Marcus watched her go and noted who looked up. Ella clocked the motion and then returned to the desk to point out a pamphlet. Tobias checked the rotation and slid his pin to the next slot on the board. Kaelan finished posting the last two polite cards, then stepped to the doorway and took a long, steady look at the threshold line, as if reading the seam where outside became in.

Marcus did one more loop, parlor to hallway to chapel door and back. He looked at shoes, shoulders, hands. No tight fists. No darting. The building breathed like a person who trusted their chair.

He called the front desk to check bell audibility one more time. "Single chime," he said into the radio.

The tone rang. In the parlor, people did what they had been taught to do. Which was to keep doing what they were doing, only with their ears open.

"Works," Marcus said softly. He wrote one more line in his notebook: norms set.

He glanced at Truth. She watched him back and thumped her tail once, slow. Outside the window, a ginkgo leaf let go and spun toward the courtyard like a coin making up its mind. Inside, the museum kept its promise in small ways, which was the only way promises ever hold.

THE FIRST SIGN WAS not the sound. It was the air. The lobby's temperature slid half a degree toward cool, the way a room does when someone opens a door and decides not to come in yet. Marcus looked up from his notes, felt Truth's shoulder lean into his shin, and answered with a light touch to her head that meant I am listening.

Two quick chimes carried from the brass in the wall niche. Not loud. Clear. Heads in the exhibit hall turned without popping up like prairie dogs. The house had taught the shape of attention in a day and a half and people were already learning it.

Marcus moved to the threshold line at an unhurried walk. Kaelan came from the desk with a quiet nod and fell in a step to his right. Charles stayed ten feet back, a little left, where he could be seen without blocking anything.

The front door stood half open. A figure waited outside on the top step, weight on one foot, hands deep in jacket pockets. Mid twenties, maybe. Brown hair cut short at home. Jacket that had been navy once and now was the color of water left in a metal pan. The person's eyes were the thing. Not frantic. Wired. Like someone who had held a thought for so long it had turned into an ache and they did not know what to do with it.

Truth sat at Marcus's heel when he stopped. She did not bark. Her tail tapped once against his boot and then went still, which was her version of telling him she was working.

Marcus did not touch the door. He stood with his palm near the seam and asked low, "May we meet at the threshold." The latch agreed. He opened enough to be a welcome without becoming an invitation, and kept his feet behind the line.

"Morning," he said. "I'm Marcus. What brings you in today."

The visitor blinked like he had not expected to be asked a normal question. "I'm just looking," he said. His voice had that tightness that comes from holding a throat stiff. "I heard things about this place."

"People do," Marcus said. "Inside, we keep a rule called hospitality. It is a promise. Everyone is safe and we ask before we act. You agree to that, and we can show you around."

The man's hands stayed in his pockets. Something in the right pocket tugged at the jacket fabric, a hard edge about the size of a matchbox. He shifted and the thing skated, catching, then sitting still again. Marcus logged it. Not a weapon. A charm. Old cloth wrapped around something that once had mattered to someone who had not taught him how to use it.

"What if I am not safe," the man said. He tried to smile and could not find the part of his face that remembered how.

"You came to a place that helps with that," Marcus said.

The house's long bell could have told him to hold the door, but it did not. It stayed quiet, present like a hand nearby but not on his shoulder. He kept his voice easy.

"What is your name," Marcus asked.

The pause was longer than a person's name should require.

"Evan," the man said finally. He did not say a last name, which was not required.

"Okay, Evan," Marcus said. "I will not ask you to take your hands out of your pockets. I will ask you to nod if you can agree to the hospitality rule while you are inside."

Evan did not nod. He rocked once toward the threshold and then back. The matchbox shape in his pocket lifted a fraction and the air near his hand grew a little colder. Truth's ears flicked. Her posture did not change.

Kaelan stood quiet to Marcus's right. She did not do anything a person could see if they were not trained to notice. She looked at Evan the way musicians look at someone who is about to join a song and cannot find their first note. Marcus watched the jacket pocket. The cloth inside had been knotted three times by someone who had been angry while tying it. He could almost feel the tightness through the space between them. The house could feel it too. He sensed the pushback in the way the threshold held its line.

"This place says no violence," Evan said. "How would you know. People say things."

"We know because it is how the building works," Marcus said. "Try it and nothing happens. We cannot hit you and you cannot hit us. That is not a dare. It is the rule. There are other places to do anger. Here, you can ask a question. Or you can walk the exhibit and let your nervous system remember how to sit in a chair. Both count."

A muscle in Evan's jaw jumped. The right pocket tightened

again, then eased. A smell hit Marcus's nose that did not belong to the lobby, a tang like old pennies and burned sugar. Kaelan's eyes flicked to his, then to the pocket. He gave the smallest shake of his head. Not yet.

"What if I already messed something up," Evan said. He was not looking at Marcus. He looked over Marcus's shoulder at the mobile of tin charms above the lobby and then at the case with the cups and balls as if those objects might be able to answer for the house.

"Then you are in a museum," Marcus said. "Museums are where people keep mistakes and make them useful."

That got him a breath that was not quite a laugh. It left Evan with a path to step onto.

Kaelan spoke for the first time. "You can hold that in your pocket and still be a guest," she said. Her voice was straightforward. "But if it wakes up and tries anything, the house will turn it into nothing. You will be left with cloth and a pebble. Better to ask it to wait."

Evan looked at her like she had said a thing he had not known he was allowed to know. "Ask it."

"Tell it," Kaelan said. "You do not need fancy words. Just a decision."

Evan nodded once, almost invisible. His shoulders dropped a centimeter. The tight smell in the air let go. Marcus did not relax his knees. He did not move at all in the way that counts.

"Welcome," he said. He stepped back one step and gave a small gesture to the right. He could have offered his hand. He did not. He chose the path that required less from the other person.

Evan stepped inside. The matchbox shape in his pocket stayed still. Kaelan slid to one side and angled her body the way ushers do when they want to guide someone without pushing. "Exhibit A starts to the left," she said. "Restrooms are signed. If you need a person, I am the person."

Evan's eyes landed on the printed map at the desk. He took one without asking permission because maps are permission. Charles offered a simple nod, nothing that would draw attention. Evan turned toward the cases like a person who had not set foot in a museum since a fourth grade field trip and was suddenly trying to remember how to be that version of himself again.

Marcus held the door half open for three heartbeats after Evan passed the line, then let it close. The house's chime did not sound. It did not need to. Truth exhaled slowly, her breath a warm line against his pants. He rubbed one ear and felt the softness of a dog that had decided to trust everything about her job today.

"Charm," Marcus said, low.

"Cloth over a coin," Kaelan said. "The coin was warm. It is not now."

"Pocket gave me burned sugar," Marcus said.

"I got pennies," Kaelan said, equal weight. "Old grudge flavor."

Charles came up to the line. "Well handled," he said softly.

"Not done," Marcus said. "If he loops back hot, we seat him. Reading room first, not the parlor."

"Agreed," Charles said. He did not ask why reading room first. He knew. Tables helped. Walls with books help people remember they are not the first or the last or the only.

Marcus keyed the radio once without speaking. A small click went out and came back. The team knew that click. It meant be where you said you would be. The lobby volunteer shifted her stance from friendly to friendly and ready. Tobias came into view at the edge of the hall like he had been passing through and chose to pause where he could see everything without looking like he was trying to see everything. Ella leaned a hip against the staff desk and adjusted the angle of the phone basket so someone approaching would not miss it.

Evan did one slow lap of the first exhibit, the one with the mirror tricks and the old show posters. He stopped in front of a photograph of a woman holding up a mirror that refused to show her face and instead showed a field of sunflowers. He stood there for a while and then he breathed out. The breath did not sound like surrender. It sounded like someone whose shoulders had just stopped telling lies about how heavy they needed to be.

He turned back toward the door, and for a second Marcus read the angle as a problem. Then he saw Evan was not rushing. He was just moving the way people move when they have remembered there is a world to be in.

"I have a question," Evan said when he reached the threshold again. He did not step over it this time. He stood on the inside line, looking at Marcus instead of past him. "If I bring something dumb that someone told me would help, and it makes trouble at the door, am I banned forever."

"No," Marcus said. "You are asked to stop bringing that thing. You are not banned unless you try to hurt someone on purpose after being told you cannot."

Evan nodded again. Smaller this time.

"What do you need answered," Charles asked from two steps back.

Evan shook his head. "I do not even know how to ask." He dug into his left pocket and pulled out a folded flyer. He held it up and then down again. "This said you help. It did not say with what."

"We help with rules," Marcus said. "This house keeps one. You tried it and it worked. That might be enough for today."

Evan looked at the fox masks in the case by the wall. He let out a breath that sounded like the smallest trophy and then backed up one step.

"Thank you," he said. He meant the words. He looked like someone who did not always mean them.

"Come back," Kaelan said. "You know how now."

Evan left. He did not look over his shoulder. The door closed on air that warmed a fraction back toward normal.

Marcus did not move right away. He waited for the echo of whatever had been in the pocket to finish dying in the seam. The house held its line. The mobile above turned, making almost-music that felt more like breathing than sound.

"Basement vent," he said to Kaelan.

"Yes," she said. "Same taste."

"Log link," Marcus said. He took out his notebook and wrote: threshold incident, cloth charm on coin, pennies and burned sugar, polite exit. He added a line under that: ward-scar near vent likely same family, still do not poke.

"Lunch in five," Charles said. He did not push it like an order, just a reminder that the day still had to be ordinary if it wanted to hold.

"Two minute drill first," Marcus said. "Escort handoff."

Kaelan smiled a little. "You love homework."

"I love no surprises," Marcus said.

They ran it with Tobias at the threshold playing the part of a visitor who wanted to argue about phones. Ella handled the first pass with policy and a real voice, not a copied tone. Kaelan mirrored body angles so the path inside felt like a choice. Marcus kept his feet light and his hands visible. The handoff to the desk took nine seconds on the first try and seven on the second. He wrote seven and circled it.

Truth watched each run like a referee who also happened to be a dog. She did a small wag when the second run hit seven seconds.

In the parlor, the metronome sat quiet on the table. Mia and Mariah were back, hands around warm cups. Sia had left her sketchbook on the arm of a chair and gone upstairs with Eric to check a window latch for a thing he thought he had seen. The museum kept breathing its steady, even breath.

Marcus posted the day's Ops Notes on the small corkboard by the staff door where only the people who needed to see would see.

Rotations live. Parlor, hall, reading, courtyard. Truth with floater at lunch.

Bells verified. Single, double, long hold audible and understood.

Threshold test pass. Cloth charm on coin, de-escalated, guest departed calm.

Basement vent seam. Logged. Related flavor to threshold charm. **Do not poke.**

Tomorrow focus. Courtyard night lighting layout, delivery timing confirmation at eleven.

He capped the marker and stepped back. Kaelan read over his shoulder, then tapped the line about do not poke with the back of the pen.

"Thank you," she said.

"For not poking," he said.

"For writing it," she said. "People listen to the board when the day gets loud."

Charles came by with two mugs and set one in Marcus's hand. "Lunch," he said. "And for what it is worth, well done."

"Thanks," Marcus said. He meant the coffee and the words.

He looked out through the glass at the steps and the small square of sky over Main Street. A gust tugged at the ginkgo leaves in the courtyard and one let go, spinning like a coin trying to decide which side mattered. Inside, the mobile of charms made their almost-tune. Truth leaned into his leg and he leaned back just enough to let her know he noticed. The promise held, built in small pieces, one ordinary choice at a time.

CHAPTER 3

Songs & Vents

Sia

United by love, fortified by loyalty, family remains the sanctuary even in a chaotic world.
Aloo Denish Obiero

THE DOWNSTAIRS CORRIDOR CARRIED the kind of quiet that
helps people hear themselves. Lamps with green shades warmed
the reading room tables and made little circles of permission
around books and elbows. The air smelled like paper and lemon
oil and the faint hum of the building being patient.

Mariah set her phone faceup on the table, the metronome
app asleep for now. "Low volume," she told Mia. "Speak it like
you are filling your own chest, not the room."

Mia nodded and focused on a spot just past Mariah's shoulder. Mariah sang a line first, simple and clear, no decoration. Mia followed, softer but steady. The pitch lived clean in the quiet and rolled across the table like water on glass.

Sia sat a little off to the side with her notebook open, pencil lifted. She was not drawing faces or the curve of Mia's mouth. She sketched the angles of sound in the room the way other people sketch chairs. The bell tone lived in the wood of the desk at her right. The song tone from her mother and sister braided around it and changed the way the wood felt. She marked a small circle where the two tones met and wrote patient beside it.

Kaelan slid into the chair at Sia's table without announcing herself. She set a ceramic cup down and tucked a foot under her. Bracelets clicked once and then stilled. "You draw the way electricians map a house," she said softly so as not to cut across the line Mia was holding.

Sia kept her eyes on the page. "I'm making sense. Lines help."

"That is what we do," Kaelan said. "Make sense so people have something to stand on."

"Who's we," Sia asked.

"White Circle." Kaelan rested her elbow on the table and let her hand hang, relaxed. "It's a group that works on boundaries and consent in places like this. We help houses and people agree about what is allowed. We do it with training and with care. No drama if we can help it."

Sia drew a small square for the reading room and shaded the

corners. "Your magic is church magic," she said. It was not a question.

"Yes," Kaelan said, like she was answering a friend. "I am a shrine attendant. A miko. I grew up with it the way some people grow up with piano. There is practice, and there is listening. The work is faith and habit and community. If I am doing it right, you see the results and not the effort."

Sia finally looked up. "You talk about it like work."

"It is work," Kaelan said. "Good work. I file reports. I clean floors. I run bell drills. I make sure a stranger who is nervous can breathe when they step through a door. If people want fireworks, they need a different place."

Mia sang another line. This one moved a half step down and held. Mariah joined and they shared the note until it stopped wondering which voice it belonged to. Sia felt it against her wrist like a small current and had to fight the habit of pressing her palm to the sketchbook cover in case it wanted to answer. She didn't. She listened.

"White Circle is Christian," Sia said, testing the word in her mouth.

"Some of us," Kaelan said. "Some Buddhist. Some of us belong to no temple and still keep the work. The name is a shorthand for the vow, not the brand."

Sia nodded. "And you are a fox."

"Something like that," Kaelan said, eyes amused. "Kitsune is the word people use. The older word is more of a cluster. Our family is a kind of kami. Where you might say Fae. The edges do not line up one to one, but they rhyme."

"People here call that Fae," Sia said. "In the way people call every tissue Kleenex."

"That." Kaelan smiled. "It can be useful language as long as we do not let it flatten things."

Sia drew a little triangle in the corner of her map and colored it in. She wrote fox near it in tiny letters, then scratched the word out and wrote cousin. "Do you live with the White Circle or near it."

"I live with my work," Kaelan said. "Sometimes that is a house like this. Sometimes it is a small building on a hill with a bell rope that will take your shoulder out if you pull it wrong. Sometimes it is a motel room and a notebook and a list of things to try before I call Charles and say the word help."

Sia liked that she said help like a tool, not a failure.

From the lobby, Eric's voice drifted in. "It is not a selfie if the house takes it, that is a portrait," he said to someone. Sia could hear the grin without seeing it.

Ella answered with her normal voice that still managed to sound like a posted sign. "Phones off in the halls. You can take pictures upstairs in the exhibits. Down here, we keep it quiet."

"I am documenting my growth as a person," Eric said.

"Do it with your eyes," Ella said. "And put the phone in the basket."

Sia smiled without showing it and added a small basket icon to the corner of her map.

Mariah set a hand flat on the table. "Pause," she told Mia. "Sip of water. Then two more."

Mia took the cup and drank without slurping, the kind of small skill that counts more than anyone tells you. She set the cup down and wiped a thumb across the ring of condensation to erase it.

Sia heard it then. The way the tone in the room changed near the floor vent. It was not louder. It leaned. The harmony from Mariah and Mia stacked clean and then bent a hair when it reached the square of metal. Not wrong like yesterday. Just not true.

Sia turned her head like she was checking a clock. She looked at the vent without staring it into shyness. She drew a circle around the vent on her map and wrote bend.

Kaelan followed her eyes. "You hear that," she asked without moving her mouth.

"It makes the note kink," Sia said. "It is small."

"Small is where we live," Kaelan said. "You tell Marcus. He will sniff it and either shrug or write a plan."

"I will," Sia said. She added a thin arrow from the circle to the hallway where the mural landing sat. The pencil line corrected itself a tiny fraction when she looked back at it, like it had been thinking about being straight and then decided to commit. She did not comment on that. She made a small dot on the edge of the page to mark that the page had chosen to be stubborn.

Mariah hummed a single pitch and Mia matched it again. Their sound ran across the room and touched everything inside it like a light hand on the back of every chair. The bell in the desk wood did not answer in tone. It answered by holding still in a way Sia trusted.

"Why bells," Sia asked quietly. "Why not words."

"Bells do not argue," Kaelan said. "They are not about content. They tell people and rooms when to lift their heads."

"Do you ever wish for lightning instead," Sia said.

"Lightning is for outside," Kaelan said. "Inside, people need things that help them stay."

The lobby sent another shape of sound down the hall. A couple of visitors laughed, the echo rolling and then dying before it reached the reading room. Someone asked if there was a student discount. Charles answered in his polite voice that did not sound like money. Ella said, "Thank you," in a tone that meant Yes, you did the thing I asked. Eric said, "Growth," in a way that made Sia think he was actually trying.

Sia flipped to a fresh page and wrote the rules again in smaller handwriting. Ask before shaping. Hold consent like a key. Do no harm here. If harm gets in, take it outside or transform it. Listen before you name. She added a small box next to each line, the kind you would check if a task were done, and left them all unchecked.

"What is the White Circle's rule," she asked Kaelan.

"Hospitality and consent," Kaelan said. "Same as Charles keeps. No hitting. No coin tricks that take the person with them. No raising your voice like it will change physics. We hold the boundaries so people can choose something else."

"Choose," Sia said, liking the word.

"Choice matters more than talent," Kaelan said. "People get that backwards."

Sia looked at Mia. Her sister was not a loud person. Mia's voice came out gentle even when she did not want it to. The tone she and Mariah were making together did not try to be pretty. It was steady. Sia drew a line that matched that steadiness. The pencil did not argue this time.

"Can I ask a rude question," Sia said.

"You can ask," Kaelan said. "I may say no."

"Do you shift," Sia asked. "Like fox to person."

"Not in public," Kaelan said, and smiled with her eyes. "And not for demonstrations."

"Okay," Sia said. It felt like a boundary and not a secret. She liked that difference.

She heard footsteps in the hall and did not need to turn to know they were Marcus's. His walk was quiet and carried an angle that felt like planning. He paused in the doorway and took in the room without making the room feel observed. Truth slid in ahead of him and found the sliver of sun that always seemed to show up wherever she might want it. She put her chin on her paws and watched Mia with the steady attention of a dog who has chosen a job.

"The vent bends the note," Sia said before Marcus could ask anything else.

He crouched by the grille and listened without putting his ear to metal. He closed his eyes like he was looking at something from the inside out. "I get metal and something sweet," he said.

"Small. Not active."

"Same spot as yesterday," Sia said.

"Same seam," Marcus said. He touched the paint with the back of one finger and then put his hand on his knee so he would not be tempted to do it again. "Thank you," he told Sia. "I'll log it and check the run in the hall after lunch."

"Do you need me," Sia asked.

"Later," he said. "When we walk it, yes."

Kaelan watched them both and said nothing. Sia appreciated the choice.

Mariah let the note go and set her phone screen dark. "Two more tomorrow," she told Mia. "No more today."

Mia nodded, a little flushed and a little proud. She glanced at Sia's notebook like she might ask to see it and then chose to keep the moment for herself. Sia approved.

The reading room settled back around them. Kaelan nudged her cup with one finger and then sipped. "You like rules," she said to Sia.

"They make room for people to be people," Sia said.

"They do," Kaelan said. "They also make room for houses to be houses. The building does not have to pretend to be a person. It can be what it is."

"What is it," Sia asked.

"A place that keeps a promise," Kaelan said. "When places keep promises, people get brave in quiet ways."

Eric appeared in the doorway like a person who had just re-membered his legs had speed settings. He caught himself before he talked over the room. "Sorry," he said low. "Ella is making me better."

"Slow is a speed," Ella said behind him, dry. She held up a small stack of maps like flash cards. "Delivery drivers got lost twice last week. I redrew the arrows. Charles says to ask you if the new ones make sense."

Eric gave her a slight bow like he was turning a bit into a joke and then took one of the maps seriously. "This is clean," he said. "I can read it without thinking."

"Good," Ella said, and turned to go tape them up.

Eric lingered long enough to tap the vent grille with his knuckle. Marcus cleared his throat once. Eric pulled his hand back. "Not touching," he said. "Personal growth."

Sia felt the corner of her mouth try to raise itself. She let it.

Kaelan stood and smoothed her skirt like she was resetting the room. "I will be in the lobby," she said. "If the vent tries to make art, please tell it to wait for me."

"It is not making art," Sia said.

"Yet," Kaelan said, and walked out, bracelets giving a small rhythm to the doorframe.

Mariah gathered her phone and cup and stood with Mia. "Ten minutes, then upstairs," she told Sia. "If you need air, take it."

"I need drawing," Sia said.

"Also a kind of air," Mariah said, and kissed the top of Mia's head.

When they were gone, Sia watched the doorway empty and

the light lie down where it had been before. She added one more square to her map for the reading room, then set a small dot where Marcus had paused his hand so he would not touch the seam. She colored the dot in and wrote wait.

The lobby sent a brief flare of sound down the hall. A pair of kids laughing. A bell chime urging someone to stop and listen. The room held.

Sia closed the notebook, pressed her palm to the cover, and felt the faintest tap from the other side. Not a knock. Not a name. Just an agreement to keep going.

AFTER LUNCH THE MUSEUM felt like it had taken a deep breath and decided to keep going. The visitor hum rose and fell like a tide against the lobby steps. Downstairs, the air held that cool, careful quiet the living floors liked. Sia waited by the mural landing with her notebook in both hands. The road on the wall ran into a bright lake and held the sun still. She didn't touch the frame. She didn't need luck. She needed listening.

Marcus came down the stairs with Truth close on his left. He wore the look he put on for checks, not hard, just tuned. He stopped beside Sia and scanned the corridor without looking like he was scanning it. Truth's ears tipped forward. Her tail did the slow one-two that meant focused.

"Ready," he said.

"Yeah," Sia said. "The bend was strongest in the reading room under the vent grille. It felt like the note caught on something."

"We'll run the line," Marcus said. "No poking. If anything wakes, we step back and call it."

"Copy," Sia said. She liked that he didn't make it bigger than it was. Small is where we live, Kaelan had said. Sia believed her.

They started at the reading room. The green-shaded lamps were on, but the room was empty for the moment. Sia led him to the floor grille near the stacks. Truth lay down with her chin on her paws and watched the metal square like it might decide to tell a joke.

"Same vent as before," Sia said. "Yesterday it tried a laugh that wasn't. Today it only bent the harmony."

Marcus crouched. He didn't put his ear to the grille. He closed his eyes, set one hand on his knee, and let his shoulders settle. When he breathed, Sia felt the room match him a little, like it trusted his pace.

"I get the building," he said after a moment. "Clean. Stone, paper, dust that behaves. Under that, metal, sweet, and old-coin." He opened his eyes and looked at her, not the grille. "That taste comes and goes. Small. Nothing is pushing."

"Kitsune cousin said pennies yesterday," Sia said.

"She did," Marcus said. He stood and followed the baseboard to the corner where the vent run probably turned. He didn't touch the wall. He walked ten paces, slow. Truth rose and paced with him, nose low, tail level. Sia followed, keeping enough distance that she didn't change his read.

He stopped at the corridor junction where the hall bent toward the mural landing. "Here," he said, and crouched again. The paint looked normal. The shadow line at the floor looked normal. Sia felt the tiny tug she'd marked on her map, the one pencil had straightened without asking. Not a pull. More like the idea of a pull.

"What," she asked.

"Brush," Marcus said. "Like someone walked past the wall from the other side. Not today. Not loud. A day or two."

"Demonic," Sia asked. She didn't whisper. Whispers make small things bigger.

He didn't answer fast. He closed his eyes again and breathed the way he did when he wanted his body to be an instrument instead of a barricade. "Not a person," he said. "Not a building. Not one of us. There's a touch of heat that doesn't belong. Not the right kind for Fae. That coin-sugar taste rides with it. Could be low demon, could be something demonic-adjacent that borrowed a tool. Either way, small. The house flattened it when it tried to laugh yesterday. Today it's residue."

"Like static," Sia said. "After you take a sweater off in the dark."

"Yeah," he said. "Exactly that."

He moved on, ten more paces, then stopped at a second vent grille lower on the wall, almost hidden behind a narrow table no one used. Truth circled once, sat, and stared at the corner where the baseboard met the stone. Her ears tipped back and forward.

"Do you want to touch," Sia asked.

"No," he said. "I want to call it and see if it answers anyway." He set his hand near the paint, not touching. "We're inspecting the run," he said to the wall like he was speaking to a person who hadn't decided if they wanted to be helpful. "We won't poke. If you've got anything to say, do it without waking up."

The air cooled half a degree. Sia felt it on the inside of her wrist where skin is thin. A sound like someone rubbing a coin across dry wood tried to be a laugh and failed. Truth huffed once, not scared, just telling them she heard it too.

"Okay," Marcus said, calm. "Thank you. That's enough."

The not-laugh died the way a match dies when you close a jar over it. The hallway settled back into patient building.

"Minor," he said. "Low. But I don't like coins on cloth in pockets at the front door, and I don't like coin rub in vents."

"Same family," Sia said.

"Feels like it," he said. "Someone played with something dumb. Or someone handed them something and said it would help. It bounced off the threshold, looked for a seam, found one it could whisper into without breaking the rules, and got flattened. It's trying corners because corners are what little cowards try."

Sia made a small sound that might have been a laugh if she'd let it. "You hate corners."

"I hate surprises that pretend to be corners," he said. "Come on. One more junction."

They took the bend toward the mural landing. The painting held noon like a secret even in the low hall light. Sia paused and let the road do to her what it did to her every time: line up the inside of her chest with a horizon that felt honest. Marcus didn't hurry her. He set a palm near the frame and didn't touch. "We're walking by," he told the wall. "We're not asking you to do anything."

The air stayed the same. Sia liked that about this place. It didn't perform for them. It worked.

They stopped at the seam she had circled yesterday. Up close, the paint looked like paint. The tiny line where two coats met looked like a tiny line where two coats met. Sia didn't press a finger to it. Marcus didn't either.

"Same taste," he said. "Less today than yesterday. If I were cheap trouble trying to find a way in, I'd run this line and see if anyone was dumb enough to chase me."

"We're not," Sia said.

"No," he said. He took a photo with his phone, no flash, then measured from the molding and the corner to log the exact spot. He dictated a note without looking at the screen. "Basement vent run, seam at mural turn, low demonic residue, consistent with coin-charm at threshold yesterday. Passive monitor recommended. No poke."

Sia watched his mouth when he said passive. It wasn't the way some people say passive, soft and useless. It meant let the house do its job and give it tools.

"Okay," he said. "We're good. Walk back."

They didn't talk for the first stretch. The hall's orbs chimed their not-melody. Sia let the quiet sit and match her insides to it. Truth brushed her leg once and then drifted to Marcus's side again, keeping the line between them like a habit she loved.

At the landing, Sia stopped. She didn't plan it. Her feet did. Marcus stopped too, not crowding her. The mural's lake held the sun the way the bell in the desk wood held the tone. She put her hand on the notebook like she was keeping a page from blowing over in a breeze that wasn't there.

"Thank you for not touching the seam," she said.

"Thank you for catching the bend," he said.

"Do you think it's going to get loud," she asked.

"Not today," he said. "Loud things want an audience. Whatever this is keeps trying to find a back door and getting embarrassed."

She let out a breath she hadn't noticed holding. "Good."

He watched her for a second like he was trying to decide whether to risk saying something. He did. "You doing okay in the house," he asked. "Not the work. You."

She let the question land and sit. "I like rules," she said. "They make room for people to be people."

He smiled a little. "You said that yesterday."

"It's still true," she said. "Also I like that Charles writes them down like grocery lists. It makes the magic feel like posture instead of performance."

He nodded. "You don't have to be impressive for the building to help."

She looked up at him. The stair light made his eyes look like a color she didn't have a word for yet. He didn't lean in. He didn't move at all. She stepped half a step closer so their sleeves almost touched and didn't, and let that be what it was.

"I'm glad it's you checking the halls," she said. "That's all."

"I'm glad it's you hearing the bends," he said. "That's all."

Truth yawned one of those big dog yawns that resets a room. Sia laughed, quiet. They moved again together without needing to say they were moving.

By the time they reached the parlor, Charles had the low table cleared and a notepad open. Kaelan stood by the fireplace with her bracelets quiet. Ella passed behind the sofa with a handful of folded maps and then slipped out. Tobias leaned in the doorway long enough to hear the first two sentences and then took his post by the hall to run interference if a visitor wandered too close.

Charles gestured to the sofa. "Report," he said, and did not make it a pressure word.

Marcus sat at the corner where he could see both the door and Sia's face. Sia took the cushion beside him and set her notebook on her lap but kept it closed. Truth stretched under the table and made a small circle with her body where sunlight happened to be.

"Minor residue along the basement vent run," Marcus said. "Same flavor as the threshold incident yesterday. Coins and burned sugar. Nothing active. The house flattens it when it tries to be clever. We found it strongest near the reading room grille and at the seam by the mural turn. It fades toward the volunteer hall."

Kaelan's mouth tightened a millimeter. Not fear. Focus. "Demonic," she asked.

"Low," Marcus said. "Could be a cheap familiar tied to a coin. Could be someone with a pocket charm and a bad idea who walked near a seam a few days ago and left a film behind. Either way, it's trying corners, not the front door."

"Which means it is either shy or testing," Charles said. He wrote three short lines on the pad, not a paragraph, just a list. "We do not give it attention. We do not let it learn us."

Sia lifted a hand a little. "Can we set passive monitors," she asked. "Not alarms. Just listening."

"Yes," Charles said at the same time Marcus said, "Yes."

Kaelan exhaled through her nose like a laugh that didn't need sound. "Good. I will ask the house to hold a tighter silence along that run," she said. "Not a wall. A hush. If something tries to rub a coin along it again, it will find felt instead of wood. It will be bored and go away."

"I'll place scribe tags at the junctions," Marcus said. "Ink only, no metal, no heat. If they pick up anything, they will give us a pattern without feeding it."

Sia looked at her hands on her notebook and then at Kaelan. "If we map it, Charles can lock it out," she said. "Not by force. By policy the building agrees to."

Charles nodded. "Consent works for doors and for rules," he said. "If the house knows the shape, it can say no to it without thinking. That is better than cleverness."

"Do we want the White Circle to look," Kaelan asked

Charles.

"Yes," he said. "But not today. We start small. Let the house lead."

"Copy," she said. She didn't write anything down. Sia suspected she would remember the three lines by the way the bracelets sat on her wrist.

"Visitor crowd?" Marcus asked, turning the question toward logistics instead of theory.

"Normal," Charles said. "Ella's maps helped. The phone baskets are working. Two polite reminders and one dictionary."

"Good," Marcus said.

Sia pushed her notebook a half inch onto the table. "I can draw the run with the two strong points and the relative fade," she said. "It won't be schematic. It'll be how it feels to the building."

"That is exactly what I want," Charles said.

Sia opened to a fresh page. She drew the reading room as a rectangle and set the grille where it belonged. She drew the corridor bend, the mural landing, and the seam. She used a softer pencil and shaded where the coin taste hung heavier. The graphite darkened on its own at the corners, a little, and then stopped when she lifted her hand and thought that's enough. She didn't look at anyone when that happened. She added a thin line of white pencil along the run to mark Kaelan's hush. The white sat on top of the gray like a quiet promise.

Kaelan leaned in without crowding. "Good," she said. "This is what the house understands. Not rulers. Shapes."

Marcus pointed at the seam mark. "Passive tag here and here," he said. "Nothing complicated. The house will use them if it wants."

Charles turned the notepad and wrote four short bullet points.

Passive listen along vent run

No touching seams

Kaelan hush tonight

Map updates daily

"Schedule," he said.

"Tags before close," Marcus said. "Hush after the last tour leaves." He glanced at Sia. "Walk at nine? Quiet. You and me."

She felt heat in her face and decided not to be embarrassed by it. She nodded. "Nine."

"Good," Charles said. He tore the page from the pad and pinned it to the small corkboard by the bookcase where only staff would notice. "We are not interesting to whatever this is. We are thorough. That is better."

Truth sighed like a dog who had just won a small argument with gravity. Her tail thumped once against Sia's shoe. Sia reached down and rubbed the soft place behind Truth's ear and felt the steady beating of a dog heartbeat anchoring the room in a way rules can't write.

"Anything else," Charles asked.

"One more small thing," Sia said. She tapped the corner of her drawing where the white line met the reading room. "When Mariah and Mia sing tomorrow, can we do one pass with the vent covered. A towel, not tape. I want to hear if the bend is the metal or the run."

"We can," Kaelan said. "The house doesn't mind towels. It hates duct tape."

"Same," Eric said from the doorway. He was halfway in, halfway out, holding two cups and pretending he was just a guy with coffee and not a person who had been listening since sentence two. "Sorry. I brought tea. Not eavesdropping. Much."

"You're fine," Charles said. "Leave the cups and your commentary elsewhere."

Eric set the cups down and backed out. "Copy," he said, softer than his usual.

Tobias slid an updated rotation card onto the table edge. "I moved the courtyard watch to start earlier if you're tagging tonight," he said. "I'll take first hour and stay out of your way."

"Thank you," Marcus said.

The room uncoiled a little, like a held breath exhaling. Sia closed her notebook and let her palm sit on the cover for the length of two heartbeats. Something small tapped back from the other side, polite as a librarian, and then went still.

Kaelan straightened and set her bracelets in order with a light touch. "I will set the hush," she said. "If you feel it try to become a net, tell me. We do not trap. We quiet."

"Quiet is good," Sia said.

"It is," Kaelan said. She smiled like a person who loved her job even when it was mostly floors and cards and small adjustments no one noticed. She left without rattling the doorframe.

Charles closed his notepad. "Go easy," he told them both. "Do not let a little trouble convince you to act like it is big."

"We won't," Marcus said.

They stood. Truth flowed to her feet like liquid with a tail. In the doorway, Sia and Marcus paused for the space of a breath. They didn't say anything that needed a room. She touched his sleeve with two fingers and let go. He looked at her hand like it was a check mark on a list he was glad to keep.

They walked back into the hall together. The orbs chimed their not-melody. The lake in the mural held noon without asking for a name. Somewhere upstairs a kid laughed at a poster from 1932 like it had been made for him. The building kept its promise by doing what buildings do when people treat them like partners. Sia followed the white line of hush in her head and thought about nine o'clock and passive tags and the way rules can turn into safety you can feel under your feet. It was enough for now.

CHAPTER 4

After Hours, After Rules

MARCUS

> Offering sanctuary is a revolutionary act; it expresses love, when others offer scorn or hate. It recognizes humanity, when others deny and seek to debase it. Sanctuary says 'we' rather than 'I'. It is belonging—the building block of community.
>
> Diane Kalen-Sukra

NINE O'CLOCK FELT LIKE a different museum. The lobby lights were softer, the tin charms over the desk barely turning.

Downstairs, the hallway orbs woke ahead of them like someone laying coins on a table one at a time. The air had the cool of stone and clean paper. Marcus liked nights. Buildings told the truth at night.

Kaelan stood by the mural landing with a small cloth pouch and three neat cards clipped together. She wore a dark sweater and the kind of flat shoes that never apologized to floors. Sia leaned on the rail with her notebook balanced on her palm, pencil ready. Truth sat at Marcus's heel, tail doing the slow one-two that meant on duty.

"Consent check," Kaelan said, light. "We lay hush along the vent run. You place ink tags where the line kinks. We ask the doors before we touch them. We do not poke anything that thinks it is clever."

"Copy," Marcus said. He tapped the capped pen in his pocket. "Ink only. No heat."

Sia flipped to a fresh page. "I will map intensity and where it fades when the hush goes on."

"Good," Kaelan said. She looked down the hall and spoke like she was greeting a neighbor through a screen door. "May we walk your length quietly."

The orbs chimed a small not-melody. The seam by the staff bath lost that hair of tension Sia had marked yesterday. Consent received.

They started at the reading room. The green lamps glowed like patient eyes. Sia crouched by the floor grille, listened, then drew one light circle around it. Marcus set a narrow paper tag the size of a fingernail just inside the frame, inked a tidy symbol on it, and breathed once to fix the habit into his hands. Truth watched his fingers like the tag might try to crawl away.

"Okay," Kaelan said, and took out the first hush card. It was blank, plain white. She set two fingertips to it, the way people touch a forehead in thought, and asked the wall, "May I lay a quiet here."

The card took no visible mark. The air at ankle height calmed a notch. Sia felt the bend near the grille smooth as if a wrinkle had been ironed without heat. She drew a tiny line and wrote less beside it.

"Good," Marcus said. "Next point."

They moved toward the corridor turn. The hush held like felt pulled gently along the baseboard. Marcus placed a second tag by the spot where yesterday's coin taste had been strongest. He was halfway through the symbol when a familiar set of footsteps tried to sneak and failed.

Eric slid into view at the far end of the hall like a kid who had promised to behave and then remembered he was still himself. He lifted both hands, palms out. "I am not touching anything," he said.

"Correct," Kaelan said. "Because the hallway will touch you back with a dictionary."

"That happened twice," Eric said. "I have learned."

He aimed for the volunteer corridor door without thinking about it, then stopped himself two feet short. He set his palm near the paint and said, carefully, "May I check the battery shelf."

The seam did not move. He tried again, more polite. "Please."

Nothing.

Eric squinted like the door had made a point and he was trying to accept it. "I am a good person," he told it.

Kaelan hid a smile in the shadow of her hand. "Ask the hall, not the door," she said. "You are trying to skip the line."

Eric turned ninety degrees to face the long stretch of wall. "Hallway," he said, serious. "May I walk to the volunteer corridor and check the battery shelf without messing up your vibe."

The light along the baseboard warmed a fraction. The seam at the volunteer door softened. The latch clicked.

"Oh," Eric said, pleased. He stepped forward. Then he paused, looked back at Kaelan, and said, "Thank you."

The hallway did nothing that a person could see. The air felt happier anyway.

Marcus could not help himself. He said, "Channel one, no chatter."

"Copy," Eric said, doing his best to walk like a person who belonged in a museum after hours. He got to the door, reached, then caught himself and asked the door too. The latch said yes. Progress.

Kaelan put down the second hush with two fingers and a quiet, "May I." The coin-sugar taste along the seam tried a tiny scrape, then found felt instead of wood and gave up.

Sia drew another circle and shaded it lighter. "Less again," she said. Her pencil line decided to straighten at the corner and she let it.

Eric came back with a neat stack of labeled battery packs and a tangle of cables already sorted with twist ties. "Do you people just absorb chaos through the walls," he asked. "Because I swear this was a mess earlier."

"The building likes order," Kaelan said. "We try to honor that."

Eric looked down the hall, at the glowing orbs and the patient doors. "Hey," he told the hallway, sincere. "Thanks."

For one second the lights along the baseboard did a soft wave like someone had run a hand under water. Eric grinned, delighted, then caught himself and made his face normal again.

"Do not get cocky," Marcus said. "Hallways can smell cocky."

"I can too," Truth added by wagging once.

They reached the mural landing. The lake held noon. Sia always felt steadier here. Marcus set the third tag near the place he had measured yesterday and looked at Kaelan. She set her fingertips to the last card and asked the wall again. "May I lay a quiet here."

A small scrape rose from inside the vent run, like a coin dragged across dry wood. It tried to become a laugh. The hush took it apart the way a pillow takes noise apart. What remained was the shape of someone who had lost interest.

"Good," Marcus said, and wrote the time down. "Direction from south alley to mural turn. Intensity low. Hush absorbs without echo."

Eric, who had been standing with his hands behind his back

like a museum kid on a field trip, took two careful steps toward the seam. "Do not," Marcus said without looking up.

"I was going to ask," Eric said.

"Ask from there," Kaelan said. "Consent does not only belong to doors."

Eric faced the wall like it was a person he had annoyed earlier and wanted to do better with now. "We are walking by," he said. "We are not poking. Please do not be weird while my friends are working."

It was ridiculous. It was also polite. The hallway did not answer, which Sia decided was the best possible reply.

They continued down the service corridor for a quick pass. At each turn, Kaelan asked. The walls said yes in small ways. At one door, Eric forgot himself and gave it a push with the casual confidence of a teenager who had never met a boundary he couldn't charm. The door stayed shut like it had invented the idea.

He blinked, backed up, and reset. "Door," he said. "May I open you to check the list."

The seam softened. The latch clicked. He turned the handle with a face that said I am learning even if it kills me.

"Better," Kaelan said.

"Character growth," Eric said.

He finished his check and tried to come back out without asking. The door leaned stubborn again. He stood there for a second, then said, "Okay. Sorry. May I leave."

The door opened smooth like it had never had an opinion.

Eric stepped through, rolled his shoulders, and muttered, "Yeah, well, your mom is a willow tree."

Sia snorted. Kaelan coughed into her hand and failed not to laugh. Marcus kept a straight face because he was good at his job.

"Did you just insult a hallway," Sia said.

"I complimented its lineage," Eric said. "Willows are elegant. They have boundaries and vibes."

"The hall is not offended," Kaelan said, smiling. "But next time, thank you is enough."

"Thank you," Eric told the hallway, more earnest this time.

A dictionary thumped off a shelf inside the volunteer room. Eric jumped and looked wounded. "That was not me," he said.

"Consider it a reminder," Kaelan said. "Polite in, polite out."

"Copy," Eric said, holding the battery packs like an offering. "I am going to put these away where they belong and then leave before the building assigns me homework."

"Too late," Marcus said. "You are on courtyard watch at ten. No ideas. Just eyes."

"I have so many ideas," Eric said. "I will write them down and not do them."

"Growth," Sia said, and this time it did not sound like a joke.

Eric disappeared in the direction of the staff door. The hush along the baseboard stayed where Kaelan had laid it, quiet like a blanket, not heavy like a weight. The not-laugh in the vent did not try again.

They finished the run and circled back to the mural. Kaelan

touched the frame with two fingers and took a breath that set everything inside her to the same tempo as the room. "Consent held," she said. "Hush is seated. If anything scrapes, the house will turn it into nothing before it thinks of being a noise."

"Tags are live," Marcus said. He checked the time and wrote it. "Sia, anything on your map we missed."

Sia turned the notebook so both of them could see. She had drawn the vent run as a soft gray line and shaded three spots a little darker. The white pencil she used for hush sat on top like chalk on slate. Along the mural turn, the white line thickened on its own for a fraction of a second and then settled. Sia lifted her hand and the pencil stayed still.

"That," she said, tapping the thicker segment, "was the not-laugh. It tried to become a shape and then decided to be bored."

"Good," Marcus said. "We love bored."

Truth leaned against his shin and sighed like someone letting go of a long day. Kaelan tilted her head, listening the way she always did.

"Thank you," she told the hall. "We will leave you to your evening."

The orbs dimmed a single notch. Lights listening. Consent answered.

On their way back past the staff bath, the corridor denied Eric again, gently, because he volleyed a quick, "Can I grab a snack," at a door that had never once in its life been a kitchen. He stopped, frowned at it, then shrugged.

"Fine," he said, walking off. "Your mom is a willow tree."

This time the dictionary did not fall. Somewhere, very faintly, a bell sounded the shape of a laugh. Not a ghost. Not a demon. Just a building that had decided to enjoy a joke as long as the person making it meant no harm.

Marcus let himself smile as they took the turn for the parlor. Nights were good for learning. Hallways had patience. Teenagers sometimes did. Doors liked being asked. The hush sat quiet along the baseboard like a promise, and the room felt like it had accepted their part of the deal.

THE PARLOR AT MIDNIGHT felt like a room that knew how to hold voices without letting them echo. Fire wasn't lit. The green-shaded lamps gave enough light to make edges honest. Truth circled once under the low table and settled with a sigh that sounded like a period.

Charles set a plain notepad on the table and slid a pen beside it. Kaelan leaned a shoulder against the bookcase with her bracelets quiet. Sia came in a step behind Marcus, notebook in both hands, hair pulled back like she wanted nothing in her face while she thought.

Marcus sat at the corner of the sofa that let him see the door and the hall. Habit. He took a breath and let the day line up in his head the way tools line up on a pegboard.

"Report," Charles said. Not heavy. Just the word.

"Tags placed," Marcus said. "Reading room grille, mural turn, service corridor junction. Ink only. No heat. Hush seated along the vent run." He kept it short so the room didn't have to hold a lecture. "Two light scrapes tried to become laughs. Hush absorbed both. No echo. Intensity low."

"Timing?" Charles asked.

"Nine thirty-two and ten oh eight," Marcus said. "Direction south alley toward mural. Faded near volunteer hall."

Kaelan nodded once, eyes half-closed like she could hear the run under the floor. "It felt like a pebble thrown down a long pipe," she said. "By the time it got to us, all the speed was gone."

"Late delivery tried the door at eleven," Marcus added. "Ticket moved without permission. Driver just wanted to be done. Helper had a pocket charm. Threshold killed the charge when he yanked it out. We rescheduled for eleven tomorrow. Ella logged plates, names, time."

"Bowl out in the morning," Ella said from the doorway, already holding the ceramic dish. She set it on the bookcase and tapped the index card she had printed. **Leave pocket charms here. Pick up when you go.** Friendly font. No red. "I'll keep the bowl in sight."

"Good," Charles said. He wrote four bullets on the pad in clean block letters.

> Tags live, hush holding
> Two minor scrapes, no echo
> Late delivery refused, rescheduled

> Charm bowl out, signage gentle

"Flavor?" Kaelan asked Marcus.

"Coins and burned sugar," he said. "Same as the threshold kid's pocket yesterday. Same as the whisper at the grille when Sia first caught it. Low demon or something playing at it. Not a push. Testing corners."

"We keep corners boring," Charles said. "Bored trouble goes elsewhere."

Sia set her notebook on the table and turned it so they could see. Her map showed the corridor in graphite, hush in a thin white line, darker shading where the residue had been strongest. She had marked two small times in the margin. Nine thirty-two. Ten oh eight.

"This matches," Marcus said. He liked that her map made the shape obvious without needing legend keys and arrows.

Kaelan studied the white line. "The hush took," she said. "If it tries again, the house will yawn and that will be the end of it."

"Exterior grilles," Marcus said. "I want a cover-story check. HVAC vendor. No magic notes on the work order. They'll look at screens, we look at edges."

Charles wrote another bullet. "HVAC walk this week. I'll call in the morning."

"Tobias moved courtyard watch up an hour," Ella said. "He is taking first post. Eric has second. I am giving Eric a thermos so he doesn't invent reasons to come inside."

"I told him no ideas," Marcus said.

"He is writing them down," Ella said. "He's proud of that."

Truth thumped her tail once under the table. Marcus reached down and scratched the soft place behind her ear. She leaned into it in a way that pulled the stress out of his hand without asking permission.

"Anything else on the run," Charles asked.

"Yeah," Marcus said. "Tomorrow we keep passive only. No poking. I'll walk it twice, early and late. Kaelan can refresh hush if it thins. If a scrape tries to be clever, we let the house make it boring again."

Kaelan touched her bracelets. "Copy."

"Good," Charles said. He tore the notepad page and pinned it to the small corkboard near the bookcase where only staff ever looked. The list sat there like a grocery note. Useful. Unexcited.

The room loosened a notch. Sia closed her notebook with her palm flat on the cover for two heartbeats and then took her hand away. Marcus saw the way her shoulders eased when she did that and filed it as data, not a question to be asked out loud.

Charles picked up the charm bowl and set it on the desk by the fireplace. "We are not interesting," he said. "We are clear. That is better."

"Agreed," Marcus said.

Ella peeled off toward the desk to draft a short email to the shipper confirming the new time. Kaelan stepped to the threshold, listened to the hall, and nodded like she was hearing a pulse she liked.

"Go easy," Charles said to both of them. "We do not let little trouble convince us to act like it is big."

"We won't," Marcus said.

Sia stood when he did. They stepped into the hall together. Truth flowed between them, tail brushing both their legs like she had decided they were a matched set.

They walked without filling the space. The orbs chimed their almost-melody. Somewhere upstairs a chair scraped and stopped. Marcus waited until they were between the parlor and the mural before he spoke.

"Thanks for flagging the bend," he said.

"Thanks for not touching the seam," she said.

They both smiled a little at the symmetry. He wanted to say other things and didn't. She looked like she wanted to draw something and also didn't. Good. Private things could be private without being secret.

"You okay with the night walks," he asked. "We can rotate you out."

"I like learning the hall," she said. "It likes being learned."

"Yeah," he said. "It does."

They passed the mural. The painted road slid into the lake and held the sun still. Sia slowed the way she always did. He didn't move around her. He waited. She took the second she needed and then kept going.

At the staff door, she paused with her hand near the paint. "May I go write this down," she asked the door.

The seam deepened. The latch clicked. She looked at Marcus, then at the door again like she was thanking it for minding the rule.

"Nine tomorrow for the early walk," he said.

"I'll be there," she said.

Truth pressed her shoulder into his knee and then into Sia's leg like she was rearranging them on an invisible grid. Sia laughed under her breath and slipped inside. The door closed without a sound. The hush sat quiet along the baseboard, doing its job without asking for attention.

Marcus checked the line of the lock, the light in the hall, the time. He made a quick note on his phone: **Ops Notes — passive holds, bowl out, HVAC cover, early walk 9, late walk 10.** He sent it to the staff thread and put the phone away.

Kaelan's head appeared around the parlor door. "Hush still seated," she said. "I am going to sleep before it thinks it can do without me."

"It can," he said. "But sleep anyway."

"I plan to," she said, and left with a small wave.

The building breathed the way buildings breathe when the people inside have decided to keep their promises one more day. Marcus put a hand near the bell niche and didn't touch.

"Thank you," he told the room, quiet enough that only a building would hear.

The brass warmed a fraction. The reply was not a sound. It was a feeling like a yes you could stand on. He took it, turned off the last lamp in the parlor, and walked the hall one more time before bed.

CHAPTER 5

Mages & Patterns

Sia

Believe in your heart that you're meant to live a
life full of passion, purpose, magic and miracles.
Roy T. Bennett, The Light in the Heart

THE DAY BEGAN WITH fur on the steps.

Sia noticed it first as a scatter of downy hairs near the door-
mat, silver-brown and soft as dandelion seeds. Then the group
rounded the banister in two neat lines, small bodies in matching
yellow field-trip scarves, and the lobby air filled with the warm,
clean smell of moss after rain.

Sasquatch children were smaller than the campfire stories,
rounder in the cheeks, and absolutely focused. Their elders

walked at the edges, tall and quiet, long coats cut like forest shadows. The kids' voices were breathy and low, like the start of a yawn that turns into a whisper. When they laughed, it came out in chuffs that made Truth perk her ears and thump once.

Ella stood behind the desk with the ceramic bowl placed where small hands could see it. A card sat propped beside it in friendly font: **Leave pocket charms here. Pick up when you go.** Next to the card, she'd stacked a sheet of **sticker badges** and a little coupon book that said **Hot Cocoa — One Cup**.

"Welcome to the museum," Charles said, warm but not loud. "We're glad you're here." He bowed his head to the elders and then to the kids as if both were equally important.

The lead elder, silver in the beard and eyes the color of river stones, returned the nod. "We thank your house," he said. His voice carried like the low part of a song. "Our young ones learn rules and wonder today."

"Good," Kaelan said from the threshold to the hall. "We keep both in the same rooms."

A small sasquatch boy reached for the mobile of tin charms overhead, then stopped himself with visible effort. He stuffed his hand in his vest pocket and looked very proud. Sia watched the outline of a coin press against the knit. It made a neat circle, heavy enough to show.

Ella tipped her chin at the bowl. "Before you start, we have a house habit," she said, tone friendly. "Pocket charms go here while you visit, then back in your pockets when you leave. You get a sticker and a cocoa ticket for trading for an hour."

A few hands went to pockets. A few more followed when the first clink of metal hit ceramic. The elder watched, approving but not commanding. Most of the kids came forward, solemn about the ritual. Tiny hands dropped buttons, a tooth on a string, a smooth stone painted with an eye, two metal washers like pretend coins, and three actual coins with old presidents worn nearly flat.

The boy with the yellow vest hesitated. He stroked the coin in his pocket with one thumb, eyes on the bowl like it might bite.

"It comes back to you," Ella said to him, softer. "We just keep the house from getting noisy."

He shook his head once. "It's for luck," he said. His breathy register turned the k into something softer.

"Luck works better when you ask first," Kaelan said. "You can borrow our luck for a while. It fits everyone."

He clutched his pocket tighter. An elder behind him put a gentle hand on his shoulder and bent to murmur in a language Sia felt in the bones more than heard. The boy listened, then scrunched his mouth sideways.

"Tell you what," Ella said. "Cocoa now or later. Your pick. But the coin stays here while you explore. You can decide in the next room."

He nodded once, reluctant truce, and kept his hand inside the pocket like he was keeping a frog from escaping.

Marcus drifted to Sia's side, which always made rooms feel more organized. "Hush is steady," he said low. "Bowl helps."

Sia nodded. The air along the baseboard felt like white chalk on slate again, the way she had drawn it. She opened her notebook and marked a small dot near the staff hall mouth, then drew a line to the bowl and wrote smoother.

In the reading room, Mariah waited with a towel folded over her forearm like a cafe server. The green lamps were on. The elders took the benches along the wall. The kids gathered in a half circle, breath fogging the edges of the glass where they leaned closer than the glass liked. Truth took a place by the door with the patience of a dog assigned to count heads.

"Song first," Mariah told Mia. "Then science."

Mia smiled and dipped her chin. Sia took the seat just outside the circle, notebook on her knee.

Mariah placed the towel over the floor grille with two fingers and a quiet, "Please." The house did not mind towels. It hated tape. The towel settled and held. Sia drew a small square over the grille on her map and shaded it in.

"Listen to the air," Mariah told the kids. "You do not have to hear anything special. Just notice if the room feels like it's breathing."

The kids nodded with grave seriousness. A fuzzy girl near the back lifted her face and sniffed like she could smell scales. Sia tried not to smile.

Mia sang one pure tone. It was small and honest, the kind of note that doesn't try for effect. It rolled across the room and sat down in the wood like it belonged. Sia felt it lift the tiny hairs along her wrist and loved it for being exactly itself.

"Now again," Mariah said, and slipped the towel off.

Mia sang the same tone. It sat where the first one had and then bent a hair near the grille, a wobble like heat on a road. The kids leaned in as one, tiny black noses twitching.

"Did you feel that," Mariah asked.

"Yes," three kids said at once, breathy and pleased to be asked.

Sia marked two circles around the grille on her map and drew a little arrow toward the hall. She wrote bend returns uncovered.

Marcus crouched by the baseboard and closed his eyes for a second. "Same coin-sugar, very faint," he said. "Hush keeps it bored."

Kaelan stayed by the door and let the elders watch her work without turning it into a show. "Our rule," she told them, voice pitched to their quiet, "is hospitality. That includes your young ones. It also includes this building. We ask, it answers. We do not force."

The elder with the river-stone eyes inclined his head. "Your house keeps promises," he said. "We respect this."

In the front row, the yellow-vested boy still had his hand in his pocket. He kept shifting his weight like his coin wanted to turn. Sia saw it in the way the air leaned near him. The hush line didn't break. It adjusted. She added a note: coin proximity increases bend attempt.

Mia finished the tone and took a breath that didn't scrape. Mariah smiled and nudged her hand with her own, a small touch that meant good.

"Questions," Mariah asked the room.

A furry hand went up, claws tidily filed. "What happens if you sing mean on purpose," the girl asked. Her blank, curious stare reminded Sia of a fox.

"Then you have to apologize to the room," Mariah said. "And you'll probably get dictionaries."

"That happened to me," Eric said from the doorway, holding three clipboards and a bundle of pencils like he was directing traffic in a stationary store. "Thanks for the memory."

The kids laughed. It came out in breath-chuffs that softened every corner.

The elders stood to herd the group to the lobby tour. Kaelan walked backward like a trained usher. "Phones off in the hall," she said gently. "If you hear a bell, just pause. You can take pictures upstairs after."

The yellow-vested boy lingered by the towel. Sia watched him look at it, then at the bowl in his mind, then at Ella's stickers, then back at the towel again like the towel was winning the debate.

"You could trade the coin for cocoa now," Ella said from the doorway as if she had been reading his shoulder blades and not his mind. "Before you see the mirror."

The kid wavered like a sapling in a wind and then nodded. He walked, still clutching the coin, to the bowl. Truth stepped aside politely to let him pass like she knew this was important work.

He hesitated, then dropped the coin. It hit ceramic with a sound that was more thunk than ping. The hush along the baseboard brightened a notch Sia could feel on the inside of her wrist. She drew a tiny star by the bowl icon on her map and shaded the hall run a hair lighter.

Ella beamed, handed him a cocoa ticket and a sticker with a fox and a bell on it, and whispered, "Thanks for trusting us."

He pressed the sticker to his vest. It sat a little crooked. He didn't fix it. He looked lighter.

In the lobby, the elders guided the group past the mobile of charms and toward Exhibit A. Marcus leaned against the staff door frame with his shoulders loose and his eyes on the flow. The mobile turned just enough to pretend it was picking a new song and then settled into almost-music again.

"Good trade," Sia told Ella as the group moved on.

"Bribery is hospitality's cousin," Ella said. "Charles approved the cocoa book. We are very official."

"Your font helps," Sia said, deadpan.

"Thank you," Ella said, entirely sincere.

Sia followed the group to the mouth of the staff hall and paused. The hush line lay there like a white pencil had drawn it along the baseboard. She put her palm near it without touching and asked, small, "Still good."

The answer wasn't a chime. It was the way the room stayed exactly itself.

Downstairs, they walked the corridor once with the elders and a pair of teachers. Sia kept half an eye on the kids' feet and how the hall behaved around them. The ones who had dropped things into the bowl moved like summer water. The ones who had nothing but lint in their pockets moved like summer water too. The yellow-vested boy kept glancing back toward the reading room as if checking that his coin wasn't lonely. The hush did not care. It kept being a hush.

Marcus listened at the grille one more time with eyes closed, then stood. "We're steady," he said. "Good job, towel."

"Good job, bowl," Ella said.

"Good job, kid," Sia said, and drew a check mark next to the note that read coin vessel hypothesis.

Kaelan fell into step with the elders and translated a few of the museum's house phrases into the measured cadence of the hidden village. "Ask before you act," she said. "Hold consent like a key. Do no harm here. If harm arrives, we take it outside and change its shape."

An elder glanced at Truth. "Your dog understands," he said.

"She does," Kaelan said.

Truth wagged once, slow.

Back upstairs, the tour flowed into the exhibits without breaking. The mobile turned once and then not again. Sia closed her notebook and felt the faintest tap from the other side of the cover, not a name, just the sense of a page agreeing to be a map. She breathed out, tasting dust and old lemon oil and the new smell of sticker glue.

Marcus looked over her shoulder at the blank space she had left near the south alley vent icon. "You leaving room," he asked.

"For whatever tries to be clever next," she said. "Or for nothing. Nothing is good."

"Nothing is excellent," he said.

The yellow-vested boy returned from the cocoa table with a paper cup and whipped cream on his upper lip like a mustache. He waved at the bowl, now holding his coin like a sleeping frog, and then rejoined his group in front of a poster of a magician pretending to levitate. He didn't try to jump.

Sia made a final note: **Bowl visible, hush brighter, bend suppressed.** Then she wrote a line in the margin and boxed it twice so she wouldn't forget: **Coins can be vessels.** She underlined can. Not must. Not always. Just can. Enough to change how you walk into a room.

She shut the notebook and tucked the pencil in the spiral. The house kept being a house. The kids kept being kids. The elders kept being patient. The bowl kept being a bowl. It was the sort of morning that made maps worth drawing.

THE UPSTAIRS FLOORS WORE their quiet like a pressed suit. Afternoon light came in soft through tall windows and laid squares across the parquet. The school group's footfalls faded toward the poster hall. In the hush that followed, Charles tipped his head toward the roped-off wing.

"Walk with me," he said.

Sia matched his pace. Truth stayed downstairs with Marcus. Kaelan had drifted toward the lobby to intercept a stroller. The air up here smelled like paper, lemon oil, and a little metal from the frame screws.

They stopped at a mirror in an oak frame. The glass held a pale gray like winter sky. It did not throw back Sia's face. It offered grain, as if a forest had decided to be glass for a while.

"This one refuses people," Charles said. "It will show a room, but not a person in it. The story says a stage magician used it to vanish volunteers. The truth is it kept volunteers safe by declining to show them at all. When he retired, he sent it here rather than let it be repurposed by someone careless."

Sia tilted to check the angle. The frame showed the far wall, the column, the window. Not her. The space where her head should have been was paper. She liked it more for not cooperating.

"Why keep it on display," she asked.

"To remind people that not all old tricks were lies," he said. "And that objects can decide their use if you let them."

They moved to a glass case with a short wand resting on velvet. It was not dramatic. The wood was plain and slightly scarred near the tip.

"This cancels small glamours," Charles said. "If you are making yourself taller by an inch, it will not let you. If you have freckles and you ask the mirror to pretend you do not, it puts them back for an hour."

Sia imagined running the tip across a stage backdrop and watching glitter fall off lies. "Did the owner use it for shows," she asked.

"He used it backstage," Charles said. "On himself and on assistants. There is a line between art and harm. He lived on the right side of it. Not everyone did."

They passed a velvet-lined drawer under the case where a deck of cards rested in a cracked leather tuck box. Three cards were missing. The box label admitted it.

"Oracle," Charles said. "Three cards were deliberately removed by the owner. The deck reads like a person telling the truth when you make room for it. Without those cards, it cannot imply a death that is not inevitable, it cannot promise a love that should not happen, and it will not map war as entertainment."

"Who decided which three," Sia asked.

"The deck owner," Charles said. "A woman who decided war did not get to be a parlor game in her house. She lived longer than anyone predicted."

They lingered. The museum had more of these quiet pieces than Sia had guessed. A pocket watch that ran only in dreams and refused seconds entirely. A rope that always untied itself if left in a room with a closed door. A cloak that stayed true stage black even under noon sun. A ledger with names redacted not with ink, but with something that pulled the names back into the paper.

"Some of the famous ones," Charles said, moving without hurry, "were Mages. Some were plain people who learned to keep company with magic without needing to own it. Some were showmen who made good money and stayed out of the way when serious work was required. The overlap between stagecraft and actual craft is larger than the histories admit. We keep a little of that overlap here. Carefully."

Sia thought about the way the house let her ask for ordinary frameworks and then made volunteers remember the right shelf at the right time. "You always talk about it like work," she said.

"It is," he said. "Work with beauty in it, but still work."

They stopped at a photograph on the wall. A black-and-white street scene from the early twentieth century. The museum facade was the same. The people were not. A man in a vest stood with his hands on his hips, looking like the day belonged to him because he had decided to act like it did.

"Alastair Blackstone," Charles said. "My great-grandfather. He wrote the hospitality rule the house decided to keep."

"What about the hotel," Sia asked. "When did that happen."

"In the beginning," Charles said. "My family kept a circle we called Blue. Our work was containment and care. We built rooms below us because sometimes the best place for a dangerous thing is under your own feet where you can hear it breathe." He smiled without warming it into something soft. "Turns out the rooms wanted to be more than locks. Travelers found us. Strange people in a strange continent needed a door that would not turn them away. We stopped pretending we were only keeping things in. We wrote policies to keep people well while they passed through."

"Refuge," Sia said.

"Refuge," he agreed. "It looks noble from a distance. Up

close it is towels, schedules, soup with enough salt in it, and someone at the desk who can say a clean no when no is the kindest answer."

They took the stairs to the mezzanine. From here the exhibits looked like a town, each case a house with a story inside. Out the window, the town square made itself small and tidy under a comb of wind.

"Chicago is not far," Charles said, almost to the glass. "If you have been paying attention, you have probably felt it."

Sia had. The air around the lake had a habit of deciding which moods a city would have. Trains, water, roads, stories stacked a century deep. It felt like a place that could hold a door open without losing its balance.

"We call it a Border Town," Charles said. "Other people have other names. Crossings thin there. Doors like to appear where there is motion and story. Rails. Rivers. Stockyards. Markets. People who came to start over. Architects who made grand gestures and forgot to account for what else might like to use a high arch. Border places are not good or bad. They are useful. The trick is to know when you are walking through one and behave like it matters."

"Rules louder there," Sia said.

"Yes," he said. "And consequences are quicker. Hospitality keeps more than museums open. It keeps borders from biting."

They turned into a small side gallery with a map pinned to the far wall. It showed the lake like a bright coin, the grid of streets, and a scatter of hand-marked circles where the museum had known doors would try to be born. Someone had dated each circle in Charles's tidy hand. Some had been put to sleep with rituals that read half like building code and half like the way you talk to a horse.

"Do we go there," Sia asked.

"Sometimes," he said. "To close a door that should not have opened. To walk someone to a threshold and make sure they cross into the place they meant. Not as heroes. As staff."

He smiled at that word, staff. Sia liked the pride he took in being ordinary on purpose.

"Kaelan said kami is a cousin word," Sia said. "For Fae. Not equal. Just close."

"It is close enough to be careful," Charles said. "You will hear people say Faewild. It is a good map for some of it. Two courts. Summer and Winter. Stories told their names long before we were tall enough to reach the bell rope."

He led her to a case that held three small things on separate plinths. A brass acorn. A shard of blue glass. A ring of woven grass, brittle but intact. No labels, only accession numbers.

"Summer," he said, nodding at the acorn. "Growth, heat, harvest, favors done with one hand while the other hand picks your pocket. The best of it heals. The worst of it smothers. If you promise out of joy and forget to write a limit, Summer will keep you to the spirit of your joy until you cannot breathe."

"Winter," he said, nodding at the glass. "Stillness, memory, cold that preserves. The best of it keeps people honest and lets hard stories survive the heat. The worst of it starves for the pleasure of order. Winter loves exact words. Do not make casual vows there unless you plan to live inside your sentence."

"And the grass ring," Sia asked.

"Mortals," he said. "Us. We braid things so we can carry them. We make rules and tables and bowls and hotel lobbies because the middle is the safest place when other forces are pulling. The grass dies in winter and returns in spring because someone remembers to plant."

Sia looked at the acorn and the glass and the brittle ring. None of them shone. None needed to. "Are they at war," she asked. "Summer and Winter."

"They are in opposition," Charles said. "Sometimes that looks like war. Sometimes it looks like a dance neither can leave. When they fight in public, mortals get hurt because we are soft and brief. When they keep it to their places, the world continues without noticing. Your job is not to pick a side. Your job is to keep thresholds honest and make sure people who do not belong on the field find their seats."

He walked her past a set of photographs of outdoor theaters. One had grass grown up through the stage boards. One had frost lacing the seats in a pattern too pretty to be weather. Sia felt the pull behind both. The urge to run barefoot in clover that would never stop growing. The urge to stand in clean cold and let everything slow until naming things did not hurt.

"Iron," she said, testing. "Does it help."

"Often," he said. "But not all the time. Folk rules are helpful until they are not. Better tools are consent, clarity, and the refusal to treat hospitality like a trick. Summer and Winter both understand a door that is held closed with a posted sign and a person beside it who means what they say."

"Do not eat or drink without invitation," Sia said, remembering a line from a book that was probably half wrong.

"Better," Charles said. "Do not accept invitations you did not ask for. Know who is offering what. Pay for what you take. Debts are a language in the courts. Mortals survive by keeping theirs small and simple."

Sia thought of the bowl downstairs and the cocoa tickets. "Offer food compensation," she said. "We did that today."

"Yes," he said. "We keep people out of debt by paying for their cooperation in public and ordinary ways. It looks like cocoa. Underneath, it is an oath kept small and clean."

They paused by another case. Inside sat a folded scrap of parchment with an ink blot the size of a thumbprint. Next to it, a small brass stamp with a cracked handle.

"A seal from a treaty between two small courts far from here," Charles said. "The ink blot is deliberate. Someone decided the document should not carry a name out of its border. They spilled ink over the word and then agreed to pretend the spill had always been there."

"That worked," Sia said.

"It did," Charles said. "Names are doors. Sometimes closing a name is the only mercy."

She felt behind her ribs the place where words live and thought about not naming things before they are ready. Her pencil hand itched. She did not open her notebook. She let the urge quiet on its own.

"What do you want me to know before Summer and Winter show up at our door," she asked. The question came out before she could edit it. It felt accurate and a little like standing at the edge of a lake in shoes.

"That they will show up as people," Charles said. "Not as opera. You will know them by how your skin reacts when they speak. You will feel taller or smaller than you are. You will smell heat that isn't from the room or cold that lives without wind. They will be charming. When charm fails, they will be strict. They will treat rules like a game until the moment they need rules to save face, and then they will act as if they invented them."

"And we," Sia said.

"We will have the rules written down," he said. "We will already have practiced when nothing is wrong. We will be polite without becoming food. If they ask for what we cannot give, we will say no and offer tea instead. When you are not sure, you say you are not sure. Summer respects joy that does not lie to itself. Winter respects honesty that does not flinch."

He touched the cane tip gently to the floor, a small dot to end a sentence. "You will hear stories that sort one court into good and the other into bad. Do not bring that into my building. Bring listening. Bring consent. Bring the habit of asking the house before you shape a thing that touches its bones."

Sia nodded. The map of it settled against the maps she was

already drawing. Summer as growth that needed pruning. Winter as stillness that needed doors. Mortals as the ones who built chairs and decided to sit before arguments turned into storms.

"Kaelan's language helps," she said. "Cousin, not copy."

"Good," he said. "Keep it respectful and loose. We survive sloppy metaphors by labeling them as such and moving carefully."

They walked back toward the main hall. The school group chattered near the posters, small breathy voices full of awe at a photograph of a woman in a white dress lifting a mirror that refused to show anything but sunflowers. Sia watched two of the little ones press their noses to the glass and then pull back without smudging. Good chaperones.

Charles paused at the top of the stairs and looked down into the lobby. Ella was explaining the charm bowl to a new set of visitors with her patient-aunt voice. Tobias stood by the staff door, hands tucked in his pockets, not rigid, just present. Marcus listened to the room the way he always did, like it had something to say worth hearing.

"My family thought we were building a vault," Charles said. "We built a porch. Turns out porches save more lives."

Sia pictured the threshold line at the front door and the way it had held for the late delivery the night before. Not a barricade. A posture. "I like porches," she said.

"Me too," he said.

They descended. At the landing he slowed beside the photograph of Alastair again. "You asked me earlier why we keep some things behind glass," he said. "We do not put our best work behind barriers. We put our warnings there. The best work happens at the desk, in the parlor, on a Tuesday with a school group from a hidden village dropping coins in a bowl."

"And in a downstairs hall with a hush that works," Sia said.

"And that," he said, smiling for real now.

They reached the lobby. The building breathed like a person who knows where their chair is. Sia put her palm on the notebook she still hadn't opened and let the idea of a map settle without demanding lines. She did not need to draw this part to remember it. She wanted to hold it as posture.

"Thank you," she said to Charles. "For the tour. For the words."

"Thank you," he said. "For being the kind of person who uses them." He tapped the cane once, light, and headed to the desk to answer a question about group rates as if he had not just drawn the borderlands for her on a gallery wall.

Sia stood a second longer and watched the stories hold. The mirror that refused faces. The wand that canceled small lies. The bowl that kept coins from becoming vessels. The hush that made trouble bored. The porch that stayed open. She opened her notebook then and wrote five words without boxes or arrows.

Ask. Listen. Name last. Keep promises.

She closed the cover and went to find Mariah and Mia, because the day kept going and so did the work.

By late afternoon the parlor felt like after school. Lamps on, soft light, one empty cup on a coaster. Truth was under the table, chin on paws, tail giving a tiny sweep when anyone came in.

Charles set his notepad down. Kaelan leaned against the bookcase with her bracelets quiet. Ella brought a small stack of cards and a roll of tape. Tobias stopped two steps inside the doorway like he'd practiced taking up the right amount of space. Marcus took the corner chair with a clean view of the hall. Sia sat on the sofa arm and opened her notebook.

"Report," Charles said.

Sia turned the book so they could see. She'd layered the day's sketches: a darker ring where the bend showed up with the vent uncovered, a lighter wash after the towel test, a small star by the bowl.

"Coins can be vessels," she said. "Not always. Enough to matter. The bend disappears under the towel, comes back a little when we pull it, and drops when coins go in the bowl. Hush keeps the vent run dull."

"Works for me," Marcus said.

"Bowl's pulling its weight," Ella said. She put one of her cards on the table: **Leave pocket charms here. Pick up when you go. Cocoa ticket for trades.** "People cooperate when you keep it human and give them something."

Kaelan tapped the line Sia had drawn along the baseboard. "I'll refresh the hush at close," she said. "It's holding."

"Writing it down," Charles said. He numbered as he spoke. "One, maintain hush on the run. Two, keep the bowl and signage visible. Three, collect coins at entry with a friendly script and food comp."

"I'll have cocoa and cookie tickets printed by morning," Ella said.

"Good," Charles said, and added it under the third point.

"Passive tags stay where they are," Marcus said. "I'll check them at nine and again at close. No poking. If something tries to get cute, the hush can ignore it."

"I'll set hush to ignore performances," Kaelan said. "No echo if someone tries to make it a bit."

"Noted," Charles said.

Tobias cleared his throat. "I want eyes on the south corridor during peak hours," he said. He held up a small stack of index cards with hourly slots. "I'll take first two hours each day for a week. Not to posture. Just to be there so the space stays calm."

"Rotation?" Marcus asked.

"I updated it," Tobias said, passing a copy to Ella. "Eric asked for a slot with a thermos. I said yes with one rule."

Ella raised an eyebrow. "Which is?"

"He writes ideas down and hands them to me. He doesn't workshop on the radio."

Ella smiled. "Thank you."

Sia drew a small circle by the south hall and marked a T next to it. "A witness helps hush," she said. "Rooms like someone already paying attention."

"I'll bring a chair that doesn't scrape," Kaelan said.

Truth lifted her head and watched Tobias. He looked at Marcus. "If she wants the slot sometimes, I'm in."

"She likes work," Marcus said. "She'll tell you if she's bored."

Truth's tail thumped once.

"Entry script," Charles said to Ella. "Keep it plain."

Ella slid two versions across the table. The first read: **Pocket charms rest here while you visit. You get them back when you go. Have a cocoa on us.** The second: **We keep the building calm by resting metal-on-cloth charms. Trade for cocoa and a sticker.**

"First one," Sia said. "Sounds like a person."

"Script A it is," Charles said.

"Delivery at eleven tomorrow," Marcus added. "Same company. We sign at the door, not the curb. I'll be at threshold. Ella logs. Kaelan on my right. Sia, can you stand near the south hall if the truck idles."

"I've got it," Sia said.

"We'll keep the threshold boring," Kaelan said.

"Good," Charles said.

Sia rested her palm on her notebook. The page felt steady. She let it be.

"Anything else?" Charles asked.

"Two small things," Ella said. "I printed a tiny sign for the bowl that says **no names on charms please**. Also moved the stair map two inches lower so kids can see it without jumping."

"Add both," Charles said, and wrote them down.

Tobias glanced at Sia. "For the coin read, how do I spot it if I'm not you?"

"Watch hands," Sia said. "People touch pockets when they're hiding help. The air near them feels like metal rubbing cloth, not a ring, more a scuff. If you're not sure, steer them toward exhibits and away from the hall. The bowl does the rest."

"Got it," he said.

Marcus set his radio face down. "If a kid keeps a coin after the script and cocoa, we don't make it a scene. We keep them away from the grille and the hall, hand them a map, and let the place teach them. The bowl's there when they're ready."

"Agreed," Charles said. "Dignity first."

"I'll ping White Circle with a courtesy note," Kaelan said. "Not an alarm. Just 'coin vessels in the wild, keeping it calm.' If they see it elsewhere, they'll share."

"Thanks," Charles said.

He pinned the short plan to the staff corkboard. It looked like a grocery list. That felt right.

Marcus looked over. "Walk?" he asked Sia.

"Yeah," she said.

They stepped into the hall. Tobias took the parlor doorway like he meant it. Ella headed for the desk with her tape. Kaelan went to check the hush. Charles paused to scratch Truth's ear, then moved toward a visitor with a question.

Sia and Marcus walked to the mural landing. The orbs along the wall kept their soft light. The painted road slid into the lake the same way as always. Sia stopped to look. Marcus didn't crowd her.

"Thanks for letting the rules do the work," she said.

"Thanks for catching the bends," he said.

They stood there a second, quiet. She didn't open the notebook. She didn't need to.

From the lobby, two quick chimes sounded. Not loud. Clear.

They turned together. Truth read the shift and came up into heel. Ella set her tape down without losing her place. Charles faced the door like he'd been expecting it. Kaelan paused at the corridor, listening once to the hush.

A figure hovered on the top step outside, unsure. The door waited. The bowl was ready. The hush held the line.

"Ready?" Marcus said.

"Ready," Sia said.

They headed for the threshold.

CHAPTER 6

Guest at the Door

MARCUS

A house doesn't make a home. When the place has got history, family, emotions, worries, joys worked into the wood, that's when it gets a solid threshold.

Jim Butcher, Dead Beat

THE PERSON ON THE top step had the kind of stillness that belongs to a freezer aisle. Not dramatic. Just cold at the edges. He held a small satchel against his ribs like a waiter guarding a bill, and he hadn't decided whether to knock or run.

Marcus took his spot a half step behind the threshold line. He didn't crowd the door. Truth sat at his left, ears up, tail in the slow one-two that meant she was working. Kaelan slid to his right, where she could see the street and the sidewalk both. Charles was ten feet back, cane grounded, eyes clear. Ella had the logbook open with a pen ready. Sia stood just outside the staff hall, watching, quiet. Tobias kept the south corridor in view without staring. Eric hovered near the desk until Ella pointed to a chair. He sat.

"Evening," Marcus said through the gap when he cracked the door an inch. "Welcome to the museum."

The man on the step blinked like the word welcome wasn't the one he'd expected. Late twenties, maybe early thirties. Dark hair cut neat. Coat that belonged in a winter catalog. His eyes held that frost-clean stillness Marcus had learned to clock. Winter on the clothesline, not in a blizzard way. The air around his mouth made a tiny curl when he exhaled.

"I'm a courier," he said. Voice formal. Accent nowhere in particular. "I request sanctuary for the night and permission to deliver a sealed letter to Charles, caretaker."

"Okay," Marcus said. He kept it simple on purpose. "We keep a hospitality rule in here. No violence on site. Ask before you act. If you hear a bell, you listen. If you hear a long bell, you stay put and a staffer will come to you. Phones off in the living halls. You agree to that, we can invite you in."

The courier's posture didn't change, but the skin at his throat eased a little. "I agree," he said. "I understand bells."

"Great," Marcus said. "Second thing. Pocket charms rest in the bowl while you're here. You get them back when you leave.

Ella will give you a cocoa ticket for the trade."

The courier's mouth tugged like he wasn't used to that part of a script. His hand drifted toward his coat pocket and stopped. Then he nodded once. "Understood."

"Last piece," Marcus said. "We don't host calls or castings from the lobby. If you need to send a message, you can hand it to staff and we'll figure out a safe way. Deal."

"Deal," the courier said.

Marcus opened the door wider, still standing inside the line. "Come to the threshold and wait one step back. We'll get you squared away."

The man stepped up. The temperature in the gap dropped a notch, the way it does when a freezer door opens and all the air tries to leave. Truth didn't flinch. She watched his hands, then his face, then relaxed a hair when he kept both hands visible.

"Name for the log," Ella said from the desk.

He hesitated just long enough to make Marcus ready to say it was okay to use an alias. "Austin," he said. "Like the city."

"Thank you," Ella said, writing it down. "Time is nineteen fifteen."

"Crossing point," Charles asked from his steady place behind Marcus.

"Chicago," Austin said. "Train to bus, then on foot. It was the least rude door."

"Border Town," Marcus said.

Austin's eyes flicked to him like he'd passed a test. "Yes."

Kaelan nodded once, reading his edges. "You're holding well.

Bowl's on your left."

Austin reached inside his coat and took out a small bundle of cloth the size of a matchbox. He didn't make a show of it. He held it like a person carries a fragile egg and a secret at the same time. Marcus smelled silver under clean cold.

"Is this sufficient," Austin asked. He didn't say what it was. He didn't need to.

"It is," Marcus said. He stepped back enough that Austin could reach the bowl without crossing the line. The ceramic sat on the desk corner in full view, card propped beside it: Leave pocket charms here. Pick up when you go. Have a cocoa on us.

Austin set the wrapped coin in the bowl. It thumped more than it pinged. The air by Marcus's cheek warmed half a degree, the way a room does when someone remembers to close a window. Truth's tail tapped the floor once. Kaelan's bracelets made a single soft click and went quiet.

"Thank you," Ella said. She handed Austin a small ticket. "Cocoa coupon. That's the policy."

Austin took it like he wasn't sure whether to thank her or bow. He settled for, "I appreciate the clarity."

"Letter," Charles said, gentle. "If you still want to deliver it, I'm listening."

Austin touched the satchel with the back of his fingers and looked at the threshold line again. "May I step inside."

"Say yes to the rules one more time," Marcus said. "It makes the door happy."

"Yes," Austin said. "I agree to hospitality, the bells, and no violence."

The door hinge felt like it loosened under Marcus's hand. He stepped back and held the opening without turning it into theater.

Austin crossed the line. He didn't track snow in. He didn't drag a mood behind him. He came in like a person who knew how to walk into rooms without taking them over. Marcus liked that.

"Welcome," Kaelan said.

Austin answered with a short nod that still managed to be polite. He took the satchel strap over his head and set the bag on the intake table by the parlor, then opened it with care. Inside sat a slim leather wallet and a smaller flat box. He placed both on the table and slid the box forward.

"For Charles," he said. "Care of the Arbiter's desk. There's a clause under the seal that grants you consent to open as care-taker."

Charles approached at an easy pace, set his cane against the table, and studied the seal. The wax was pale and matte, stamped with a simple circle and a tiny hash mark in the rim. No dramatics. Marcus felt the plainness like a relief.

"I see the clause," Charles said after a beat. "Thank you." He looked to Marcus, then to Kaelan, then back to Austin. "We'll read this together. You can sit while we do."

Austin's shoulders lowered a centimeter, which was probably a Winter-sized exhale. "Thank you."

Before he sat, his eyes flicked to the bowl, then to the staff hall. Marcus watched the glance because the glance mattered. Nothing moved along the hush line. Good.

"Water," Ella said, already setting a cup on the table.

"Yes, please," Austin said. He didn't gulp it. He took a steady sip like a person who understood what floors and cups and rules were for.

"Marcus," Charles said, tapping the box with two fingers. "Once I break this, we're in a conversation. Let's make sure we've set the room right."

Marcus keyed his radio once, a silent click. Tobias replied with a click from the south corridor. Sia gave one from the staff hall. The building held the kind of quiet that can handle news.

"Conditions," Marcus said to Austin. "No calls out while you're seated here. If someone tries a call in, ignore it. If you feel your temperature drop too far, tell us and we'll move you to the reading room where the wood's thicker."

"I can follow those," Austin said. "May I keep my phone for timekeeping."

"Phones stay at the desk," Ella said, pointing at the charging basket. "You can check it on request."

"Understood," Austin said. He took a phone from his inside pocket and set it near the bowl with a care that said he didn't want to pick a fight with any more furniture tonight.

Truth left Marcus long enough to sniff the air by Austin's chair, not touching him, just making sure the room understood that she was tracking this new person. Austin held still, let her do the work, then gave her a small nod like he'd read the rule about dogs and consent before he arrived.

"Ready," Charles said.

Marcus moved to the corner of the table where he could see the door, the desk, and the south hall. Kaelan took the other side, hands easy at her belt. Ella stood by the desk with the log open to a fresh line. Sia stayed near the staff hall, notebook closed, attention clean.

Charles broke the seal. No smoke. No theater. The paper inside was ordinary stock, printed, not handwritten, the way smart people send messages when they don't want anyone to argue about fonts. He scanned, then read out loud.

"To Charles Blackstone, caretaker, and staff. A request for a neutral window under your house rules for a meeting of proxies in regard to coin-carried nuisances and unlicensed binds noted in your district. Proposed duration: one hour. Proposed number: two and two, with one observer per side. No summons and no binding on site. Reply by three days."

He looked up. "Signed by Arbiter Desk, Lake Division. Co-marked by one Summer proxy and one Winter proxy. No insult language. Plain."

Austin hadn't moved. "I'm authorized to carry the reply," he said. "I am not authorized to argue it."

"What's your read on the streets," Marcus asked. "Since you crossed through Chicago."

Austin considered that for a half second. "Summer's restless. Winter's tight. People who carry small favors are stacking coins in their pockets like it's a game. I saw two scrapes at a threshold on my way here. Both flattened by a hush that wasn't yours."

"Border Town," Kaelan said, satisfied.

"Yes," Austin said.

Ella wrote three lines on a small card and slid it to Charles. He glanced, nodded, and kept the card under his hand.

"Here's our answer for now," Charles said. "We'll consider hosting, strictly under our rules, with our script, after we set the room. No off-site law sneaks in because people say the word neutral too loud. We'll send a formal reply after we run it past our staff and check the calendar."

Austin dipped his head. "That matches what my desk hoped you'd say."

"Good," Charles said. "You need a chair."

Austin gave a small, real smile. "Yes."

"Reading room," Marcus said. "Quiet corner, lamp on, water. We'll do a long-chime drill once you sit so you know how it sounds in here."

Austin stood, steady but careful, like someone whose shoulders weighed more in winter and had learned to move anyway. Marcus walked him as far as the reading room threshold and stopped. He didn't enter. He pointed to the corner where the light pooled and the chair didn't squeak.

"That one," Marcus said. "If the air gets too cold, tell the room out loud. It'll listen."

"I believe you," Austin said. He took the chair, set the cocoa ticket facedown on the table like a marker, and rested both hands on his knees.

Marcus went back to the lobby. He looked at Charles. Charles looked at the bell niche. Marcus nodded.

"Long hold," Charles said.

Kaelan pressed the bell. The tone filled the lobby and ran along the halls like warm water. People paused where they were. Ella set her pen down. Tobias stopped mid step and looked to his right so anyone watching would follow the look and see a staffer. Sia stayed still, visible and calm. In the reading room, Austin froze his hands and didn't try to be helpful. Good.

The bell faded. For a breath the building felt taller. Then it settled into normal again.

"Thank you," Charles said, pitching it to the room. It answered by being the same.

Ella closed the logbook and looked at Marcus. "Do you want the bowl moved an inch," she asked. "Feels like the line of sight from the step to the card could be cleaner."

"An inch left," Marcus said.

She nudged it, stepped back, and nodded. "Better."

Eric stood up like he couldn't stop his legs from having opinions, then caught Tobias's eye and sat back down. Progress.

"We'll draft a reply," Charles said to Marcus. "I'll keep it in the plainest language I've got. We'll ask for their four names in writing, arrival on time, and we'll put water and chairs where they can't argue about them."

"No coins in," Ella said. "We can print the script on the invite."

"Good," Charles said. He tucked the letter back in the flat

box and set it on the intake table like a normal bit of mail that happened to matter.

Marcus checked the threshold line one more time. The pane glass held a faint image of the steps and the square of streetlight beyond. The air wasn't doing tricks. The hush along the base-board felt like white chalk on slate again. He liked that.

He looked toward the reading room. Austin sat the way some people sit in cold churches, serious and present without trying to impress anyone. Sia had vanished into the hall with her note-book closed, which meant she was giving the building space to digest. Truth stood and stretched, looked up at Marcus, then toward the staff door like she had an opinion about who should walk her next.

"Not yet," he told her. "We're still on intake."

Her tail tapped once anyway.

"Okay," Marcus said, mostly to the room. "Welcome to the part where we make boring look easy."

The building seemed to agree. It didn't warm up or cool down. It just held steady while a Winter courier finished a glass of water in a reading room chair, a bowl babysat a wrapped coin, and a desk started a reply in a font that wouldn't scare anybody. That was the job. And it worked.

Austin sat in the reading room like someone who'd learned

how to take up less space than he needed. Lamp on, hands on knees, eyes on the wood grain. The air near him stayed a notch colder, but it wasn't spreading. The hush along the baseboard held like chalk on slate.

Marcus took the parlor side of the threshold and checked the angles. He could see the lobby desk, the bell niche, and the south hall mouth. Kaelan stood where she could watch both doorways without making a map of herself on the floor. Ella set a glass pitcher and a stack of paper cups on the intake table. Sia lingered in the hall, notebook closed, head tilted just a little like she was listening for room tone. Tobias posted up two steps inside the south corridor with that steady watchman posture he'd decided to practice.

"Ground rules," Charles said, voice even. He'd moved to the intake table and rested his cane against his chair. "They're simple, and they're firm. No violence on the premises. Ask before you act. Phones stay at the desk. If you hear a bell, you follow it. Long bell means stay put and staff will come to you. If you feel unwell or pressured by anything you brought with you, you tell us. We'll move you to a better spot."

"I can keep those," Austin said. He glanced toward the lobby, not the door, the bowl. Good.

"Zones," Marcus said. He kept it practical. "Lobby, parlor, reading room are open with staff. Living hall's for us. If you need a real quiet, that corner in the reading room is the best. If you need to leave fast, you say so and we'll walk you to the steps. We don't do surprises."

"No surprises sounds great," Austin said. The way he said great landed flat and honest, not like a joke.

Charles tapped the flat box with the letter once, then set it aside. "We'll consider the neutral window. We'll answer after we check our calendar, set the room, and write a script everyone can follow. If the courts don't accept museum rules, we won't host. That's the whole thing."

"That's consistent with what my desk expected," Austin said. He sat a touch straighter, like the sentence had taken a weight off the spot between his shoulder blades.

Eric drifted a foot closer to the reading room doorway, curiosity bright on his face. Tobias slid one half-step forward without turning it into a scene.

"Back on your mark," Tobias said, quiet.

Eric raised both palms and grinned. "I'm literally on it," he said, and then actually stepped back onto the scuff he'd made in the floor wax last week. Progress.

A ripple of cold lifted off Austin's coat and died at the hush line. Marcus felt it on the inside of his wrists and filed it: pressure test, minimal. Sia didn't move. She just breathed in and out like a metronome the room could borrow.

"Do you need food," Ella asked Austin. "We've got soup."

"Not yet," Austin said. "Water's good."

Ella poured, set the cup where he could reach without standing, and left it alone. Kaelan eased a fraction closer to the reading room threshold and spoke to the house, not the guest. "We're keeping it quiet," she said. "Thank you."

The air warmed half a degree. Austin noticed. He didn't comment.

"Let's log it clean," Charles said. He nodded to Ella.

She flipped to a fresh card. "Name Austin, arrived nineteen fifteen, coin surrendered, phone checked. Letter from Arbiter Desk opened with consent clause. Request for neutral window under house rules. No decision yet. Guest seated reading room."

"Good," Charles said.

"Two more things," Marcus said. "If someone comes looking for you, you don't answer in the doorway. You let us work the threshold. If you've got a second coin or anything else you forgot about, the bowl's still here."

Austin's eyes flicked to his other pocket. He stopped, breathed, and then reached slowly into his coat. He came up with a thin steel washer on a string. He turned it in his fingers. It didn't read like silver. It read like habit.

"This one's sentimental," he said. "No work on it. I can put it in the bowl anyway."

"Up to you," Marcus said. "If it starts acting like a friend with opinions, we'll evict it together."

Austin gave the smallest smile and set the washer in the bowl. Ceramic, light clink. Nothing moved in the air. He looked lighter anyway.

Sia shifted her weight, the kind of move that means a person has decided a room's doing fine. She caught Marcus's eye. He nodded. She took that as permission to step in, not to prod, just to put a word on the table people could use.

"Maps help," she told Austin from the reading room doorway. "If you want to know where the quiet is at any hour, ask. We won't give you a tour like a show. We'll point."

"I'd appreciate that," Austin said. "My sense of direction dies in buildings."

"Same," Sia said. She left it there and backed out again. Good distance, no press.

Kaelan glanced toward the bell niche, then at Charles. "Do you want a second long hold later tonight with fewer bodies," she asked. "Sometimes guests hear it different the second time."

"After closing," Charles said. "We'll warn him."

Austin lifted a hand. "You can run drills as you need. I won't mind."

Marcus checked the lobby again. A pair of teens finished reading the poster about a mirror that refused faces. Ella redirected them upstairs with a smile and a card for the scavenger hunt. Eric went back to highlighting a map, doing the job Ella had given him like he'd chosen it himself.

"You say you came through Chicago," Charles said to Austin. "Anything we should hear beyond what the letter covers."

"Coins are a fad," Austin said. "People like the way they feel strong when the metal talks back. Half the trouble starts because someone wants a party trick. The other half is people who think they can force open a door the way they force open a locked app. The Arbiters are trying to keep it small. They'd rather you set terms than find out by accident when someone shows up with friends."

"Understood," Charles said. "We'll draft clean terms. No coin-carry in the room. Four names in advance. On time. One hour. Water on the table, no gifts, no food unless we serve it and we won't. We run the bell once at the top so everyone understands the rule."

Austin nodded. "I can carry that back."

"You'll carry our reply after we sleep," Charles said. He stood, rested his palm on the table for a second, then picked up his cane. "You're a guest tonight. Not a messenger who has to stay on his feet."

"Thank you," Austin said. He meant it.

"Marcus will place you," Charles said. "Kaelan will keep the hush seated. Ella's your point for normal things like cups and directions. Tobias is eyes on the south hall. If Eric bothers you, he's practicing not bothering people, so tell him nicely and he'll feel proud later."

"I can do that," Austin said, amused.

Tobias checked his watch like the idea of being a posted time mattered to the hallway as much as it did to him. It probably did.

Marcus walked to the reading room threshold again and stopped there. "That corner's yours. If you need the bathroom, it's left, first door. If you need sleep, we'll find a blanket and a better chair. If you need out, say out."

"Copy," Austin said, using the word like he'd earned it. He crossed to the chair and sat. The cold pulled in tight around him the way a person pulls a blanket up. It didn't seep.

"Pressure's fine," Kaelan said, half to Marcus, half to the wall. She set her fingertips on the door frame like a pianist finding middle C. "We'll keep it that way."

Eric drifted again. Tobias lifted a brow. Eric drifted back with an exaggerated innocent face that made Ella snort-laugh into her sleeve.

"Okay," Charles said. He gathered the flat box and the printed page, slid both into a folder, and wrote a single line on the outside: **Neutral window request. Draft reply tonight.** He set the folder on the desk where he'd pick it up when the last visitor left. "We're done making this a moment. Back to normal."

Normal resumed on cue. A couple asked about hours. Ella answered. The mobile of charms gave one lazy turn that decided to stop before it made a melody. The door held the line it always held. The hush stayed put.

Marcus checked the bell niche, then the bowl, then the reading room again. Austin had his hands flat on his knees and his shoulders down. He looked like he could sit for a week if the chair let him.

"Do you want a book," Sia asked from the hall.

Austin thought about it, then shook his head. "I'll watch the wood," he said. Not poetic. Just honest.

"Fair," Sia said. She looked at Marcus. "I'm going to take notes and then see Mia and Mariah. If you need me, I'll have my radio."

"Good," Marcus said. He felt the tick in his chest that meant systems were set and the job now was staying boring.

Ella slid a small laminated card onto the intake table for Charles to sign. Visitor agreement. Plain language. No gotchas. He signed, handed it to Marcus. Marcus walked it to Austin.

"Read it," Marcus said. "If you're good with it, sign and I'll stick it in the folder."

Austin read every line. He didn't rush. He signed in a clean, blocky hand and slid it back. "I appreciate you writing it like a person," he said.

"Helps us too," Marcus said. He took it to the folder and clipped it on.

The room cooled half a notch and then returned. Marcus didn't like the dip, but he liked the return. He looked to Kaelan.

"Still us," she said. "It tried to test the edge and got bored. Hush is tedious on purpose."

"Favorite kind," Marcus said.

Tobias stepped over, kept his voice low. "I'll start the watch earlier tonight," he said. "If anything pings near the south corridor after close, I'll log and sit. No heroics."

"Thanks," Marcus said.

"Do you want a second pair," Tobias asked, eyes flicking toward Eric.

"Not yet," Marcus said. "Let him sort maps. We'll use him when the room isn't learning a new person."

"Copy," Tobias said, and returned to his mark.

Sia finally slipped off down the staff hall, pace unhurried. Truth watched her go and gave Marcus a look that belonged to a dog who had an opinion about who should be walking her next.

"Later," he told her again. "We're almost through the part with clipboards."

Truth sighed like a small huff and put her chin back on her paws.

"Anything else before we break," Charles asked.

"Just one," Ella said. She pointed at the bowl. "I want it an inch left so the first thing a person sees from the step is the card, not the ceramic."

"You already moved it an inch," Marcus said.

"I want the second inch," Ella said.

"Take it," Charles said.

She nudged it. The card lined up with the door sightline perfectly. She gave a short, satisfied nod, then penciled a note on a sticky for morning setup: **Bowl two inches left of desk edge.**

Marcus let himself breathe a little deeper. The intake was done. The letter was open and parked. The guest had a chair. The rules were on paper. The hush had held. Nobody had tried to win the room with volume.

He keyed his radio. "Ops note," he said. "Austin seated reading room, coin in bowl, phone at desk, letter open. We're in consider mode. Hush steady. South hall under watch."

Clicks answered from Kaelan and Tobias. Sia clicked once from down the hall.

"Back to work," Marcus said, mostly to himself. The job was

making sure work stayed what it was. He took one last look at Austin, who had closed his eyes without sleeping, like a person who'd found a way to rest with a wall at his back. Good. Marcus turned toward the desk to help with the next line of questions about hours and parking, because keeping the porch open was still the point.

CLOSING CAME QUIET. UPSTAIRS lights clicked to night settings. The mobile over the desk did one last lazy spin and quit. Austin had drifted deeper into the reading room, lamp on low, shoulders settled. Marcus checked the air by the baseboard. Hush held. Good.

Sia tapped her radio once. "I'm crashing," she said. "Truth, walk?"

Truth looked up so fast her ears made a small flap. Marcus laughed under his breath.

"Take her," he said into the radio.

Sia appeared at the hall mouth with a blanket folded over her arm and that end-of-day tilt to her shoulders. Truth trotted over like she'd trained him, not the other way around. She leaned into Sia's leg, pleased with her life choices.

"Traitor," Marcus told the dog, low.

Sia grinned. "She picked me. Don't be jealous."

"I'm not," he said, and absolutely was a little. "Ten minutes around the block. Don't take the south alley."

"Copy," Sia said. She clipped the leash without asking, because Truth liked the ritual more than she needed it, and headed for the stairs. Truth didn't look back. Marcus put a hand to his chest like he'd been abandoned by a coworker who owed him rent.

Ella came out from behind the desk with three paper cups and a grin. "Want to blow off steam without breaking anything," she asked.

Tobias stepped out of the south corridor on cue, hands in his pockets, posture that gentle kind of ready he'd been practicing all week. "Training window?" he asked.

"Side reading room," Marcus said. "Short rules, short rounds."

They took the room off the lobby, the one with low shelves and a table that didn't wobble. Marcus shut the door most of the way so Austin could rest without hearing them, but he didn't latch it. Museum habit. Doors stay askable.

Ella set the cups down. "Water," she said. "And a timer. No blood. No flinging. We log it as training."

Tobias slid a notebook onto the table and wrote the header: **After-hours drills, consent-based.** He looked up. "First drill?"

"Arm wrestling," Ella said, already rolling up her sleeve. "Fast rounds. Thirty seconds max. Willing contest, call stop any time, we reset if the table complains."

Marcus pulled a chair in and put his forearm on the wood.

"Consent?"

"Given," Ella said. "No wrist torques. No leaning your entire torso like you're shopping for discounts."

"Given," Marcus said. He looked at Tobias. "Ref?"

Tobias set his phone on the table, timer open. "Three, two, go."

They pressed. Ella didn't waste time with theatrics. She met him straight on, grip firm, elbow planted right. Marcus felt the shove in his shoulder first, not his hand. Dragon muscle wanted to win and didn't care how. He let it settle into form and pushed, steady, just enough to test.

Ella smiled like someone who enjoys a puzzle. "You're not even trying," she said.

"I'm trying politely," he said, and gave her five percent more.

She gave him ten back. Her forearm corded under the skin in a way that said gym work and something else. He felt the something else. It tasted like warm metal and old smoke.

"Fifteen seconds," Tobias said.

Marcus leaned a hair. The table didn't complain. Ella's wrist dipped, then recovered in a quick, neat line that belonged on a whiteboard diagram. She wasn't fast. She was efficient.

"Twenty," Tobias said.

Marcus decided not to prove anything and took it home, gentle enough that her knuckles hit the wood like a tap, not a thud.

"Time," Tobias said.

Ella shook her hand out, not mad, not huffy. "Okay," she

said. "Again, but swap sides. Left hand."

"Consent," Marcus said.

"Given," she said.

They reset. Tobias counted. Left-hand grip is always a little weird, but Ella handled it like she'd practiced. Marcus pushed, then checked his own form to keep it safe. Ella grinned at him and changed angle mid-push in a way that made his wrist wobble. He almost lost it out of surprise alone.

"Twenty-five," Tobias said.

Marcus pulled focus back to the shoulder, not the wrist, and edged her down. It wasn't clean. It worked.

"Time," Tobias said.

Ella laughed. "Almost had you."

"You almost did," Marcus said. "I didn't expect a switch."

"Active Dragon Blood," she said, tapping her own shoulder. "Not the same as yours, but it's not a museum exhibit either."

He blinked. "You've been running hot this whole time and didn't tell me."

"You didn't ask," she said, easy. "Also I don't lead with it. File me as 'can lift the heavy box' and 'will argue the sign should be two inches left' and 'hey, nice forearm.'"

He snorted. "Consent to put that on your HR card."

"Given," she said, and took a drink.

Tobias had been writing notes in tidy block print. "Form looked safe," he said. "No torque. We should set a rule about finger flex if someone cranks on tendons. Tap out with the free hand."

"Add it," Marcus said. "And log that this counts for strength and focus, not dominance. The point isn't winning. It's practicing rules that keep everyone safe when adrenaline tries to make decisions."

"Logged," Tobias said.

Ella lifted her brows at Tobias. "Your turn."

"I'm not beating either of you," he said, amused. "But I'll show up."

They reset. Tobias gave consent, Marcus matched grips, and they went. It wasn't a contest. Tobias was strong enough, but the lever arm wasn't in his favor and his shoulder didn't have dragon help. Marcus took him down in seven seconds, careful as putting a coffee mug on a shelf.

"Again," Tobias said, already smiling. "Left."

Left was slower. Ella watched their elbows, ready to call a stop if anyone started cheating without meaning to. Tobias exhaled in a steady count and rode it down without dragging. Marcus liked him for that. Most people fight the last inch like it's personal. Tobias treated it like a rep at the gym. Done, reset, no drama.

"Okay," Ella said. "We've proved Marcus is a problem and I'm a surprise. Switch drill. Brain."

"Chess," Tobias said immediately. "Same consent rules. Timed turns. No gloating, no trash talk that turns into a scene."

"Fine with me," Ella said. "Marcus, do you play."

"A little," Marcus said, which was true if you defined little as grew up with an uncle who played blitz in bars and taught him to castle before he learned to drive.

Tobias set the battered plastic set on the table. The kings wobbled a little on their bases. He clicked the clock down and looked at both of them. "Consent."

"Given," Ella said.

"Given," Marcus said.

"Three minutes," Tobias said. "Increment two. Say 'stopping' if you need to knock it off."

They started. Ella opened clean and simple, center pawns out, knights developed. Marcus mirrored with a small grin he tried to keep inside his face. The room had the good quiet of a library with a door half closed. Outside, the lobby settled into night jobs. Austin's lamp stayed a warm coin on wood.

"Not trash talk," Ella said, moving a bishop. "But if I take your knight it's going to be because you got cocky."

"Noted," Marcus said. He moved a pawn and she took the bait without blinking. She was building something that looked like a pretend mess and wasn't.

Tobias watched their shoulders more than the board. "You're both leaning when the clock ticks," he said. "Rule: both feet flat on the floor or you lose a tempo."

"That's not a real rule," Ella said, smiling.

"It is now," Tobias said, deadpan, and wrote it down like he had a handbook to update.

Marcus moved his queen and immediately regretted it. Ella's rook slid across like a guillotine. He lost the knight she'd promised to take and had to win it back by trading out of a cramped center. She arched a brow when he got loose again, impressed.

"You're better than 'a little,'" she said.

"You almost beat me at arm wrestling," he said. "I didn't want to give you two wins in one night."

"Almost is not two," Ella said. Her rook took an open file like she'd saved it for dessert.

They played two games. Ella took the first on time, not material, because she ran his clock down while keeping the position even. Marcus took the second by building a small net around her king that she saw a half move too late. Each time Tobias said "good" like a coach who liked form more than score. He logged openings, mistakes, and the rule tweaks they would keep. It felt like filing, not flexing. Marcus liked that too.

When they stopped, Ella stretched her fingers and checked the hall. "Austin?"

"Steady," Marcus said. "Hush is bored. That's my favorite setting."

"Same," Tobias said.

Sia's footsteps sounded on the stairs. Truth came in first, tongue out, happy with the world. She walked straight past Marcus and pressed against Tobias like he was a very important lamppost. Tobias froze, then remembered to ask. "Can I pet you," he said.

Truth sat. Consent given.

Sia leaned in the doorway, hair damp from the mist outside. "She hog you," she asked Marcus, cheerful.

"All night," he said. "She left me for better company and didn't even leave a note."

Truth wagged at his voice like she had heard the accusation and found it cute.

"Training went well," Tobias said, still petting like he'd found a button that made his day better. "No broken tables. Marcus is strong. Ella is stronger than she looks. I want to try a grip drill next week with bands so we don't wreck anyone's wrists."

"Good," Sia said. She looked at the board. "Who won."

"Split," Ella said. "He took one. I took one."

Sia nodded like that sounded correct for the universe. "Austin's fine," she added. "He's got that winter church sit going. The lamp helps."

"Thanks," Marcus said. He tried not to look too pleased to have her back even though his insides did the dog-tail thing Truth had been doing all evening.

Ella packed the chess set. "We should formalize this," she said. "Short drills, clear rules, fifteen minutes max, log it like any other training. We can even put a sign on the door that says practice so nobody thinks we're goofing off."

"We're allowed to goof off," Sia said.

"Sure," Ella said. "But we're very proud of being responsible dorks."

Tobias finished the log line and capped his pen. "Next time I want to run scenarios," he said. "Two people in, one person out, verbal scripts only, no hands. It'll make the threshold drills easier."

Marcus nodded. "Tomorrow we'll start the reply draft after breakfast. Neutral window, our rules. Four names in advance. On time. One hour. No gifts, no food. No coins."

"And chairs that don't squeak," Sia said.

"Ella will move them two inches left," Marcus said.

"Don't tempt me," she said, smiling.

From the lobby, a long, soft creak rolled through the boards. The building doing a stretch. The hush line didn't waver. Austin's lamp stayed steady. The night had landed the way nights should land.

Sia yawned once and covered it with the back of her hand. Truth yawned in sympathy, then turned in a slow circle under the side table and flopped with a grunt that sounded like the period at the end of a good sentence.

"Sleep," Marcus said. "We're on early."

"Copy," Sia said. She gave him a small salute that made his chest feel like a lighter thing and headed for the staff hall with Truth at her heel.

Ella stacked the cups and took the notebook to the desk. Tobias killed the timer and taped the log line to the training section of the corkboard by the door: **Arm wrestling, consent rules, 30-second rounds. Chess, 3+2, posture rule added. All drills voluntary, logged.**

Marcus checked the reading room one last time. Austin had gone from statue still to sleep, real sleep, jaw unclenched. The cold tucked in close to his coat and didn't leak. Good.

He turned back to the side room. "Board stays out," he said, tapping the king. "Clocks too. We'll keep this under the same rules we keep everything else. Ask first. Stop when someone says stop. Make it boring to be a problem."

"Deal," Ella said.

"Deal," Tobias echoed.

They pulled the door nearly shut and left the table ready for tomorrow. In the lobby, the bowl caught the last throw of light and the card beside it read the same simple thing it had read all day. Marcus let that be the last check on his list. Then he took the long look around he always took before he called a night done. Doors where they should be. Chairs where they should be. People where they should be. Rules written down. Boring, on purpose.

It felt like the right kind of strong.

CHAPTER 7

Dreaming on Paper

Sia

The future belongs to those who believe in the beauty of their dreams.

Eleanor Roosevelt

MORNING MADE THE LOBBY look honest. The big front windows took sky and turned it into squares on the floor. The mobile above the desk hung quiet, like it had already had its coffee. Sia stood at the parlor threshold with her notebook open to a fresh page and let herself match the room's pace. Truth nosed her knee once and sat, tail thumping twice like a rhythm check.

"Quick status," Charles said. He had the intake table cleared, a plain folder to his right, a capped pen aligned with the edge. Marcus stood near the bell niche, arms loose, looking like he had slept and then remembered how to be awake without rushing. Kaelan leaned against the bookcase, bracelets quiet. Ella rolled in with the logbook and a stack of small clipped sheets. Tobias took his watchman spot two steps inside the south corridor, calm as a museum bench. Eric hovered with two maps and the energy of a golden retriever trying to look professional.

"Hush line," Marcus said. "Seated. No pings overnight."

"Tags?" Charles asked.

"Stable," Marcus said. "Reading room grille and mural seam read the same as last pass. Bored."

"Favorite setting," Ella said, and made a tiny check mark in the margin of her card.

"Bowl placement," she added. "Two inches left of the desk edge. Card angled toward the door. Sticky note on the setup binder so we remember it forever."

Sia drew a small square for the desk and marked the bowl with a dot, then sketched the sightline from the front steps. She wrote card first in her tidy print.

"Good," Charles said. He tapped the folder. "We draft, we read, we send. Plain and clean."

Austin was already in the lobby, the same chair as last night. He looked better in daylight, less like a freezer aisle and more like a person who had brought winter in his pockets and set it down politely. He had a paper cup of water, hands wrapped around it, eyes attentive without being nosy.

"Thank you for staying," Charles told him.

"Thank you for the chair," Austin said.

Truth's ears tipped toward him. She did not stand. Her tail did the one-two again, slow and steady.

Sia took a breath and settled on the sofa arm where she could see Charles's pen and Marcus's shoulder and the door at once. The words would matter more if they sounded like people. That was her job today.

"All right," Charles said. He flipped open the folder. Inside sat the Arbiter letter under a paper clip and a sheet of museum letterhead. The letterhead was not dramatic. The name and address sat at the top in a font that would not make anyone's aunt nervous. He uncapped his pen. "Opening."

Sia wrote as he spoke so she could see the sentences land. He had a cadence that made paragraphs behave.

"To the Arbiter Desk, Lake Division," Charles said. "We received your message carried by Austin. We can host a neutral window tomorrow at eleven a.m., under our house rules. We will seat two and two with one observer each, as you requested. We will keep the space safe and boring on purpose."

He looked at Sia. She nodded and lifted a finger. "Move 'tomorrow' to an exact date," she said. "No room for confusion."

"Right," he said. He added the date. He did not use numbers alone. He wrote the month out, then the day, then the year. He glanced to Ella.

"Script block," Ella said, already sliding a small typed paragraph across the table. "Plain language, same as the entry card."

Charles read it, then read it again out loud so the room could hear it. "While you are here, you agree to our hospitality rule. No violence on site. Ask before you act. Phones stay at the desk. Pocket charms and coins rest in the bowl until you leave. If you hear a bell, you follow it. We will run one long bell at the top so everyone understands how we run safety."

"Good," Marcus said. "Add water only on the table. No food. No gifts."

Charles wrote, "We will set water only. No food will be served. Do not bring gifts."

"Seating," Marcus said. "Chairs, two feet off the wall so no one can wedge. Witness chairs placed with clear lines to the door. No one sits with their back to the bowl."

Sia drew a tiny diagram while Charles translated that into sentence form. She put a little X for the bowl and two squares for the chairs, then drew sightlines and wrote water on table. She felt the room nod when the picture made sense.

"Names in advance," Ella said. "We need four names before ten thirty. Printed. No titles."

Charles wrote, "Provide four names by ten thirty a.m., printed. No titles."

"Arrival," Marcus said. "On time."

"Arrive on time," Charles wrote. "If you are late, we will hold the space for ten minutes and then we will close it."

"Coins again," Ella said. "A separate line so they cannot pretend they missed it in the paragraph."

Charles made a small space and wrote, "No coins or metal-on-cloth charms in the meeting room. We will collect them at entry and return them when you leave."

"Bell again," Kaelan said, voice even. "Say we ring once at the top. Say we do not ring for show."

Charles added, "We will ring one long bell at the start. We do not ring for show."

Sia slid her finger under the opening to check flow. "Tone is good," she said. "Keep 'boring on purpose' in the opening. It tells them we mean this to be work, not theater."

"I like it," Charles said, and left the phrase in.

He continued, slower now, checking each block as he set it. "We host this as a museum and hotel under our policy. We will not enforce court law. We will enforce our rules. If you cannot agree, we will not host. We will not take sides."

"Remind them about the building," Kaelan said. "Without naming it like a person."

Charles wrote, "The building is set for quiet. Do not try to wake it."

"Thank you," Kaelan said.

"Closing?" Charles asked.

Sia glanced at Austin. "Something that keeps it human," she said. "We look forward to a safe hour and clean exits."

Charles wrote, "We look forward to a safe hour and clean exits." He signed it with his name and title. He did not add flourishes. He underlined nothing. He looked up at Austin. "Read before we print."

Austin stood, came to the table, and read every line. He

moved his lips as he did it, a habit Sia found weirdly comforting, like he did not want to assume he knew what words would do before they were in the air. He tapped the sentence about the bell.

"Will the bell startle anyone here," he asked.

"It will ask people to pause," Charles said. "No one on our staff runs from bells."

"Good," Austin said. He tapped the line about the bowl. "If someone tries to sneak a coin, will you eject them."

"We will collect the coin," Marcus said. "If they argue, we will walk them out. We have a script."

"Understood," Austin said. He pointed at the arrival window. "If they show at ten forty-five, will you seat them early."

"No," Charles said. "We will seat at eleven."

Austin nodded. He stepped back. "I can carry this."

"Perfect," Ella said. She had already slid the letter into the printer queue and was standing by with a staple. The machine hummed. She clipped the reply to a copy for the file and placed both on the table with a short, satisfied sound.

Sia wrote reply draft approved beside her little diagram and drew a circle around the bell line. She liked circles better than stars. Stars felt like shouting. Circles felt like a held breath.

"Last checks," Marcus said. "Bowl angle still good. Phone basket set. Chairs chosen. Water pitcher in the reading room cabinet. Witness rotation by the south hall."

"Rotation card posted," Tobias said, lifting the corner of a small index card on the corkboard by the parlor door. "I'm on the first half hour. Eric does maps. Ella stays desk. Kaelan floats. Sia stands by the mural where she can see and hear without being in their faces. Marcus runs the threshold. Charles hosts."

Eric raised his hand. "Consent script is printed for me in big letters so I do not make up jazz."

"Good," Ella said, pleased.

Charles turned the reply toward Austin. "Ready for send-off."

Austin took the letter, folded once, slid it into a plain envelope, and sealed it with a small press of his thumb. No wax. No special mark. The ordinariness of it made Sia like him more. He glanced at the bowl. "Coin?"

Ella lifted the card that said pocket charms here and tapped the rim of the ceramic. "Still resting," she said. "Phone basket?"

Austin handed his phone over without commentary. Ella slotted it into a charger with a small sticker that read visitor. She set a numbered ticket on the desk beside it like this was a coat check at a very calm theater.

"Ready," Marcus said.

They gathered at the door. Not in a huddle. In a line that made sense. Marcus stood half a step behind the threshold. Kaelan took his right. Charles held the handle. Ella had the log ready. Sia stood back far enough that the morning light could hit her notebook. Truth heels were tidy, head level, eyes on the step. Austin stood one pace from the line, envelope in his left hand, coat buttoned even though it was warmer inside than out.

"Say yes again," Marcus told him. "Makes the door happy."

"Yes," Austin said. "Hospitality, bells, no violence."

The door hinge loosened. Charles pulled it open. Outside, the square was starting to fill with people who had decided to like the day. The air smelled like wet concrete and coffee.

"Thank the house on your way out," Kaelan said. "It likes being included."

Austin glanced at the ceiling like he could see the rafters. "Thank you," he said, formal and clean.

Truth walked him to the step. She did not crowd his legs. She matched his pace and then stopped dead at the threshold line because she had learned that trick and liked using it. Austin paused like he understood that was part of the ritual. He looked at Marcus.

"You are good at your job," he said.

"Same," Marcus said.

Austin descended two steps, turned, and lifted the envelope slightly in a half-salute. Then he headed toward the street like a person who had maps in his head and shoes that liked pavement. He did not leave a temperature drop behind him. The gap he had occupied warmed back to normal in one breath.

Ella wrote the time. "Reply sent ten twenty-two," she said. She underlined it once.

Charles closed the door. It landed with the solid sound of a habit kept. The mobile above the desk turned once and decided that was enough for now.

Sia walked to the Ops board in the parlor and pinned a fresh card. She wrote, in tidy print, **Reply sent 10:22 a.m.** Under that she drew the corridor line with a small white chalk mark where the hush lived and wrote pressure even. She hooked the marker back on the cork strip and stepped back. The board looked like a grocery list again. She loved that.

Ella finished her part of the morning and came to stand beside Sia. "Plain enough," she asked.

"Plain is perfect," Sia said.

"Good," Ella said. "I didn't want to use any words that would make someone feel like they had to change shoes."

Marcus joined them with his radio on his belt and his hands quiet. "We're set," he said. "We rehearse after lunch. Sia, I want your ears on the mural during the rehearsal bell."

"I'll be there," Sia said. She flipped to a new page and drew a box for rehearsal, a circle for the bell, a square for chairs, and a dot for the bowl. She made a note to ask Mia if she could lend her voice to the top-of-hour tone later in the week, not for the meeting, just to hear what it did to the room. Not today.

Kaelan checked the hush along the baseboard with that two-finger touch she used when she wanted the building to feel seen. "Still seated," she said. "It will handle attention if attention arrives."

"Let's keep it low," Charles said. "Museum open as usual. If anyone asks about a meeting tomorrow, we say private booking, museum open, nothing to see."

"Copy," Ella said.

Eric pointed at the bowl. "Do you want a second card that says no tokens, or is that too much."

"Add a line to the first card," Ella said. "No tokens is good but say it like a person. Like, please don't use tokens here."

Eric wrote it on a sticky first and brought it over. **Please don't use tokens here.** The font was a hair too large. Ella redid it in her friendly script and taped it under the main card. The bowl sat there like a small moon that had decided to help.

Truth stood, stretched, and leaned her shoulder into Sia's shin. Sia scratched behind her ear until the dog's eyes went soft. Truth's tail tapped the floor. Consent and contentment in one small motion.

Sia went to the mural landing and checked her map against the real wall. The painted road slid into the bright lake, holding the painted sun where it liked it best. She put her palm near the seam and asked, quiet, "Still good."

The air answered by staying exactly itself. She smiled and closed her hand like she was putting that yes into her pocket for later.

Back at the intake table, Charles slid a copy of the reply into the folder and wrote the simplest line on the outside. **Sent. Expect reply.** He underlined nothing. He stacked the folder with others that had normal words on their covers. Sia trusted people who used normal words when the stakes were high.

"Lunch in twenty," Ella said. "Then rehearsal."

"Make it soup," Marcus said.

"Always," Ella said.

Austin's absence left no chill. The house didn't sag. The hush kept its white line. The card on the bowl looked like something a person would read and obey. Sia took a last look at the Ops board and the door and the bell and the faces in the room and decided the morning had landed the way mornings should land. She put her pencil under the spiral and closed the notebook with a quiet tap.

"Back to work," Charles said.

They broke, not like a team on a field, just like staff in a building that knew how to be itself. Sia slipped past the mural and let the quiet ride along her shoulders. She had a meeting to rehearse, coins to keep out of rooms, and a map in her head that matched the chalk line on the baseboard. For now, that was enough.

THE READING ROOM KEPT that after-lunch hush that makes pages sound louder. Lamps were on, green shades throwing soft circles onto wood. Truth settled by the door like she was counting visitors with her ears. Ella stacked a few returns on the side cart and looked over at Sia.

"Eric says he has a training idea," Ella said. "I told him he gets ten minutes and a safety plan."

Eric arrived exactly then with two pillows under one arm and a folded hand towel over his shoulder like a lifeguard. "Great news," he said, stopping a foot inside the threshold, palms out. "I have the wisdom of a world class slacker and I'm finally going to use it for good."

Sia eyed the pillows. "That sentence makes me nervous."

"It should," Ella said, amused. "Pitch it clean, Eric. No jazz."

"Right," he said. He set the pillows on the carpet by the low table, then stepped back so he wasn't looming. "Here's the angle. You want to tap the Dreaming without losing the whole afternoon. We can practice a controlled slide. Daydreaming on command. It's a micro-nap with boundaries. You're anchored. You stay in the chair. You can talk. If anything gets weird, I tap your shoulder and you're out."

Sia glanced at Ella, who had already pulled a small index card from her pocket and scribbled anchors at the top. "What are your anchors," Sia asked.

"Me at your right," Ella said. "Truth at your feet. Eric on timer with a phrase to bring you back. You hold the mug so your hands have a job."

"What phrase," Sia asked Eric.

"I'm going to say, 'Class is over,'" he said. "Because your brain knows what that means and it's not dramatic."

Sia couldn't help smiling at that. "Okay."

Eric held up the hand towel. "This is for the grille if the air decides to be a jerk. I'll put it down with a please."

"Thank you," Ella said. "Consent stays on even when we're being weird."

Truth thumped her tail once, as if she agreed to all of it.

They moved a chair so Sia could sit with her back to a book-case and her face to the lamp. Eric set one pillow behind her lower back and one under her feet without touching her. He put the towel within reach of the floor grille. Ella placed a warm mug of water in Sia's hands so the weight would register even if her attention wandered.

"Talk me through it," Sia said.

"Okay," Eric said. He pulled a chair close enough to see her face and far enough not to crowd. "Step one, we set a timer for four minutes. That's less than a nap and more than a blink. Step two, you pick a dumb image to watch. Clouds, dust motes, whatever. Step three, we do box breathing. Four in, four hold, four out, four hold. Step four, you let your eyes drift without closing them. If they close, it's fine. You're allowed. The trick is, when your body tries to fall, you follow it just a little. You don't go deep. You stay shallow and nosy."

"That's the slacker wisdom," Ella said.

"Exactly," Eric said. "Experts in not doing things are very good at almost sleeping."

"Safety," Ella said.

"Right," Eric said. "If I say class is over, you come back. If Truth nudges your knee twice, you come back. If you need out, you say out and we stop. No heroics. No ghost hunts."

Sia nodded. She looked at Truth. "If I get weird, nudge me twice."

Truth licked her nose and set her chin on Sia's shoe. Agreement.

Ella sat to Sia's right, knees angled, posture easy. "I'll watch your hands," she said. "If the mug dips, I'll fix it. You don't have to perform. Just try."

"I can try," Sia said.

Eric set his phone on the table, timer open. He placed the towel over the grille with a quiet please. The air settled.

"All right," he said. "Pick your dumb image."

Sia looked at the dust in the lamp light. Each mote did its private dance. She picked one that moved slightly slower than the rest and decided it was worth a short relationship.

"Got one," she said.

"Cool," Eric said. "Breath now. In four, hold four, out four, hold four."

They counted a few cycles together. Sia felt her shoulders let go of their fake job. The mug was warm, not hot. Truth's breath made a small breeze against her ankle. Ella's pencil tapped once, then didn't. The room agreed to be a room.

"Eyes soft," Eric said. "You can close them if they want to. If they stay open, let them blur."

The lamp halo fuzzed at the edges. Sia followed the slow dust mote until it wasn't a mote anymore, just a dot that threaded through light. Her hands held the mug on autopilot. The chair's back pressed where a person likes to be held when they don't want attention.

"Let your body fall a half inch," Eric said. "Catch it with breath, not with muscle."

Sia's chin tipped a fraction. Her grip didn't slip. The floor moved further away and then settled under her feet again. She heard the room and also something below it, like water under boards. Her mouth felt a little numb. She heard herself say okay and wasn't totally sure she'd said it out loud.

"You're good," Ella said, the way nurses talk when they put a needle in clean.

Sia saw the dust change shape. It wasn't a dot. It was a line that connected to another line. She could talk if she wanted. It would come out slow. She didn't need talking. Movement came easier. She lifted one finger off the mug and set it down again. The mug stayed where it was.

"You're in the shallow end," Eric said. "Try saying hi."

"Hi," Sia said. Her voice sounded like it had cotton on it. Not heavy. Just padded.

"Can you see anything different," Ella asked, calm.

Sia blinked, slow. She looked at Ella and at the same time not at Ella. The room had two layers. The top layer was chairs and lamps and dust. The second layer was light that had opinions. Ella carried a bright that wasn't lamp bright. It came from shoulder level and above her head. It wasn't a color she could name. It was like gold, if gold had been washed in morning sky and drawn with clean lines. The edges rotated in a pattern that wanted to be a wheel and a wing at once.

"Ella," Sia said, slow. "You have... not a crown. Like a circle. It's sharp and soft. It keeps looking like it wants to be a wing."

Ella's mouth tugged. She didn't act surprised. "Uriel," she said, quiet. "It shows when people are safe enough to see it."

Sia could see the lines inside the bright now. Geometry and scorch and calm. It wasn't scary. It was like looking at a tool that knows what it's for.

"That's new for me while I'm awake," Sia said.

"Noted," Ella said, like she was writing it down in her head. "Keep it easy."

Sia turned her head a little. Truth's shape had layers too. The top was the dog she loved, all black nose and funny toes and patience. Under that was a light that stacked like stone tiles. Old. Polished by feet. It ran from her chest to the tip of her tail and back to her paws, braided with a thread that looked like sunlight pulled through water.

Truth looked up at Sia and, in the space where words aren't the point, said, clear as a bell without sound, Kaelan promoted me.

Sia's hands tightened on the mug. "What," she said, and heard the mug clink against the table. Ella steadied it with two fingers without breaking eye contact.

Truth blinked once and wagged once. Temple Dog now, she said in that same not-voice. It came with a picture instead of a certificate. The picture was a doorway with paper charms, a porch with shoes lined up, and Kaelan's hand resting gently on Truth's head. The feeling that went with it tasted like rice and bells and work you do because you love the people who need it.

Sia tried to shoot up in the chair and couldn't because her body was asleep in a very polite way. Her mind was awake enough to ask questions.

You can talk, she told Truth, halfway laughing inside her own face.

In here, Truth told her. Out loud I'm still a dog.

Eric's voice came from the top layer, careful. "How's your ride."

"Truth is talking," Sia said. "In the dream part. She says Kaelan made her a Temple Dog."

Ella breathed out and smiled with her eyes. "That tracks," she said. "Kaelan would do it the second Truth did the job without asking for a title."

Truth looked very proud and also like she wanted a treat.

"What else do you see," Ella asked.

Sia let her gaze drift again. The room held steady. No seams flexed. The hush stayed like chalk under the baseboard. When she looked toward the hall, she saw a faint thread run along the floor, not white like her pencil, but clear like a fishing line that knew where it belonged. It hummed the idea of yes.

"I can see the hush," Sia said. "It's like string for holding fish, but smarter."

"Good," Eric said, thrilled and trying not to sound like he was thrilled. "Do you feel stuck."

"No," Sia said. She flexed her toes. Felt socks, not water. "I can move. I'm talking. I think I could stand up if I had to."

"Let's not," Ella said quickly. "New trick, small steps."

Truth put her chin back on Sia's shoe and sent a warm wave up Sia's shin without moving. Sia understood it meant stay. Okay. Got it.

"Class is over in fifteen seconds," Eric said. "You'll hear me, then you'll let go of the image and squeeze the mug once. Then you'll blink until the lamp is just a lamp again."

Sia looked back at her dust mote. It had stopped being a line and turned back into a point. It didn't care about any of this. It was living its best dust life.

"Class is over," Eric said.

Sia squeezed the mug once, then again. The chair got heavier under her. Her throat felt like it had a zipper and someone had zipped it back to normal. She blinked. The room clicked into its usual layer. Ella's face was just Ella's face. Bright still sat on her shoulders, but it relaxed into the kind of glow Sia only noticed when she was paying attention. Truth was only a dog with a very expressive tail and a look that said she was ready to brag if bragging were allowed.

Sia breathed once, then twice, then grinned because that had been a lot and also fine. "Okay," she said. "That worked."

Eric pumped a fist like a tiny kid at a spelling bee. "Nice."

Ella touched Sia's forearm, light. "Any pressure behind your eyes," she asked. "Any nausea."

"No," Sia said. She checked. Her body felt regular. "I'm good. I could eat."

"We'll do snacks in a minute," Ella said, pleased. She jotted three notes on her card in small, tidy letters: anchors held, talk/move while asleep worked, aura noted.

Sia looked at Truth. The dog wagged like a metronome set to patient. "You're a Temple Dog," Sia said out loud, because it should be said out loud too.

Truth smiled with her whole face. It didn't look like a human smile. It looked like a dog being herself and knowing she'd done well.

"Does she get a hat," Eric asked.

"No hats," Ella said. "She gets extra chicken."

Truth wagged harder.

Sia put the mug down. Her hands weren't shaking. She loved that. The world hadn't shifted under her feet. It had opened a window and then closed it on command.

"So," Eric said, sitting back like a coach after a decent drill. "You just learned to pull yourself toward dreaming without going full sleep. That's huge."

"Yeah," Sia said. "It felt like standing in a doorway. Not in or out. I could talk."

"That's exactly where we want you," Ella said. "Doorway, not the river."

Sia nodded. The word river made her chest do a small weird thing. She shelved it for later.

"Again tomorrow," Eric asked, trying to sound casual and failing.

"Let's do it," Sia said. "But we keep the timer and the anchors. I don't want to get cocky."

"Agreed," Ella said. "We'll log it. We'll tell Kaelan about the promotion so she can make it official with her circle."

Truth puffed a little at the word official.

Sia stood slowly and the room stayed room. She stretched her hands and rolled her shoulders. No pins and needles. No vertigo. She felt like herself, plus a trick.

"Thank you," she told Eric.

"Thanks for trusting me," he said. "I know I'm the intern who wants to do science fair. I'm trying to be useful."

"You are," Sia said, and meant it.

Ella collected the towel from the grille with a soft please and folded it like a napkin. "Let's grab those snacks," she said. "Then we set the chairs and run the bell rehearsal."

Truth stood and bumped her head lightly into Sia's thigh, then looked toward the staff hall as if to say, walk me later and I'll forgive the lack of chicken right now.

Sia scratched the soft spot behind Truth's ear. "Temple Dogs negotiate, huh."

Truth's tail said, obviously.

They left the reading room with the pillows stacked and the chair back where it belonged. Sia felt like she'd learned how to breathe in a new way without making a big deal out of breathing. She could call the Dreaming closer now and send it away. It felt like holding a door she owned. That was a good shape for a skill.

EVENING SLID OVER THE museum the way a librarian closes blinds. The last of the school crowd had drifted out. The bowl stayed visible with its friendly card. The Ops board had a new index card pinned in Charles's clear print: **Arbiter acknowl-**

edgment received. Arrival tomorrow at 11:00 a.m. Four names attached. Museum rules accepted. Ella underlined the time and added a small note about water only. Marcus checked the bell rope once and left it alone.

Sia read the card, nodded to herself, and headed for the staff hall. Truth matched her steps, tail doing the slow metronome that meant off shift. The living floor smelled like soap and tea. Sia's room had the corner with the small window and a sliver of sky.

She flipped the light and set her notebook on the desk. The day sat inside it in clean lines already, so she didn't push more words at it. She reached for the sketchbook instead. Paper felt kinder than prose right now.

"Pose," she told Truth.

Truth did an exaggerated stretch that made her toes spread, then arranged herself on the rug the way she liked for being admired. Head up. Ears forward. Tail tucked politely out of the way so it wouldn't smudge charcoal. Her eyes said she took the job seriously and also that she expected a treat later.

"You're very professional," Sia said. She sat cross-legged on the floor with the sketchbook propped against her knees and started with the shape of Truth's head. Light pencil first, then darker when the lines told the truth.

Drawing slowed her down in a way nothing else did. You can't lie to a curve. If you try, it looks wrong and the page tells on you. She worked from nose to eyes, then the square angles of Truth's shoulders under fur. The lamp made a warm pool on the floor. Outside, a car passed and went quiet again.

Halfway through the ear, Sia felt that familiar prickle at the edge of the page. Not a draft. Not words. Just the sense that the space inside the picture had decided to be larger than the paper.

"Okay," she said, low. "You can watch."

A dot landed in the white space above Truth's head. It wasn't a smudge and it wasn't an accident. It sat there like a seed thinking about roots. Sia didn't name it with her mouth. She tested the shape with charcoal and waited.

The dot elongated, then tucked, then tried again. It became a tiny curl, like the start of a question mark, and then two feet that were barely feet at all. It perched on the drawn outline of Truth's ear like punctuation. The curl lifted and fell as if it were breathing.

Truth didn't move. Her eyes tracked Sia's hands and then flicked to the place on the page where nothing should have been. She wagged once, slow, the way a person nods at a friend peeking around a door.

"Hi," Sia said into the space between the pencil and the paper. "If you're staying, pick a spot."

The curl scooted a hair and settled on top of Truth's head in the drawing. It looked proud of itself, which was ridiculous for a dot with ideas. Sia let herself smile because pretending she didn't see it never worked. Respecting small things worked better.

She added two light strokes to suggest weight where it sat. The line of Truth's ear carried the extra without complaint. The pencil felt warmer in her fingers. The page felt like a room with a window open.

"I should call you something," she said, mostly to herself. The curl bounced once, very faint. Sia thought about the job this small presence kept trying to do. It liked margins. It liked living between lines. It turned up where idea and picture met and pressed until they noticed each other.

"Scrib," she said quietly. "Short for scribble. Short for the thing a hand does when it's finding what's true."

The curl brightened. Not light. Not color. Just a feeling like a sparkler you're not allowed to hold indoors. It settled deeper into the drawn fur, as if the name had given it gravity.

"Okay, Scrib," Sia said. "You can sit with Truth for now."

Truth's real ears did a tiny flick. She didn't ask for permission to be a perch. She didn't need to. That was her brand.

Sia finished the sketch. The likeness landed right around the eyes, which is where any real drawing starts and ends. She sat back and looked. Truth looked like Truth. The tiny curl on drawn Truth's head looked like a secret that wanted to behave.

"All right," Sia said. "Bed."

Truth stood and shook once, the polite kind that doesn't send hair everywhere. Sia set the sketchbook on the desk and propped it open to dry. Scrib stayed in the picture, or that's what it looked like. The page felt heavier now, like it had learned a new trick and was practicing.

Sia brushed her teeth, washed her face, and pulled on a soft shirt. She checked the hallway out of habit. Quiet. A single lamp glowed at the far end. Someone had left a note on the cork strip by the stairs: **Meeting tomorrow. Privacy in parlor. Museum open.** Ella's handwriting again. Friendly even as a reminder.

Back in her room, Sia slid under the blanket. Truth took the spot on the rug near the bed that let her see both the door and Sia's face. Temple Dog posture. Proud and practical. Sia reached down to scratch her shoulders.

"Thank you for modeling," she said.

Truth sighed like she'd been thanked for putting a traffic cone in the right place.

Sia turned off the lamp. The window held one square of city light. She did the box breathing out of habit. Four in. Four hold. Four out. Four hold. The day ran a highlight reel behind her eyes all by itself. Bowl angle. Austin at the door. Bell rehearsal. The letter written like a person. The way the hush had hummed when she looked at it from the doorway of a waking dream.

She didn't force the Dreaming. She asked it.

"May I come through," she said into the pillow, like talking to someone in the next room.

The drop came gentle. Not like falling off a cliff. More like stepping down one stair in the dark and finding the next one exactly where it should be. The air thickened into water that didn't get her wet. The room slipped sideways and then righted itself as a different room with sky that wasn't a real sky and a river that was always the same and never the same.

She stood on the bank without standing up in the bed.

Dream rules, door rules. Consent first. She said hello to the shore in her head and with her feet. The shore accepted her weight without making a fuss.

The River King was where he always was when he meant to be easy to find, sitting on a smooth black rock with water running around his ankles like it had elected him chair. He wore clothes that belonged to any time and none. He had a face that made people tell secrets and feel better afterward. The water leaned toward him in a way that wasn't physics and didn't need to be.

"Evening," he said. His voice carried like the part of a song that never gets loud and never goes away. "You smell like paper and a new name."

Sia felt her cheeks go warm. "I named a small thing," she said. "Scrib. It lives in my sketches."

"It will like that," he said. "Names are doors. Small doors make safe rooms."

"I figured it needed one," she said. She put her hands in her pockets even though pockets weren't a thing here unless you wanted them. They showed up obediently because this place respected effort.

Truth appeared at her left the way dogs do when the rules let them. Dream-Truth looked like ordinary Truth, just a little shinier around the edges, like someone had cleaned her outline. She sat and watched the river. Scrib wasn't here. That felt right. Some things belonged in paper.

"We got an acknowledgment," Sia said. "Arbiter desk. Meeting at eleven tomorrow. Two and two. Our rules."

The River King nodded. "Good. Porch rules hold. They prevent hunger from pretending to be law."

"Is hunger Summer," Sia asked. "Or Winter."

"Yes," he said. He smiled without showing teeth. It was the kind of answer that wasn't a trick. It meant both.

"Thanatos is nearby," he added, as if he were telling her the wind direction. "He's watching, not asking."

Sia felt it before she saw it. A pressure like the drop in a room when someone sets a heavy book on a table in the next room. Not scary. Just present. She turned her head. On the far bank, in the shade where the reeds bent, a figure stood still in a way that wasn't human stillness. The absence around him made the colors more honest.

She lifted a hand in a small hello. The figure inclined his head. No drama. No opera. Witness, not entrance. She let her hand fall.

"Do I need to do anything with that," she asked.

"Not tonight," the River King said. "He's learning your edges the way you learn a hallway. He prefers to watch before speaking. Respect serves you both."

Sia sat on the bank with her shoes off, simply because you can sit with your shoes off here and never get cold. Truth lay beside her with her chin on her paws. The water managed to be busy and calm at the same time. It made a sound that didn't read as music and still had tempo.

"We set the letter in plain words," Sia said. "I helped make it boring."

"Good," he said. "Boring is a shield that does not look like a shield. Courts underestimate it."

"Summer and Winter accepted our rules," she said. "On paper, at least."

"Paper matters," he said. "So do chairs and water and a bell everyone hears. The courts will bring theater even when they promise not to. You bring policy and posture. It evens out."

"I can see things now when I daydream on purpose," she said. "Ella's bright. Truth's layers. The hush like a string. Eric taught me the doorway trick. I can move and talk while I'm there."

"That's a good path," he said. "Doorways are places of power when you remember to hold them instead of rushing through. Do not live in them. Use them."

She picked up a small flat stone and set it on her knee. It chose not to be a skipping stone. That was fine. "I named Scrib," she said again, because saying it twice made it more real. "That felt like drawing a circle around the job, so it doesn't wander."

"Names are leashes if you pull," he said. "They are handholds if you agree to hold gently. You have a good grip."

"Thanatos," Sia said, glancing to the far bank again. The shape hadn't moved. "He was at the edges last time too."

"He is a threshold that does not brag," the River King said. "He respects rules. He will not cross your porch without invitation. He will stand where people forget to look and remind them to behave."

"I don't mind him watching," she said. It surprised her to

admit that. "It makes the edges feel honest."

"Then you are listening correctly," he said.

Water slid over his ankles and didn't make him wet. Sia let that be a thing instead of a puzzle. She liked him better when she didn't try to turn him into a homework problem. He had saved her life once by being himself. That felt like enough.

"Tomorrow," she said. "Eleven."

"Before that," he said, "breakfast. Chairs. Scripts printed. Cocoa tickets where people can see them. Think small. Leave the big to those who think they need it."

She laughed. "Ella already moved the bowl two inches left."

"I expected nothing less," he said.

Truth made a small sound that meant content. Sia scratched her behind the ear out of habit. Dream-Truth closed her eyes for a second and then opened them again. Consent given, consent received.

Sia looked downriver. A curve waited there, same as always, a bend she hadn't walked yet. She didn't stand. She didn't push. Doorway rules. The Dreaming didn't need her to prove she was brave.

"I should go," she said. "We have a meeting to rehearse."

"Go with your ordinary voice," the River King said. "It will carry farther than a speech."

She stood, which in this place meant she decided to be standing and the ground agreed. She put her shoes back on because she liked the gesture. She touched two fingers to her forehead and then to the water, a habit she'd made so the exit felt like a courtesy, not an escape.

"Good night," she told him.

"Good work," he told her.

She turned. Thanatos on the far bank inclined his head again. It felt like being seen by a well that never ran out. She nodded back. He did not move to follow. Good.

The return was a breath and a corner and a soft click. The room put itself back around her in one piece. She woke in her bed with the blanket pulled up to her shoulder and the air in her nose the exact temperature it should be. Truth snored once and stopped. The square of city light sat on the floor in exactly the same spot. Sia looked at the sketchbook on the desk. Scrib stayed where she'd left it, perched on paper Truth's head like a tiny punctuation mark that had finally earned a name.

She checked her body. No headache. No float. No cold in her fingers. She felt how she always wanted to feel after sleep: real.

"Okay," she whispered to the ceiling. "Tomorrow."

Truth's tail thumped once against the rug without her opening her eyes. Sia smiled, rolled to her side, and let the normal night carry her the rest of the way.

CHAPTER 8

Neutral Window

MARCUS

I believe in everything until it's disproved. So I believe in fairies, the myths, dragons. It all exists, even if it's in your mind. Who's to say that dreams and nightmares aren't as real as the here and now?

John Lennon

THE SQUARE OUTSIDE LOOKED like a postcard that had decided to be helpful. Clear sky, clean light, the bus stop empty for once. Marcus put one hand on the door handle and the other in his pocket and let himself breathe with the building. He wasn't a bouncer. He wasn't a priest. He was a guy at a door who knew how to keep a porch honest.

Ella slid the bowl two inches left so the card faced the step dead on. Please don't use tokens here was taped under the main line in her tidy script. She adjusted it a hair without looking like she cared. Charles stood back from the threshold with his cane grounded and that host calm that made people behave. Kaelan took her usual spot at Marcus's right. Bracelets quiet, eyes steady. Tobias lingered two steps inside the south hall, present without broadcasting. Eric had a map on a clipboard and instructions not to improvise. Sia leaned at the mural landing in the angle of wall that let her hear the room without making it a performance. Truth sat where she could see the door and the bowl both. Her posture said Temple Dog like it was a job description.

At 10:56 the sunlight on the steps warmed a notch. That was the only warning. Two people turned the corner with the easy glide of people who believe the day belongs to them. Summer read like that even when it was subtle. A woman in a simple dress that looked expensive because it didn't try, a man in a jacket open to the air like November had no vote. They smiled as if the porch had told them a joke already.

"Morning," the woman said, stopping one pace short of the line. "We're early, but early is polite."

"Morning," Marcus said. "Early waits until eleven."

The man grinned and held up a transit token on a chain like a necklace from a retro arcade. "Bus fare for the bowl," he said. "I could use store credit."

"Funny," Marcus said. He didn't smile. "Tokens don't cross. Coins and charms rest in the bowl while you're here. You get them back when you leave. Entry is at eleven."

The woman looked at the card, then at Truth. Truth looked back, calm as a rock that had decided to be friendly. The woman unhooked the token and dropped it into the bowl with a soft clink. Then she reached into her pocket and set down a coin without pretending it was anything else. The man followed with a coin of his own, silver-slick, edges worn. The bowl took them like it had been hungry for exactly three things and had been promised lunch.

Ella tore two cocoa tickets and set them on the desk like name tags. "Thanks for the trade," she said. "Phones at the desk too."

"Of course," the woman said. She placed her phone in the basket without sighing. The man did the same and looked only a little like he'd lost a pet.

"Names for the log," Ella asked.

"Primrose," the woman said. "And Cal."

"Got it," Ella said, writing them down. She didn't write titles. She never did.

Marcus stepped half aside so they could see the interior and not mistake that for an invitation. "We seat at eleven," he said. "You can wait on the step. Door stays cracked."

Primrose tipped her head like she wanted to see whether the house would flinch. It didn't. She stepped back one pace without losing the smile.

Cal glanced past Marcus to the mural, then to Sia. He was

charming in the way of someone who thought charm was a shared language. Sia didn't give him a place to land. She looked at the seam by the painting and nothing else. Cal's grin adjusted to neutral like a shirt collar he hadn't meant to button wrong.

At 10:59 a cool edge threaded into the door gap like the line where shade meets sun. The Winter pair came up the steps without hurry. They moved like neat handwriting. The woman wore a black coat without lint. The man's tie was straight. Their eyes took the world in like a ledger takes numbers, not unkind, just exact.

"Morning," Marcus said.

"Morning," the man said. "We are on time."

"Good," Marcus said. He nodded toward the bowl. "Pocket charms rest here."

The woman produced a small cloth-wrapped coin that matched the one Austin had surrendered the night before. No speech, no commentary. She set it in the bowl. The air at Marcus's cheek warmed half a degree as if someone had closed a refrigerator door. The man placed a flat ring of plaited wire beside it and looked at the sign as if he appreciated fonts.

"Phones," Ella said, holding out the basket.

They complied. Ella set two more tiny tickets on the desk. "Water only inside," she said. "You can grab a cup when you're seated."

"Names," she added.

"Vera," the woman said.

"Reed," the man said.

Ella wrote them clean. Marcus watched the bowl and the line. Nothing clever pushed. Good.

He glanced back at Charles. Charles gave him the smallest nod. It meant go ahead and make it simple.

"Rules out loud," Marcus said, back to the four of them. He kept his voice conversational. "No violence on site. Ask before you act. Phones stay at the desk. Water only. One long bell at the start so everyone hears it. Big one. No coins past the line. If you brought one, we already took care of it."

Cal opened his mouth like he wanted to make the bus token joke again. Primrose touched his sleeve. He closed it. Vera's face didn't change. Reed's eyes cut to Truth, then to the baseboard line where the hush lived, as if he could taste rules and liked the flavor.

"Seating happens at eleven," Marcus said. "We start on time."

The hall clock clicked to the hour. Kaelan lifted the bell and looked at Charles. He lifted a hand. "For the house," he said. "Not for show."

Kaelan rang a single long bell. It rolled through the lobby and down the halls and came back to itself without echo. People paused where they were. Eric set his pencil down. Tobias tipped his head to the right so anyone looking would see a person who knew where to look. Sia breathed in and out twice like the room could borrow her rhythm. Truth flicked an ear and then went still. The air settled into a shape that knew its job.

"Thank you," Charles said, not to the guests, to the building. He let the tone fade all the way before he moved. Then he turned to the four and smiled like a person who runs a hotel that is also a museum and wanted this hour to be a clean one. "Welcome. We'll seat two and two with your observers."

He gestured, not wide, just enough. Marcus stepped back from the line and put heel to threshold so the door knew where he was. Primrose and Cal crossed first, Summer heat taken down to room temperature by the bowl. Vera and Reed followed, chill zipped up and put away. Truth stood as they passed, not blocking, only being witnessed by a dog who had been promoted and was doing the work.

Reading room, two chairs on each side of the table, pulled two feet from the wall so no one could wedge. Witness chairs angled to see the door and the bowl. Water on the table in plain glasses. No food. No paper except the copy of the agenda that said Agenda in a font you could read from across a grocery aisle. Ella's clock sat on the corner where she could tap it and no one else could.

"Primrose and Cal on the left," Charles said. "Vera and Reed on the right. Observers in the chairs behind. Water is on the table. We'll keep this hour boring on purpose."

Primrose's eyes lit at the phrase as if she was tempted to peel it open and see if it squeaked. She didn't. She sat. Cal followed her lead and kept his hands on the table. Vera sat with her coat folded over the back of her chair in a line straight enough to be a ruler. Reed poured water as if water deserved respect.

Marcus took the spot where he could see door, desk, and south hall. He checked corners. No tilt in the air. The hush lay along the baseboard like white chalk on slate again. The bowl held three coins, one ribbon charm, and a loop of wire that looked like it wanted to pretend it was nothing. It did not move.

"Phones are at the desk," Ella said. "If you need the time, I'm keeping it."

"We accept," Vera said. Her voice made words behave.

Primrose leaned her forearms on the table and smiled like this was brunch. "Your sign is charming," she said. "The token note. We'll circulate it."

"Thanks," Ella said. "We wrote it for people who like being talked to like people."

Cal glanced at the mural again as if the painted lake had personally invited him. Sia stayed in her angle and gave him nothing. He adjusted his attention to the water in front of him. Smart.

Charles didn't clear his throat. He didn't need to. He set his palm on the tabletop, a small anchor gesture, and everyone looked at him.

"Neutral window," he said. "Our house rules. One hour. Water only. We are not a court. We are a museum that keeps a hotel under it and a porch in front of it. You will leave your coins here. You will keep your hands on the table when you feel like saying more than you should. If you hear the long bell, you stay in your chair and a person will come to you. Do you agree."

"Yes," Primrose said.

"Yes," Cal said.

"Yes," Vera said.

"Yes," Reed said.

"Good," Charles said. He nodded to Ella. She tapped the clock. 11:01. He nodded to Marcus. Marcus flexed his fingers once, not because he needed to, but because his body liked rituals. He looked at Truth. She blinked slow and settled her chin on her paws. Witness, not judge.

Kaelan stood just behind Marcus's right shoulder where her voice could reach the wall if she had to. Her bracelets didn't make a sound. She had tuned the hush to eat show. The building held that like a recipe it enjoyed.

Marcus took one more slow scan. Summer warmth pressed from the square outside but didn't seep. Winter neatness watched its own edges and seemed pleased. The two flavors balanced. Sia's attention held the seam by the mural. The threshold line under Marcus's heel felt like a door that knew exactly what it was built to do.

He let his hand fall to his side. "Let's start," he said, and meant all the simple things that sentence could mean.

CHAIRS SET THE TONE. Four at the table, two behind, water in plain glasses. No paper piles, no props. Marcus watched hands. Calm hands make calm rooms.

Charles opened with exactly what the room needed. "This is a neutral window under our rules. One hour. Water only. No gifts. If you need a break, say so. We're here to stop small trouble before it turns into something people write poems about. Agenda is two items: coins and binds."

Ella tapped the clock. 11:02.

"Coins first," Charles said, and looked to Marcus.

Marcus stood where he could see the door and the bowl and still talk without raising his voice. "Pattern's simple," he said. "Coins carried through thresholds are acting like little batteries. Not always. Enough to matter. We saw 'bends' along our vent run when coin-carriers stood near the grille. Bowl collects coins at entry, bends go flat. We set a towel when we needed to and it stayed flat. When coin-carriers kept their pockets, the air tried to lean. Today, your coins are in the bowl, and the room is boring. That's how we like it."

Primrose had art-gallery posture that tried to make listening look like a compliment. She glanced at the bowl without moving her head. Cal actually turned to look, then caught himself and turned back. Vera didn't blink. Reed folded his hands on the table like a picture in a training manual.

Ella slid a small card forward, one sentence on it in friendly print. "Compliance numbers for the last day," she said. "Visitors who read the card and traded charms: ninety-two percent. People who joked about bus tokens: eight percent. People who argued after the cocoa ticket: zero."

"Map?" Charles asked.

Sia stepped in just enough to set her notebook on the corner of the table and open to a clean diagram. "Time-of-day spikes," she said. "Lunch hour is our warmest pressure. I'm calling it Summer-flavored attention. Even then, the hush handled it as long as pockets were light."

Cal smiled at the word flavored like he appreciated the metaphor. Vera didn't reward him.

Marcus kept it direct. "We need both courts to tell your people the same thing in the same words. No coins through public thresholds. Leave tokens at entry. Pick them up on your way out."

Primrose's mouth shaped an almost-yes and then settled into a question. "Even dead coins?" she asked. "No charge, no whisper, just metal on fabric."

"Even those," Marcus said. "Good habits beat clever workarounds. We're not checking battery levels at doors. The rule has to be simple enough to work when you're late and hungry."

Reed nodded once. "Simple rules survive the night," he said.

Vera folded one finger inward, then flattened it again. "We can discourage binding favors to coins," she said. "In public, at least. Some of our young make games. Games become habits. Habits become thresholds."

Cal leaned back an inch. "Summer can message it," he said. "We like short rules. Make it a poster and people will actually read it."

Ella slid a second card, already drafted in her head and now on paper. **No coins through public doors. Leave tokens at entry. Follow posted bells.** She set it between the four glasses like a centerpiece. "This is the tone," she said. "Not a threat. Not legalese. We'll hang it beside our bowl card for a month."

Primrose read it, then looked at Charles. "You'll post that even if we don't," she said.

"Yes," Charles said. "We'd rather be consistent than fashionable."

"Fair," she said.

Vera tapped the edge of the card once. "We'll send the line to our border walkers," she said. "Their circles like rules that keep them from apologizing to strangers."

"Good," Marcus said. He pointed with two fingers to the baseboard. "Our hush is tuned to eat show. It doesn't replace grown-ups making better choices. We'd like your help with that."

He let the table breathe. Ella's clock ticked like a polite reminder that time was a real thing.

"Second agenda," Charles said. "Unlicensed binds. We're not here to lecture you about history or theater. We're here because people are sticking favors where they don't belong. Doors. Phones. Coins. We keep a hotel under this museum. We don't run a stage. We need simple language both sides can circulate that turns strangers into neighbors instead of props."

Reed slid a sheet out of a slim folder and stopped himself from smoothing it. "Our position is that binds off-circle and without consent are improper in any shared space," he said. "Youth or not."

Cal made a face like he'd swallowed a peppermint too fast.

"We don't mind favors," he said. "We mind stupid."

Kaelan stepped half a pace forward, hands loose, voice even. "Script it," she said. "Short. Clean. No metaphors that make people angry on purpose."

She looked at the four like she was checking their faces for a fever, then spoke to the room, not the courts. "Ask before you act. Don't bind strangers. Don't bind in shared spaces. Don't bind to coins. If someone says stop, stop. If you mess up, apologize and undo it in public."

Reed's eyes warmed a fraction. Vera wrote the lines down in a small notebook with slow, exact strokes. Primrose listened like she was deciding whether the phrasing would play on a poster. Cal's leg bounced once under the table and then remembered the hush and stopped.

"We can circulate that," Vera said. "We'll add a line about consequences."

"No threats," Charles said. "Consequences are fine. Don't write like the poster wants to fight the room."

Primrose grinned, approving the phrase. "We do love a room that refuses to be an audience," she said.

Marcus watched her eyes. Summer liked to test edges with charm first, pressure second. He didn't mind charm when it stayed in its lane.

"Contacts," Ella said, tapping her pen. "We'll need one name from each court for follow-up. Someone who can read a map and answer a phone without making it a poem."

"Cass," Primrose said. "She runs clean and doesn't waste

adjectives."

"Linn," Vera said. "He writes like a grocery list. You'll like him."

Ella wrote both names and their contact lines on a card and clipped it to the folder labeled **Neutral Window**. Marcus liked that folder. It looked like Every Other Tuesday and not like a crisis.

Halfway through the hour, the room tried to test itself. It was small. Primrose shifted her shoulders and let a tiny nudge of attention slide across the table like a candle trying to be a spotlight. It wanted eyes. The hush noticed and ate it. The air flattened, polite and uninterested. Truth's ear flicked once. Marcus didn't change his tone.

"No show," he said.

Charles nodded as if Marcus had mentioned the weather. "We don't perform," he said. "We host. If you want applause, we'll lend you a mirror."

Primrose's mouth tilted with the humor of someone who knows she'd been caught and doesn't resent it. "Noted," she said.

Cal blinked like he'd missed a cue and was embarrassed to realize the cue had been there. Sia didn't flinch. She marked something in her notebook and then let her pencil rest. The mural's painted lake held light the way a real lake holds boats. Boring on purpose was working.

Ella lifted a new card. "We'll post our policy for thirty days," she said. "Same tone as the bowl card. Doors up front, lobby, reading room. You're welcome to steal our wording. Flattery that prevents fires is good manners."

Reed gave the tiniest bow from the neck. "We accept the theft," he said.

Vera checked the clock and then the water level in her glass. "Our messenger asked us to arrive and leave on time," she said. "We'll honor that. Half hour left."

"Good," Charles said. "Second half is making sure the words stay in people's pockets when they walk out of here."

They talked logistics. Primrose liked posters and suggested three spots where Summer travelers actually read signs instead of pretending to. Cal volunteered to send the sentence to three social feeds that connected to buskers and street magicians. Vera offered a tight paragraph for Winter's bulletin that didn't sound like a sermon. Reed said he would speak to a pair of people who managed doors two neighborhoods over and ask them to add a bowl out front with a card like Ella's.

Ella wrote as they spoke, not verbatim, just the bones. Sia drew a small circle around the noon hour on her pressure map and drew a little arrow that said attention economy. Marcus pretended not to see it and was glad she'd said it on paper.

Near the end, Charles asked each side to repeat deliverables out loud. He liked people to hear themselves agree.

"Summer will message no coins through public doors, leave tokens at entry, follow posted bells," Primrose said. "We'll push the wording to buskers and border kids. We'll add a friendlier bowl sign at two doors we use a lot. Contact is Cass."

"Winter will circulate the same line, in our own words but not fussy," Vera said. "We'll discourage binds to coins and binds in public spaces. We will note consequences without threatening. Contact is Linn."

"Museum will post policy for thirty days," Ella said, "and keep the bowl card front and center. We'll answer questions with the same script we used today."

Marcus added his piece because clarity liked chorus. "We will keep the hush tuned to eat show and keep staff at the threshold. We will keep the coin rule simple and enforce it calmly. No one comes through with coins. If you do, the bowl gets them until you leave."

Reed's mouth made the shape of approval. Cal nodded like he had finally accepted that the bowl was not a personality test. Primrose's smile turned into something more practical. Vera looked mildly satisfied, which was probably a Winter version of joy.

Ella tapped the clock. 59:30. "Time," she said.

Charles placed his palm on the table and spoke like a person ending a meeting in a church basement. "We said what we needed. We kept it calm. We'll post the words we promised. You'll do the same on your side. If you need us, you have a contact. If you show up with coins, they go in the bowl. Thank you for keeping the hour boring."

The four stood. No chair legs scraped. Reed folded his glass napkin with a precision that would have made a linen supplier weep with gratitude if this had been a restaurant. Vera lifted her coat. Primrose set both hands flat on the table for one second as if to promise she wouldn't press harder than she had to. Cal shot one last longing look at the mural, then made a good decision and didn't turn it into a comment.

Marcus walked them to the threshold and stopped with his heel on the line. The bowl waited. Ella held out the basket. Phones were returned. Tokens and coins came out of the ceramic and into their owners' hands only after each person had crossed back onto the step. No gifts changed pockets. No invitations were extended. Truth stood and held their exits with her quiet eye contact that made people behave without knowing why.

"Thank you," Charles said, and meant it in the way hosts mean it when the dishes are already done.

"Thank you," Vera said. "We'll send the wording back for the bulletin."

Primrose paused on the step and smiled at the bowl card like it was an inside joke she enjoyed. "We'll quote you," she said. "We won't pay you."

"Pay us by following the sign," Ella said.

"We will," Primrose said, and headed down.

Cal gave Marcus a small salute that actually landed respectful and then followed. Reed checked the time and nodded, pleased. Vera put her gloves on without fuss. They turned the corner and were gone. The temperature in the gap evened out in one long breath.

Ella wrote the time in the log. 12:01. She underlined clean

exit.

Marcus felt the room release in a way that didn't sag. Just a notch of permission. Chairs were still chairs. The hush stayed chalk-flat along the baseboard. The water on the table tasted like water and not attention. He liked that.

Sia closed her notebook with a soft tap that sounded like finishing a sentence. Kaelan touched the door frame with two fingers, a thanks the building always seemed to hear. Truth stretched her front legs, then her back, and sneezed once like punctuation.

A soft scrape came from the floor near the door. Not the squeak of a shoe. Paper. Marcus looked down. An unsigned card had slid under the gap. Ella bent, picked it up, and flipped it over. Four words in tidy block print.

"Thank you for boring," she read, and handed it to Marcus.

He smiled before he could stop it. "Same," he said, and pinned the card to the Ops corkboard with a pushpin between **Policy posted** and **Cocoa tickets restocked**.

Charles exhaled like he'd put a box on a shelf exactly where it belonged. "Lunch," he said.

"Soup," Ella said.

"Always," Marcus said. He checked the bowl one more time, touched the bell rope with the back of his fingers, and let the building know it had done good work. The hour had stayed what it needed to be. No coins crossed. No performance took over. Words were on paper. Contacts were in a folder that looked like any other folder. The porch held. That was the job.

And it worked.

THE ROOM RELAXED. NOT a slump, just normal again. Ella took the timer back to the desk. Charles filed the folder. Kaelan checked the door frame with two fingers and gave a small nod. Tobias walked the south hall once. Eric started labeling a map and caught himself before narrating. Truth did a slow loop, looked in each corner, and sat where she could see the door.

Sia stood by the mural with her notebook, thumb in the spiral. She looked tired from paying attention for an hour. Marcus walked over.

"Hey," he said.

"Hey," she said. "That went well."

"Yeah. Boring worked."

She smiled. They moved to the parlor. The couch had its usual dent. Truth followed, then peeled off to shadow Ella at the desk. Temple Dog duties.

They sat. Not close, not far. Late light through the windows. The mobile did half a turn and stopped. Marcus leaned forward with his elbows on his knees. Sia tucked one leg under, notebook on the cushion between them. Neither of them opened it.

"How'd the bell feel from your spot," he asked.

"Clean," she said. "Room said yes. Summer didn't love it, but they dealt. Winter liked it and pretended it was just fine."

"Sounds right."

She slid the notebook toward him with one finger. "I added a note to the map. Lunch spike, like we thought. There's also a thin bump right at eleven. Might just be the bell. I want to test it next week."

"Do it," he said. "We'll keep the script the same."

She leaned back and let her head rest in the corner. Her cheeks were a little pink, shadows under her eyes. He could read tired. He waited.

"You okay," he asked.

"I'm fine," she said, then added, "Mostly sleepy."

He patted his shoulder once. "Use my shoulder if you want."

She narrowed her eyes at him like she was rating a product. "That's not a pillow."

"Try anyway."

She scooted closer and eased her head onto him, careful at first, then sure. Her hair smelled like soap and outside air. She was warm. He kept still.

"You're actually comfortable," she said, surprised.

"I try."

She laughed once and went quiet. Her breathing slowed. He felt himself relax with it.

"What'd you do with the card," she asked after a beat. "The 'thank you for boring' one."

"Pinned it near the cocoa tickets."

"That tracks," she said, amused. "Very you."

Truth wandered past, checked that Sia was settled, gave Marcus a look that said don't screw this up, and trotted back to the lobby. He kept his hands to himself. He set his breathing to match Sia's so she could borrow it if she wanted.

"You ever think about leaving," she asked, voice already softer. "Like, not doing doors and bowls anymore."

"Sometimes," he said. "Mostly when I skip lunch."

She snorted. "Same."

He let the rest out slow. "I like porches. I like simple rules. I like when people exhale because a room is set up right. When I was a kid, I wanted to be the guy who knows which switch fixes a bad mood. This is the closest I've found."

"That's very you," she said. Her eyes were closed now. Not performing, just done for a minute. He watched her face settle.

He liked her. He didn't need a speech about it. He liked how she watched walls like they were worth listening to. He liked that she kept maps light and changed them when the room asked her to. He liked that she didn't push him to act like a guard when he called it caretaking.

He also knew better than to turn feelings into a job for someone else. No pressure. Ask first. Keep it simple. He set that rule next to the coin rule in his head.

Her head shifted a half inch on his shoulder and stayed. Sleep was taking over. He didn't move. He looked at the mural. The painted road met the painted water. Fine.

He thought about coins. No coins through thresholds. Easy rule. Feelings should be the same. No demands through hearts.

Ask first. Keep it plain.

She murmured something that wasn't a full word. His name might've been in it. He kept his voice low.

"You're fine," he said. "Just rest."

Her fingers twitched once on the notebook. Ink stain on her finger. Small callus where the pencil sat. He wanted to trace it with his thumb. He didn't. He stayed still.

Truth came back, checked Sia's knee, checked Marcus's face, and posted at the doorway facing the hall. Good dog.

The lobby ran like a normal afternoon. Charles answered a call about hours. Ella found a pen that worked and sounded happy about it. Kaelan told the door it had done well. Tobias radioed a soft okay and went quiet.

"Doorway," Sia said in her sleep, barely.

He answered under his breath. "Right here. Take your time."

He let himself picture a small life. Breakfast. Soup. A bell when needed. A bowl sign people actually follow. Sia drawing at the end of the day. Truth patrolling like it matters, because it does. No drama. Just steady. He didn't think that was naive. He thought it was a plan.

She shifted again and whispered something that might've been a laugh. A piece of hair had stuck to her cheek. He slid it back carefully, slow enough that she could wake and swat him if she wanted. She didn't. The curl let go.

"Not a pillow," she said, half asleep.

"I'll try to be one," he said.

She didn't answer. He didn't need her to. He watched the

hall.

He set a few promises where no one could trip on them. He'd say what mattered when it was time. He wouldn't turn this into pressure. He'd protect the quiet she used to work. He'd protect the room she used to sleep. He wouldn't walk her through any door she didn't choose.

He checked the bowl from where he sat. Still there. Card still clear. No tokens line easy to read. The bell rope hung straight. The hush line along the baseboard was the same chalk-still it had been all morning.

Sia breathed deep, the real sleep kind. He gave her the hour, or as much of it as she wanted. He could be a person and a chair at the same time.

He looked at the mural one more time. The road and the water shared space. That was enough. He kept the watch and let the quiet hold the rest.

She stirred after a while and blinked up at him. "How long did I crash," she asked.

"Twenty minutes," he said. "You snored once. I will deny it in court."

She made a face. "Rude."

"Accurate."

She adjusted but didn't move away. "Thanks for the shoulder," she said. "You can put that on your resume."

"I'm adding it to special skills," he said. "Right under bowl placement."

She smiled and looked at his hand on the cushion. "You can

hold my hand if you want," she said. "Not a big deal."

He paused long enough to give her an out. "You sure."

"Yeah," she said. "Clear yes."

He slid his hand over and laced their fingers. Her grip was warm and steady. No fireworks. Just good.

"This okay," he asked.

"It's good," she said. "You're steady. I like steady."

He let that sit where it belonged. "I like being around you," he said. "That's not a grand speech. It's just true."

"Same," she said. "Let's keep it simple. Slow is fine."

"Works for me."

Truth lifted her head, checked the hands, then put her head back down like she was logging it for later.

Sia's voice went soft again. "Small plan," she said. "Hot chocolate after close. You, me, a table that does not wobble. We can make fun of Eric's labels and pretend we are not doing that."

He grinned. "That is a strong plan."

"Great," she said. "It's a date. Or not a date. We can keep it light."

"We can call it cocoa and not label it," he said.

"Even better."

She squeezed his hand once and then relaxed again, eyes drifting shut. "If I fall asleep again, wake me in ten," she said. "If I talk about weird river stuff, ignore me."

"I'll wake you," he said. "And I won't quote you."

"Good," she said, already half under.

He watched her settle and let the quiet stretch. He noticed

small things. The way her breathing synced back to his. The way her shoulders had dropped since the meeting. The way Truth's ear flicked when a board creaked and then settled when nothing followed. He liked all of it.

"Marcus," she mumbled, eyes still closed.

"Yeah."

"You're not just a chair."

"I know," he said. "I'm trying to be a good one anyway."

She smiled without opening her eyes. "Keep trying."

He sat there with her hand in his and let the afternoon slide toward evening. Ella put a small sign on the desk about the private booking earlier and then came by the parlor, saw them, and pretended the couch was a national park you were not allowed to talk in. Kaelan gave Marcus a short look that said proud of you, then went to check the baseboard again. Charles crossed the lobby with two mugs and set one on the table near the couch. He didn't say anything about it. It smelled like cocoa.

Sia cracked an eye. "Perfect," she said. "Great staff."

"We're not staff," Marcus said.

"We act like we are," she said. "It works."

He squeezed her hand. "Cocoa later. Nap now."

"Copy," she said, and slipped back into real sleep with a small smile that felt like a green light and also a seat belt.

He kept the watch. He liked the job. He liked the person leaning on him more. He could like both without breaking either. That felt right. He looked at the bowl and the bell and the line at the baseboard and thought, rules still hold. Then he let the minute be quiet and easy and theirs.

CHAPTER 9

Singing Truths

MIA

Life is not a game. Still, in this life, we choose the games we live to play.

J.R. Rim

THE READING ROOM HELD the right kind of quiet. Lamps on. Green shades steady. The wood table didn't wobble. Along the baseboard, the hush line stayed flat, like chalk that had nothing to prove. Truth circled once, chose a spot by Mariah's chair, and flopped with a sigh. Her eyes drifted half closed. If dogs could purr, she would.

Mariah warmed up with a soft hum that wasn't about sounding pretty. She rolled her shoulders like she was shaking off a nap. "Ready," she asked.

Mia nodded. Her throat felt fine. Her hands were the problem. She sat on them, then pulled them free because she needed them to count.

Eric set his phone face down and tapped the table with two fingers. Slow. Even. "Same plan," he said. "Fifteen seconds you can run on command. You lead. Mariah takes the low. One beat of silence so attention drops. Keep tempo boring. If hush twitches, we adjust."

"I won't trip hush," Mariah said. "Promise."

Truth's tail tapped once without her eyes opening. She liked when they sang. Mia tried not to smile and failed a little.

"First pass," Eric said. "Whisper level. Words first."

Mia kept it plain. "Answer the room. We help at the desk. Front door only."

"Good," Eric said. "Breathe after room. Count four. Then finish."

She set the breath where he wanted it. "Answer the room." Inhale on a quiet four. "We help at the desk. Front door only."

"Now cadence," he said, tapping quarter notes. "Two bars on answer the room. Hold one beat. Then your second line. Mariah, stack the low only under answer the room. Keep it smaller than you want. No swell."

"Copy," Mariah said. She glanced at Mia with that steady look that meant lean if you need to.

They set in. Mia kept her voice just above a whisper. "Answer the room." She held the beat, then, "We help at the desk. Front door only."

Mariah slid under, barely there, enough to put a floor under Mia's line. The hush didn't move. Eric watched the baseboard like it had a heartbeat. His tapping stayed even.

"Again," he said. "Same volume. Shorter vowel on room. Don't let it ring."

Mia tightened it. "Answer the room." Beat. "We help at the desk. Front door only."

"Better," he said. "Now really give me the hold. That beat is the drop. The door loses the thread there."

Mariah nodded. "That's the point."

They ran five at whisper. Truth eased from eyes-half-closed to full nap. Her breathing lined up with Eric's tap. The hush stayed bored. Good.

"Take it to normal talking," Eric said. "Same shape."

Mia lifted the volume to regular inside-voice. The nerves in her hands moved into the line and settled. "Answer the room." Hold. "We help at the desk. Front door only."

Mariah's harmony sat lower, close to a hum. She didn't try to make it pretty. She made it stable. The air did nothing at all, which was the goal.

"Volume is right," Eric said. "Mia, clip front. One syllable. No pitch on it."

She ran it again. "Front door only."

"Yeah," he said. "That."

They did a set of ten. By the fourth, the hold felt like a brake she could find without thinking. On the ninth, she rushed the breath and heard it. Mariah tapped two fingers on the table. Mia reset on ten and hit it clean. Truth's tail answered with one soft thump.

"Noise test," Eric said. He played a low clip of lobby chatter from his phone. Just enough to be annoying. "Run over this."

They did. Mia felt her throat try to push. Mariah shook her head once and stayed small. Mia followed her down. The cadence slipped under the chatter and didn't fight it. It still worked.

"Good," Eric said. "That's the feel. Not a show. A floor sign."

"Try it at door volume," Mia said. "Firm, not loud."

"Once," he said. "Then back down. If hush twitches, we stop."

She tallied a slow breath. Eric clicked a soft tick on the phone. Not a fancy tone. Just a clock sound.

"Answer the room." She held the beat without flinching. "We help at the desk. Front door only."

Hush stayed flat. No echo. Eric nodded. "Mark that volume. Don't go higher. If you need weight, add Mariah, not decibels."

"Agreed," Mariah said. "We can add a second low on the hold. Lead stays clear."

"Try the two-stack," Eric said. "Mia lead. Mariah under. Then add a second note under the hold. Keep it quiet."

They tried it. On the hold, Mariah added a note you feel more than hear. The silence got heavy without turning into a stunt. It felt like a door choosing not to move.

"Okay," Eric said. "Use it if the first pass doesn't land."

Mia rolled her shoulders, shook out her hands. "Again."

They ran it again. Each pass, one small fix. Shorter vowel. Softer s. Don't lean on help. Breathe here. The boring adjustments that turn a line into a tool. Her throat stayed fine. Her hands stopped being a factor.

"Timing tell," Eric said. He sat across from them and used the fake voice he and Ella used in drills. Not spooky. Modern and dumb on purpose. "Hey. Mia. Can you crack the side door for two seconds. It's heavy."

He nailed the tone enough to be annoying. Mia didn't look at him. She aimed at the table. "Answer the room." Hold. "We help at the desk. Front door only."

He tried to answer before she finished. She didn't fill the space. The hold cut him off clean.

"That's the move," he said. "If something jumps the beat, let it hit the hold, then finish your line."

"Put that on the card," Mia said.

"Noted," he said, jotting.

They ran three more with fake asks. Worried friend. Flirty. Angry. Angry was the one that made Mia want to push. Mariah shook her head again and kept the line quiet and low. Angry fell right off the hold. That felt good.

"Last block," Eric said. "Normal volume. Six clean. If you grab a breath wrong, we reset the count."

"Rude," Mia said, which made Mariah laugh.

"Accurate," Eric said, grinning.

They hit six. On the fifth, Truth made a sleep noise like a tiny engine, then went still. Mia decided that counted as applause.

"Record time," Eric said. He opened voice memos. "Fifteen seconds. Mia lead. Mariah low. Silent hold. Tag once so it loops."

Mia set the rhythm in her chest, a quiet drum. Eric counted them in with a finger. They ran it. Clean. The words landed like a posted sign. He stopped the recording, played it back at low volume, listened for hiss and echo. None.

"Name the file," Mariah said.

"Escort Cadence v1, teen-safe," Eric said as he typed. He glanced up. "You want a better name."

"That's the better name," Mia said. "Label it boring so no one tries to make it artsy."

He laughed. "Done."

He airdropped the file to the museum phone and copied it to the small passworded folder he and Ella kept for scripts. Then he pulled a card and wrote the beats the way a person would read them.

Escort Cadence v1 - Teen Safe

   1. Lead: "Answer the room."

   2. Hold one beat.

   3. "We help at the desk. Front door only."

   Notes: keep volume normal. Clip vowels. If the door "answers" early, let it hit the hold, then fin-

> ish. If pressure rises, add low harmony, not volume.

He slid the card to Mia. "Tone check."

"It sounds like a person, not a spell," she said.

"Good," he said.

Mariah squeezed Mia's wrist. "You're solid," she said. "That felt like you."

Mia nodded. The sentence landed in a spot that mattered. She didn't need to be a soloist. She needed a tool that worked.

"Two more reps," Eric said. "Then one at whisper over the lobby clip. We're done after that."

They ran them. On the last one, the click track bugged Mia. She nodded at his phone. "Swap the tick. It sounds like a smoke alarm."

He picked a softer click. "Better?"

"Way," she said.

They finished the set and sat back. The room stayed steady. Truth rolled to her back with her paws up, held it until Mia snorted, then flipped over and pretended nothing happened. Classic.

"Printing the card," Eric said. He sent it to the small printer in the corner and grabbed two clean half-sheets. One for the desk. One for the practice folder.

Mariah snapped a photo of the card and the baseboard line. "I'll send it to Kaelan and Ella," she said. "If someone messes with the side hall sign, they can reset without asking."

"Thanks," Mia said.

Eric handed Mia the printed card. She read it again and heard her own line in her head without trying. It didn't feel like a performance. It felt like a pocket tool.

"What are we calling the silent beat," she asked. "We need a word we can shout during drills that doesn't sound like we're casting something."

"Hold," Eric said. "Or drop."

"Hold," Mariah said. "Short. Boring."

"Hold," Mia agreed.

Eric wrote it on the card.

Truth got up, shook, and leaned against Mia's shin. Mia scratched her chest. "You like the song," she asked.

Truth pushed her head into the hand like obviously.

"One more," Mariah said. "Pick the one you want on muscle memory."

Mia chose the middle. Not whisper. Not firm. Everyday. Eric counted them in. They ran it. It landed where it should. No buzz. No edge. Clear and simple.

"Stage-ready," Mariah said, smiling like a coach who'd seen a form they could build on.

"No stage," Mia said, but she was smiling too. "It's a tool."

"Best kind," Eric said. He clipped the card to the folder, tucked a second copy into a plastic sleeve for the desk, and added the audio to the tablet they used for tours. "Backup for when I forget my phone."

"When," Mia said.

"When," he echoed, deadpan.

Mia stood and stretched until her shoulders clicked. "The vowel notes helped," she said.

"Vowels are sneaky," Eric said. "They add drama without permission."

"Rude," she said.

"Accurate," he said, then laughed.

Truth sneezed once like punctuation. Mia checked the baseboard out of habit. Still flat. Good.

"Food," Mariah said. "Then back to the desk. You did real work."

"Feels like it," Mia said.

They cleared the table. Eric scooped printer scraps. Mariah tapped a tiny click pattern on the tabletop for Mia to steal. Tap tap tap. Hold. Tap tap. Mia matched it on her thigh until it stuck.

On the way out, Mia pinned the extra card in the practice section of the Ops board. It sat next to the door note she'd written earlier. If a door uses your name, don't answer the door. Answer the person next to you. We help at the desk. The two cards looked like they belonged together. She liked that more than she planned to say out loud.

"Cocoa after close if you still have the ticket," Eric said.

"I do," Mia said. "I earned it."

"Yeah," he said. "You did."

Truth headed for the lobby like a worker clocking back in. They followed. The hush stayed calm. The table hadn't shifted.

The cadence sat in Mia's chest like something simple and solid. Not a song for applause. A tool. She liked tools.

By close, the lobby felt normal again. The bowl card stayed obvious, the cadence card sat on Ops like it had always been there, and no one tried the side hall. In Mia's room, the lamp threw a small circle of light across the rug. The door was half open by habit. That is how they liked it on the living floor.

Sia knocked with her foot because both hands were full. Two mugs of cocoa, a bag of chips, and a taped bundle of cookies. Truth slid in first and claimed the rug like she had a reservation.

"Delivery," Sia said, setting the mugs on the desk.

"You didn't have to," Mia said. She was already reaching for a mug.

"I wanted to," Sia said. "You did great today."

Mia tried to hide a smile in the steam and failed. Sia did a quick room sweep. Blanket folded, sketchbooks stacked, hair ties in a dish. She cued a lo-fi playlist and sat on the floor with her back against the bed. Mia joined her. Truth settled between them, pleased with her workload.

"Door voice okay now," Sia asked.

"Yeah," Mia said. "It tried my name and Eric's. The timing was off. The cadence held."

"Good," Sia said. "Needy trouble. Not sharp."

They let the music fill the quiet for a minute. Sia bumped her knee against Mia's. Mia didn't flinch. Small win. Sia pulled a tiny mirror from her pocket, tipped it toward the lamp, and checked Mia's eyes like a sibling who refuses to be subtle.

"What," Mia said.

"Science," Sia said, flat. "No glow. You look like you."

"Yeah," Mia said. "They haven't glowed in a while."

Sia set the mirror down. "Glowing eyes are overrated."

"I liked them," Mia said. The honesty came out smaller than she meant. "I know they were a problem. The horns were worse. It was also me. Now it isn't."

"You're still you," Sia said.

"I know," Mia said. "Sometimes it feels like I quit a team and everyone else kept the jerseys."

"You didn't quit," Sia said. "You got free. Jerseys itch."

A soft knock hit the door. Two taps and a pause. Kaelan's rhythm. Mia called for her to come in.

Kaelan edged through with a quilt, a pillow, a net of tangerines, and a pack of sticky notes. She stacked everything with neat hands and kept a straight face. "Sleepover," she said. It sounded like a question and a plan.

"Yes," Sia said. She was already dragging the quilt toward two chairs.

Truth stood to greet Kaelan, then stole the first pillow and lay on it like a queen. Kaelan didn't argue with a Temple Dog. She produced a second pillow from the bag with magician timing and dropped onto the rug.

"House rules for sleepovers," Kaelan said, counting on her fingers. "Sugar within reason. Lights low by midnight. No doors for whispers. No jump scare videos."

Sia raised a hand. "I reserve the right to throw a pillow if you talk like a temple aunt for more than ten seconds."

"Noted," Kaelan said, amused.

They built a small pillow fort between the two chairs. The quilt drooped, then decided to cooperate. Sia sorted snacks into a pretend store. Kaelan lined up sticky notes like tickets. Truth crawled under the quilt and parked at the entry as security.

Kaelan peeled a tangerine and split it, handing halves to both girls. "I heard about the door," she said to Mia. "Clean work."

"It was small," Mia said.

"Small wins become habits," Kaelan said. "Habits become walls that don't need to look like walls."

Sia translated with a grin. "That means we'll be less tired next week."

"Good," Mia said.

They ate in a loose triangle on the rug. The playlist switched to something with a soft drum. Sia clapped along and lost the beat on purpose until Mia corrected her. Both of them laughed.

"So," Sia said, nudging the chips toward Mia. "One thing you like about not glowing."

Mia stared at the ceiling and picked something real. "People talk before they stare," she said. "That helps."

"Counts," Sia said.

"Another," Kaelan said gently.

"I don't break phone cameras anymore," Mia said. "That was annoying."

"Also counts," Kaelan said.

"Your turn," Mia said to Sia. "One thing you like about mapping everything."

"I can hear when a room needs help," Sia said. "And I can stop drawing and it still exists."

"Two things," Mia said.

"I'm bad at counting," Sia said, smiling.

Kaelan stretched out and propped on one elbow. "Hospitality is more than safety," she said. "It protects identity. If you know the house rules, you don't have to guess who you're allowed to be."

"I keep thinking I should pick a lane," Mia said. "Human or not. Quiet or not. I'm stuck between."

"You're allowed to be between," Kaelan said. "Between is a place. Doors connect there."

Sia tossed a pillow at her. "Ten second rule," she said, laughing. "Less temple aunt."

Kaelan hugged the pillow like a fine. "Plain version," she said. "You can be yourself here. No jersey required."

"Thanks," Mia said. She meant it.

Sia held up a sticky note. "We need a code word for when Mia spirals about being different."

"No," Mia said. She was already half smiling.

"Yes," Sia said. "Pick one."

Kaelan thought for one second. "Cocoa," she said. "Short.

Safe."

Sia wrote cocoa on the note and stuck it to Mia's sleeve. "Perfect."

"I'm not wearing this," Mia said, and left it there because it made them both happy.

They traded stories. Sia told the one about Eric mislabeling a box as mysterious jars and creating a cursed drawer by accident. Mia reported Ella's new policy, cocoa tickets for cards that make sense to normal people. Kaelan said Charles tried to fix a squeaky board with a look before he got the nails. All small stories. All better than silence.

"Sing the thing once," Sia said. "I want to hear it without lobby noise."

"It's a tool, not a show," Mia said.

"We like tools," Sia said.

Mia gave in and ran the cadence quietly from the floor. "Answer the room." She held the beat. "We help at the desk. Front door only."

Sia matched a simple harmony and didn't overdo it. Kaelan hummed low for three seconds and stopped. Truth rolled onto her back with her paws up and stayed like that, very proud of her listening skills.

"That feels like turning a sign around," Sia said.

"Exactly," Mia said.

They added star stickers to each other like grade school. Mia got one for answering the room. Sia got one for being annoying on purpose. Truth got one on her collar for Temple Dog excellence. Kaelan accepted one for not going full temple aunt for twenty minutes.

Lights went lower. The lamp stayed on. The room changed shape the way rooms do when the bright things are off. Mia lay back with her feet under the edge of the quilt. Sia flopped beside her and tucked cold toes under Mia's calf like a space heater. Kaelan took the chair for a minute, then slid to the floor because the floor felt right. Truth adjusted so she covered all three like a quiet blanket.

"Last check before we shut up," Sia said. "Mia, tell me who you are."

"You're exhausting," Mia said, but she answered. "I'm Mia. I sing when I need to. I don't glow. I like cocoa. I keep the room calm."

"Favorite," Sia said.

"Your turn," Mia said.

"I'm Sia," Sia said. "I draw maps. I listen to walls. I carry snacks."

"Accurate," Mia said.

"Kaelan," Sia said.

"I'm Kaelan," Kaelan said. "I ring bells. I ask the door before I ask the person. I tell rooms to be kind."

They let that sit. The playlist rolled to soft drums again. Mia glanced at her wrist. The faint pattern under her skin caught the lamp and didn't do anything dramatic. It was just there. She touched it with one finger and waited for feelings to sting. They didn't.

"You're perfect," Sia said. Not mystical. Just sure.

Mia tapped the sticky note on her sleeve. "Cocoa," she said.

Sia huffed a laugh. "Cocoa," she echoed.

"Cocoa," Kaelan added, smaller from the rug.

They shut up. The room stayed itself. Mia wasn't a demon or a project. She was a person on a rug with her sister, a friend, and a dog with a new job title. That felt like enough. She drifted off to the sound of the playlist switching tracks and Truth scratching her paws on the rug one time, the kind of small noise that means all clear.

The Annex Incident

TOBIAS

"Oh no." I said panic rising in my chest. "No, no, no, Somebody get a can opener. I've got a god in my head!!"

Rick Riordan, The Red Pyramid

THE ANNEX FELT LIKE a hallway that forgot how to echo. Tobias liked that about it. Concrete underfoot, clean paint on the walls, storage doors with numbers that actually matched the map Ella kept at the desk. He ran his route with the sheet in his back pocket, squares boxed out like a chessboard. Corner by the fire extinguisher. Vent above the coat rack. Utility hatch at the T-junction. He had written small notes in his own words, not magic terms. Cold spot. Weird hum. Watch the light.

Truth padded at his side with a pace that matched his. When he stopped to listen, she stopped and listened too. Her ears tilted at the vents. Her nose did a slow sweep. He scratched her shoulder once. She leaned in without breaking stride.

He paused at the first vent and held his hand in front of the grille. Air should have pulled in. Instead he felt a faint push against his palm, like someone blowing from the wrong side of a straw. Backward draft. He looked down the corridor. Nothing moving. The Annex lights hummed at their regular pitch. Somewhere in the main hall, a tour group laughed, then faded. He closed his eyes and stood still long enough to let his body catch the pattern. The push came in little pulses. One two, then a long pause. Not random.

He tapped his radio. "Annex check," he said. "No drama. Noting a backward draft at vent A."

Ella's voice came back easy. "Copy. Guests are light. You have space."

"Got it," he said.

He walked to the T-junction and sniffed. Metallic tang. Not blood. Not rust. Something like a penny you held too long. He marked it on his sheet. Penny smell. Midline. He crouched by the utility hatch and listened. A thin tap sounded behind it. Tap. Pause. Tap. Wrong tempo for the building. Pumps and heaters had their own songs. This did not match. He put his ear to the metal. Tap.

Truth gave him a look. Not alarmed. Focused. He nodded to

her and stood.

"Ella," he said into the radio. "Can you ask Eric to give me one notch less glare in the Annex. I want to see the edges."

"On it," Ella said.

Three seconds later the left bank of fluorescents stepped down a setting. The concrete looked calmer. He could see dust float near the vent lip. He moved closer and watched. The dust drifted toward the hall, not in. That matched the push on his hand. He took painter's tape from his pocket and stuck a small flag to the grille so he could watch the direction without standing under it. The flag lifted and pointed into the hallway. Wrong way.

"Flagged," he told the radio.

Sia's voice stepped in, steady. "Mark your three nearest corners. Floor, lintel, vent lip. Do not draw yet. Just note the triangle."

He pulled his pencil and put tiny dots on the floor and along the door frame. "Marked," he said. "No chalk yet."

Truth turned her head toward the far vent at the other end of the T. Tobias looked up. The dust there moved the same wrong way. The air between the two vents felt thicker by a hair, like a room before a storm, but the storm did not live here. He rubbed his fingertips and tasted copper on the back of his tongue the way you do when you run in cold air. He did not love that.

"Two vents reading weird," he said. "Both pushing. Something in the hatch keeps tapping."

"Copy," Charles said over the radio. Calm as a person reading off a grocery list. "Hold position. I am coming to you."

Kaelan's voice followed. "Do not give the room your attention. Make the room follow yours."

"Understood," Tobias said.

He put his back to the wall where he could watch both vents and the hatch. He did not stare at any one thing. He scanned like he was watching a field for someone to wave. Truth sat with her front paws on the line he had chalked last week. She did not growl. She did not show her teeth. She watched.

Footsteps approached from the main hall. Mia reached the Annex mouth first. She did not step inside. She stood where the light and sound from the lobby could still touch her and set her voice at the level people use in libraries when they are allowed to talk. "Hey folks," she said to the few visitors drifting near the doorway. "If you want the mirrors, they are open upstairs. Water and maps at the desk. We will bring the Annex tour back in ten."

A pair of teens looked past her as if the word Annex had turned into a magnet. Ella walked up behind them and slid a scavenger map across her palm like a card trick. "Blue stickers start your route," she said. "Mirrors are better before lunch. The Annex unlocks later."

They turned because good maps are stronger than magnets when you are bored and thirsty.

Sia came to the mouth next. She held her notebook, not a piece of chalk, and leaned into the wall at a point where she could see the triangle of space Tobias had marked. She did not ask him to move. She put three small pencil dots on paper in a shape that matched the floor, lintel, and vent lip. "Watch this," she said, quiet enough that only Tobias and Truth heard.

Eric arrived and killed a little more glare in the middle bank of lights. The hallway got clean. Charles's cane clicked on the tile in a steady rhythm. He did not hurry. Kaelan came with him and stopped beside the fire extinguisher, bracelets quiet, eyes on Tobias's hands.

"Tell me what you noticed," Charles said.

Tobias kept it simple. "Backward draft at both vents. Penny smell at midline. Tap behind the hatch. The pushes come in twos with a long pause. The dust flags point into the hall."

Kaelan nodded. "Good eyes," she said. She turned to Sia. "Anchors."

"Floor by your right foot," Sia said, nodding. "Lintel at the left corner. Vent lip where the tape flag sits now."

Charles set the tip of his cane to the tile and spoke one plain sentence to the building in a tone that sounded like thank you and please hold at the same time. The air felt like a person had put a hand on the small of its back and asked it to stand up straight.

Kaelan moved to the first point and pressed her palm to the floor. No gesture bigger than that. Her mouth shaped a word Tobias could not hear. She stood and crossed to the lintel and did the same, hand flat, bracelets still. The air between the two points lost something slippery and gained something solid. She looked to Tobias for the count.

He held up three fingers, then two, then one for the hold they had all learned to share. She placed her hand against the vent lip with the tape flag and pressed like someone closing a cabinet door that did not like to close. The tape lifted. The dust moved, then slowed. The tap behind the hatch tried to go faster and failed. The second vent's flag fluttered once more and then hung limp.

The grille lip showed a thin black line like charcoal dragged along metal. It forked at the end, crooked in a way that made his eyes want to slide off it. Sia pointed with the end of her pencil. "There," she said.

Eric held a small glass jar open and nodded to Tobias. "You want to catch it," he asked.

"Yeah," Tobias said. He took a square of card from his pocket and scraped the lip. A few grains fell into the jar. They looked like ash and were not quite ash. Eric twisted the lid on and wrote Annex vent trace, time, date in short plain letters. He did not draw a symbol on the label. He did not add the word demon. It would go on the shelf above the corkboard where they kept all the small proofs that the house was doing its job.

Mia stood at the mouth of the Annex and ran one line of the escort cadence at whisper to drift a pair of curious adults back toward water. She did not make it a show. Ella posted the small side card at eye level for volunteers. No name calls answered here. Come to the desk.

Truth moved to the center of the T and sat facing the hatch. She looked like a dog in a painting of a train station who knew when the train would arrive. She did nothing else, and that was enough.

The tap behind the hatch fell silent. The metallic taste eased off the back of Tobias's tongue. He felt his shoulders drop a half inch and let them stay there.

"Report," Charles said.

Tobias kept it in human words. "We had two points poking at once. It tried to write something along the vent lip and had a mirror at the hatch. The triangle held when Kaelan pressed the third point. Air is normal. Towel would be good if it starts again."

"Good," Charles said. "Sia."

Sia circled the time on her map. "The spike lines up with yesterday's lunch pressure," she said. "Same ten-minute window. The pattern smells like someone testing, not charging. Frequency is a repeat. Angle is new."

"We have watchers who learn," Kaelan said. There was no drama in it. Just fact.

Tobias took the damp towel he had brought in a plastic bag and laid it over the vent lip so the grille was half covered. He taped the corners so the towel did not flap. He liked tools that did not care about names. Cloth and tape rarely cared about anything other than physics. He pressed the tape down with the flat of his hand and thought about the fork in the black line. It had looked sloppy. Not art. A lever.

"Anything from below," Mia asked. She asked it the way a person asks about weather. She stood far enough back that the room could ignore her question if it wanted to.

Tobias tested the air again. The penny smell had walked away so quietly that he could have believed he imagined it. He did not think he had.

"Not here," he said. "But something took a look."

Charles stepped back so he was out of the Annex mouth and let the hallway breathe without him. "We are done for the moment," he said. "We do not feed the room when it does not need us."

"Copy," Ella said. She slid the desk bell back to its usual spot and wrote one clean line in the log. Forked push at Annex vents. Three-point hold, no show. Trace jarred.

Eric held the jar up to the light like a science fair kid who wanted a blue ribbon for labeling. He put it in the tray for Charles to sign and moved his attention back to the light bank. No more glare. Good.

Guests walked past the Annex without seeing a story to tell. That was the goal.

Sia stayed on the wall another few seconds, then closed her notebook and tapped the pencil once against the cover. "Triangle is steady," she said. "I am moving to the main hall to listen."

"Go," Charles said.

Kaelan touched the vent frame again, not to push, just to thank the metal for holding a line it had not asked to hold. She turned to Tobias. "Good timing," she said. "Good count."

He nodded once. He did not do compliments well in public. He pointed at the towel instead. "I will come back in five to make sure it is still flat."

"Do," Charles said.

They started to pull back from the Annex in a smooth reset. No one said crisis. No one took a victory lap. Tobias liked that about these people. Boring was a choice they made on purpose.

He walked the T once more. He looked for anything that wanted to be a hook. He checked his squares. The corner by the fire extinguisher was fine. The utility hatch sat quiet. The tape flag on the far vent did not lift. Truth followed and sniffed the towel and seemed satisfied with how it smelled. She gave him a glance that read like a nod.

He put his route sheet against the wall and added three things in pencil. Add towel to kit. Keep spare tape on hall hook. Circle this time block for the next three days. He boxed the notes so he would not forget them when the next job tried to take their place in his head.

At the Annex mouth, Mia tipped her chin at him. "You good," she asked.

"Good," he said.

"Want me on the cadence again if anyone drifts," she asked.

"Yeah," he said. "Light, not loud."

She gave him a mock salute that did not turn into a joke and tilted her body just enough to suggest the right path to the next pair of wanderers. Ella smiled at them without showing teeth and pointed to the blue sticker on their map like a secret only three people knew. They went where she pointed because most people will take a path if you make the path look easy.

Sia had already gone. Kaelan and Charles turned toward the lobby in step. Eric took the jar to the tray and wrote the time on the binder clip before he forgot. Truth stayed with Tobias because that is what she did when he had a job in a hallway.

He stood for one more minute and listened. The building made the sounds of a building that liked its job. The Annex did not hum wrong. The tap did not return. The towel lay flat. He let the last of the tight feeling leave his shoulders and rolled his neck once.

"Walk me out," he told Truth.

They headed for the main hall, slow. He did not stop thinking. He did not stress it either. He kept the rhythm that let him see what he needed to see without making the room feel watched. He liked that balance. He liked that someone had tried to pry at the vent and the house had said no with three calm touches and a towel. He liked that the jar on the tray would make the corkboard smarter. He did not like the fork at the end of the black line. It looked like a signature from somebody who liked cheap tools.

At the mouth, he checked the clock on the wall. He wrote the time on his sheet and circled it. Lunch window. Again. He thought about yesterday's Neutral Window hour. He thought about the lure at the staff door the day before that. It might all be noise. It might not.

Ella looked over the desk and lifted her chin in a small question. He shook his head once to say no emergency. She wrote another line on the log anyway. Second check clear.

Truth bumped his shin, a light touch that said move. He moved.

Behind him the Annex stayed quiet. The triangle held. The thin black fork on the grille lip had been scraped. The jar that held the ash that was not ash sat in a tray with a label that did not pretend to know everything that could be known. It was enough for now.

Tobias put his route sheet back in his pocket and felt the pencil marks there like a small map pressed into paper. He liked maps he could carry. He liked jobs he could do twice if needed. He liked that nobody clapped when the thing did not happen. He and Truth took the corner into the main hall and let the Annex be a hallway again. There would be more to do. He had time.

THE ANNEX SETTLED. THE towel lay flat. The flags stopped moving. The tap behind the hatch gave up. Tobias marked his sheet and stepped into the main hall with Truth at his heel.

Crowd noise came back in a low wash. Schoolkids drifted past the diorama cases. A stroller squeaked and then fixed itself. The smell of the café rode the air from upstairs. Coffee and sugar. Under it, just a thread, came the cold-soot smell he remembered from one late night on a lower level. It was faint enough to ignore if you wanted to. He did not want to.

He stopped at the corner and pretended to check a poster. Truth lifted her nose and made a small adjustment, just enough to say she smelled it too. He nodded and moved.

Ella looked up from the desk. He touched his route sheet with two fingers. The sign meant maybe. She gave him a tiny nod and straightened a stack of maps that did not need straightening. It made the desk look like a landing pad.

He took the next minute for a slow scan. He did not stare. He watched the way people moved. A dad with a toddler on his hip. A pair of teens laughing at a statue's toes. A woman checking her phone near the bowl card and then putting it away when she read the line about phones at the desk. No problem there.

The smell did not come from vents. It threaded through bodies. It got stronger when a cluster walked past the Annex mouth and weaker on the other side of the hall. He traced it with his body more than his nose. Truth paced with him, three steps behind and a little to the left. She watched feet and hands like a coach on the sidelines.

Mia drifted out of the reading room and parked near the desk with her notebook tucked under her arm. She did not ask him anything. She just caught his eye and tapped the rhythm for the escort cadence on the back of the chair. Tap tap tap. Hold. Tap tap. He nodded once.

Eric dimmed the middle bank of lights another notch. The glare off the polished floor dropped. People looked better without the shine in their eyes. Tells were easier to read when faces were not fighting light.

Tobias set up a simple pass. He stepped to the desk and grabbed two maps. He walked five feet into the flow and held one up like a person offering a flyer near a subway entrance.

"Maps," he said, easy. "Water at the desk if you want it."

Most people smiled and waved him off or took a map and kept moving. He was watching for the ones who would not look at the bowl card or the bell rope or Truth. He was watching for pupils that did not change with the light. He was watching for the flinch when Ella's pen clicked by accident. He clicked it himself and watched the way heads turned.

Three possible guests showed up fast. A woman with a scarf who would not step near the bowl and moved away when Truth looked at her. A man in a suit who stood too straight and blinked too slow. A family with a teen and a little kid. The teen kept his hands in his hoodie pocket and stared past the desk like he was trying not to make eye contact with a teacher. On another day that would just be teen. Today the cold-soot smell ran right through that group when they walked.

Tobias kept it calm. He walked two steps closer to the woman with the scarf and held out a map. "Exhibits upstairs are open," he said. "Mirrors are quiet right now."

She took the map with two fingers and veered away from the desk. When she passed Truth, the dog's ear flicked. Not a warning. A note. The smell did not spike. He let her go.

He shifted toward the suit. "Water," he offered. "We keep it cold."

The man looked at the cup like it was a test. He glanced at

the bowl card, then at the bell rope. No twitch. His breath was normal. The smell did not change. Tobias stepped back and dropped him from the list.

He pivoted to the family. He smiled and held a map at the teen's eye level. "You want the scavenger route," he asked. "Blue stickers. Fast track."

The teen did not take the map. He kept his hands in his pocket and stared past Tobias's shoulder like there was a screen there. The little kid looked at Truth and made a face that meant he wanted to pet and was not sure if he was allowed.

"You can say hi," Tobias told the kid. "Ask her name first."

"Truth," the kid said.

Truth wagged once. The kid held out his hand. Truth sniffed and did a short dog smile. The smell flared, then thinned. It was like something had to make a choice about being seen by a dog. Tobias felt the tiny shift and filed it.

Mia took a half step closer to the desk and tapped the rhythm on her thigh. Tap tap tap. Hold. Tap tap. Ella poured water and set three cups where a person could grab them without breaking stride. Eric unplugged a buzzing sign in the corner and set it behind the desk so quiet could be the default.

"Annex tour starts later," Mia told a couple near the corridor mouth, friendly and plain. "Try the skylight room first. Better light for photos."

They turned away from the Annex without arguing. The teen looked after them with a tight jaw and then looked away when Truth looked at him. The cold-soot thread gathered around the family again and then thinned when the little kid giggled at Truth's ears.

"Maps," Tobias said again, still easy. He did not push. He waited to see what the group would choose.

The dad took one and glanced at the bowl card with a normal face. The mom asked Ella about bathrooms. Ella pointed and added a line about the water fountain. The kid took a cup and drank like it was the most amazing thing in the room.

The teen finally pulled one hand out of his hoodie pocket and took the map. His fingers were too cold. Tobias could feel the cool from a foot away. That was wrong for a person who had been inside for ten minutes. The teen's pupils did not match the light from Eric's dimmer change. They felt slow. Tobias stepped a little to the right so the teen would have to pass him to get to the Annex mouth. He did not block. He made a path look easy in the other direction.

"Reading room is open," he said to the family. "Table's free if you want to sit for a second. Water on the corner. Maps can live there while you plan."

The mom liked the idea of sitting. You could see it in the way her shoulders dropped. The kid tugged toward the dog. The dad followed the map with his eyes like a person who had been politely lost and did not want to say that out loud.

"Reading room," the mom said. "Two minutes."

The teen did not move until the little kid pulled his sleeve. The smell spiked and faded with the tug, like it did not want to go and did not want to stay. He twitched his head and went.

Tobias let them pass. He looked at Ella and touched his shoulder with two fingers. The signal meant privacy please. Ella nodded. She slid out from behind the desk and set two cups on the reading room table, then angled two chairs so the family could sit facing the door, not the hall. She moved the bowl card on the side shelf so it was visible without being in their faces. She did all of this with the care of someone setting a table at home.

Mia stood at the reading room entrance with her weight on the back foot and her eyes soft. She did not block. She set the tone. "You can park here," she told them. "Bathroom is around the corner. If you need anything, just ask."

Truth crossed the hall and sat by the doorway, not inside. She faced outward and watched the flow. Her tail moved once and then stopped.

Eric cut the café music a little from upstairs, just enough to let voices sit on top of the sound. The building felt like a place that was listening instead of performing.

The family settled. The kid put the map on the table and traced the route with his finger. The mom drank water. The dad checked the opening hours on the card Ella had set down. The teen took the chair farthest from the door and leaned back like he wanted to look casual. His feet were too still. His gaze kept sliding to the Annex mouth and back like a magnet that had learned to breathe.

The cold-soot thread stayed near the teen. It was thinner than it had been in the hall. That mattered. It meant the room was helping. The hush loved rooms where people sat with water.

Tobias liked that about this place.

He parked himself two steps off the doorway where he could see both the family and the Annex mouth. He kept his hands at his sides and his shoulders down. He did not look like security. He looked like a guy who might be able to find a trash can. Most people felt better around guys who could find trash cans. That was his experience.

Ella slid a bowl of wrapped mints onto the corner of the table like a person who believed in tiny comforts. The kid took one and said thank you around the wrapper. The teen did not touch the mints. He stared at his cold hand like it belonged to someone else. Tobias saw the breath in the kid's chest and the mom's chest and the dad's chest. Three normal patterns. He saw a small hitch in the teen's inhale. Not fear. Not asthma. More like a cough that never formed.

Mia hovered near the door and put one palm on the frame for a second like a hello to the house. Then she brushed the cadence under her breath, just enough to set the room's rhythm. "Answer the room." Hold. "We help at the desk. Front door only." There was no door to answer in here. The line just told the walls what kind of room this was.

The teen blinked slow. His gaze snagged on the bowl card, then jumped to Truth, then to Tobias, then down to his hands. He wrung them once and shoved them back into his pocket. The smell thinned again. Tobias let his breath follow the room instead of the teen. The room helped more than any stare could.

The little kid reached for a second mint. The mom raised an

eyebrow without speaking. The kid pulled his hand back and grinned. The dad unfolded the map and asked Mia which way the arrows pointed, left to right or right to left. Mia turned the map and traced the path with a finger, simple and silly, like the arrow game you do with toddlers. The dad laughed and said thanks. The teen watched the finger. The cold thread twitched.

"Crowd is fine," Eric said quietly from the desk. "I am going to swap a flicker in the side hall."

"Good," Ella said. "Keep the sound low."

Sia walked past the reading room and gave Tobias a small look that meant call me if your nose says below. He lifted two fingers once for hold. She kept going toward the statue hall. She was listening for patterns. He knew she did not need to stand over him to do that.

The smell floated up once more, a thin band that pressed against the reading room doorway and then eased when Truth leaned forward on her front paws. It felt like a draft that wanted to be a hand. It did not get to be one. Tobias stayed where he was and waited to see if the thread would choose a face. He wanted it to choose in a room with witnesses and water, not in a hallway with a corner.

It chose nothing. It sat on the teen like a coat that did not fit. The teen's eyes were dull for one long blink and then a little clearer. He tugged his sleeve and said, "I'm fine," to nobody in particular. The words sounded like he had copied them from a line he used on a different day for a different problem. The mom put a hand on his shoulder and squeezed. She did not make a speech. She just did the hand.

Tobias glanced at Ella. She nodded toward the front door. There were two benches outside and a patch of sun where people could sit and not feel watched. Good.

He checked the Annex mouth one more time. No flags moved. The towel stayed flat. The hallway acted like a hallway. He turned his body an inch toward the reading room and let his stance become a guide. He made the front door look like the next normal step in a day.

"Fresh air is good," Ella said to the family. "There is a bench on the porch. We have blankets if you get cold."

The mom nodded. The dad stood. The kid grabbed the map. The teen took a second to lift his hands out of his pockets. He looked at the dog first, then at Tobias, then at the door like it had been waiting for him longer than he had been waiting for it. The thread wavered. It was almost gone. Almost was not enough.

Tobias fell in on the right, not crowding, just present. Mia moved to the left with water. Truth took point, slow and calm. Ella held the door. The air in the doorway felt a little cooler than the hallway. He filed that. The building agreed with fresh air.

They stepped through together. The porch had clean light and a view of the square. Traffic noise softened the edges of voices. The bench was open. Mia set a cup in the teen's hand and another beside the mom. Ella pulled a spare coat from the standing rack and offered it without fuss. The dad sat and kept one foot on the sidewalk like a person who wanted to be useful and did not know how.

Tobias stayed at the edge of the porch where he could see the room inside and the square outside. He did not speak. He watched the way the teen held the water. He watched the way the kid looked at Truth and at the pigeons and back. He watched for the moment the thread would try to make a scene.

The door behind him opened with a soft click. Charles stepped out like he had been on the way already. He had the Key in his palm, not raised, not hidden. It looked like a piece of metal a custodian would carry. He took in the bench, the faces, and the way the teen's shoulders did not know whether to stay up or settle.

"Good place," Charles said to Ella, quiet. "Thank you."

"Bench looked right," Ella said.

"May I," Charles asked the mom, nodding toward the teen. He waited for her yes. He got it as a nod and a small "please."

He moved in a way that did not spook and knelt until he was at the teen's eye level. "We are going to make this boring," he said, like a promise. He set his palm lightly against the sleeve, Key under his hand, and spoke one clean line that made sense even if you did not know what the word Key meant. "Inside to step," he said. "Step to air."

The world folded without a jerk. The teen's eyes blinked once on the bench and opened on the porch edge. He was sitting in the same position, hands around the cup, breath catching like a person who woke up too fast from a nap. There was no flash. No noise. The air had moved him the way a hallway moves you when you are walking and not thinking about it.

The thread broke like string in water. It did not snap and fly. It unraveled and sank. Truth's head tilted like she had heard a high thing stop. She wagged once and then looked at the square like the job was done and she was back to counting buses.

The teen stared at the water in his cup and frowned. "I feel weird," he said.

"That is normal," Charles said. "Drink. Sit in the air. The room will do the rest."

The mom put her hand back on his shoulder. The dad let his foot rest on the porch. The kid petted Truth once and then sat on his hands like a person who knew how many pets counted as enough.

Ella set a folded blanket on the bench beside the teen and did not force it on him. "If you get chilly," she said.

"Thanks," he said, and then blinked like the word surprised him.

Mia posted herself two steps back with her shoulder to the door frame. She did not sing. She did not talk. She made the porch feel like a porch and not a stage.

Charles looked once at Tobias. Tobias kept his face neutral and let the air come all the way back to normal before he nodded. The look Charles gave him back said good work without the words. Tobias let the compliment land and did not dodge it this time.

Inside, Sia wrote the time on her map. Eric added a small note to the log. Ella breathed out with her mouth closed so no one would hear the last of the worry leave. Truth watched the square like buses could learn from her.

Tobias stood and watched the edges. If the body goes wrong, block and hold. The Key moves people, not harm. He put that sentence in his head where it would be easy to grab later. He would write it on the Ops card when they went back inside.

The porch stayed porch. The bench stayed bench. The teen drank water and stared at the cup like he was trying to remember what story he had been told before this one. He looked up at his mom and then at his dad and said, "I'm okay." This time it sounded like him.

"Good," Ella said, simple as a sigh. "Take your time."

THE PORCH STEADIED. THE teen drank water and kept both feet on the ground. The blanket sat beside him like an option, not an order. Charles stayed until the kid's breath matched the street noise, then gave Ella a small nod. She stayed to keep the family company. Mia leaned on the door frame and let the porch be a porch.

Tobias stepped back inside with Truth at his heel. The lobby felt normal again. The smell was gone from the air near the door. It lingered in a thin thread farther inside, past the reading room, where the main hall widened before the Annex mouth. He filed the line in his head and followed it with his body, slow enough not to put weight on it.

A staffer from the museum floor came off the staircase with a tray. Cups of water. Napkins. Small things that made people settle. She walked like someone who had done this a thousand times. Left hand steady under the tray, right hand ready to pass a cup to anyone who needed one.

Tobias clocked the cluster near the corner before she reached them. Two adults reading an exhibit plaque and not really reading it. A guy in a thin jacket standing wrong for his size. The wrong part was in the shoulders. They were pulled a little too high, like an invisible coat hanger lived under his shirt. He kept glancing at the Annex mouth and then away. His jaw worked like he was chewing air.

Truth's ears tipped toward the cluster. Tobias shifted his path to put himself between the tray and the corner. He did not block the man outright. He made a better route for the tray.

"Water," the staffer offered, smiling. "Free if you want it."

The guy in the jacket turned too fast. His eyes had that glazed, slippery look that tells you a person is not fully in their body or is in it with a bad passenger. He stepped toward the tray. His hands came up empty, then closed in a way that made Tobias move. It was not a grab for a cup. It was a grab for a wrist.

Tobias planted and slid right to take the line. He did not shove. He let his body be where the wrist would have been, then put his forearm up in a clean bar that did not strike. The tray cleared behind him. The staffer stopped short but kept the cups level. No spill.

"Hands down," Tobias said, voice flat and steady. "Take a

breath. Sit."

The guy's hands stalled an inch from Tobias's forearm. His eyes skittered to the bell rope like a thing inside him disliked the shape of it. Truth stood and leaned forward until her paws touched the baseboard line. She did not bark. She set her eyes on the man's sternum like she knew where the center of him was.

The man froze. It was not a polite stop. It was like a clutch disengaged. His fingers hovered, then twitched. His jaw worked and then let go. A sound came out that wanted to be a swear and turned into a small cough.

"Got you," Tobias said, same calm. He kept his forearm where it was and set his other hand near the man's elbow without touching. "Sit."

Mia's voice came from the desk at a whisper, the cadence she had made with Mariah earlier. "Answer the room." She held the beat. "We help at the desk. Front door only." It was not aimed at the man. It was aimed at the space. The people around them heard the tone and eased back instead of crowding.

Sia stepped into Tobias's sightline and took one small step to the side to close off the Annex mouth visually. Not a wall. A suggestion. Eric cut the middle bank of lights one more notch. The glare left the floor. The air felt less sharp.

The man's hands dropped a fraction. He took a breath that did not belong to him, then one that did. His eyes lost some glass and found a little context. The wrong set in his shoulders did not let go. It hid.

Charles's cane touched tile behind Tobias. He had taken the

inside route from the porch and crossed the lobby without anyone noticing. He stopped on the man's left where he could be seen without being a threat.

"May I," Charles asked, looking at the museum staffer first, then at Tobias, then at the man. He waited on both yeses. The staffer nodded. Tobias narrowed his eyes at the man, saw a tiny blink that looked like a human left behind a window, and gave Charles the second yes.

Charles kept his voice quiet and plain. "We are going to make this simple," he said. He set his palm lightly on the sleeve, the Key caught under his hand, and spoke the line he had used on the porch. "Inside to step. Step to air."

The space did the fold again. No show. The man was standing in front of Tobias, off-balance and ready to grab something that wasn't a cup. In the same breath he was on the front steps, seated against the railing with both hands open and empty, blinking hard like he had walked through a door without seeing it first.

Tobias stayed where he was and felt the wrongness unhook. It did not fly off like a bird. It loosened, like a tight knot under water that gives one loop at a time. Truth's tail tapped once and then went quiet.

The museum staffer kept the tray level because she was a professional. She exhaled and adjusted her grip. Mia moved to take two cups and carry them toward the steps. Ella opened the door and let in a drift of outside air. The man shivered. Not from cold. From change.

Charles spoke to the log as much as to the room. "Transit

shakes hitchhikers," he said. "It does not hurt the person. They will feel confused. Give water. Give air. Do not ask questions for one minute."

Ella nodded and took two cups outside. She handed one to the man and set one down beside him. "Sip," she said, the way she said it to anyone who needed the reminder.

The two adults at the plaque had backed up three steps with their eyes wide. Sia turned her shoulders and showed them the map like nothing wild had happened. "Skylight room is open," she said in the tone you use for pointing out a window view. "Better light for photos right now."

They moved. People follow a simple road when you make one.

Tobias lowered his forearm. His heart had jumped at the grab and was already finding its rhythm again. He looked at the staffer. "You okay," he asked.

"Fine," she said. Her hands were steady. "Thanks."

He nodded and stepped to the door to check the porch. Outside, the man in the thin jacket was sitting with the cup to his lips. His eyes had lost the sheen. He looked around like he was trying to remember where he had left his car in a lot and was not embarrassed to admit he forgot. Ella stood a few feet away, present without hovering. Truth took the threshold and watched both directions at once.

Mia posted a small handwritten card next to the door, waist-high where volunteers would see it. Give them space. Water first. No questions for one minute. The handwriting matched the other Ops cards. Plain. Clean.

Charles stayed outside long enough to watch the man's shoulders stop pretending to be a hanger. He spoke to him in the tone you use for a person who looks lost at a bus stop. "You had a faint," he said, which was not a lie. "Sit as long as you need. The air helps."

The man nodded like he was agreeing to a plan he understood. "I'm okay," he said. It sounded more like him with each syllable. He took another sip and let his shoulders drop the last inch.

Tobias stepped back into the lobby and wrote two lines on the Ops pad with Ella's pen. If a grab starts, block and hold. The Key moves people, not harm. He added one more, because he liked when cards told you what to do, not what not to do. Water first. Air next. Then questions.

He put the pen down and rolled his shoulders once. The tightness there let go. Sia walked by and tapped the time on her map with her pencil. "Same window," she said. "This felt linked. Push, then a ride-along."

"Agreed," Tobias said.

Kaelan checked the Annex mouth one more time. The towel lay flat. The tape flags did not lift. She touched the vent frame with two fingers in a quiet thank you and moved on.

Eric labeled a new jar. Annex corner dust, after grab. He did not know if dust mattered. It was habit. Habits made patterns visible later. He set the jar on the tray with the others and marked the time on the clip.

Ella came back inside and pulled a coat from the rack to lend to the man outside for the next ten minutes. "He is clear," she said, quiet. "He will be confused." She added, "He said thank you like he had been holding it back all day."

"Good," Charles said. He tapped the cane once and looked at each of them in turn. "We keep doing it this way. Simple. Witnessed. No force unless bodies are in danger."

"Copy," Mia said.

"Copy," Tobias said.

Truth sat at his heel and looked up at him like he had passed a test no one had made. He scratched behind her ear. "Chicken later," he told her. She wagged exactly once like a promise.

He took his route sheet from his pocket and added a star next to the Annex square and a second square by the reading room door. He drew a small arrow to the porch to mark the path Charles liked for transit. He boxed the notes. He liked having a map he could hand to anyone on a shift.

The lobby settled into normal. Someone asked for bathrooms. Someone else asked what time the mirrors closed. Ella answered both questions like the day had been average. Mia slid the cadence card a quarter inch straighter on the board. Eric fixed a squeaky sign. Sia wrote a small circle on the map and tucked it away.

Tobias looked at the tray and then at the staffer. "I can walk with you," he said.

"I'm good," she said. She picked up the tray and smiled like the joke was that nothing had spilled. It had not.

He went back to the Annex mouth with Truth and listened. The towel breathed like cloth does when a room forgets about it. The vents held. The hatch stayed quiet. He stood there and let his breath match the building again. He liked this part, the after. Not victory. Not relief. The part where the room chose calm and he got to witness that choice.

He wrote one more line on the Ops pad before the hour turned. If the body goes wrong, block and hold. Then call Charles. The words looked boring on the board. Perfect. He wanted boring to be the thing people saw when they looked up.

Outside, the man in the thin jacket leaned back on the bench and looked at the sky. Inside, the museum kept being a museum. Tobias slipped the route sheet back in his pocket, patted Truth's side, and kept watch. He had time. There would be more to do.

CHAPTER 11

Between Seasons

Sia

I was very much provoked. Of course, I knew there are no fairies; but that needn't prevent my thinking there is.

L.M. Montgomery, Anne of Avonlea

SIA'S GARDEN MET HER like it always did, with light that understood how to be soft. Gravel held the last of a glow that wasn't from a sun she knew. The path curved once around a small stone basin and then reached a place where it both split and didn't. To the left, air carried warm leaf smell and a sweet green taste she felt on her tongue. To the right, frost lay like quiet chalk at the edge of shade, and breath came out a little whiter than it went in. The garden itself sat between them, steady as a table.

She let her sneakers scuff the gravel so the sound would tell the place she was here. Then she touched the low wall with her fingertips and counted to four. Thanatos had taught her that. Places like to be greeted the way people do.

He was there when she lifted her hand. No footsteps. No big entrance. Just a figure in dark clothes that didn't cast the kind of shadow regular lights make. He watched the split in the path the way a lifeguard watches water.

"Evening," he said, like a neighbor.

"Hey," Sia said. She checked the left and right without turning her head. "It's louder today."

"Because you are listening for it," he said. "And because it is listening back."

She breathed in summer for a second. Heat without sting. A violin string kind of brightness behind the leaves. She breathed in winter for a second. Cold without bite. Air that knew how to be clean. She centered on the gravel, where it just smelled like rock and dust and the last of the basin's water.

"Something from Summer put a card under our bowl," she said. "Real seal. Bad phrasing. It named roles."

"Roles are shortcuts," Thanatos said. "Shortcuts tempt courts when they are bored or when someone hopes to skip a line."

"Kaelan says Summer didn't write it right," Sia said. "Which means someone is pushing a boundary with borrowed paint."

Thanatos's mouth tilted. "That is a good phrase for it."

"She wants me to write a clause," Sia said. "Scope. Cost. Sunset. I can feel it sitting there, but I don't want to write something that makes a mess."

"That is why you practice here," he said, and pointed at the gravel in front of her. "Show me the rule in the smallest possible piece. Do not use a court's name. Do not use a person's name. Tell the ground what kind of place it is."

Sia chewed the inside of her cheek. Then she spoke in the same voice she used for map labels. No drama. Just truth.

"Paths observe the border," she said. "No summons across the line without a guest's yes."

The gravel didn't glow. There was no sound effect. The change felt like math. The left and right stayed left and right. The fuzzy seam between them went from blur to a clean stripe the width of a bread knife. The stripe ran from the basin's lip to the low wall and stopped where the garden ended.

"Good," Thanatos said. "You asked for behavior, not obedience. Roads and rivers listen when you speak to behavior. They want to know what they are allowed to be."

Sia looked at the stripe. It wasn't marble or paint. It was a decision the ground had made. The summer air didn't cross it without a pause. The winter chill didn't either. The garden breathed easier between them.

"Again," he said. "The same rule, but smaller."

She pointed at the basin. "Water observes this rim," she said. "No spill without a hand to carry it."

The meniscus tightened. A curl that had been thinking about becoming a drip changed its mind.

"Smaller," he said.

She pointed to her shoes. "Gravel stays underfoot," she said. "It doesn't jump into shoes."

His eyes warmed like someone who had just been handed a good joke. "That is a charitable clause. Your toes will thank you."

She felt the shift under her soles. The little pieces of rock that liked to fling themselves against socks sat down and agreed to be a path.

Thanatos hooked a finger at the line where summer and winter met. "Tell the stripe when to end."

Sia took a breath and aimed for light and boring. "This border holds until I sleep and wake," she said. "Then it asks me again."

The stripe agreed. She felt it without seeing it. The rule had a sunset. It would not linger past usefulness and start protecting the wrong thing.

Thanatos circled the basin once, hands in his pockets. "That is your craft," he said. "Not power that throws, not fire that eats. Jurisdiction. You do not command people. You tell places the way you want them to behave, and places choose to like you."

Sia let the sentence sit in her chest until it felt like it belonged there. Jurisdiction. She liked the sound of it. It reminded her of teachers who wrote classroom rules in marker and then actually kept them, not the ones who yelled and forgot.

"What about cost," she asked. "Kaelan said every clause pays for itself."

"Costs keep you honest," Thanatos said. "They also tell a place you understand what you are asking. Here, cost can be as simple as attention. You give the room your eyes when it needs them. You update the rule when the facts change. You accept that a border that protects choice might also keep a friend on the far side until they choose to cross."

Sia grimaced. "So I don't try to write around consent."

"You do not try," he said. "You refuse. The more your rule protects choice, the stronger the rule stays when you walk away. If you write to control people, the rule will go dull in your hand. The place will forget it. That is a kindness built into the world."

She thought about the card under her pillow. Present the Singer and the Caretaker. The handwriting had been pretty. The sentence had felt like fingers on the back of her neck.

"What about invitations that name roles," she asked. "Is there a best way to answer those besides throwing them out?"

"Rewrite pressure into a door," Thanatos said. "Do not hurl the words back. Turn them into a doorway with a knob on the inside. You can do it in one line."

He looked at the stripe again, then back at her. "Try it."

Sia pictured the card. She pictured Ella's calm voice at the porch and Mia's cadence near the Annex. She pictured the desk and the bowl and the signs that worked because they were boring and everyone could understand them.

"In this garden," she said first, to keep the practice anchored.

"No court may issue summons by title. Invitations come in plain names. If an invitation touches a role, the garden will turn it into a polite sign that says 'ask the person at the desk' and then drop it by sunset."

The air didn't change temperature. The stripe widened a hair. On the summer side, the leaves moved as if someone had read the line and shrugged and seen that it didn't try to tell them what music to play. On the winter side, frost held its crisp edge and did not creep just to make a point.

"That one felt good," Sia said.

"It is good," Thanatos said. "You wrote scope. You named a cost. You placed a sunset. You did not punish. You refused to be pushed."

Sia kicked the gravel with the side of her shoe and watched it move just enough to show her the rule had not turned the path into concrete. She liked that. Rules are not prisons when they are written right.

"What about courts that pretend they did not hear," she asked. "Or polite hands that use real seals to nudge."

"Then you do what you do at the hotel," he said. "You post a rule where anyone can see it. You send a copy to both courts so no one can pretend they missed it. You make the rule so clear that people who want to follow it feel better when they do."

Sia took her notebook out of her hoodie pocket. The paper here never tore. She tried anyway. It bent and came back like a leaf. That seemed fair. She sketched the stripe and wrote three words beside it. Scope. Cost. Sunset.

"Tell me the difference between a rule and a dare," Thanatos said.

She thought of the bowl under the desk lamp. "A rule makes space," she said. "A dare tries to collapse it."

He nodded. "Say that back to yourself before you write anything important."

She wrote it under the three words and boxed it in pencil. Then she looked at the left-hand path again. The summer smell tugged at her like someone's hand in a crowded hallway, not mean, too firm. The right-hand path did the same in the opposite direction. She had never noticed the tug so clearly. It made the garden feel more like a place she had chosen, not just a place that happened when she slept.

"Can I keep the stripe," she asked. "Or does that make me a border cop in my own head."

"Keep it while you are awake here," Thanatos said. "Borders are not bad. They are only bad when you use them to hide from love or when you make them permanent because you are scared. You can let it fade when you leave."

Sia checked the basin one more time. The water had not spilled. A star on the surface uncurled and lay flat. She reached out and dipped two fingers in, then touched the stripe with a wet thumb. The line stayed.

"Tomorrow I want to post a clause on the Hotel," she said. "I want it to be boring and human and impossible to mistake."

"Then write it now," he said. "Say it twice. Once to the garden. Once to yourself."

She faced the door that wasn't a door. She pictured the Hotel's front glass and the spot near eye level where a person would read when they came in. She pictured Ella's pen and the way Ella preferred Times New Roman for cards because it felt friendly.

"Inside the Hotel," Sia said, "no court may issue summons by title. Invitations in plain names at the desk. Invitations expire at dusk. A copy goes to Summer and Winter at close."

The gravel agreed. The line didn't widen. It didn't need to. The agreement felt like a hum in her shins.

"Again," Thanatos said, quieter.

"Inside the Hotel," she said, "no court may issue summons by title."

He tipped his head as if he were listening to a radio only he could hear. "That part will carry by itself," he said. "It has the tone of something the House already wanted to say."

"Good," she said. "I don't want a fight."

"You want a door," he said. "With a knob on this side."

She put the notebook away and rubbed her thumb over the line she had touched with water. It left a darker mark for a second before it dried.

"Can you walk with me to Summer," she asked. "Longwang said he'd hear me if I needed him. I want to show him the seal and ask whether that card was theirs."

"I can walk to the curb," Thanatos said. "I will not walk the path. My presence changes conversations you need to own."

"That's fair," she said.

He looked at the winter side for a heartbeat, the way you look at a friend out of the corner of your eye. "You will want Winter to read your card too," he said. "Not because you owe them, but because courtesy keeps dogs from barking when you walk past the fence. That is true of courts and neighbors."

"Copy to both," she said. "It's in the clause."

"Good," he said.

They stood at the split together and let the air speak. Summer's side was bolder. Winter's side was patient. The garden held both without apology. Sia felt herself settle in the middle the way a good chair settles when you sit right in it.

"Last thing," Thanatos said. "Your rule can ask for silence."

"Silence," she said.

"Not forever," he said. "A clause that gives the House quiet hours is a gift. Tell it the window you want. Ask guests to make their asks at the desk in that time. You are not forcing anyone. You are telling the room to protect its own breath."

Sia smiled. "Like the hush line."

"Like the hush line," he said.

She tried the practice version here. "In this garden, from now until I sleep, no calls across the stripe," she said. "Questions at the bench. Answers at the bench."

The stripe felt pleased. That was a silly word for a line of gravel, but the feeling matched. Thanatos's eyes softened, which was another word that didn't sit right on him and also was the only one that fit.

"You're ready," he said.

She looked down at her shoes. No gravel had jumped into

them. She laughed, small and real. Then she looked up again.

"Walk me to the curb," she said.

They stepped toward the bright side together. The garden did not yank her in. It opened the way a store opens when a person turns the sign. Thanatos stopped where the stripe ended and the path's green light began.

"You have the habit of writing for people to feel safe," he said. "Write for places to be honest and you will make more safety than you can carry in your hands."

Sia nodded. "I can do that."

"Good," he said. "I will be where I always am."

"Thanks," she said.

He stayed. She took the first few stones of the Summer path and felt the water sound rise under the leaves, warm and fast, like a river running beside a city sidewalk. In her pocket, the photo of the seal might as well have warmed a degree. The card under her pillow in the other world felt less heavy from this distance, like it had realized there was a right way to answer it.

She looked back once. The stripe held. The basin stayed full. Thanatos had already turned away, not as a snub. As a gift. This part was hers.

SUMMER MET HER LIKE a warm hand on a railing. The path widened into a curb of dressed stone beside quick water the color of tea in sunlight. Heat sat on the air without turning heavy. Insects worked somewhere out of sight, steady and small.

Longwang waited at a bend where the curb stepped down into a shallow stair. The city coat, the calm posture, the check of her breath before anything else. It was him.

"You brought a question," he said.

"Yeah," Sia said. "A card showed up under our bowl. The seal's real. The wording's wrong."

He glanced along the path the way people glance down a line of cars before crossing. "Good place to check it," he said.

Another figure stood in the shade of the stair. Taller by a head. Older without looking tired. Dark coat, quiet hands, pale scales over the knuckles that caught light like river stones. Ember eyes that did not glow unless they wanted to.

"Fuzanglong," Longwang said. "My brother. He keeps treasure when it needs a keeper. He writes law for things that prefer to stay out of sight."

"Hi," Sia said.

Fuzanglong stepped forward and tipped his head once. It felt like courtesy, not a quiz. He held out a hand for the paper. Sia had brought a photo of the seal and her quick sketch. She passed both across.

He studied the sketch first. He turned it, found the wobble where the vine met the ring, and looked up.

"You saw the join," he said.

"Couldn't miss it once I looked," she said.

He checked the photo without touching the screen. "Seal's

ours. Hand that used it isn't."

"So someone borrowed your stamp," Sia said.

"A clerk stamped a card that never got written," Longwang said. "Old trick. It does not travel well."

Fuzanglong returned the phone and sketch. "You didn't come to name the person," he said. "You came to set rules at your door."

"Right," Sia said. "I want a clause that says courts can't call people by titles inside the Hotel. Invitations have to use names at the desk. They time out at dusk. We send copies to both courts."

Fuzanglong faced the river and listened. Sia could not hear words in the water, only the sense of attention.

"Keep it short," he said. "Three parts. Scope. Cost. Sunset. You have the shape. You also need a mark to tell the room where the clause starts and ends."

He took a small stone from inside his coat. It was the size of a coin, dull as a pier rock, with a tight circle cut into one face.

"This marks borders for rooms," he said. "No power on its own. Press it to a place and speak your clause. The room reads the span between the marks. If you try to use it to control people, it goes dull."

"What does dull mean," Sia asked.

"It becomes a rock," he said. "You can skip it across a pond. That is all."

She nodded and took the marker. It did not heat up. It felt like a tool that liked hands more than pockets.

"I'm not writing for people," she said. "I'm writing for

places."

"Then we agree," he said.

Longwang stepped down one stair and drew his fingers through the surface of the river. The water lifted and settled like it trusted him. "Say your clause out loud," he said.

Sia did not check the paper. "Inside the Hotel, no court may issue summons by title," she said. "Invitations in plain names at the desk. Invitations expire at dusk. Copy posted to Summer and Winter."

The stone curb under her shoes felt like it had nodded.

"Scope is clear," Fuzanglong said. "Cost lives inside courtesy. Sunset keeps it from turning into a wall you forgot to take down."

"Who writes it on the door," Longwang asked.

"I'll draft," Sia said. "Ella will pick the font and placement. Eye level. Charles will sign. No show."

At Ella's name, Longwang's expression shifted. Interest, and something that sounded like memory.

"You say her name with respect," Fuzanglong said.

"I hear it when she talks to rooms," Longwang said. "She settles a crowd without forcing them. I've heard that tone in good places."

Sia thought of Ella at the porch and almost smiled. "She'd roll her eyes at the compliment," she said.

"Then I will tell her myself," Longwang said. "I'd like to meet her. Not for ceremony. For tea."

"I'll ask," Sia said. "She decides."

"Good," he said. "Ask."

Fuzanglong moved two steps along the curb and looked downriver. "Summer didn't deliver the card," he said. "Someone used our seal to see if you'd chase. Winter will see the shadow and knock soon. If both knock, hand them the same page."

"I will," Sia said. "The card on the door will read like posted hours. No drama."

Fuzanglong's mouth twitched at posted hours. "Yes. Make it that dull."

He nodded toward the marker in her palm. "Marking is simple. Press the stone on the inside of your front door where people read. Speak the clause. Press again at the other end of the frame. Post a paper copy for eyes. The marks are for the room."

"What if someone rips the paper down," Sia asked.

"Rooms don't learn from paper," he said. "They learn from how you talk to them. The paper is for people. The marks are the rule."

Longwang put his hands in his coat pockets and looked up through the leaves. "Your garden sits between Summer and Winter," he said. "You like the middle. That makes you a better host than most."

"I like bridges," Sia said. "They feel honest."

"Write honest bridges," he said.

Fuzanglong made a small rectangle in the air with two fingers. Teacher habit, not a trick. "There's a cost to you," he said. "Hold the clause in your attention for a week after you post it. Not as strain. As a check. After that, if the House likes it, it will carry it for you. You only revisit when facts change."

"I can hold it," Sia said. "That's easy."

"One more line," he said. "Write it for yourself, not the door. You won't answer cards that name roles. Keep that in your head for the days you're tired."

Sia thought of the words on the card under her pillow. Leave. Granted. Present. The way those verbs tried to move people around. "I can do that," she said.

Longwang looked toward the turn of the river. A slow shape passed under the surface and did not rise. "Send your copies to both courts when you post," he said. "Not before."

"Same time," Sia said. "I'm not asking permission."

"Correct," Fuzanglong said.

"I'll date the copy and keep one on our board," Sia said. "If anyone pretends they missed it, the board answers."

"Clerks love boards," Longwang said, amused. "They save you ten arguments in winter."

Sia stored that. "Good tip," she said.

The marker warmed once in her palm, a small pulse of presence.

"If you ever use it to push people, it will go dull," Fuzanglong said. "You can bring it back one time by saying out loud that you pushed, in the room you tried to boss. Ask for a do over. You get one."

"Only once," Sia said.

"Only once," he said.

Longwang glanced at the leafy walk that would take her back

to the garden. "When will you ask Ella," he said, casual on purpose.

"When she says yes," Sia said. "She's not a prop."

"That is why I asked," he said. "Tell her the river is polite. Tell her we serve tea."

"I will," Sia said.

She turned from the curb and started back under the leaves. The heat stayed kind. The insects kept time. At the edge she looked down at the marker again. The ring cut into its face held a thin line of light, like chalk under glass. She curled her fingers around it and pictured the spot on the Hotel door where the clause would live. Eye level. Friendly font. Signed. Dated. Boring by design.

She pictured Ella reading it and nodding once. Charles tapping the cane to tile and saying thank you and hold in the same breath. Mia brushing the paper edge because straight edges make her happy. Tobias drawing a tiny door on a route card and adding the line. Truth sitting under the posted copy like it was a dot on Sia's map.

The path carried her toward the garden without making a big deal out of it. She stepped across the border stripe. Air cooled. Thanatos was not there, which felt right. The basin held its water. The gravel stayed out of her shoes.

She opened her notebook, added courtesy under scope, cost, and sunset, and boxed all four. The marker went in her hoodie pocket. In the morning the door would get its clause. The courts would get their copies. Ella would get an ask, not a push. That felt like the right kind of magic.

249

CHAPTER 12

Below the Line

CHARLES

I'm not upset that you lied to me, I'm upset that
from now on I can't believe you.

Friedrich Nietzsche

CHARLES PREFERRED THE LOWER levels when they were honest. Concrete, pipe, old paint that had the decency to peel in straight lines. He took the south service tunnel with a work light in one hand and the Key in the other, palm open, metal quiet against skin. The air held the kind of damp that belonged to basements, not to rivers. Good. If there was a river smell, something had come where it did not belong.

He paused at the first grate and swept the beam across the lip.

Coins sat in the mesh like someone had tried to feed a parking meter that used air. Pennies mostly, two nickels, one old token with a star. He touched the nearest with the tip of his little screwdriver. It ticked against metal and refused to fall through.

"Eric," he said into the radio. "South tunnel. I've got coin scatter in grates. Log it."

"Logged," Eric said. "Want me to cut the fan for a minute so you can hear your own head."

"Hold for now," Charles said. "I'll call it."

He crouched, examined the edge of the grate, and found a smear that looked like candle wax after a prayer. It had a scalloped edge. Burned seal, thin, like someone had tried to make an official shape with a Bic lighter. He scraped a curl into a jar and labeled it because habits make patterns visible later.

He moved on. The sump corridor followed the spine of the building and bent once, a clean right angle. The bend was where trouble liked to knock. Corners collected old air, and old air kept secrets.

Halfway down, he found a pipe collar with a mark painted on the steel. The circle and thorn line wanted to read Winter, but the left edge didn't close on itself. Off by a hair. It matched the wobble Sia had sketched upstairs from the Summer borrow.

He photographed the collar and sent it to Sia with four words. Wrong Winter mark, sump.

Her answer came back as a dot and a time stamp, then one word. Noted.

He smiled at the economy and kept moving.

At the end of the corridor, the paint changed from museum cream to a gray he didn't remember approving. The old archive door sat in that gray like a blind window. The handle looked ordinary and it wasn't. If you have lived in one building long enough, you can tell when a door has learned a new trick. This one held its breath.

He stood to the side of the frame and leaned in just enough to see the floor. There were coin shims under the sill, thin stacks that lifted the wood a fraction of an inch from the tile. Each stack sat at a measured angle. If you opened the door wide and stepped through, the coins would slide, the air would bounce off three faces, and a person's sense of where their feet were supposed to be would tilt.

Kill boxes did not need teeth. Angles and echo could do it if you let them.

"Eric," he said. "Give me ten seconds of silence on lower fans."

"On your count," Eric said.

"Three, two, one." Charles waited, and the world took a breath. The fans wound down. The only sound left was the building thinking. In the quiet, he heard a thin, wrong tap behind the door. Not a pump. Not a valve. Human impatience performed by something that didn't have hands.

"Thank you," he said. "Bring it back in ten."

He set the work light on a crate, tilted so it would wash the frame, not glare. He took Fuzanglong's marker from his pocket. The small stone felt like a normal rock that liked jobs.

He pressed it to the inside of the door frame at eye level and spoke in a voice you could use at a desk.

"No passage by borrowed sign. Tools only read the hands that own them. Sunset at shift end."

He pressed the marker low, near the floor, to finish the span. The painted circle on the pipe collar down the hall did nothing and that was information. On the door wood, the counterfeit attention that had made the coin stacks matter went slack. Two shims slid out from under the sill and clinked against his shoe.

He set the marker away, picked up the Key, and waited. Riders hate when you remove their leverage. They try a new one.

The air on the far side of the door folded like cold glue peeling from glass. Something flattened itself along the culvert bend and then realized the bend no longer belonged to it. It reached for echo. The clause made the echo read as air, not as handle.

It tried a role-call. The word did not make it past the frame. Above them, the posted clause lived in glass. Words spoken here took the same path as words spoken at the door. They fell out of the sentence like a moth hitting a window and beating itself quiet.

"Enough," Charles said. He did not put power in it. He put a decision there.

He held the Key flat to the air and gave it the same line he used upstairs for a human who needed to be moved without being harmed. "Inside to bench. Bench to still."

The building obliged. It never made a show of it. The space between him and the wood made a shape only the Key could see.

Air became a place that held. The rider's weight was a cold on his forearms and then it wasn't. In the light spill from the work lamp, a ring on the tile near his boot took a shadow it hadn't held a second before. The shadow had edges and a calm center, and the center was occupied.

"Good," he said. He did not say it to the rider. He said it to the room.

"Fans up," Eric said in his ear.

"Bring them back," Charles said. The hum returned, settled, and made the corridor honest again.

He knelt, touched the ring with two fingers to confirm it read as holding, then reached for the jar and scraped a line of residue from the edge of the door frame where the painted attention had been. It looked like ash. It wasn't ash. He labeled it with the time and place and set it beside the coins.

He swept the coin stacks into a bucket with a small brush. Coins clicked like rain in a tin. He found three more stacks he hadn't seen in the first pass, and a dime that had been filed at the edge to make it sit at a tilt. Someone had given this trap patience. He respected the craft and stole the tool.

He took two photographs. The frame with shims gone. The ring with its quiet center. He texted Sia only what he would want to know at a desk upstairs, nothing more.

Rider benched, south sump. Continuing.

She replied with one character. K.

He stood, rolled his shoulders once to put his back where his back belonged, and listened at the door again. The wrong tap had stopped. The wood held the kind of still that told you a room had made up its mind. He touched the Key to the latch. It was not a command. It was a courtesy.

"Open one inch," he said. "No more."

The latch eased. The door moved just enough to break the seal of old paint. The hinge made a sound the building had never made for him before, a quiet, oiled yes that did not belong to museum carpenters. Cold air breathed through, not outdoor cold. The kind that lives in places that have no windows.

He lifted the work light and took the space in with his eyes before he moved his feet. The corridor beyond was clean, newer gray, edges sharp, dust even. The tape line along the baseboard was museum straight. Someone had laid floor with a string and a rule. On the wall, at shoulder height, a stencil he recognized because he had approved its font five years ago.

DEAD LETTER.

He did not step. He let the House have the first chance to tell him no. It did not.

He glanced down at the holding ring. The rider stayed where it was, a cool weight in the center, as obedient to boredom as to command. That was the point of a bench. It let a thing stop being in motion without turning the stop into pain.

He put one foot through, then the other, and stopped after one pace. The Key sat warm in his palm. The corridor bent left and rose three shallow steps. He went up without changing his breath and followed the light the building offered him. It was not bright. It was exact. The kind of light you get in a back room when someone who cares about eyes chooses bulbs.

At the end of the bend, there was a room the maps did not have. It was not big. It was clean. Two rings were set into the floor, one farther in, one near the door. They matched the temper of the ring outside, but these were built, not borrowed. Between them ran a low bench that had not existed a minute ago and now looked like it had been here since the museum opened its doors.

On the far ring sat the shape he had felt the night they fixed the vents the first time. The Annex push had left a residue on him that his hands had memorized without meaning to. The older thing had taken a seat like it had accepted a bus stop by mistake and was too proud to stand back up. It had weight. It did not have a face. The ring held it without drama.

On the near ring, the new rider settled. It tried the edge, found no lip, tried the echo, found no handle, then stilled as if boredom had finally won an argument with hunger.

"This room was never built," Charles said, softly, to no one and to the House. "Good."

The air pushed back against his clothes a hair, the way old wood pushes when it likes a sentence. Policy had a new hallway. He could work with that.

He backed out one step and reached for the bucket of coins he had left in the corridor. He set the bucket against the wall out of reach of the rings. Pennies, nickels, two tokens, one filed dime. He would count them later. For now, they were a hazard he had taken away.

He laid a printed Ops card on the doorframe with one strip of blue tape. He wrote the rest in pen while his hand was steady.

Ops hold. Logged by Charles. Do not enter.

He clicked the pen closed, set it in his pocket, and looked once more at both rings. The far shape had not moved. The near ripple quieted with the work light's second click. Above him, the fans turned. Water ran in a legitimate pipe farther down. He noted that too. The world below had to stay boring so the world above could be pleasant.

He took a final photograph for the record, then let the door sit where it was. He didn't close it tight. He didn't wedge it open. He balanced it so the latch would not bite the frame and the hinge would not think it had been forgotten. That was enough to tell the room it was occupied without making it feel like a closet.

At the threshold, he lifted the radio. "Topsides," he said. "South sump. Rider benched. Found a response room labeled Dead Letter. Two held. I'm going to ask a few questions before I come up."

Sia's answer carried the sound of a pen ticking paper. "Logging. One sentence when you can."

"I'm all right," he said. "Room is quiet."

"Good," she said. "We're steady."

He almost told her about the hinge sound, about the way the font on the wall matched the cards they used for exhibit copy, about how rooms prefer plain letters when you write rules that last. He did not. That would be for the board, not the radio.

He checked the Key one more time, felt the tool choose his hand again in the way it always did, and stepped back into the chamber that was not on any blueprint they owned. The rings waited. The air listened. Somewhere up there, the clause on the glass read like hours. Down here, it made a place for those hours to matter.

"Let's talk," he said to the room, not to the shapes. Then he set the work light at his feet and took the low bench that had appeared for exactly that purpose. He had time. He would use plain words. The House would hold the rest.

THE DOOR HELD AT one inch like it understood limits. Charles let it. He kept his shoulder off the frame and checked the hinge again with his ear. The sound wasn't museum wood. It was the kind of quiet yes you hear in a new file room when a clerk opens a drawer that was machined to fit.

He lifted the work light, angled it low so it wouldn't blind him if anything glossy waited, and eased the door another hair. Cold slid out, clean and dry. Not swamp. Not sewer. The good kind of below that concrete learns when it's done curing.

The corridor beyond had fresh paint. The line where wall met floor was straight enough to please an inspector. A strip of blue ran along the baseboard at knee height. It wasn't painter's tape. It read like a path line. He held still until his eyes told him the color wasn't a trick of the lamp. It stayed. The House had laid a runner without cloth.

He stepped through with the Key flat in his palm. One pace. Two. Enough to own his footing without offering it to anyone else. The air kept its temperature. The light fell true. He looked left. The corridor rose three shallow steps to a bend. On the wall, halfway up, a neat stencil sat at shoulder height in the museum font he'd signed off on five years ago.

DEAD LETTER.

He half smiled without meaning to. The House had a sense of humor that filed its jokes where staff would understand them. Dead letter meant a message that never reached its person. It also meant a place where messages wait without causing trouble.

"Good name," he said to the paint, quiet.

The blue path line climbed the steps and turned. He followed it. The third step gave a tiny answer under his shoe, not a squeak, a settle. That told him the floor had learned his weight and agreed to hold it. He made the bend and came out into a small room he had not known existed.

It was simple. Two circles set into the floor, brass rings flush with tile, one nearer the door, one farther in. The nearer ring was empty and not empty. He could feel the rider in it the way he felt cold when someone opened a walk-in freezer. A presence without a face. The far ring held a shape that made his hands remember the night they'd steadied the Annex towel and tasted soot too clean to be fire. The older thing had weight like a bad mood. It sat as if a bus stop had mistaken it for a passenger and was embarrassed, so it acted like it had meant to wait all along.

Between the rings ran a low bench, plain wood, no back. A copy of the bench sat against the wall under a light that didn't hum. A shelf beside the door held a stack of blank cards, a pencil cup, and a small date stamp in a metal tray. There was a wastebasket with a fresh liner. Nothing expensive. Everything correct.

"This room was never built," Charles said, because the House liked hearing conclusions out loud when they were true. "We made it with policy."

The air pressed against his shirt just enough to count as approval. He set the work light on the shelf so the rings would stay evenly lit and put the bucket of coins on the floor where a hand couldn't reach it even if it learned a trick. He checked the near ring again. The rider's cold lived in the center. The circle held it without anger. That was the point. You don't punish gravity. You set rules and let weight keep its dignity.

He stepped to the far ring and stopped short of the line. The Annex demon's presence had a different feel. Less scrape, more soak. It had learned corners the way a leak learns a basement. He didn't talk to it yet. He looked at the room first, making a map in his head. Vent here. Drain there. No vents cut in shadow lines. Someone had thought about echoes and angles. The place didn't collect them. It let them pass.

He took a card from the shelf and wrote in block letters, the kind you use when you expect to read this in a hurry later.

Ops hold. Logged by Charles. Do not enter.

He taped the card just inside the door with blue tape, flush to the frame, where a person would see it and stop without having to think about their feet. He added the time and date in the corner. The pencil left a clean line, not soft. That made him like the pencil.

He lifted the radio. "Holding two," he said. "Dead Letter room. I'll question before I come up."

Sia's reply clicked through with the background hush of the lobby. "Logged," she said. "One sentence when you're safe."

"I'm safe," he said. "Room's honest."

He could hear Ella's porch in the way the radio stayed easy. He could hear Mia's habit of lining tape along the counter. He could hear Eric not breathing into his mic because he'd learned not to years ago. Good. The House above was doing its job. He let the comfort of that soak in, then put it away. He had a job too.

He took the bench that waited between the rings. It was the right height for questions. Not low enough to make a back ache. Not high enough to look like a judge's seat. He set the Key across his knee, palm over it. The tool did what it always did when it knew it would be needed. It got warm enough to say I'm here.

He didn't speak to the shapes yet. He spoke to the room. "I need the rings to hold neutral and true," he said. "No pull. No push. If a word tries to be a handle, drop it before it gets clever."

The lights held steady. The air didn't ripple. Agreement enough.

He eyed the shelf again. There was a pen in the cup that

wasn't like the others. He picked it up. It had weight. It was the kind you sign receipts with when you want the paper to feel the choice in it. He put it back and took a regular pencil. Plain tools keep a room honest.

He looked into the near ring, at the place where cold piled up into a center. "You're benched," he said. "You can sit still without losing anything that belongs to you. If you try the door by a role-call, the house will ignore you. If you try echo, the ring reads echo as air. If you talk like a neighbor, I'll hear you."

The cold shifted from braced to bored. That was good. Bored things tell stories.

He looked to the far ring. "You were here before I got smart enough to notice," he said, plain. "That's on me. You're held. You won't be hurt. We'll do this in short lines."

The older presence didn't strain. It didn't get loud. It made the air feel like a little room with carpet where arguments get lost because no one wants to stand up. He filed that. Carpets teach you what shape a thing prefers.

He took the date stamp from the tray and clicked it on the back of a blank card, then wrote a header.

Dead Letter - Intake

Under it he added three fields and left them empty for now:
Name, Route In, Borrowed Tool.

He looked to the near ring again. "Let's start with you," he said. "Name."

Nothing. He waited. He didn't threaten. The ring kept cold in the center like a bird keeping eggs warm.

"Name," he said again. "If you don't have one you can give me, give me the sound you'd answer to in a crowd."

A faint static brushed his ear. Not a hiss. A shape in sound. Something like two nickels tap-tapping in a pocket. He wrote **Taps** on the card. If it hated the name, he'd change it later.

"Route in," he said. "Who pointed you at our corners."

Another brush. A memory of a narrow place under a bridge where people don't go at night because they want to give themselves a reason they can say out loud. He wrote **footbridge underpass** and circled it.

"Borrowed tool," he said. "Seal. Who handed it to you."

Cold flattened, then rose like mist over water. A picture without a picture. Fingers that didn't belong to Summer or Winter. The habit of a clerk without the job. He wrote **the Borrower** and underlined it once. He didn't look up. He didn't let his voice change. If you dignify a tease, it grows teeth.

He slid his gaze to the far ring. "You. Name."

The air pressed. Heat under cold, like a hand over a candle at arm's length. It didn't give him a sound. It gave him a laugh you hear in bar basements when a jukebox is between songs. He wrote **Basement** and waited.

"You used coins like shims," he said. "You made angles into a door. Where did you learn that."

The press got smug. A memory he didn't own tried to sit in his body. He didn't let it. The ring kept its shape. He got a line instead of a shove.

Coins are keys when you don't own the lock.

"That's a saying, not an answer," he said. "Try again."

Silence. The kind that hopes you'll fill it and say too much. He didn't.

He looked back to the near ring. "Who told you to pull me to that door. I want a pronoun if that's all you can do."

A cool draft leaned toward the far ring and away. He wrote **they** and drew a very small arrow between the two entries. Not proof. A pointer.

He kept his tone even. "Why us. Why this place."

The far ring lifted the heat under the cold like a man lifting his chin. The voice when it came had no bass to it. It wasn't a sound he could replay. It just reached the top of his spine and pressed a word there like a stamp.

"Because the Merlin keeps a small hotel and thinks no one sees him."

The line landed. Charles let it be a line. He didn't stand. He didn't flinch. He stamped the date on a second card, wrote **Title used** and the word **Merlin** in the same neat hand he used for budgets, then set the card aside to file later.

He kept his focus small. "Who taught you that word."

The near ring got colder and smaller at the same time. The far ring warmed. He had his answer, which was not an answer. He wrote **shared vocabulary** with a question mark.

He went back to the list. "Intent," he said. "Was this about breaking something or measuring it."

The near ring tugged sideways and then corrected. The far ring lifted heat and set it back down. He wrote **measure** and under it **learn posted hours**. He circled hours.

He looked at the Key on his knee. The metal sat steady. He looked at the shelf. The date stamp sat where he'd set it, ready to say yes to any paper that needed a time.

"Here's what's going to happen," he said to the room. "You'll be fed. You won't be hurt. You won't be moved until a court clerk collects you by name with a receipt I can file. If anyone tries to trade roles for names, the door won't hear them."

The floor agreed with the smallest tilt of pressure. The rings settled like bowls on a table when a bus passes and the table chooses not to vibrate.

He raised the radio again. "Topsides," he said. "Holding two, quiet. Intake card started. One used my title. We'll want a receipt when we hand them up."

Sia's voice came back calm. "Copy. I'll make a receipt template."

"Thank you," he said, and meant it in three directions.

He pulled the bucket of coins close enough to count without giving anybody ideas. Pennies thick, nickels thin, two tokens with stars, the filed dime. He made four stacks by type. The filed dime got its own index card. **Filed edge for tilt**. He snapped one more photo.

Then he stood, not fast, not slow, and walked to the door. He left it at the same careful inch he'd found. He pressed the blue path line with his shoe and felt the floor give that tiny approval again. The dead letter name sat on the wall where staff would understand it. He touched the stencil with two fingers.

"Hold," he told the room, the way you tell the front desk to hold a call while you check a number. The House didn't hum. It didn't flare. It kept the quiet it had made for him to work in.

He stepped back into the corridor with the Key in his hand and the intake card in his pocket. Upstairs would get the news without drama. The board would get a clean entry. The next scene in his day would be questions and a short list of screws and mesh and words. That was enough. He followed the blue line back to the hinge that knew his weight and paused one breath to listen. The yes was still there.

"Good," he said, and meant the corridor, the bench, the policy, and the small room that knew how to welcome messages that didn't belong anywhere else. Then he climbed to the level where the House wore glass and names and tape, and where posted hours were already earning their keep.

THE BENCH WAS THE right height for work. Charles set the intake card on his knee, kept the Key warm in his palm, and looked between the two rings. The near ring kept the rider like a cold held in one place. The far ring held the older presence, the one that moved through corners like water through drywall.

He started simple. Simple saves time.

"Near ring," he said. "You gave me a sound. I wrote Taps. That good enough."

The cold gave a small click in the middle. Not loud. There was the sense of two coins knocking in a pocket. He kept the name.

"Far ring," he said. "You didn't give a name. I wrote Basement. That annoy you."

The pressure in the room shifted the way a person leans back and smiles without moving their face. Not yes. Not no. Good enough. He left it.

"Here are the rules," he said. "You can talk. You can not talk. Talking is smarter. If you try to yank me with a title, the room will ignore you. If you try echo for a handle, the ring reads echo as air. If a question feels too sharp, say skip. We will get more done with short sentences."

Silence from both rings. Honest silence. He liked that. He wrote it in his head as a point in their favor.

He clicked the date stamp on the top of the card again. Sometimes the sound gets a room moving. He went back to the near ring.

"Taps," he said. "You came in from a footbridge underpass. Who sent you there."

A small drag of cold toward the far ring. The old presence warmed. Charles wrote **pointed by Basement** with a question mark. Not proof. A start.

"Borrowed tool," he said. "Winter seal. Who handed it to you."

The cold fanned out and then tightened. A thin shape like a paper slip with a clean ring pressed on it formed at the edge of his hearing and vanished. He wrote **the Borrower** again and underlined it. "Describe the Borrower."

Taps offered nothing this time. The far ring moved instead. Heat rose, settled, and left him with a memory that was not his. A desk. Ink that never smudges. A hand that never shakes. A clerk's motions done by someone who is not a clerk anymore.

Charles wrote **former clerk habits** and kept his voice level. "Taps, how did the Borrower find you."

Static brushed like sand. He got the sense of coins in the same pocket as keys, an old jacket, and a corner where a phone light never quite reached. He wrote **found near coins** and let it stand.

He looked at the older presence. "Basement. Why coins."

Silence again. A little more smug. He waited. Smug likes to fill a pause.

"Because the house is wood with good grain," Basement said finally. The voice came without echo. It did not sound like a throat. It sounded like someone speaking through a coat. "Coins sit where grain does not notice them."

"That is cute," Charles said. "It is not an answer."

"You saw what they do," Basement said. "They lift a sill. They make a line false by a finger. Angles give you a corner and echo gives you a handle. You have staff who pull doors open politely. They make very simple machines."

Charles wrote **coin shims lift sill** even though he already knew it. Writing makes knowledge stay where you can point to it.

"You had a kill box ready," he said. "Step wide, angle wrong, echo bad, feet shame you. Where did you learn that. Phrase, not poetry."

"Basements," the demon said, in a tone that made the word a trade. "Parking. Storage. Your old rooms. Forgotten stairs. Humans teach the lesson when they leave a bucket at the bottom step and get angry at their foot instead of the bucket. We watch. We learn. We build."

"Who told you to try it under our archives," Charles said.

"The Borrower," Basement said. "They wanted you angry at your foot."

Taps shifted, a small slide in the near ring that felt like embarrassment. Charles glanced at the cold and kept his voice calm.

"Taps, why me," he asked. "Why this house."

The cold gathered and made a point toward the Key. Not a push. A reference. It was not about Charles as a person. It was about a tool and a place and the way both had been used in the last two days.

"Because I moved a thing without hurting it," Charles said, answering his own question in a sentence that would file clean. He wrote **targeted Key user**. Then he lifted his eyes.

"Basement. Did you tell this one to test me."

"Not me alone," Basement said. "The Borrower sent messages. I tuned them."

"How," Charles said.

"Coins," Basement said. The word came with humor now. "You wrote the rest on your door. Names. Hours. You think rules keep you safe. They do. They also mark who writes them. They make a map of your hands."

"That is the point," Charles said. He did not rise to it. He wrote **rules reveal author** and that was a fact, not a crime. "You used the Winter seal to borrow a clerk. You used the Summer seal to borrow a stamp. Why not use your own."

Basement gave him the feeling of a shrug. Taps made the tiniest click, a rhythm like two taps and a pause.

"Because your seals would die at my door," Charles said. "Smile if I am wrong."

Neither ring smiled. The light did not change. He filed it as confirmed.

He shifted on the bench, checked the Key with his palm, and addressed what had been dropped like a knife.

"You used the word Merlin," he said.

Basement's presence turned pleased again. It had the joy of a child who finds the lever that makes a toy speak.

"You used it to get a rise," Charles said. "You did not get one. Where did you learn it."

The near ring pulled cold tight around its center, a defensive move he had seen from frightened things in labs when a door shuts a second too loud. The far ring warmed a fraction. He had his axis. He wrote **Basement used title** and drew a short line to **the Borrower**.

"Name your teacher," he said. "If you cannot, give me a shape."

Basement waited. He let it. Time down here felt like a long

hallway. In that hallway, a minute was cheap and a mistake was expensive.

"Your teacher writes through other hands," Basement said at last. "Their tools do not squeak. They do not lose stamp pads. Their lines hold when you forget to look at them."

"Has the teacher been here," Charles asked. "Not through borrowed hands. Here."

"No," Basement said. "They will not kneel to your entry."

"That is a choice," Charles said. "Not a power."

The older presence did not take the bait. Good. He did not want a fight. He wanted a list.

He went back to Taps. "If I opened the near ring and told you to leave by your own choice and not by a role, where would you go."

Cold lifted, turned, and pointed in a direction that was not a direction humans would write on a map. It pointed toward water, but not out. It pointed toward pipes inside pipes. He wrote **pipes within pipes** and circled it.

"You do not get to leave," he said. "Not until a clerk collects you by name with a receipt we sign together."

Taps cooled. Not angry. Resigned. That was the right line.

"Basement," Charles said. "Same question."

Heat rolled. It had the shape of someone lifting a trap door. He got the sense of an old elevator shaft and a set of stairs that had been bricked up and then unbricked by someone who liked bricks. He wrote **vertical shafts** and **tampered stairs**. He underlined **tampered** twice.

"That is not a place," he said. "That is a method."

"Yes," Basement said. "You asked wrong."

"I asked the way I meant," Charles said.

He flipped the intake card and made a second header.

Dead Letter - Notes for Ops

Under it he wrote: **Mesh for Annex vents. Screws for two collars. Check south sump fan rattle. Inspect staff stair for tamper. Map older shafts.**

He added **Receipt template** and a box for signatures. He would hand that part to Sia and Ella. They would make it something humans could use when they were tired.

He spoke again. "The Borrower. Human or not."

"Was," Basement said. "Is not anymore."

"Used to be a clerk," Charles said. "Now a thief with old habits."

"Yes," Basement said, and sounded bored to admit it.

"Who do they serve," he asked.

"Borrowers serve themselves," Basement said. "The teacher serves a ledger."

"Whose ledger," Charles said.

"No one you invite," Basement said.

Taps clicked again, two coins, pause, one coin. He had no translation for that yet. He wrote the rhythm anyway.

"Did the teacher tell you to use my title," he asked. "Or did you hunt for it and get lucky."

"Nothing about you is luck," Basement said. "You are a filing error that kept good handwriting."

"That is an answer without a noun," Charles said. He wrote **teacher knows title** and **goal: provoke**.

He let a beat pass. Then he put the Key on the bench beside him and leaned his elbows on his knees. "We are done with this part," he said. "Here is what happens next. Winter already knows you borrowed their seal. They sent a warning. They will collect you when it suits their record. If Summer wants to argue about the stamp you forged, they can argue with the receipt. You will be fed until then. No one here hurts you."

Basement made the air feel heavier for a second, a room that wanted a fight and was disappointed. Then the weight left. He took that as a yes.

He looked at Taps. "When you sit, is there anything you want that makes sitting easier. If it is dumb, I will say no and we move on."

The cold gathered and held. There was the sense of running water, not to drink, just to hear. He wrote **sound of water** and nodded.

"We can set a pitcher on the shelf with a drip," he said. "Not in the ring. On the shelf. That is as far as it goes."

The cold eased. He would do it on the way out. A pitcher on a tray, a paper towel set flat so the drip would make a small, ordinary noise.

He looked at the older presence. "Same offer."

Basement gave him a memory of a fluorescent light that hums right above a table. He wrote **no hum** and pointed at the fixtures.

"They already do not hum," he said. "If you mean silence, you have it."

Basement did not thank him. He did not need it. The room held neutral and that was a kind of courtesy.

He stood. The bench did not scrape. He set the intake card on the shelf next to the date stamp and wrote **two rings occupied** and the time. He put the pencil in the cup and left the pen where he had found it. He picked up the Key and felt it choose his hand again, a simple weight that said ready.

"Dead Letter holds," he said to the door. "If anyone knocks with a role, do not answer."

The door sat with that small readiness he had come to trust.

He lifted the radio. "Topsides," he said. "Two held. Interrogation done for now. We have notes for Ops. One used my title. No movement. I'm coming up."

Sia answered with the scratch of paper and a softer undertone that meant Ella was near the desk. "Copy," she said. "We're steady. Water at the desk. No new cards."

"Good," he said.

He picked up the bucket of coins and set it on the corridor side. He took one last look at the rings. The near cold kept its center. The far weight sat like a person who could do patience all day because patience was a hobby. He let that be their work.

At the threshold he paused. The stencil on the wall read DEAD LETTER with a small serif at the top of the E that always made him think of librarians. He touched the paint with two fingers.

"Hold," he said again, because rooms like to end the way they began.

He closed the door to the one inch he liked, felt the latch rest against the strike without biting, and turned away. The blue path line met his shoes where he expected and carried him back to the hinge that had learned to say yes. He listened for that yes. It answered. He climbed.

At the foot of the staff stairs, Truth waited with her chin on the landing, like a sentry who admits she sits because sitting gets better results. She stood when she saw him and wagged once. He touched her head.

"Good girl," he said. "Two to watch."

She turned and paced up two steps, then looked back to check that he followed. He did. The air warmed on the way up. The damp turned into the lobby's clean humidity. He heard water poured into cups. He heard people reading a sign. He heard Mia's tape pulling free in tidy strips and Eric's foot falls that never rushed.

He reached the staff door and stepped through. Ella looked up from the board. He set the bucket on the counter, placed the intake card beside it, and wrote three lines in clean hand:

> *Dead Letter room open below. Two held.*
> *- Coins collected. Filed dime noted.*
> *- No harm. Await clerk by name, with receipt.*

He capped the marker and set it down exactly where she kept it. His voice when he spoke stayed cool, but the blade had gone back into its sleeve.

"It's quiet," he said. "We're fine."

He did not say the title that had been used. He would say it once, at the board, in a short line, and then let it sit where it belonged. The House had posted hours. The House had a new room. The rest would keep until they needed it.

CHAPTER 13

Polite Request

SIA

All our knowledge begins with the senses, proceeds then to the understanding, and ends with reason. There is nothing higher than reason.
Immanuel Kant, Critique of Pure Reason

BY MIDMORNING THE BOARD was clean. Sia liked seeing it that way before she added anything new. Ella had wiped the glass last night so the dry-erase ink came off in one smooth pass, and the room smelled faintly like citrus from the cleaner. Good. A board should feel ready to hold the day.

Charles set a small stack of cards on the rail and rested the cane lightly against the wall. He didn't stand at the head of the table. He took the spot you use when you want the work to look shared.

"Quick," he said. "Below is quiet. Two separate pushes tried to make corners into doors. They used coin shims under sills and borrowed marks painted a hair off center. Both failed."

Mia's eyes flicked to Sia's map. Sia already had the south sump curve circled in pencil and the Annex bend marked with a neat X. She wrote coin stacks and underlined it.

"The wrong marks were trying to read as Winter," Charles went on. "But the left side didn't close. Same wobble you caught on the Summer stamp, Sia. That wobble is our tell."

Eric nodded, satisfied in a quiet way. Kaelan tilted her head, bracelets soft. Tobias stood with his route sheet tucked against his forearm, ready to start moving the second the briefing ended. Truth lay by the staff door with her chin on her paws, watching him like she could see the route forming.

"What about the source," Ella said. "Who's pushing."

"Names we have are flimsy," Charles said. "The rider didn't have much. The thing in the basement calls itself a lot of jokes, but it gave me enough to set policy. The person who staged the borrowed seal acts like a clerk who forgot they quit. We'll call that one the Borrower until they hand us the right word."

He slid the top card forward. Bold header in his square print: **DEAD LETTER policy**. Sia's stomach did a small flip at the phrase, then settled when she read the lines. It wasn't a room announcement. It was rules.

No entry below without two witnesses.

Removals require receipts in **names**, signed and logged.

No titles at any threshold. Titles get no answer.

Visits log in ink. Sunset at shift end.

"Good," Ella said. "It reads like a person wrote it."

Sia pinched the card to the board with two magnets, then pulled Fuzanglong's marker stone from her hoodie pocket. It sat in her palm like it always did, unshowy and ready.

"We'll set the door," she said.

They crossed to the staff stair. Sia pressed the marker to the frame at eye level, the same spot she'd use for hours, and spoke the clause in a voice you could use across a counter.

"Removals by receipt in names only. The House will not answer titles. Clause ends at handoff."

She pressed the marker low near the baseboard to finish the span. The change didn't shine. The hush in the hall got a touch heavier, like a book slid onto the right shelf. Truth lifted her head and flicked an ear, then settled again.

"That's the feel I wanted," Sia said.

"Assignments," Ella said, turning back to the board.

Tobias was ready first. "Lower rounds every fifteen," he said. "I'll add a watch square at each corner and a coin check at every grate. I'll log time, location, and type."

"Perfect," Sia said. "Call out filed edges. Those are tricks, not tips."

"Got it," he said.

Eric tapped his pencil against his knuckle. "I'll walk the staff stair and the south hall for tamper," he said. "If I find old shafts,

I'll sketch and flag. I'll put cones at the Annex mouth and the mirror corridor so the easy path looks obvious."

"No tape across doorways," Ella said without looking up from the board. "Cones only."

"I like my job," Eric said. "No hazard webs."

Mia had already pulled a template onto the counter. "Receipt form," she said, flipping it so they all saw. "Name, date, case number, clerk, collected by, countersigned by, chain of custody. I'll print three copies. Clerk keeps one, we file one, the third lives on the board until close."

"And lanyard cards," Sia said.

Mia wrote as she spoke. "If someone asks for the basement by title, point to the sign and call Sia."

"Make a second set for volunteers," Ella said. "Small enough to live behind the name tag."

Kaelan rested two fingers on the door frame like she was feeling its pulse. "This is good," she said. "Names make a place breathe easier."

The bell on the front desk gave a single polite tap. Not the lobby chime. The little brass bell volunteers use when they want someone rather than everyone. Truth stood, ears forward. Sia glanced at Ella. Ella glanced at the posted clause on the glass. Okay.

Through the lobby, a figure in a storm-glass coat paused at the posted card and read it the way people read hours. No title call. Good. Min stepped inside with a sealed folio and the kind of calm that made the room calm around them.

"Ella," they said with a small nod. Then to Sia, "I'm Min. We spoke yesterday. I have a removal order written in names."

"Thank you," Sia said. "We'll handle it at the threshold."

Min didn't try to see past the door. They didn't lean. They followed Ella's lead to the staff hall like someone who respected houses. At the frame, Sia held up the marker again and touched eye level and floor so the room would understand the version of the rule they were about to use.

"Removals by receipt in names only," she said, clear and steady. "Clause ends at handoff."

Min opened the folio and set three papers on the counter that jutted just inside the doorway. The first was the order. The second was their copy of the policy acknowledgment from yesterday with a neat stamp that read **read into record**. The third was a blank receipt template with Winter's letterhead, clean and plain.

"Name of the being you're collecting," Sia said.

"Taps," Min said, neutral as a water temperature.

"Status," Ella said.

"Neutral hold," Min answered. "No harm reported."

Sia wrote the time in the corner of the board copy and read the name and status out loud so the room had to hear it. Min signed the receipt first, then turned the page without flair. Charles stepped forward and countersigned with a clean signature that matched the posted clause copy upstairs. Ella initialed the chain of custody. Mia stamped the date and time with a neat thunk. Sia printed Taps on the line for collected by, under

Winter's clerk column, and added Min's name in parenthesis.

"Truth," Sia said softly. "Stair."

Truth posted at the top step, angled so she could see both the hall and the lobby. She didn't growl. She didn't need to.

A faint vibration scratched the baseboard. Sia felt it in her teeth before she heard it. Not fan hum. A buzz like a phone left on a wood shelf. She crouched and ran her fingers along the hinge line. There, tucked flush with the metal, sat a dime with a shaved edge, nudged under the plate like a shim waiting to lift the line of the sill.

"Not today," she said. She pinched it out with a key tip and dropped it in a stainless tray Mia slid into her hand without looking up from the stamp. The buzz died. Min's eyes flicked to the tray and back.

"We've seen three filed edges," Min said, almost conversational. "They like the hinge because no one checks it."

"We check it," Sia said.

Min's mouth softened a hair. "Yes," they said.

Ella didn't make an announcement. She looked at the frame and said, "Ready."

Sia pressed the marker to the low corner inside the door and spoke so the room would obey the boring shape of the moment. "Open to the ring for transfer. Names only. Close at handoff."

Cold slid across the tile in a straight line, like a shadow of a ring moving from one room to another without touching anything that wasn't its job. Sia didn't try to see the being. She didn't need to. The paperwork was the point.

"Taps," Min said, clean in the air.

The cold answered by settling. Min held out both hands palms up, like a librarian taking a book that shouldn't have left the building, and stepped back half a pace when the room finished moving. Nothing bumped. Nothing scraped. The ring shadow left the tile and was gone.

"Collected," Min said, for the record. They didn't smile. They didn't bow. They put the fact in the air.

Sia put her finger on the "clause ends at handoff" line in her head and felt it go quiet. She wrote **Collected, 11:47** in the corner of the board copy and blew on the ink because she'd learned to stop smearing things the hard way.

Min signed their copy, slid Sia's across for a countersign, and waited while Mia added the stamp. Mia handed the third copy to Ella, who clipped it to the board with the red clip that meant paper trails live here.

"Thank you for keeping this boring," Min said. "The Borrower will probably try to follow your paperwork next. Keep logs clean, and if you see a seal in the wrong place, write the word wrong in ink on top of it before you put it in a sleeve. It sounds silly. Clerks hate seeing wrong on a seal."

"Clerks are people," Ella said. "People hate it when their tools get used to lie."

Min dipped their head in agreement. "We'll see you again," they said. "By name."

"By name," Sia said.

They left without touching the frame. Truth watched them

pass the clause on the glass and then looked back at Sia like, see, that is how you leave.

Back at the board, Sia pinned the signed receipt under the Dead Letter policy and wrote a small card for the rail in her neat print.

Paper Trail:

- Sign everything. Names only.
- Receipts live in the red folder.
- Log stray seals and coin finds.

Mia set the stainless tray with the filed dime on the counter and labeled it with tape: **hinge pull**. Tobias added a tiny X on his route card at the staff door hinge so he wouldn't forget to check again, even if the day got noisy. Eric drew a box on his sketch with a note about the south stair risers and wrote check under it because he liked verbs more than nouns.

"Questions," Ella said.

"How far down was the wrong mark," Tobias asked Charles. "Just to know where to put my eyes."

"Pipe collar in the sump corridor," Charles said. "Left side of the circle didn't close. I got that from Basement and from the paint."

"What's Basement," the volunteer at the back asked, eyes wide and trying to be small about it.

"Not a place," Charles said, voice mild. "A habit that likes to live in places. It will keep trying old tricks. We'll keep using new tape."

That was enough for the volunteer. It was almost enough for Sia. She still wanted to ask if he'd stood in the room when he said it, if he'd looked at the rings and made a bench appear by being himself. She didn't. The privacy sat on him like a jacket he wasn't ready to take off, and it wasn't her job to untie it. Her job was to make sure the rules worked when she wasn't in the room.

"Speaking of tape," Mia said, holding up two lanyard cards. "Volunteers. Read."

The teens at the back read out loud in chorus, a little sing-song. "If someone asks for the basement by title, point to the sign and call Sia."

"Thank you," Mia said, delighted that they hit the cadence without being told.

Sia added one more card under the receipt for her future tired self.

> **If a card names a role, it isn't for us.**
> **Point to the glass. Call Sia.**

Truth bumped Sia's knee with her nose and then went back to the top step like she'd put herself on a timer. Good. Sia put the marker stone in her pocket and glanced at the staff door clause one more time. It read to her hands. That always felt like the real test.

"Rounds start now," Tobias said. He had his pen clipped to the top of the route sheet and the look he got when corners wanted to be seen by a person who understood them. "Every fifteen. If anything buzzes, I'll log and ping."

"Ping me and Eric both," Sia said. "I'll update the live map. Eric will make the easy path louder."

"I love making easy louder," Eric said.

Kaelan had been quiet, watching the way the air moved on its own when names got read aloud and receipts landed. She finally stepped closer to the board and touched the edge of the Dead Letter card with a fingertip. "Paper makes borders," she said.

"Paper makes memory," Ella said. "Borders remember what we ask them to."

Sia looked at the receipt again, at the crisp stamp, at Min's legible name, at Charles's steady signature. The whole thing felt like a small door that closed exactly the way it should. None of it was dramatic. All of it would keep them from bleeding hours into arguments later. Boring was a gift.

"Okay," she said, capping the marker with a click she liked. "We keep it human. We keep it dull. If the Borrower wants to play clerk, they can stand in line and use a name."

Eric grinned. "I've always wanted to watch a demon take a number."

"Save that for the memoir," Ella said.

Tobias headed for the service hall. Truth stood and tracked him for three steps, then settled back into her notch. Mia slid the receipt copy into the red folder. Sia added a dot to the map where the hinge dime had sat and drew a tiny triangle over it to remind herself that tricks love corners more than walls.

At the board, there were no gaps begging for panic. Just cards, a policy, a receipt, and the promise of a day that would move the way you wanted a day to move in a place people brought children and old knees and curiosity. She liked that more than she could say.

The bell at the desk chimed once. Not a signal. Just the sound of a person who needed a map. Ella moved without hurry. Sia watched the door, let the posted clause sit in the corner of her vision, and felt the House answer to the shape they had written on it.

Min's warning lived next to her thoughts. The Borrower would chase paper next. Fine. That was a game Sia understood. The rules were already on the glass. The folder was red on purpose. If someone wanted to lie with a stamp, she'd write wrong in ink right across it and file that too.

"Next," she said to the room, because that is what you say when a job is done and you're leaving space for the one after it. The board held. The stair held. The marker stone warmed her palm in her pocket. The day kept moving on rails they had chosen. That was enough for now.

Sia asked for the garden the way she had learned to ask for water. Calm breath. Plain words. She lay down on her bed with the receipt filed and the board clean in her head, closed her eyes, and named the bench once under her breath. The drift took her without a bump.

Light met her soft and honest. The gravel remembered her shoes. The basin held a thin star on the surface where it liked to hold one. The stripe ran from basin lip to the low wall, a clean bread-knife line that kept Summer's warm leaf smell on one side and Winter's chalk-cold air on the other. She checked it first thing, because that made the rest of the place sit right. It held. The middle stayed the middle.

"Morning," she told the garden, because places liked to be greeted the same way people did.

Nothing answered with words. The path shaped itself a degree more solid under her sneakers and the bench looked like a friend who had been waiting and didn't mind the wait. She sat and let her shoulders drop.

She felt the tug before she saw it. The stripe pulled tight as if someone had plucked it like a string and then held it down with two fingers. The air at the middle grew busy in the quiet way heat gets busy above a stove when water is just about to boil.

"Okay," she said, out loud and calm. "I see you."

A hand slid across the stripe and into her side of the garden. It did not drag an arm with it. It did not belong to a body. It was a clerk hand, narrow and neat, with clean knuckles and short nails and ink that never smudged anywhere it had ever worked. The fingers held an envelope by the corners like it weighed nothing and also mattered. Sia's name sat on the front in careful script.

She did not stand. She didn't want the place to think she had been chased off her own bench. She put both feet flat on the gravel and let the stripe sit in the corner of her vision so she would not lose track of it.

"Plain names or nothing," she said.

The ink on the envelope tried to creep toward a job word anyway. She watched the N in her first name lean, felt the push toward Singer, and put her thumb on the loop before it could complete. The letter tried to resist. It failed. Her name stayed her name.

"Not here," she said, and let her hand fall.

The hand did not yank the envelope back. It held, polite to the point of being rude. It waited like a person who will keep a door open past courtesy because they want you to feel like you owe them.

The garden gave her a quiet that felt like a held breath. Then Thanatos was there. No footfalls. No cold. He stood half a step off her shoulder and a little forward, left side to the stripe, as if they were sharing a curb and watching traffic together.

His coat was black without shine. His face read like someone who could stay still for a year and not make a point out of it. For the first time, Sia saw the thing she had always felt more than seen. The Scythe hung along his back like a tool carried home from a shift. It did not glow. It did not threaten. The curve of the blade put a thin line of shadow on the stripe where it crossed it. The pole rested against his palm like a broom rests against a janitor's hand when they pause for one second to look down a hallway they keep clean.

"Hey," Sia said, because she didn't need a title for him either.

"Hey," he said. He kept his eyes on the hand and the line. "You were going to say no. I came so the hand knows what a no looks like from both sides."

"That's generous," she said.

"It's a job," he said.

The hand pushed the envelope another inch toward the bench. It did not touch the gravel. It hung there as if resting itself on manners.

"You have my name," Sia said to it. "Who are you."

The envelope didn't grow a reply. The script didn't add a sender. That was a choice and she knew it.

The edge of the Scythe moved the smallest amount, not to swipe, not to warn, the way a person might shift a tool to show they were holding it on purpose. The shadow line across the stripe sharpened and then relaxed. The garden understood it. The hand understood it too. It stopped inching.

"Plain names," Sia repeated. "You want a conversation, you use one."

The hand did nothing.

Thanatos's voice stayed low, like he didn't want to wake a baby in a room over. "Let the bench do its job," he said. "If you want to read, read from there. Not at the line."

Sia stood, because the bench had asked to be included and benches like to be treated like part of the work. She kept her breath even. She put her fingers on the envelope and said out loud, "I'm taking this to the bench. You will not follow me over my own ground."

The hand released the corners without making a show of it. It didn't retreat. It hovered at the stripe at the exact limit she had allowed things to hover. Thanatos didn't speak to it. He didn't need to. His presence made the stripe visible in a way it had never needed to be visible before.

She sat and broke the seal at the bench. No wax. No court mark. The paper warmed in her palms like it had been held under a lamp. The lines on the first page slid as if they wanted to be headlines about roles. She put her finger on the top line and said, clear, "Plain names or nothing."

The letters snapped into sentences you could read without stumbling. No titles clung. She recognized the tone even before the words finished resolving. It had the boredom of a job done out of habit and the neatness of a person who likes forms.

Sia,

Advice about vents and drains. You have more than you know. You are checking the wrong corners, and you are counting the wrong fans. I can teach you a counting method that will save you three hours a week. In exchange, you will unlock one door of my choosing for one hour, once, during the Neutral Window. Your House can choose which day. I will not push a role. The door will hold for you if you stand there with your hand on it. I will not use a court seal. I do not need one. Reply with a yes by putting this page in your red folder.

Regards,
The Borrower

Sia kept her face boring so the garden wouldn't get ideas. The left edge of the page itched like a cheap sweater. She didn't scratch it.

"I hate that this is tempting," she said.

"It's designed to be," Thanatos said. "Count the lies and you'll hate it less."

"The part where standing at a door keeps it safe," she said. "That's a lie."

"It's a theft," he said. "It tries to borrow your presence to borrow a threshold."

"And the part where they don't need a seal," she said.

"Also theft," he said. "It tries to treat your home like a hall-way."

The hand waited at the stripe without tapping finger or showing nerves. It was professional, which was worse. She looked at the script again, at the neat way it had stacked the offer like a grocery list of sins.

"Plain names," she said once more, quieter. The letters did not try to crawl anymore. They knew the rule had been posted in a place that would outlast the paper.

"Leave the garden," she said to the hand. "You can wait beyond the boundary if waiting is your hobby. But you leave the garden."

The hand didn't pop like a soap bubble. It rolled back at a steady, clerk pace. It crossed the stripe and stopped with its fingers just beyond it, letterless now, like someone standing on a curb keeping their shoes out of a puddle.

"Good," Thanatos said, almost to himself. He set the Scythe's butt on the gravel, not hard enough to dent it, just enough that Sia could see where the line of the pole wanted to live. Up close, the blade didn't look big. It looked efficient. It did not gleam. It drew light along its edge the way a good blade draws light when you hold it under a single lamp to check for nicks. The tool made the stripe feel like a sign that had always been there.

"What is the rule when a hand tries to do a job the person will not own," he asked.

She didn't have to think. "We talk at the bench, not at the line."

"Good," he said. "What is the rule when an offer uses your home as a lever."

"We turn pressure into a door and close it."

"Good," he said.

Sia looked down at the page. The words didn't try to slide anymore. They sat in a paragraph like they belonged to a chapter she did not want to read. She pulled the pencil from her hoodie pocket and wrote beneath the signature, at the bench, in her everyday hand.

The garden accepts no trades that cost other people's safety. Offers in names at the bench, not at the stripe. Offers expire at dusk.

She did not add please. The garden did not require please. It required scope, cost, and sunset. She felt the bench carry the sentence the way a desk carries a posted form when you pin it under glass.

The paper warped a little under her fingers, like something inside it had lost pressure. The ink at the top loosened and blurred and then crisped again as if it had understood it could not be roles here. She folded the letter along the center so the fold would break the habit of reaching like a hand. It resisted. Then it gave. She set it on the bench to see what the room would do with a yes-that-is-no.

A wind the width of a finger moved across the paper. The letters browned the way paper browns when you leave it in a car window. The fold darkened first. Then the rest dried in a pattern that looked like ash without mess. She brushed it into the tray on the bench that kept seeds from rolling. The ash did not try to spell anything on its way down.

"Okay," she said, mostly to herself. "Okay."

Thanatos angled the Scythe off the stripe again until the blade sat behind his shoulder. It vanished like a phone screen goes dark. Not gone. Not present. Waiting.

"Thank you for bringing the tool out," Sia said. "It helped."

"I didn't bring it out," he said. "You finally looked where it lives. That is different."

"That also helps," she said, because it did.

The hand remained at the far side of the line. It hadn't left. It would wait until dusk. She knew that in her bones. Some people make a job out of waiting. Ledgers make a pride out of it.

"Leave," she told the hand again, because repetition was part of the work. "You can post a note at the bench tomorrow if you find your name."

The hand didn't move.

"Good," Thanatos said. "You didn't try to push it with the blade."

"It isn't my blade," she said.

"That has never stopped anyone from trying," he said.

She almost laughed. She didn't. The stripe wasn't the place to joke. The stripe was the place to be exact.

"What happens if I had read at the line," she asked. "Would the words have stuck to me."

"They would have tried," he said. "The stripe is a tool that reads the person who owns the room. Reading at the stripe makes you easier to put into the math. You read at the bench. That keeps the math with the furniture, where it belongs."

"Is the garden my home," she asked.

"Yes," he said, simply. "It is your home in the way a studio becomes a home when a person sweeps it every morning, names the plants, and fixes a squeak that bothers no one but them. The stripe is the part that learned you keep it. It prefers you. That preference is the only magic that works forever."

"And that is why the hand couldn't come farther," she said.

"That is why it tried anyway," he said. "Some people make a living pretending preference is negotiable."

She let the truth of that sit next to her on the bench. It felt right. It felt like something she would know even if no one told her. Home wasn't a wall. Home was a place that learned you and decided to like you back.

The hand stayed just beyond the line. It didn't twitch. It had more patience than she did. That was fine. She had rules and a sunset. Those beat patience over time.

She put the tray with the paper ash on the lower shelf where she could throw it out later or let the garden decide whether it wanted to eat it. She didn't need to control that much. She needed to write the part with her name on it and leave the rest alone.

"Morning," she said to the garden again, because the moment felt like it wanted a start, even if it was an end. "Thank you."

The basin star uncurled and lay flat and then curled again. The stripe didn't shimmer. It kept line the way good tape keeps a straight run on a wall you meant to paint right the first time.

"Tomorrow I'm posting a Paper Trail card," she said. "And a No Trades policy in human language. And I'm putting coin checks in the route forever, or at least until I get bored of being right."

"Good," Thanatos said. "Keep receipts. Let ledgers chase what they understand. They will hate that you made paper a door."

"That is their problem," she said.

"Yes," he said.

She stood and the bench took the compact of her weight without complaining. She walked to the stripe and planted her feet the way she had been taught for balance in gym. The hand changed nothing in its posture.

"Leave the garden," she said, one more time.

The hand withdrew a final inch so the fingers were not even tempted to poke. Then it went still again. It did not turn into smoke. It did not try to make her flinch. It did the most annoying thing it could do. It waited.

"Dusk," she said. "Then you can find a different hobby."

"Dusk," Thanatos agreed. "Then the paper will be too tired to pretend."

He stood with her at the stripe for another minute. He didn't fill it with stories. He didn't do anything grand. He kept the tool where it belonged and let her home be a home without turning into a lesson. That kindness counted.

"I'm going to wake up now," she said. "I have a card to write before lunch. I will not be dramatic about it."

"You are learning," he said, and there was humor in it without any edge.

She stepped back from the stripe and the bench and the basin star and let the garden keep its breath. The drift reversed and the weight of sheets and pillow returned. The ceiling in her room made its own line, not as straight as the stripe, but close enough for morning.

She sat up and wrote the Paper Trail card in the notebook on her nightstand in clean block letters, twice, so she wouldn't forget one word when she did the real version at the desk.

Sign everything. Names only.
- Receipts live in the red folder.
- No trades that cost safety. Offers at the desk in names. Expire at dusk.

She underlined names and safety because those were the pieces you forget when someone tries to be clever and helpful at the same time. Then she checked the clock, checked the clipboard by the door where she kept her own small posted hours, and got up.

In the corner of her mind, the hand still waited at the line. She let it. Waiting was cheap. Rules were cheaper to write than chaos was to clean. She could afford to let an enemy be bored for six hours.

She looked at the marker stone on her dresser. It looked back the way a good tool looks back, with zero interest in being anything but itself. She pocketed it, patted the hoodie chest where she kept her pen, and headed for the desk to write the first card in real ink.

Sia stayed on the bench until her breathing matched the garden's. The hand waited at the far side of the stripe, whoever held it patient enough to make waiting look easy. Thanatos stood with his weight even, the Scythe quiet behind his shoulder again, more like a broom left ready than a weapon.

"All right," Sia said. "Teach me the part I don't know. I can guess, but I'd rather be right."

"Thresholds," Thanatos said. He did not make a speech. He set facts on the table like tools.

"A Threshold is what a place grows when a human claims it as home on purpose," he said. "It is not a wall. It is a preference. Rooms learn you because you sweep them, feed them, name them, keep them, and post rules that leave people better than you found them. That learning turns into a boundary the world can feel."

"Like the porch," Sia said.

"Exactly," he said. "Porches earn it faster than bedrooms. Kitchens earn it best. Homes that never get cooked in stay shallow. Your bench and stripe learned you because you come here and you work. You write in names. You refuse trades that cost other people their safety. You do it again and again. Repetition sets the line."

"Why do vampires need an invite," she asked. "People told me that as a kid like it was folklore, not a policy."

"It is both," he said. "A vampire is a predator that relies on leverage. A Threshold kills leverage. It is a place choosing the people who live there. It makes invitation a key. Without an invite, a predator is just a stranger with nothing to stand on."

"And the Fae," she said. "Why do their deals fall apart inside."

"Because bargaining needs a market," he said. "A Threshold refuses to be a market unless the owner turns it into one. If you invite a Fae into your kitchen by name to eat soup, the Threshold stays a kitchen. If you invite them in to trade your voice for power, the Threshold collapses because you asked it to. It does what you said, not what you meant."

Sia looked at the stripe. It was a line of plain truth. It did not glow. It did not care about angles or echo. It cared about who cared for it.

"So when the Borrower pushed a letter over," she said, "it was trying to pretend the bench is part of a counter."

"Close," he said. "It was trying to treat your home like a lobby where they already work. The Threshold forces them to admit they are at the door. It is why their hand stopped. It is why your name would not change."

"What breaks a Threshold," she asked. "So I can avoid doing it."

"Neglect breaks it," he said. "Time breaks it when people stop showing up. Coercion breaks it when an owner uses a place to take away choice. That rewrites the room. It starts preferring the wrong thing. If you turn a kitchen into a place where no one gets to eat unless they say the right words, the kitchen will help you enforce that. It will also stop being a Threshold. It will become a trap."

Sia felt that land where rules lived in her head. "So the line holds because I don't use it to boss people around," she said. "I use it to keep people safe."

"Yes," he said. "Rules for places. Not for humans. Jurisdiction. You are not a sheriff. You are a host who knows how to put chairs in the right spots so a room can do its job."

She nodded. It matched the way everything else about her craft had matched. Simple first. Boring always. Kind if possible.

The hand at the stripe adjusted an inch farther back until all the fingers rested behind the line. It made a small show of following a rule. Sia refused to reward it with attention. She went back to the bench, pulled her notebook, and wrote the core in a box she drew thick with two strokes.

> **Thresholds prefer the people who live there.**
> - **They do not control people.**
> - **They govern how places behave.**
> - **They grow with care and clear rules.**
> - **They fade with neglect and force.**

She looked up. Thanatos read while pretending not to look, then gave a half nod that let her know she had it right.

"Another question," she said. "Can I carry a Threshold with me."

"No," he said. "You can carry respect for one. You can write room rules in other places that make small, useful borders. A table can have a threshold if the people at it agree to treat it like a table where everyone gets heard. Your marker helps with that if you keep to places. But you cannot pack your home and use it as a shield on a road."

"Good," she said. "Shields make people act like they are already under attack."

"You are learning," he said again, not unkind.

She set the notebook down and looked at the line. "Will the Borrower keep waiting," she asked.

"Until dusk," he said. "Waiting is part of their ledger. It makes them believe they are patient. It hides the fact that they are stubborn about the wrong things."

Sia thought about Min's warning. The Borrower would chase paperwork next. It made sense. Seals and stamps mattered to them. If you wanted to hurt a clerk, you didn't break a door. You made the file cabinet lie.

"They'll push forms," she said. "Try to send us something that looks right but smells wrong."

"Yes," he said. "They will try to make you live your day out of their folder."

"That's not going to happen," she said. "Not while we have red clips and a word like wrong we can write in ink."

Thanatos stood quiet. He had the comfortable silence of someone who liked when people reached their own sentence. Sia reached hers.

"Okay," she said. "I'm posting a No Trades card in human language in the morning. I'm adding coin checks to routes for a while. I'm making a big Paper Trail card for the desk and a small one for volunteer lanyards. Names only. Sign everything. Receipts live in the red folder. Offers expire at dusk."

"The garden will like that," he said.

"The garden can be picky," she said. "So can I."

She picked up the tray with the paper ash and set it on the lower shelf. The bench did not mind keeping trash until she decided what to do with it. The house upstairs liked tidy waste bins. The garden liked leftovers that meant a rule had worked.

The hand didn't move. It had a quality that reminded her of old buildings with offices that close at five. If it had a face, it would wear glasses and never smudge them.

"Tell me one more thing," Sia said. "Your Scythe. What is it doing when it's not cutting anything."

"Agreeing," he said.

"To what," she asked.

"To the line," he said. "The blade shows where the line wants to live. It tells rooms that borders are real even if no one is shouting about them. People see a blade and think harm. Blades are also rulers. They draw straight when hands shake. That is enough most days."

She pictured a carpenter's square and a chalk line and a steady hand. That made more sense than anything glamorous.

"Can anyone else use it," she asked. "If a person grabbed the pole and tried."

"They could pick it up," he said. "They could carry it. They could hurt themselves with the weight. It would not read their orders unless the order matched the line. The tool obeys the boundary, not the person."

"That seems fair," she said.

"It is," he said.

She glanced back at the stripe. The hand twitched at the word fair, then forced itself still. That told her more than the letter had. The Borrower didn't care about fair. The Borrower cared about numbers.

"Last thing," she said. "If the Borrower finds a name. A real one. Not a title. What changes."

"They can put a note on your bench you will be able to read without your marker," he said. "They still cannot come in without an invitation. Names are keys. They are not ladders."

"I can work with that," she said. "They can submit like any other neighbor. Paper. In daylight. Under a red clip."

"You are a delight to ledgers," he said dry, which in his mouth counted as a compliment.

Sia stood and walked to the stripe. She did not put a foot over. She did not test. She placed her hands behind her back so she would not do something with them just to feel strong. The hand waited. She smelled the ledger smell under the hand now. Paper and ink and plastic sleeves. Clean and false at the same time.

She kept her voice even. "Leave the garden," she said. "You do not get to hang a hand over my line and pretend it has rights. You can wait beyond it. You can file in names. You can bring a receipt next time you collect anything you think is yours. Until then, you wait. Not here."

The hand slid back the last half inch until it was entirely on the far side. Then it went still.

"At dusk," Thanatos said, "it will be gone."

"Good," she said. "I have enough to do without a prop in my peripheral vision."

She returned to the bench and touched the place where she had written the refusal. The wood felt the way her notebook did when a clause settled. Not heavy. Not light. Complete.

"Thanks for the lesson," she said.

"You did most of it yourself," he said. "I brought a blade to remind the line it was allowed to be a line."

She considered the day waiting upstairs. A card to write. Two lanyard slips. A corner check for the hinge where the dime had sat. She felt tired in a good way, like after scrubbing a floor and seeing it stay clean.

"I'm going to wake up and write," she said. "You good here."

"I am never in a hurry," he said.

"That sounds like bragging," she said.

"It is a job description," he said.

She smiled without showing teeth, because the stripe liked calm. "See you later," she said.

"Later," he said.

She stood, touched the basin brim with two fingers, and let the garden release her. The drift back to her body went the way it should, no snags, no cheap tricks like alarms. She sat up in her room and wrote the No Trades card in her notebook so it would be waiting for her hand at the desk.

No Trades:

- No exchanges that cost safety.
- Offers at the desk in names.
- Expire at dusk.

She underlined safety. She added a small box in the corner that said wrong in pencil, because she wanted to remember to write it in ink across any seal that tried to lie.

Then she got up, pocketed the marker stone and her pen, and went to find Ella. Paper trails, then coin checks, then lunch. The Borrower could wait outside a line until the sun went down. She had work to do that would make dusk arrive on schedule.

On her way to the desk, she passed Truth sitting where the hallway made a clean plus sign. The dog's ears tracked two corners at once. Sia touched her head.

"Good girl," she said. "Hold."

Truth blinked and held. The house did the same. The rest would keep until the board asked for it.

CHAPTER 14

Paper Cuts

TOBIAS

In individuals, insanity is rare; but in groups,
parties, nations and epochs, it is the rule.
Friedrich Nietzsche

TOBIAS LIKED TO START with corners. If corners were honest,
the day had a chance. He touched the edge of the Ops desk, the
staff hall mouth, the hinge shadow on the stair, and the Annex
line in that order. The house gave him the same plain read he
had learned to trust here, cool and even. Good. He wrote 9:15
on his route card and started the first loop.

Truth tracked him to the desk with one eye as she loafed
under Ella's stool. Volunteers were setting out maps. Mia had

the red folder clipped to the board. Sia rolled a fresh strip of tape between her fingers like someone who liked having the right tool in reach.

The first test walked itself to the counter. A man with museum shoes and a neutral smile. The paper he slid across the desk felt too smooth.

"Morning," Ella said. "What can we help with."

"Inspection," the man said. He kept his voice in the middle of his throat where it belonged in a polite lobby. He didn't say a title. He put the slip on the glass like it had always planned to be there.

Tobias watched the paper. He did not touch it. He never touched a thing until Ella was finished with it. The heading was clean, serif font, no flourish. The body read like a real permission slip. It used names. It asked to confirm "temporary basement access for inspection," then listed a routing number and a return address line.

He felt the paper chill before he found the miss. It was the kind of cold you get when a freezer door is shut and the rubber seal briefly pulls air. Not a draft. A tug. Truth flicked an ear and went still.

"Who scheduled you," Ella asked, friendly as water. She did not say that no one had.

The man considered his script. "Clerk's office," he said. He did not add Summer or Winter. He did not give a name.

Sia stepped closer and laid the slip on a rubber mat meant for pens. "Give me one second," she said, and she checked the header with the attention she gave art labels. The kerning was wrong by half a hair. The routing number had a rhythm real office routing numbers had, but the pair in the center doubled when they should have stepped. Close enough to fool a tired person. Not today.

"Dead routing," Sia said. She pulled a pen from behind her ear. "Names are fine, the numbers are ghosts."

She wrote one steady word across the seal in blue ink, the way a clerk taught to correct would write across a counterfeit stamp. **wrong**. No caps. She did not mash the letters. She made them clear. The paper twitched under the pen and tried to smudge. It failed. The ink sat like it had always lived there.

"Apologies," Ella said. She handed the man a map and a sticker sheet like nothing special had happened. "Closed areas are marked. Water at the desk if you need it."

The man retracted his hand like he had touched a stove, nodded, and left with human speed. He wanted the desk to move on. Ella moved on. Tobias did not.

"Red clip," Sia said. Mia slid the forged slip into a clear sleeve, clipped it under the red tab on the board, and wrote the time next to it. The air by the clip tightened the way a guitar string tightens when you get it in tune.

"Route," Ella said.

"On it," Tobias said.

He walked the staff door again, slower. The hinge sang at the edge of hearing, a thin metallic buzz that did not belong to fans. He crouched and ran the back of his knuckle along the plate.

A warmth hung at the metal that did not make sense this early. He took out the small flat key he used for prying and used it like a pick. The shaved dime sat tucked beneath the hinge plate like a coin under a table leg. He jarred it into the stainless tray Mia handed down. The hum died the instant the metal left the frame.

"Filed edge," Eric said from behind him. He had the kind of grin he wore when he found a new problem. "Nice try."

Tobias set the dime in the tray and wrote 9:21 hinge, dime filed on his card. Truth's ear settled. He stood and checked the corridor. It kept clean line. He gave the frame a second pass anyway. Nothing else glinted wrong.

On his way to the Annex mouth, he drifted past the volunteer table and watched two teens in matching school sweatshirts point at the skylight room on the map. Normal noise. Exactly the kind of cover good traps liked.

"Second slip," Mia called.

A woman in a denim jacket had dropped it like the first, name different, same wording. The numbers sang the same wrong rhythm. Sia wrote wrong over the seal and slid it into a fresh sleeve. Mia clipped it under the first. The air at the red clip tightened again. Tobias put a second dot on his card and drew a small line between them because patterns matter.

He cut to the staff stair. Eric met him at the top with his pencil tucked behind his ear and a look that said get ready. The down draft met them at the third step. It wasn't cold so much as off tempo, a pulse that fell neatly on the Neutral Window beats they had learned to hate.

"Feel that," Eric said.

"Yeah," Tobias said. He set a boot on the next riser and rocked his weight. The rise held normal. He squinted at the seat where the step met the riser. The screws had new heads. Not bright, just newer than the ones around them. One had a hairline shim beneath the lip of the wood, a sliver that would lift a line by a whisper. Enough to catch a person's balance if they were carrying a bucket and a worry.

"Tobias," Sia said in his ear. Her radio voice did not rush. "If it asks for our names before it gives one, it's a lure."

"Copy," he said.

On the landing someone had hung a clipboard the way you hang one in a hallway for maintenance, hook and cord, angled to invite signatures. SERVICE RECEIPT sat across the top. No sender listed. The first blank read Name. The second read Date. The rest was tidy and empty.

Tobias did not touch the pen on the cord. He slid the top sheet into an evidence sleeve and wrote 9:27 stair landing, clipboard with name-first on it in block letters on the flap. The pen on the cord swung back and forth like a cheap metronome, then went still.

"Steps carry staff by posted routes only," Sia said on the radio. "No borrowed signs. Clause sunsets at close."

"Ready," Tobias said.

She walked to the frame at the top of the stair with the marker stone. He could hear her voice through the radio and feel the rule settle as she spoke. The hush thickened through the wall and made itself comfortable under his boots. The off-tempo pulse eased off like a hiccup that decided it had been embarrassing.

"That's better," Eric said. He tapped one of the new screw heads with the tip of his pencil, then drew a box on his sketch with a quick note. "I'll swap these later. We'll keep this boring."

Tobias gave the stair one more long look and led the way back up. He wanted the trap sprung somewhere they chose, not out on the landing because his curiosity beat his training.

Back at the staff door, he stopped inside the frame so his body made a wall any stray eyes would read as uninteresting. Sia arrived a breath later with her clipboard. Ella and Mia split jobs without talking. Ella pulled the stamp. Mia pulled the receipt template they had made last night. Eric stood where he could kill a light glare in the lobby if it started to make people look at the wrong glass. Kaelan eased from the baseboard to a chair and sat like a person ready to ring a bell once if the air changed shape. Truth posted on the step, angled to watch both the desk and the door.

"Let's turn it around," Sia said. "Read it where the wall can file it."

Tobias took the template. He didn't try to sound official. Official made people feel like they should argue. He read the words in names.

"Refusal of Access," he said. "Request denied. Dead routing. Names only, no titles. Logged at the desk at nine thirty-three."

Mia pulled the date stamp and placed it on the corner with a clean thunk that made the paper admit it was paper. Ella signed. Tobias signed beneath her. Sia added the time in the right margin because she liked time to live where eyes actually go.

He walked the refusal to the red clip and slid it under the forged slips. The air at the board tightened a shade more. You couldn't see anything change. You could feel the line get honest.

The desk phone rang. No caller ID. No slow roll to the ring. A single clean sound.

Ella looked at him. He lifted the handset and kept his voice plain. "Tobias."

A flat voice on the other end said, "Accepted," and hung up. Not a tone. Not a click. Just absence.

He set the receiver down and wrote 9:34 phone said Accepted next to the refusal on the board copy. He circled the time and drew a dot next to it on his route card. He liked dots you could stack later.

"Winter," Sia said on the radio. "Do you have any inspections on file."

Min's reply came through without lag. "None at your location. If you collect a name, we will countersign. Good job writing wrong on the seal."

Mia grinned and waggled the stamp. "We like boring."

"We approve of boring," Min said, and clipped off.

A volunteer drifted up with a third slip on a tray, eyes big because teenagers think they are hiding their curiosity when they are not. Ella pointed at the paper trail card and smiled. The kid smiled back without knowing why and set the tray down.

"Same dead routing," Sia said after one glance. She wrote wrong across the seal and slid the slip into its sleeve with the same quiet satisfaction she used for filing a lab report in high school. Mia clipped it under the second forged slip and the refusal. The board now looked like a neat, small door that had closed without fuss.

The hinge hummed again, a thin version of the earlier buzz. Truth's nose swung to the left. Tobias ran a finger along the plate. Nothing under the metal this time. He checked the jamb, the screw heads, the floor seam. Clean.

"It's chasing the paper, not the door," Sia said. She had the look she got when her live map made a new sound in her head. "Let it. It will have to choose a name or keep eating its own tail."

Kaelan let her bracelets breathe and spoke like a person describing a step, not a poem. "It will learn boredom. That is a lesson worth teaching."

"Alright," Ella said. "Back to the room. Water and maps. Normal talks. We will not let stationery be the weirdest part of our day."

Tobias nodded. He logged the hinge check with a small cross-out mark that made him happy because it showed he had looked and found nothing. He wrote a line under the last entry for a space before the next loop. He would go down the stair again at quarter to, because corners liked being visited at the same times.

Mia reached behind the counter for the stainless tray. "I want a display case for crimes of stationery," she said.

"We're not making a shrine," Ella said. "We're making a shelf in the supply closet."

"Fine," Mia said. "A very organized shelf."

"Now you are speaking my love language," Ella said.

A little boy tugged his grandmother toward the skylight room, stopped to stare at Truth, and waved. Truth wiggled one paw and went back to watching the board. The room let itself be a museum again.

Tobias took the service landing clipboard from the evidence sleeve and held it up for Sia without stepping into the path. The top line still asked for a name first. The corner of the page had a tiny bend, the kind that happens when a person is bored enough to fidget. He liked that detail. It made the Borrower look like a person and not a curse.

"Bagged and logged," he said.

"Thank you," Sia said. "No signatures. We serve, we don't sign."

He slipped the sleeve into the folder beneath the red clip. The air nudged back against his knuckles like a cat brushing a hand on its way past. This house liked paper done right. He had never expected to care about folders on a wall as much as he cared about a clean door. He did now. That felt like growth he could live with.

He looked at his watch. Nine forty. He had five minutes before he wanted to walk the stair again. He used two of them to check the Annex mouth and the hallway cone Eric had set so the easy path looked like the only path. Someone had moved the cone half an inch while adjusting a stroller. Eric adjusted it back without sighing.

Sia put a small lanyard card on the volunteer station and tapped it with her knuckle. "Read this out loud for me."

The kid read without embarrassment. "If someone asks for the basement by title, point to the sign and call Sia."

"Perfect," Sia said. "You're hired forever."

"Please don't," the kid said. "I have midterms."

"Fine," Sia said. "We'll hire you part time."

Tobias checked the door once more. Nothing hummed. He wrote a small note in the margin of his route card. Get screw set from Eric for 2 risers. Swap after lunch. It felt good to put future quiet on paper. It kept his hands from looking for fights they did not need.

He turned to Ella. "If the phone rings again, I'll take it."

"You answer with your name," she said. "No speeches."

"Always," he said.

He took his second loop at a steady pace. The house matched it. The red clip sat where it belonged, a small bright square that said the story was being told by people who knew how to tell it. The forged slips were already getting boring. That was a win. Boring traps made brave mistakes.

At the stair he paused. The new screws waited like a dare. He touched the riser and felt the steady temperature of wood that belonged here. The pulse did not return. The clause held time for him. He thanked the frame with a palm pressed to the paint, then went back to the desk.

The phone did not ring again. Not yet. When it did, he would be ready with the quiet sentence the house liked best. He wrote his name on the next line of the route card so he would see it when he looked down and not forget who he was in the middle of all the paper. Then he put the card away and got ready to teach chess like it was a normal thing to do after you refused a ghost at a threshold. That was how you kept a place human. You put the most ordinary thing back in the middle of the day and let everything else settle around it.

TOBIAS SET THE WOODEN board on the reading room table because it looked like it had been waiting for a purpose besides holding brochures. The table sat far enough from the lobby to feel private, close enough that he could still hear the desk bell and the murmur of maps. Sun through the high windows made the dust look honest. Truth crawled under the table and flopped on her side so her chin lined up with the H file like she was judging pawns.

"Black or white," he asked.

"White," Ella said, already pulling the near pawn to e4. "I need the first move today."

"Sold," Tobias said. He brought a knight to f6 and let his

breath catch up to the morning.

Marcus dropped into the third chair with the look of a man who was pretending not to need a sit. He set his phone face down, rolled his shoulders once, and reached for a pawn. "I'll spot you both and heckle," he said.

"You can have the black pieces next game," Tobias said. "Let me have this one before you make me cry."

Marcus moved a pawn like he was shifting a cup. "As you wish," he said.

They played opening moves in a steady rhythm. Ella liked clean lines. Tobias liked congestion that broke late. The click of pawns against wood did what he needed a game to do in rooms like this. It set a cadence that reminded the body that time belongs to people, not to whatever crawls through vents.

"Reset," he said after ten moves, not about the board. "Say the whole morning back to me."

Ella kept her eyes on the pieces. She didn't need to look up to put a story in order. "Two forged inspection slips. Names in the body text, dead routing numbers. Sia wrote wrong in ink across each seal and clipped them under the red folder. Hinge had a filed dime under the plate. You jarred it. Buzz died. Stair had a shim under a riser and fresh screws, pulse was landing on Neutral Window timing. Sia set a steps-only clause. The pulse stopped. Clipboard on the landing with a name-first trap. You bagged it. Then you read the refusal at the staff threshold in names and filed it under the red clip. The phone said Accepted and hung up."

"Good," Tobias said. "Say the part you didn't like."

"The part where paperwork tries to act like a person," she said. "If I get tired that's the kind of trap I fall for. It looks like my job."

"Same," he said. "I'd rather fight a thing I can see. Stationery is rude."

Truth sighed like she agreed. Her tail thumped twice against the underside of the chair.

"Castle," Marcus said, sliding Ella's king into a little house behind pawns. He said it like a joke, then glanced toward the lobby, then back at the board. "Same, by the way. Give me a claw I can break. This filing cabinet war is for people with patient souls."

"That's why we play chess," Tobias said. "It burns the panic off. It makes the next decision feel like a choice instead of a reaction."

"Also I like beating you," Marcus said.

"You won last time because I was talking," Tobias said.

"You were talking about how I was going to lose," Marcus said. "It was useful."

Ella snorted and scooped a pawn. Her hands were steady. That was good to see.

They played three more exchanges. Tobias traded a knight he loved for a center he wanted. He watched Ella clock the trade and file it in whatever part of her brain kept track of mail and teenagers. She made a note at the edge of the board with her fingertip, a little tap near the file where she would push later.

She didn't need words for it. She owned the room enough to let the table remember.

"Okay," Tobias said, letting the pieces breathe. "Tell me about China."

Ella's eyes lifted from the rook to his face, then back to the board. She didn't hide the little smile that liked the idea. "Long-wang invited me. Names only, porch rules. It's training, not a court tour. He said benches and markets, how to set tone across paths. He didn't set a date. He asked me to pick a week that keeps the Museum from getting grumpy."

"You want to go," Tobias said. He didn't make it a question about permission. It was a status check.

"I do," she said. "I don't want the House to feel abandoned, and I'm not dragging the whole crew through an airport while we're running receipts for demons with office supplies."

"Good instincts," he said. "We do it quiet. We do it boring. We keep the board covered while you're gone."

Marcus looked up from the bishop he was pretending not to covet. "I'll go," he said. "Carry bags, watch corners, make sure no one bumps you into a river. You're getting training. You don't need to babysit me. I'll keep a radius and a bad attitude."

"One more seat filled," Tobias said. He moved a pawn and made Ella look at the board again so the talk stayed in the frame he wanted. No stage, just a table and plans.

"I have Church routes we can use," he added. "No fuss, no grand entrances. Small airports, quiet drivers, boring hotels with real doors and real breakfast. No titles on any paperwork.

Names only. Posted hours in a folder for any clerk you meet."

"Do we need to bring the Key," Ella asked.

"No," Tobias said immediately. "We keep the big tool off planes and off roads we don't own. We bring receipt kits. We bring copies of the clause. We bring your porch voice. We bring Marcus, who looks like he will apologize for breaking someone while he does it."

"I am very polite," Marcus said.

"Exactly," Tobias said. "You make trouble look like a misunderstanding, then you end the misunderstanding."

Ella nudged her queen one square, small move, big message. "If my porch voice doesn't work?"

"You call me," Tobias said. "You call Garren. We have a fixer who understands posted hours. They know borders and they like boring stamps. We keep you inside names the whole time."

"Dates," Ella said. "We need to pick dates that don't step on field trips or Neutral Window crunch. I don't want to leave Sia in the middle of a paperwork war."

"We won't," Tobias said. "We'll pick a week that looks like an ordinary museum week, not a festival. We'll give Sia and Ella-clone Mia the receipts to make our absence become a process instead of a hole."

"Ella-clone," Mia said from the desk, not looking over. "I'm honored."

"You should be," Ella said. "You have better handwriting than me."

Tobias took Ella's pawn because he could, and because it

would make her do the mean bishop thing he needed her to do next. "We leave the twins off every list," he said. "They're not boarding planes. They're not standing on porches in foreign cities. They are Hell's real targets, and as long as they're in a place with posted hours and a dog who thinks in straight lines, we make Hell bored to death."

"Agreed," Marcus said. The answer came fast, no debate. "They're kids. They stay with us. They learn the dull parts. They get good at dull. Dull will keep them alive longer than anything flashy."

Ella nodded. "They'll complain," she said. "But they'll be fine. Sia will keep them busy with rules. She's good at giving people jobs that feel like choices."

"Daily check-ins," Tobias said. "We send texts at posted hours. Names only, no poetry, no titles. If a clerk needs to countersign anything abroad, Garren routes the paper through a cathedral office with a stamp that's so boring angels fall asleep."

Marcus grinned. "I like him already."

"You'll meet him on the phone in five," Tobias said. He slid his rook and watched Ella see it too late. He hated doing that to her. He did it anyway. "You okay to be away from the board for a week?"

Ella looked at the queen she'd left on the wrong square and lifted it with a small breath that let him know she'd seen the trap and didn't mind learning out loud. "If I leave good cards and better water," she said. "If I leave Mia with a red clip and Tobias with a route. If Sia writes names on the glass and doesn't try to hold everything with her hands. Yes."

"Good," Tobias said. "That's the answer."

They played in silence for a minute. Truth scooted so her nose touched Tobias's boot. He pressed his heel against her jaw and felt her relax the way animals do when someone tells them that they are seen.

"I don't love leaving when the Borrower is trying to turn our desk into a puppet," Ella said after three moves. "I also don't love waiting so long that the invitation goes stale."

"Then we pick a date within two weeks," Tobias said. "We make the announcement at the board like any trip to a conference. Staff card. Lanyard cards. Posted hours won't cry."

"Two weeks gives me a shot at getting Sia steady in the garden with the Threshold stuff," Ella said. "She's close. Once she gets through the part where she thinks she has to be a sheriff, she'll remember that hosts set clocks, not courts."

"Then that's our window," Tobias said. He took a pawn and gave back a knight because he liked living with his choices. "I'll call Garren. He'll line the road. We'll keep it dull."

"Dull is good," Marcus said. He tipped a pawn over like a person cheers with a beer. "To dull."

"To dull," Ella said.

Sia slid into the room with a fresh card and set it on the corner of the table. **Paper Trail: Sign everything. Names only. Receipts live in the red folder. No trades that cost safety. Offers at the desk. Expire at dusk.** She didn't interrupt the game. She let it be background like an extra light in the right place.

"You good if we move on China," Tobias asked her.

"Yeah," Sia said. "Go be boring abroad. I'll keep boring here. We'll cross-compare boring when you get back."

"Deal," he said.

"Marcus," she said, "if your phone starts a fight while you're being boring, you call me first."

"Yes, boss," Marcus said, and saluted with a pawn.

"Don't call me that," Sia said, but she smiled a little and left with the card to pin it where it would do the most good.

Ella pushed a pawn to make room for a rook that would hurt later. "You really think this place can be a home base," she asked, not like she was fishing for compliments. Like she wanted a second opinion from a person who walked corners on purpose.

"Yes," Tobias said, and meant it. "If Sia gets her craft settled, this place is a lid on a pot. The magic is thick and cooperative. We're fighting wisps of sulfur here that would be armies somewhere else. That means the house is working with us."

Ella's shoulders eased the way he liked to see. "Okay," she said. "Then we make plans that respect that."

"Call him," Marcus said to Tobias, nodding toward the hallway. "I'll guard the queen while you step out."

"That is a lie," Ella said.

"I will guard her," he said. "By threatening her with my bishop until she learns something."

"That's closer to the truth," Ella said.

Tobias stood and set his palm on the table to let the room

know he was leaving pieces in its care. Truth rolled onto her stomach and thumped her tail once without opening her eyes. He took that as a blessing.

"Two minutes," he said. "If the phone rings again, yell my name."

"We will," Ella said. "Also I'm going to beat you because you left your rook dumb."

"I did that on purpose," he said.

"Sure," she said.

He left them to the board and the low buzz of people looking at dinosaurs on a weekday and stepped into the side hall where the acoustics made phone calls feel private. He pulled his route card, added a line that said call Garren now, and dialed.

As it rang, he looked back through the reading room doorway. Ella and Marcus bent over the board like two clerks arguing about commas. Truth had her paw over her nose. Sia's card glowed a little in the sun because paper likes doing that when it knows it matters. The day, for a slice, looked exactly like something worth defending by being as boring as a receipt.

Garren picked up on the second ring. "Tobias," he said. "Talk to me."

"Got a minute," Tobias said. "I've got two updates and a favor. First, Sanctuary is holding. Second, we're about to plan a trip to China."

Tobias stepped into the side hall where calls didn't echo. He kept an eye on the corner by the lobby and dialed.

"Go," Garren said.

"We're steady," Tobias said. "Sanctuary's holding. If Sia locks her craft, this can be home base. The place backs us. We're dealing with sulfur wisps here that would be full hits anywhere else."

"Good," Garren said. "How'd you get there?"

"Posted hours. Names on glass. Receipts for everything. We benched a rider and pulled info from a basement crawler. There's a thief working the edges. We call them the Borrower. Feels like a former clerk."

"Tricks?"

"Forged inspection slips in names with dead routing numbers. Kerning almost perfect. Filed dimes under hinges to lift lines a hair. Clipboard on the stair asking for our names first. We bagged one. Sia wrote 'wrong' across the seals. I read a Refusal of Access at the threshold and filed it. Phone rang with no ID, said 'Accepted,' hung up."

"Good response," Garren said. "Keep it on paper. Keep writing 'wrong' on any stolen seals."

"Already doing it," Tobias said.

"How's the team?"

"Solid," Tobias said. "Ella's running the board. Sia's learning place rules fast. Marcus stays calm or jokes, both help. Truth's posted. Volunteers know their lanyard line. Eric marks corners and makes the easy path obvious. Mia runs the red folder like a pro. Kaelan keeps things even."

"That buys you time," Garren said. "What do you need?"

"China," Tobias said. "Longwang invited Ella to train. Names only. No court tour. I want to take her and Marcus. Quiet flights, boring hotels, drivers who don't ask. A fixer who respects posted hours. If Winter or Summer want countersigns, we need a dull stamp. We travel in names."

"I'll set it up," Garren said. "Newark through a quiet hop. Driver who thinks you're a choir exchange. Two soft houses. Cathedral office on call for countersigns. No titles. Black ink. Very boring stamp."

"Perfect," Tobias said. "We'll pick dates inside two weeks. Ella wants to dodge field trips and Neutral Window."

"I'll have routes ready," Garren said. "How long?"

"A week," Tobias said. "Enough to learn, not enough to look like we moved in."

"Who's covering the Hotel?"

"Sia and crew," Tobias said. "Receipt kits everywhere. Volunteers trained. Truth knows the route. Charles handles doors. We stick to names. Borrower just took our refusal. Next move will be more paper. We're ready."

"I can live with that," Garren said. "Quick regional update. Benson's team is green at a bridge, Winter sent three receipts and one apology. Alvarez is on hospital duty, fixing a library basement with no posted hours. Ives is dealing with pipes and one confused ghoul. Low heat."

"Good to hear," Tobias said.

"Daily check-ins from you," Garren added. "Posted hours. Morning and evening. If the Borrower sends orders, serve the refusal in names and file it before you even parse it."

"Done," Tobias said. "I'll text you our refusal language for your file."

"And the twins?" Garren asked.

"They stay," Tobias said. "Hell's watching for them. Here they're kids with jobs and a dog. On the road they're leverage."

"Thank you," Garren said. "Anything else?"

"Yeah. We're not fortifying this place into a bunker. It's a museum. We're making it safer by running it like one."

"That's the job," Garren said. "Make us less necessary. Send dates today. I'll make the road dull."

"Copy," Tobias said. "One more: that 'Accepted' call. No voiceprint I know. No trace."

"Fine. They put themselves under your paperwork. Keep them there. When you get a name, don't celebrate. Write it down and file it."

"Got it," Tobias said.

"Tell Ella she's cleared for China. Tell Marcus cathedrals don't need his elbows. Tell Sia boring is holy."

"I will," Tobias said.

The line clicked off. Tobias wrote 10:06 Garren greenlight on his route card and went back to the reading room.

Marcus had set a trap. Ella saw it and used it anyway because it taught her something. Tobias gave them the news.

"Green light," he said. "Newark cover. Names only. Drivers who hate questions. Cathedral stamp if needed. Two weeks or less."

Ella's shoulders dropped a notch. "Good. We'll pick dates today."

"Twins stay," Tobias said.

"Agreed," Marcus said.

"Daily check-ins. No trades. Refusals first," Tobias said. He tapped the table. "Finish the game. Then we write the list and keep it dull."

CHAPTER 15

Names on the Line

ELLA

> Mathematics is a game played according to certain simple rules with meaningless marks on paper.
>
> David Hilbert

THE MINUTE HAND SLID past the mark she didn't like. The lobby's noise thinned in that way crowds do when they notice the weather change and pretend they didn't. Ella checked the board, the red clip, the posted cards, then the staff door where Sia stood with the marker stone resting in her palm.

A courier rolled a case through the glass doors like he belonged in airports more than museums. He wore a badge on a lanyard that was too clean. The plastic glare made it hard to see the printing. He didn't go to the front desk. He came straight toward Ella with the steady walk of someone trained not to hurry.

"Can I help you," she said, stopping him at the break between lobby tile and staff hall carpet.

"Signature," he said, holding up a clipboard. "Acknowledgment that you received the custody notice."

"We read and file at the threshold," Ella said. "Not in the lobby."

Sia stepped into the doorway and touched the frame at eye level. "Papers read in names. No custody changes at this door. File only." She spoke like she was setting hours again. The air cooled a notch and the hallway seemed to hear her.

Ella set a rubber mat on the counter just inside the frame and nodded at the clipboard. "Place it there."

The courier set it down. The top form looked like a receipt. It wasn't. The first blank asked for her title. The second asked for her signature. The third asked for a date. There was no published sender, no route number she could check, no presenting party section filled out.

"Before we file anything, we log who presents it," Ella said. She slid a clean form onto the mat. **Notice of Presenting Party** sat across the top in the same boring font Mia had chosen for every Ops template. "Your name, please."

The courier didn't reach for the pen. He smiled past her shoulder at nothing. "Just a signature that you received it."

Ella didn't look over her shoulder. She knew Tobias had stepped into her blind spot like he always did when the hallway needed a wall. She kept her voice even.

"We read in names at the threshold," she said. "We log in names. No titles. No signatures until paper is correct. Your name for the presenting party notice, please."

Truth shifted her paws at the top of the stair. Not a growl. Just the sound of a dog bracing without making a point of it. The plastic on the courier's badge lifted at one corner where the lamination had bubbled. It didn't peel, but it wanted to.

"Refusal first," Tobias said, stepping up beside her. He read from the sheet Mia had clipped to the board five minutes after breakfast. "Refusal of Access. Request denied. Dead routing. Names only. No titles. Logged at the desk at eleven twelve."

Mia stamped the refusal with a clean thunk and set it aside to be filed after this moment was over. Sia slid Ella's **Notice of Presenting Party** closer to the courier again.

"Name," Ella said.

The courier reached for the pen, then stopped. His fingers hovered above the plastic. Truth's ears tipped forward a hair. The hinge on the staff door gave a tiny, high buzz Ella could feel in her back teeth.

"Light," Ella said, one word to Mia.

Mia angled the desk lamp across the mat. Ella took the **service sticker** from her pocket and set it on the edge of the clipboard where the light hit cleanest. Heat soaked into the plastic for one second, then cooled. The faint blocks at the bottom of the sticker came up like a watermark. Name. Route. Authorizer. The lines were blank, but the structure showed itself. Whoever printed it had expected signatures to exist.

The courier flinched before his face read it. It was small, but she had seen that flinch at the museum a hundred times. It was the moment kids had when they realized a dinosaur skull wasn't a replica.

"Your name," Ella said. "We'll clip the notice with the custody attempt and the refusal. Then you can go."

Sia put the tip of her pen on the fake authority line in the courier's form and wrote **wrong** in blue along the bottom of the header. She didn't press hard. She made the letters legible. The ink sat and didn't slide.

"Name," Ella repeated. She didn't raise her voice.

Marcus shifted his stance beside the lobby rope and set his hands where he could lift or stop someone without looking like he was about to do either. Eric drifted to the far glass and killed a glare so the crowd wouldn't gather just because light made it easy to gawk. Kaelan sat on the bench by the volunteer desk and watched air instead of people, bracelets silent. Tobias kept the line. Sia held the frame. Mia watched the stamp like it had a choice.

The courier swallowed. "Hale," he said finally.

"Hale what," Ella said. She kept the rhythm slow on purpose.

"Hale Rowan," he said, and looked like he wanted to take the name back now that it was in the air.

Ella wrote it on the **Notice of Presenting Party** in block letters. She said it back one time, same pace, so the room could file it. "Hale Rowan. Presenting party."

She slid the form to Mia. Mia stamped the time and handed it to Tobias, who walked it to the red clip without leaving the threshold. He slid it under the custody notice and the refusal. The air at the board tightened like a string that finally tuned to pitch.

The clipboard's top page tried one last trick. The blank next to "title of signatory" pulsed in a way ink should not pulse. Ella put her finger on the empty line and shook her head.

"Names only," she said. "And we sign nothing on your paper. If Winter wants to acknowledge anything about this, they'll request it in names with a route that exists."

The badge at the courier's chest peeled farther at the corner. The lamination lifted and showed the same name she had just written. No initials. No title. The mask matched the paper now that the paper had a name.

"Hale," she said. "You're logged. We won't keep you. We'll send a countersign if Winter asks for one."

The radio clipped to the board hissed once. Min's voice came through in the polite tone that made rooms behave.

"We show a presenting party logged as Hale Rowan," Min said. "No inspections scheduled at your location. Countersign available if you need it."

"Copy," Sia said. "We decline pickup. We're watching to see if the paper route collapses now that a name is pinned."

"Understood," Min said. "Keep filing in names. We'll do the

same on our end."

The radio went quiet. The lobby, somehow, got quieter with it.

Hale tried again. "You should sign the acknowledgment. It closes the loop."

"Our loop closes when we file," Ella said. "We're done."

Hale didn't argue. He lifted the clipboard, slid the pen back in its clip, and pinched the peeling corner of his badge like he could smooth his own name back into hiding. It didn't take. He turned like a person leaving a church after putting a prayer card in a rack and walked out without looking back.

Ella watched his shoulders until they blended into the door crowd and the glass erased his shape. Then she breathed in, breathed out, and pressed the service sticker flat to the lamp light one more time. The faint blocks stayed blocks. No names rose on their own.

"Time," she said.

"Eleven sixteen," Mia answered, writing it next to the presenting party notice under the clip. She added a thin red tag that read **presenting party** and squared the stack.

Truth settled her chin on her paws and let her eyes half close. The hinge went quiet. The weird buzz in Ella's teeth faded.

"Min has the name," Tobias said. "That's as good as countersign without the ink."

"Desk only next," Sia said. "We need that card up before lunch. If their paper rides naps or benches, I want to starve it at the surface."

"Already drafted," Mia said. She held up a card in her tidy handwriting. **Desk Only: Paper reads in names at desks during posted hours. No service at benches, seats, or stairs. No titles. No trades.**

"Pin it," Ella said. She kept her hands on the rubber mat for one more second so the corridor would read how she wanted it to read. Then she walked the clipboard back out to the lobby and set it on the edge of the front desk where anyone could see the empty presenting party block and think twice about trying to play courier without a name again.

Marcus drifted back to her side. "Hale Rowan," he said. "Feels right to file a name."

"Names make rooms honest," Ella said. She checked the board. The red clip looked heavy in the right way. "Let's stay on schedule."

He nodded. "Stair?"

"Please," she said.

He went. Tobias followed. Kaelan stood and smoothed the front of her cardigan like a person about to help an aunt set tables. Eric gave the rope a little nudge to straighten it. The volunteer turned a map around for a kid without being asked.

The lobby noise took a breath and returned to normal volume. The Window would push harder soon. Ella could feel the pressure change the same way she could feel a storm a mile away. Small things lined up to meet it. That was the point.

Sia touched her sleeve. "We should try something after this shift," she said low. "A lesson Fuzanglong showed me. It's clean.

It involves you."

"Fine," Ella said. She didn't need the details now. She needed the next card on the glass. "After we post Desk Only."

Mia pinned the card at eye level where visitors reading hours would trip over it without feeling managed. Ella set a second copy at the volunteer station. She wrote a tiny lanyard version for the teens and pushed it across the counter.

"Read it out loud," she said.

They did. "Paper reads in names at desks during posted hours. No service at benches, seats, or stairs. No titles. No trades."

"Perfect," Ella said. She gave them a smile she saved for people who did small boring things that kept everyone safe.

A family passed by on their way to the dioramas. The dad asked if the T. rex was real. The volunteer handled it. Ella listened to the answer anyway so she would remember the cadence later when she had to say something that would make a room act like itself.

Sia checked the frame again. Truth checked the hinge. The board held. The clip held. The name held.

Ella looked at the clock. Neutral Window would hit properly any minute. She felt ready and also not ready at all. That was honest. She kept her mouth shut about it and poured three paper cups of water for whoever reached for one first. Then she slid her pen behind her ear, palmed the service sticker once to confirm it was still warm, and turned back toward the door.

"Next," she said. "We're not giving the day away."

THEY POSTED THE DESK Only card and the room got a touch quieter, but Ella could still feel the Window starting to lean on the day. The hum sat under the lobby noise like a bass note she couldn't shut off. Sia waited until a school group cleared the map rack, then touched Ella's sleeve again.

"Now?" Sia asked.

Ella nodded. "Where?"

"Here is fine," Sia said. "Sit. Put your feet flat. Hands on your knees."

Ella sat in the reading room chair that faced the wide doorway. It let her keep the front desk, the board, and the staff door in her peripheral vision. Sia pulled the second chair close and set the marker stone on the table. She took Ella's left wrist with two fingers, light and steady.

"If you feel wrong at any point," Sia said, "say stop and you'll be back here. You will not fall over. You will not lose time. It feels like an elevator, not like sleep."

"Okay," Ella said. She kept her tone even. "What do I do?"

"Breathe," Sia said. "Think about a bench and a bowl of water that holds a star. Nothing complicated. If your mind tries to decorate, let it go. I'll pull. You let me."

Ella pictured the bench like she would sketch it. Straight back, clean lines, no carvings that wanted attention. She pictured a shallow basin that belonged in a courtyard. Sia's fingers were warm against her pulse. The hum of the Window sat in Ella's ear like a warning she was tired of hearing.

The drop was exactly what Sia had promised. No falling. No dream blur. The chair pressed her shoulders for one breath and the next breath was softer air that smelled like stone and something green. The gravel under her shoes made a different sound. The light came from nowhere obvious and everywhere she needed. It was daylight that didn't pick a direction.

The bench waited. The basin held a small white point that did not move. A stripe ran between them like someone had laid painter's tape dead straight across a floor and told the room to respect it.

"Welcome to my garden," Sia said. Her voice was the same voice she used for posted hours. Calm. Friendly. Not trying to sell anything.

Ella stood because her body wanted to prove it could. She kept the board and the lobby in her head like a thread tied to her wrist. She checked for dizziness. Nothing. Her shoes left the gravel and set again without scuffing. The place didn't want her to trip.

"This is where you've been meeting him," Ella said.

"Sometimes," Sia said. She did not say Thanatos. She didn't need to. The air knew. "And where I write rules that rooms can carry. We can test a sentence here and see if it holds before we put it on glass."

"Good," Ella said. "Then let's test now."

Sia nodded. "Take out the sticker."

Ella reached inside her hoodie. The service sticker was still warm. In the garden light it felt a degree heavier, like it believed in itself. She set it on the bench. The edges squared up as if they were relieved to lie flat. The faint blocks in the lower corner showed cleaner than they had under a desk lamp.

"Presenting party, route, authorizer," Ella said. "Blank, blank, blank."

Sia set two fingers on the sticker and didn't press. "We're going to ask the garden to show us how this paper walks," she said. "It can't show us people. It can show us paths."

"Do it," Ella said. She watched the stripe and tried to feel any tug in the air that would warn her if she was about to make a mistake.

Sia touched the marker stone to the bench so the sentence would have a place to sit. "Show us where this paper walks," she said. She kept the words simple, like a label.

The stripe tightened for a second, then relaxed. A thin line of light leaked out of the sticker, not bright enough to hurt, just enough to trace. It ran to the edge of the bench, hesitated at the stripe, and then skimmed along it like a finger dragging water from a puddle. The line did not cross the stripe. It followed it to the basin, then out, hugging the edge of the path until it reached a spot that had no door and no sign.

"That's the staff hall, right side," Ella said. She could feel the shape even if she couldn't see walls.

The line winked and took a new turn. It looped past a memory of the skylight room. Ella saw benches where people napped after lunch on field trips. She saw the soft chairs by the dioramas where parents surrendered to gravity for five minutes. She felt the volunteer desk where someone's head had been on folded arms at three yesterday.

"It's riding naps," Ella said.

Sia's mouth tightened. "Daydream drift."

The line traced those rests like stations on a train. It never used a door. It never touched a hinge. It treated quiet human moments like step-stones and landed at the staff threshold already carrying the feel of having been received. It was a cheat a smart clerk would try if they were not allowed to touch a lock.

"Third way," Ella said. Her stomach hated being right.

"Dream route," Sia said. She didn't look away from the line. "That's how the phone could say Accepted without anyone touching anything."

"If we don't block this, we'll keep getting slips that act like they're signed," Ella said. "A patient thief can move influence by naps. That is gross and smart."

Sia touched the bench with the marker stone again. "We can starve it."

"How?" Ella asked.

"Make the dream spit paper back to the desk," Sia said. "No paper crosses by sleep. Paper reads at desks only, in names, during posted hours."

"Try it," Ella said.

Sia set the stone down and said the sentence normal and

plain. "No paper crosses by sleep. Paper reads at desks only, in names, during posted hours."

The bench took it like a stamp on a clean form. The stripe did not flare. It just got honest in a way Ella could feel in her teeth. The thin light line from the sticker flickered. It ran its cheat route once more, then broke in two like a fiber-optic cable with a crack in the center. Half bled off to the front desk. Half died in a nothing corner where paper should never have been anyway.

The sticker cooled under Ella's fingers. The faint blocks at the bottom of it looked less proud. The garden had taken the route apart like a junk drawer and put the screws in a jar where they belonged.

"Good," Ella said. She still felt tight across the shoulders. "It's not enough."

"I know," Sia said. "This works here because the garden is mine. We need posted cards out there that echo this. Desk Only. Nap Space is for rest, not service. We'll name seats and benches as seats and benches. No paper service. We'll add it to the volunteer lanyards so no one lets a clipboard land on a lap."

"And Tobias adds catnap checks to his routes," Ella said. "He'll hate it for a week and then love it."

"He's already drawing the boxes in his head," Sia said.

The light at the edge of the stripe shifted. A shadow laid itself thin along the border and then withdrew as if it had only come to see if anyone would flinch. Ella knew that posture now. The Borrower was waiting out there like a clerk who thinks patience is a weapon.

"Can they walk people like this," Ella asked. "Or just paper."

"Paper," Sia said. "Thank God. People are choice. The Dream can carry pressure and echo. It cannot drag a person into a room they did not choose."

"Then we anchor people," Ella said. "We make benches proud to be benches. We write Desk Only where eyes land. We label nap spaces as rest, nothing else."

"We should also ask the House to let us know when a slip arrives warm," Sia said. "Mia can tag those under the red clip as dream-route. We can tell how fast this is happening."

Ella looked at the stripe and tried to put what she was feeling into words that would lead to the right action. "I still feel the Window coming," she said quietly. "This is going to help, but I think we're late."

Sia didn't argue. "We are," she said. "But late is better than never. We can still make the surface strong."

"Can we mark the board with a sentence from here," Ella asked. "Or do we have to write it upstairs."

"I can send the clause with you," Sia said. She set the marker stone to the bench again and wrote a clean two-liner on the air so Ella could read it. "Desk Only. Paper reads in names at desks during posted hours. Nap spaces host rest only. No service."

Ella memorized the rhythm the way she memorized school phone trees. She could hear Mia reading it in her tidy voice and the teens echoing it like a chorus. She could see the card on the glass. She let the image fix.

"Okay," Ella said. "One more thing. If someone is napping and a slip lands in their lap because the Dream route is ugly, does the card handle it."

"I think so," Sia said. She didn't pretend certainty. "We'll find out."

A soft presence shifted at the far edge of the stripe. Ella did not look up to meet it. She didn't need the lesson to turn into a visit. Sia's shoulders didn't rise. That told Ella she had made the same choice.

"We should go back," Ella said. "We have to post the cards and put lanyards in hands before lunch. If this starts during Window, I want the front desk to be the only door."

Sia picked up the marker stone. "Hold my wrist again. Same as before."

Ella did. The return was simple. The garden stepped away like a room that liked you enough to let you go without asking for another conversation. The chair found her spine. The reading room air had dust in it again. The lobby noise sounded like people, not pressure.

"Time?" Ella asked.

"Eleven forty," Mia said from the desk.

"Cutting it close," Ella said. She stood and her knees behaved. The sticker in her pocket had gone cool. "Let's do the cards."

They moved fast without telegraphing panic. Sia wrote two Desk Only cards in the neat hand the house understood. Mia printed small Nap Space cards with simple language.

> **This seat is for rest.**

> **No paper service here.**

Volunteers got lanyard versions and read them out loud until the words sounded like directions, not rules. Tobias took a sharpie and added two boxes to his route card labeled catnap checks. Marcus walked the benches and leaned each one an inch so no clipboards could lie flat. Eric taped a small arrow at eye height that pointed to the desk so even the laziest paper would find its way.

Ella taped the big Desk Only card at the front desk where you read hours and decide if you're going to argue. She taped the second at the staff threshold so the wall would hear it twice. She carried the third to the reading room desk and set it by the lamp that had shown the sticker its own bones.

The hum under the noise lifted another notch. The minute hand kissed noon. A family decided against the cafe and went outside for sandwiches. The volunteer chuckled at something a kid said about a shark jaw. Ella took a breath, then another. The day was ready enough. That would have to be fine.

Sia touched her elbow. "If this blows," she said, quiet, "you stay on the desk and keep the paper path clean. I'll take the hall with Marcus."

"I know," Ella said. "You call if the line feels wrong."

"I will," Sia said.

Truth bumped Ella's knee and trotted to the top of the staff stair, then sat with a look that said she understood posted hours better than most people. Ella scratched her ear and stepped back behind the counter.

Mia lifted the red folder, squared the stack, and clipped it with a small extra tap like she was sealing a jar. The new tags looked strange against the older ones. **custody attempt**. **presenting party**. **dream-route**. The air by the board tightened one more time.

The phone rang. Caller ID blank. Ella picked up.

"Ella," she said.

Silence. Then a small click that wasn't a hang-up, just a breath held too long on the other end of a line.

"We read in names at the desk," Ella said. "If you have business, use one."

Nothing. The line stayed open for two more seconds, then went dead.

Ella put the handset back and didn't look at Sia. She looked at the posted card and the people and the water cups she had set out. She took one and drank half.

"Here we go," she said, and this time it wasn't under her breath. "Desk only. Names only. No trades."

The Window answered by breathing in. The museum breathed out. The job got simple and hard at the same time. Write where paper goes. Keep every other path boring. Hold.

She set her palms on the counter so the house could feel her choice and waited for the first real test to step into view.

CHAPTER 16

The Line Lowers

TOBIAS

If you kept the small rules you could break the big ones.

George Orwell, 1984

TOBIAS LIKED THE STAFF stair because it told the truth underfoot. Old concrete, honest grit, paint scuffs where a thousand utility carts kissed the wall and said sorry. He took the first flight at a steady pace and listened for the hum he hated. The Window was pushing from above, soft now, building. He had felt worse, but this was in the same family.

Charles followed one tread behind, key ring tucked flat in his palm so it wouldn't jangle. He moved like a person who knew every squeak and chose not to wake them.

"Ella and Sia's cards are posted," Tobias said, keeping his voice low in case the stair liked quiet better. "Desk Only, Nap Space, the whole thing. Volunteers have lanyard versions. Mia reads them out loud like a pledge."

"I saw," Charles said. "Good language." He sounded like he had slept two hours on a couch and pretended it counted. "The dream-route explains a run of odd readings. I kept marking them as noise. That was my mistake."

"You corrected fast," Tobias said. He didn't mean it as a compliment. He meant it as a status check. Fast mattered more than sorry.

They hit the landing where he and Eric had found the name-first clipboard. The hook was empty now. Tobias glanced at the screw heads by habit. New set. Eric had swapped them after lunch and filed the old ones in a bag. The draft here stayed neutral. Good. He wrote 2:05 landing clean on his route card and tucked the pencil behind his ear.

Charles unlocked the steel door at the bottom of the next flight and shouldered it open with a careful push that didn't bang. The service corridor beyond was cooler. Light bled through slim fixtures that hummed like aquarium lids. Pipes ran along the ceiling with enough dust to look normal. Tobias counted corners out of habit. Four visible, fifth around a bend.

"Parts of what we're about to see were kept quiet," Charles said as they walked. "Not because I wanted to lie. Because I didn't want the hotel to learn fear of itself."

"Say it plain," Tobias said.

"There are places where the House stores pressure," Charles said. "And places where it holds what tries to harm guests. The public mission comes first. Refuge. Hospitality. If I gave every volunteer a tour of locks and cells, this place would start to wear a uniform in their minds. I wanted them to wear aprons."

"That's fair," Tobias said. He didn't need an apology when he could get a reason. "But today you show me everything you can, because secrets waste time."

"Agreed," Charles said.

They passed a vent seam that had been resealed last week. Tobias bent without asking and ran a knuckle near the edge. His skin found a tacky patch the rag had missed. He lifted his hand to his nose. Sulfur, thin, like a match scraped once and blown out before it caught. He wiped his knuckle on a cloth square he kept in his pocket and wrote 2:08 vent seam sulfur faint on the card.

Charles glanced back. "You smell it too."

"Barely," Tobias said. "There and gone. Like someone walked through cooking eggs and regretted it."

"Flux is ahead," Charles said. "Don't trust your eyes completely. It's not trying to fool you. It adjusts while you look."

Tobias had learned to walk into new rooms like a lifeguard walks into a pool. No rush. Eyes first, then feet. The corridor opened into a wider hall with walls that looked like stone at a glance and like flexible paneling if you let yourself stare. The floor seams were straight, then not, then straight again, as if the place breathed and settled between breaths. A smell of wet dust and ozone sat under everything else, not unpleasant, like the scent that hangs after a summer storm.

"The Flux," Charles said, and it sounded like a name you speak in a library so you don't wake the stacks.

"Define it," Tobias said.

"Circulatory system," Charles said. "The House pulls magic that gathers in odd spots and moves it back through the structure. Old wards stay fed. New posts settle. Stress drops before it cracks plaster. It recycles what arrives so the public floors stay stable."

"Does it see intent," Tobias asked.

"No," Charles said. "It feels load, not motive. It's a set of good habits with no opinions."

The wall to their left rippled a finger's width, then stopped. Not a wave. More like the skin of a drum that had been tapped very lightly. A screw head gleamed new in one panel. Tobias touched it with the back of a finger and found a hint of warmth that didn't match the metal around it. He wrote 2:11 warm rivet left panel third seam on the card.

"You expected this to strain today," Tobias said.

"I expected it to strain next week," Charles said. "Today is a few days early. I think Ella and Sia kicked the right hornet nest with names. Good work often feels like trouble before it feels like relief."

A faint arc of scuffed dust curved along the floor ten feet ahead. Not a footprint. More like a skid where something had leaned and caught itself before falling. Tobias crouched and held his hand over it. No heat, no draft. Just the suggestion of weight in the wrong place.

"Someone brushed the wall," he said.

"Something," Charles said. "Dreamers walk without leaving rude marks. Thieves smudge."

They moved on. The Flux bent left, then corrected. Tobias watched the corners like they might talk. The ceiling lowered by an inch in one stretch and then gave it back by the next fixture. He kept count of lights because getting turned around by brightness is a real thing in basements. Every third fixture flickered in a pattern that felt intentional and probably wasn't. Old buildings make their own music. You learn the song and trust it until it changes.

"Blue, Red, White built this," Charles said as if he'd decided there wasn't a better time for history. "It was a joint project when the first rumors started about things that would not leave people alone. White gave us ritual clean lines and the habit of asking. Red built vessels that hold pressure so people don't. Blue learned the building and promised to only turn the lock if the world needed it."

"Who holds the keys now," Tobias asked.

"Blue," Charles said. "By agreement. Not by rank. I keep them because someone has to, and because I have fewer reasons than most to use them."

Tobias let that sit. He didn't press on rank. Titles didn't help if a person bled the same when a bolt cut skin. He would ask what he needed when he needed it.

The hall narrowed into a turn with a door that looked older than the walls around it. The steel had a skin of paint that had been refreshed a dozen times and still showed the original color at the edge where hands had rubbed it. Charles took a key from the tight ring and paused like a person giving a class one last chance to decide if they wanted to come along.

"Past this, the House stops being helpful on purpose," he said. "It becomes precise. That can read as cold if you're not ready."

"Open it," Tobias said.

Charles turned the key. The lock accepted the turn like it was doing what it wanted. The door pushed inward on heavy hinges that didn't squeal. The air beyond carried no dust and no scent. Tobias stepped in and felt his shoulders adjust to a room that hated drift. Lines held. Corners were corners, not suggestions. The floor didn't flex. The seams didn't breathe. It felt like a hand had pressed the place flat.

"Prison level," Charles said. He didn't raise his voice. He didn't need to. The room caught sound and put it down without amplification. "Antechamber first."

They walked a short hall into a gallery with a viewing rail that looked more like a catwalk in a power plant than anything in a museum. Behind tempered glass and an armature of thin, pale lines that made a lattice, a dark shape waited in a cube that wasn't a room so much as a space that had been told exactly how to behave. The first demon. The one that had tried the basement weeks ago. It looked smaller than memory made it, as things often do when they are not moving. A panel on the wall beside the glass held a grid of toggles and small lights with labels that did not use titles. West stair. North drain. Annex seam. Staff hall hinge. Language that said place, not power.

"Old work," Charles said. "Repaired often. Argues with you never."

"Rider," Tobias said, nodding to the next cube down the gallery. The human inside sat still with eyes open and no one home behind them. A luminous thread ran from his temple to a cobweb of lines in the far corner of the cube where pressure collected like fog. Not hurt. Held. His chest rose and fell. His fingers twitched when the light flickered in the hall.

"Separate lattices for separate problems," Charles said. "The rider wakes sometimes. He eats and drinks when he remembers. We remind him politely."

Tobias read the labels again. He liked how much of this was built to be understood by people who didn't love glamour. A small plate under the toggle grid read Manual Steward Board in letters that had been engraved by someone who liked straightness. No names. No signatures. Just the thing it was and the job it did.

"Why keep this off the tour," Tobias asked. He knew. He wanted to hear it from the person who chose.

"Because places learn from how we talk about them," Charles said. "If every volunteer sees locks and cells when they think hotel, the House will start optimizing for capture instead of hospitality. We cannot afford that. We hold cages only to keep guests safe, not to make ourselves feel powerful."

"Fair," Tobias said. He stepped to the rail and looked down the corridor that led deeper. His eyes tried to slide, then settled. A hairline vibration walked along the base of the gallery wall at ankle height, the way a train lets you know it will arrive soon even before the rails hum. He crouched and set two fingers close to the seam without touching it. The buzz was there, then gone.

"Something's walking a wire," he said.

"I felt it this morning and dismissed it," Charles said. "I hate admitting that."

"Save the hating for later," Tobias said. "We need your hands steady."

Charles nodded and moved to the toggle grid. "If anything moves wrong, I can arm a perimeter. The House will do the rest if the steward is free to ask."

"And if the steward is not," Tobias said.

"The system locks to prevent a bad order," Charles said. "It won't let someone inside a cell tell it to turn into a knife."

Tobias made a note he didn't like. He didn't say it.

They walked the length of the rail together. The lights beside the toggles sat boring and green. No alarms sang. The demon in the first cube raised its head like a dog catching a scent it couldn't place, then settled back as if listening to a song in another room. The rider turned his face toward the ceiling and blinked twice. Somewhere deeper, a thin sound scraped that could have been metal cooling or could have been patience running out.

"Move fast when we need to," Tobias said.

"I intend to," Charles said.

They stood at the last view window when the seam along the opposite wall lifted like bad wallpaper catching a gust. It didn't rip. It eased away from the surface in a clean line you could slide a hand into. Something did. Fingers pressed from the wrong side, pressed again, and then a shape the color of wet brick stepped from a seam that had no depth to be hiding it. Another followed behind, and another. Eyes that understood rooms in terms of exits and leverage skated right over the ward glass. Their mouths didn't open. They didn't posture. They scanned.

Tobias didn't think. He counted. Three in the open. Two shadows behind, maybe. The tall one on the right carried weight in its shoulders and had one knee that held a fraction shy of true. Weak side. The middle one's hands twitched with a rhythm he'd seen on people who liked knives. The left one was watching Charles, not him.

"We learned too late about the dreaming," Charles said, and it came out like a date on a plaque. No self pity. A fact.

The tall one pivoted and snapped a chain of shadow across the rail that cracked against the metal with a sound like a snapped belt. The middle one flicked a bone shard into the air that spun like a tiny fan and went for the toggle box. Tobias stepped in front of it and threw his forearm up. The shard clanged off the grating and skittered under the rail.

"Back," Tobias said, already moving. He put his shoulder into the tall one's chest, not to stay and wrestle, but to steal half a step of space. He dipped and drove a heel into the knee that had lied to him. It buckled. The shadow chain swung again and ate air. The left one lunged for Charles with a broad grab that said it liked putting people where it wanted them.

Tobias shoved Charles sideways. The chain cracked the rail where Charles's head had been a second before. The left one recovered quicker than Tobias liked and used the rail as a pivot to vault up. Tobias got an elbow into its ribs on the way down and followed with a heel to the temple that bounced it off a post and left it blinking in a way that meant he had time to do something else before it remembered its job.

"Board," Charles said, reaching for the toggles.

The tall one didn't bother with Tobias this time. It reached past him with a long arm, grabbed the front of Charles's coat, lifted with mechanical ease, and slung him through the open door of an empty cell like a parent throwing a bag into a closet. Charles hit the floor, rolled twice, and came up on a knee, already reaching for the door. The outside seal glowed and settled like a lid meeting a jar.

"Don't," Tobias snapped at the tall one and hit it with a bar he yanked from a latch, jamming the metal between its ankle bones and twisting. It snarled and went down on three points. Tobias turned to the board. Small red lights, not alarms, just indicators that reminded you the world had taken a vote. One line read Steward access internal. Another line under it read

Global arming locked.

Charles put his palm to the glass. His face wasn't panicked. He looked like a man stuck behind a bus window trying to tell you your stop was next. "Go," he said, calm and clear through the layered wall. "Rally them. I cannot arm the House from in here."

"You sure," Tobias said, already backing, already picking the angle that would keep two bodies in front of him and one behind where the rail kinked.

"Yes," Charles said. "I can hold this row. You need the others. The Hotel will not move for me until I am outside."

The middle demon came in with the knife hands. Tobias let it get close enough to believe in itself, then stepped past its lead foot, took the wrist, and introduced its forehead to the edge of the hatch in a rhythm that would live in his bones tomorrow. It went loose for three seconds. He used them like a gift, jammed the latch bar into the tall one's ribs to keep it honest, then hopped the low sweep that came from the left, plant foot on rail, push off light, land clean.

He didn't plan to win the room. He planned to leave in one piece with enough skin to call a war. He gave the tall one one more shot to the head for mourning and took the long side of the corridor. The seam behind the new arrivals hiccuped like a cat about to spit something ugly out of its throat. He wasn't going to wait to see what.

"Library," he said into the radio he had already lifted to his mouth. He kept his eyes up while he ran. "Now. Our fight is below."

The Flux greeted him with lines that had brightened thin as copper wire warming. Small threads ran along seams ahead like routes on a subway map that someone had highlighted with a dull pen. Not dramatic. A warning. He wrote 2:19 seams lighting thin on the route card without looking, by feel, word shapes he had traced a thousand times in other rooms. He didn't need perfect penmanship to remember.

The door to the corridor opened without catching. The service hall beyond accepted him like a lane that wanted feet on it. He cleared the stair, took two at a time, felt the building lean toward him like a coach telling a runner where the bend would be. The hum from upstairs had shifted. Not louder. Closer.

He didn't look back. Charles had chosen his job. Tobias had chosen his. He hit the landing, took the next flight, and filed the last image of the ward rail at the front of his mind so he wouldn't forget the way the lights had looked when the world decided to make him earn his lunch. Then he put it away so his hands could do the work in front of him.

THE GALLERY HAD THE kind of stillness that makes you straighten your back without thinking. Corners squared up. Lines stayed put. No shimmer, no drift. The Flux's quiet pulse ended at the threshold like a tide that refused to cross a chalk line.

Tobias let his eyes map the room before his feet did. Catwalk, waist-high rail, tempered panes set in steel. Beyond each pane, a cube defined by hair-thin filaments that read like the skeleton of a room. Labels sat on the nearest wall in neat rows, engraving deep enough to gather dust and still read clean. No names of people. All places.

Charles didn't perform this part. He walked to the nearest pane and stopped like a person checking on a patient who'd stabilized overnight.

Inside the first cube, the demon from weeks ago sat in a crouch, elbows on knees, head tipped as if listening to far water. Without motion, it looked almost human until you let your gaze rest on its skin. The color never landed. It was brick. Then bruise. Then frost-bite red with a gray underwash that wanted to be mold. The lattice cut the cube into invisible planes that the eye didn't like but the body trusted anyway.

"Old work," Charles said. "Repaired often. It has opinions about load but not about people."

Tobias leaned just enough to catch the light on the filament. There were four strands where his eye first guessed one. Each strand jittered less than a hair in the AC's breath. His skin believed the cube more than his head did, which was as it should be.

"How's it bound," he asked.

"Place rules," Charles said. "The cube's edges are defined as the only path. Inside it, the room does not host anything without a name. That makes the occupant a constant, not a guest. Constants don't leave without an external action."

"External meaning you," Tobias said.

"Or someone with the board in front of them and the right pattern," Charles said. He glanced at the panel beside the pane. A grid of toggles and tiny lights waited like an older airplane cockpit; simple, labeled, suspiciously boring. Each toggle had a little metal guard to keep casual hands from setting things on fire.

The labels were comfortingly plain:

ANNEX SEAM
STAFF STAIR HINGE
NORTH DRAIN
WEST STAIR
SKYLIGHT BENCH
GALLERY DOOR

Tobias liked the honesty. "Manual Steward Board," he read off the plate in the corner. "Show me what 'arm the House' looks like."

Charles set two fingers on the bottom row and didn't lift a guard. "I won't throw these without cause," he said. "But if we needed full posture, you'd lift by path, not all at once. The House doesn't love sudden change. Rotations are safer. And the steward has to be outside any cell or the system refuses commands."

"Safety for bad days," Tobias said. "I can live with that."

They passed the first cube. The demon's eyes tracked the seam of the floor rather than the men just outside the pane. It was looking for paths even with nothing to step on.

Two panes down, the rider sat with his head tilted back and his mouth a little open like a person who had fallen asleep in a waiting room. The lattice in this cube gathered in one upper corner where a knot of light hung like a spider egg. A filament ran from the knot to the rider's temple, but the line didn't touch skin. It hovered a breath away, vibrating so slowly that the space between the man and the pattern seemed to be doing the work.

"He's got a pulse schedule," Charles said quietly. "When the knot relaxes, he eats. Sometimes he remembers more than his name. We keep that chair soft and the water cold. The knot gets testy if we act like jailers." He nudged a carton on a little shelf beside the pane. "We keep fresh socks for him. Containment that allows dignity works better. That's not a moral lecture. It's a practical note."

"Dignity is cheaper than broken people," Tobias said. "I don't need convincing."

They walked to the middle of the gallery where a metal table held repair tools laid out in a row that made sense even to someone who didn't know the song yet. Spool of filament, brass picks, a magnifier lamp with a goose neck, three clean cloths folded small, a little tin of white paste that smelled like clean chalk and rain.

"History lesson," Tobias said. "Plain."

Charles didn't sigh. "Blue, Red, and White built this together when the circles were still arguing in public about their differences," he said. "White wrote the habits that let a place keep its word. Red designed vessels that take stress so people don't. Blue learned the building until it trusted us with its bones. The agreement was that the Hotel's first job would be hospitality. A real sanctuary. The prison was conditional. If the world pushed hard, the locks would light. If not, they would sleep behind walls that didn't need attention."

"Who signs off on waking them," Tobias asked.

"No one signs," Charles said. "The House has a threshold sense. If the field violations cross a posted line, the board will accept a shift. If they don't, you can flip till your wrist breaks and nothing will change." He moved his hand over the toggles without touching them, the way a person runs their palm over a stove to check if it's still hot. "Blue holds the keys because someone has to. The agreement wasn't rank. It was logistics. Red builds. White names. Blue stewards."

"Why keep the staff out of this," Tobias said. He didn't charge the question. He let the floor hold it.

"I didn't want a tour of cells to be the story the docents told each other," Charles said. "This place stays safe when it acts like a museum that remembers people before monsters. If the volunteers carry a picture of locks in their pockets, they'll start closing doors that don't need closing. Fear finds work. I wanted the House to choose welcome first."

"You pulled it off," Tobias said. It wasn't flattery. The upstairs felt like a place you bring a class and go home smiling. "But we need the manual now."

"You're getting it," Charles said. "I'm not too proud to adjust when the facts change."

On the far wall, the seam at ankle height let a thread of vibration walk along it, then go still. It was subtle enough to miss if your teeth weren't trained for it. Tobias's were. He went down on a knee and held his hand just above the joint where wall met floor. The buzz tapped his palm once, twice, then quit.

"Wire is live," he said. "Not power. Attention."

Charles knelt beside him, put two fingers near the same spot, and frowned. "I logged that earlier and told myself it was a breaker cycling. I should have checked again."

"You're checking now," Tobias said. He stood, eyes sweeping the ceiling, the corners, the faint lip where glass met steel. The air hadn't changed temperature. It had changed posture. The room was waiting for something to be true.

"Can the Flux leak in here," Tobias asked.

"No," Charles said. "By design. If the Flux crosses the boundary, the lattice loses authority. This level stays precise."

"Good," Tobias said. He looked across the panes and tried to see them as pathways rather than cells. If a thief wanted to walk through without touching a door, where would they pull? He didn't like the answers he found.

"Manual board again," he said, and they went.

Charles tapped the guard over **ANNEX SEAM** but didn't lift it. "There are three ways to posture," he said. "Slow rotation by wing, rapid rotation through three points, or blunt lock by area. The House hates the last one. It will stress the Flux and make the public floors brittle."

"Slow rotation then," Tobias said. "If we have to." He scanned the little lights. All green. No flashing. The panel was a polite liar when it wanted to be.

"Ella and Sia finding the dream route explains this morning's numbers," Charles said. "Pulses that didn't map to doors. I turned off two sensors because I thought they'd gone noisy. That was arrogance or exhaustion. Both, probably."

"You'll fix it after we live through today," Tobias said. He meant it. The man didn't need guilt right now. He needed a job.

They took the last stretch of rail. Tobias kept his hands light on the metal so he could feel the difference before he saw it. The rider's eyes tracked a light they couldn't see. The first demon's head lifted again and held there like a dog hearing a car it knows a block away.

"Do these things learn from watching us," Tobias asked.

"They learn patterns," Charles said. "Not nuance. They aren't clever. They are patient. Patience mimics cleverness if you don't look closely."

Tobias's mouth twitched. "Preach."

Something ticked in the pane frame to his right, so small it could have been a wire settling. The tick repeated on the left. A breath later, the long seam along the opposite wall lifted the way wallpaper lifts when steam finds a bad edge. It wasn't dramatic. It was efficient. The line opened exactly enough for a hand, then an arm, then a shoulder.

"Time," Tobias said, already shifting his weight toward the rail's corner posts.

"Time," Charles said. His hand hovered over the guards without flipping a single one. He was waiting for a reason. The House was built to punish panic.

Before anything stepped through, Tobias got one more glance at the board and the boring green lights and memorized them. If they turned red, he wanted the picture of before. Then the first shape came out of the seam like a worker stepping off a bus and checking where the exits were.

Its attention skated past the panes. It looked for rails, gaps, lever points. No ceremony. No growl. The second shape followed, smaller, hands twitching. The third put its palm on the wall and pushed like it was checking what it could steal. The air tightened across the catwalk like a room holding its breath.

"Do you want posture," Tobias asked, because even now he asked for consent when the decision belonged to the person holding the systems.

"Give me cause," Charles said, eyes on **GALLERY DOOR** and **WEST STAIR**. "One wrong move and I'll take the hit the House hates."

Tobias nodded, slid his foot to change his line, and breathed once through his nose to slow his pulse. The seam flexed wider behind the shapes. The rider blinked three times in a pattern that wasn't random. The first demon in its cube never moved, but the room around it felt like it was leaning toward the seam.

"Cause will show up," Tobias said.

He didn't have to wait long.

THE SEAM LIFTED IN a clean line like someone had sliced wallpaper and pulled just enough to test the edge. A hand came through first. Not claws. Fingers, long and wrong, knuckles set too far apart. Then a shoulder. The skin kept changing shades the way oil does on water. Two more bodies pressed close behind the first, patient and practiced.

"Eyes on the rail," Tobias said, not loud. He shifted to put the corner post at his back and the manual board in his sightline.

"I have it," Charles said. His hands hovered over the guards without flipping any. He was waiting for a reason. The House punished panic.

The lead demon stepped into full view and angled toward the rail. It didn't roar. It didn't reach. It measured the room like it had studied a floor plan. The second one kept its hands at stomach height, fingers twitching as if it held a knife it wanted to throw. The third touched the wall with the curiosity of a thief who respects good locks.

"Cause," Tobias said, half to himself.

The second one flicked something small and fast at the toggle box. Tobias saw the spin in its wrist and moved before his head finished naming it. He brought his forearm up. The bone shard pinged off metal and skittered under the guard rail. The sound drew the first demon's eyes for a half second. That was enough for Tobias to step in and steal space.

"Back up," he told Charles. He didn't take his eyes off the bodies in front of him. "If they want the board, they get me first."

The lead demon snapped a strip of shadow toward the rail. It hit with a belt crack that made Tobias's teeth buzz. He slid inside the next swing, put his shoulder into the demon's sternum, and drove through. He didn't try to stand and trade. He wanted imbalance. He wanted the knee he had clocked earlier. He found it with his heel and gave it a reason to remember him. The joint bent and the swing went wild.

The third demon reached for Charles. It didn't lunge. It went for a grab at the coat like a person hauling a bag into a car. Tobias crossed the gap and caught ribs with the point of his elbow. The body folded enough to make room for a heel to the temple. It hit the hatch frame and dropped. Not out. Out of the way.

"Railing," Charles warned.

The shadow strip came again, low this time. Tobias hopped it and felt air bite his ankles. He had no interest in taking that hit more than once. He ducked under the rail, slid, and popped up into the first demon's space before it found its rhythm again. He gave it a quick two-beat. Palm to the chin to snap the head back. Bar across the ear when it started to turn away. It reeled, but it didn't quit.

The knife-hands demon went for the toggle box again. Tobias drove his boot into the guard face and barked his shin for his trouble. Pain made the moment honest. The tiny fan of bone whirred past his hip and nicked the rubber on the rail.

"Think," Tobias told himself. He stepped left so the corner post took the next obvious angle away from the board and forced the demons to change their plan or eat steel.

Charles lifted a guard halfway on **GALLERY DOOR**, then stopped. The House groaned in a low way, the way old buildings tell you they heard you.

"Not yet," he said, eyes flicking to the rider's cube and back. "If I lock too fast, the Flux will buck and the public floors will go sharp."

"I get it," Tobias said.

The lead demon reached past Tobias and grabbed Charles by the coat. It lifted him like weight didn't matter and slung him through the open door of an empty cell. The motion was clean enough to look practiced. Charles hit the floor and rolled like someone who had practiced that too. He came up on a knee at the doorway and put his hand to the frame. The outside seal lit and set with a soft sound like a jar lid being closed by a polite machine.

"Stop," Tobias said to the wrong thing. He jammed the latch bar between the tall one's ankles and twisted until it went down. He turned to the board to throw anything he could throw and saw small red indicators lit where he didn't want them. Not alarms. States. Steward access internal. Global arming locked.

Charles pressed his palm flat to the glass. His voice came through thin but clear. "Go. Rally them. I can't arm the House from in here."

"Can you hold this floor," Tobias asked. He took two steps toward the cell, then stopped himself. He could put his body in the doorway and die in a corridor. Or he could bring back the people who turn bad days into morgues that never open.

"I can hold it," Charles said. "This wing doesn't lose to five ugly things. It loses to the wrong person pressing the wrong lever. I won't be that person. Go."

The knife-hands demon came at him fast. Tobias let it commit, slid past its front foot, and took the wrist with a grip that made the bones line up whether they wanted to or not. He bounced its forehead off the edge of the hatch frame with a quick rhythm that would make him ache tomorrow. It loosened. He shoved it into the tall one to tangle their legs and bought two breaths.

The first demon snapped the shadow strip at knee height. Tobias jumped it and planted a foot on the rail to clear the sweep. He came down on the other side of the corner post and forced the fight to reset around a different angle. He was done trading. He was here to leave.

He backed toward the corridor, eyes on hands, on hips, on knees. He gave the tall one one more shot to the ear for the road, then turned his shoulder and ran the second his line was clear.

The seam behind the demons hiccupped. Another hand tested it like a blind man feeling a curb. He didn't look back to count. He had enough data to decide.

"Library," he said into the radio. His voice stayed even because people listen better when you make it easy. "Now. Our fight is below. Charles is locked. We need the team."

"Copy," Mia's voice came back at once. "Moving."

"On me," Eric said. "Grabbing the kit."

"Marcus with you," Marcus said. He didn't waste words.

Sia's voice cut across the channel. "On route. Posting door cards. Truth with me."

Ella didn't hit the button. He pictured her picking up the sword and letting it sit in her hand like a thing she had always owned. He didn't need her voice to know she had moved.

The corridor door accepted his weight and gave without catching. The service hall smelled like old paint and fresh dust. He took two steps and stopped. The Flux had changed. It wasn't loud. It wasn't dramatic. Thin lines along the seams glowed like someone had threaded warm copper under the edges of panels. He could see routes the way a mechanic sees wiring diagrams when he closes his eyes. They ran ahead like a map lit by a dull pen.

He wrote 2:19 seams warm on his route card without looking. The shapes his hand made were automatic. He didn't need pretty. He needed memory.

The stair met him where he expected it to be. He took it two at a time, twice, then once because his knee told the truth. He counted the landing like a friend. Behind him, a dull clatter said the tall one had finally found the rail again. Let it. The door at the top of the stair would have a body in it by the time he reached it. That body would have a plan because they wrote plans on glass and said them out loud until they stuck.

He hit the last flight and felt the building tilt toward him in that way houses do when they like you and want you to make it to the kitchen. He came out into the service hall, cut right, and ran the last length with his palm sliding along the paint to stay honest in case the light decided to be cute.

The staff door opened into the lobby. The boards were full and square. The volunteers had their lanyard cards in their hands. Sia stood at the threshold with the marker stone in her palm. Mia held the red folder like a life vest. Eric had a coil of tape on his wrist. Marcus was already moving. Ella lifted her chin at him and he tossed the sword across the short distance because muscle memory is faster than words.

"Below," he said. He didn't waste the rest. "Charles is locked. The House won't arm for him."

Ella caught the sword and nodded. Her mouth flattened into a line that meant work, not speech. Sia tapped the frame once. The air cooled. Mia slid a card into the clip and added a tag that said present in a neat hand that made Tobias smile despite the taste of metal in his mouth.

"Move," Tobias said. "We hold the stairs and take the fight to the cells. Keep people asleep, not hurt. Keep paper on the desk. We fix the House or we live here forever."

Truth trotted past him and took the first step like a dog who had already memorized the route two flights down. The team fell in without argument. They weren't a squad. They were a crew that had learned to be boring together until it was time not to be.

Tobias hit the stair again and felt his heart settle into a rhythm he recognized from nights when rooms tried to become worse than they were. Not a rush. A job. He held the rail and took the steps clean. The seam lines below pulsed once like a taunt.

"Keep them off the board," he said over his shoulder. "And keep my corners honest."

"Always," Sia said.

"Always," Ella echoed.

Mia tapped the red folder with two fingers and tucked it under her arm like a shield. Eric killed a glare on the glass with the back of his hand. Marcus rolled his shoulders and grinned without humor. Truth made a small sound in her throat that meant ready.

They went down into the part of the Hotel that wanted promises kept.

CHAPTER 17

Cold Hands

MIA

The villains were always ugly in books and movies. Necessarily so, it seemed. Because if they were attractive—if their looks matched their charm and their cunning—they wouldn't only be dangerous.

They would be *irresistible*.

Nenia Campbell, Horrorscape

MIA FELT IT FIRST in her teeth. Not a sharp ache, more like a low buzz that didn't belong to her. The North exhibit's floor had a gentle sway that didn't match the building, like the museum had taken one slow breath and forgotten to let it out. The air tasted used, sleepover stale, the way a hallway does when everyone laughed too much and nobody cracked a window.

A dad stood at the bison glass with a stroller parked sideways, one foot jammed against a wheel like he meant to anchor it and then forgot what feet are for. He wasn't looking at the diorama. He was looking through it, past painted grass and faux sky to nowhere. A teenage girl at the map rack tracked a single dot like it might run off if she blinked. At the volunteer stand, Tommy answered two different questions with the same sentence in the same voice, then stared at the brochure like it had personally disappointed him.

Possession had a rhythm. Mia knew it by now. The full thing came like a wrong song that wanted to wear your body. This wasn't that. This was a thin copy. Rides, not sits. Veil over face, not a hand on the back of your neck.

She set her palm on the rail so the room would clock her as a person with a job, not noise. "Hey," she said to the dad, easy and present. "You with me?"

His eyes twitched like rain on a windshield and kept sliding. The toddler in the stroller puffed that pre-cry breath that warns everyone nearby. Cheeks blew out, eyebrows made the little tent they make, then the kid made a sound like a kazoo trying to learn opera. The dad didn't flinch.

Mia took a breath for both of them and let her voice carry the shape of it. She sang one low note at speaking volume. No words. Just tone. The note asked the air to cool jittery nerves and asked lungs to copy a reasonable pace. Old trick. Kitchen table medicine. Her mother had used it for stomach bugs and three a.m. terrors when Mia was small and thought closets had politics.

The dad blinked and folded onto the bench like someone had unplugged a cord behind his ear. The toddler let out a sigh so heavy it sounded professional, then collapsed sideways in the stroller and went to war with gravity in his sleep. Bless that gene.

The map girl didn't soften. Her lips moved in a not-language. Next to her, a couple in matching museum pins turned their heads at the exact same time as if invisible birds had flown across the ceiling and only they were invited to notice. That synchronized turn made Mia's skin crawl. Thin rides liked to imitate chorus lines.

She widened the note into two and pulled them apart a hair. The interval dragged breath down to an actual human speed if you let it. One of the pin pair swayed, sat without arguing, and blinked at her like someone who had just remembered what knees are for. The other set both palms flat on the rack like the plastic was a sacred text. Their knuckles went white. Great. Hands were forgetting they had blood.

"Water," Mia said to Tommy without breaking the hum. "Three cups, please. Slow walk."

He blinked like a camera shutter and became a person again. "Yes," he said, then corrected himself mid-step. "Yeah. I got it." His hands shook on the first cup, steadied on the second.

The tiles under Mia's shoes went cool. Sia came up from the

lobby, marker stone in one hand, the other already lifted in a calm ask that never failed to make rooms remember their jobs.

"What are you getting," Sia said. Her voice stayed conversational. She did that on purpose so rooms didn't feel scolded.

"Rides," Mia said. "Veil-thin. Breaths wrong. They're copying each other."

Sia tapped the floor with her heel and spoke to the strip like she was posting hours. "This strip hosts rest. No harm and no command."

Frost feathered at the edges. Not dramatic. Just a shade brighter, like the tiles remembered winter. The map-rack pair moved together, slowed as if they had stepped into a shallow pool, and sat on the bench without dropping. Hands opened. The plastic lost its worth. Their thumbs looked like thumbs again, not clamps.

"Good," Mia said, easing the tone toward lungs. She looked at the teen. "In on four," she said, gentle. "Out on six."

The girl copied without meaning to because bodies are cooperative when you let them be. On the second cycle her shoulders gave up their audition for coat hanger and sagged the way shoulders are supposed to sag on a weekday. She blinked, saw the room, and covered her mouth like embarrassment could hide in a hand. Mia gave her a nod that said you're fine, you did nothing wrong, you survived a paragraph. The girl didn't cry, but it was a close thing.

A teacher shepherding a knot of fourth graders did that double clap teachers do. "Eyes on the mastodon," she said, too cheerfully. The kids looked at Mia instead because the human voice with the hum under it was more interesting than bones. Mia smiled and pointed at fossils so the teacher wouldn't think she was losing her grip on her small kingdom.

At the volunteer stand, Tommy returned with cups and the face of a person trying not to drop anything while his heart argued about tempo. "Do I need to call security," he whispered like the word might summon a clipboard demon.

"You're doing great," Mia said, taking two cups. "Tell folks there's an extra bench if they feel floaty. Use that word."

"Floaty," he said, testing it for weight. "Okay. Floaty bench. Got it." He went to be useful, which he liked.

Sia ran her fingertips along the map bench as if checking for splinters and left a second card taped at knee height where tired people would read it with their shins. **Nap space hosts rest. No paper service.** The font was plain, the tape neat. It looked like a sign and not a threat and that was the point.

Somewhere west, a cough sounded like a drain trying to be a throat. The hair along Mia's neck prickled. She glanced at Sia.

"Staff wing," she said.

"With you," Sia said.

They crossed the lobby edge together. Mia kept the tone low, just enough to make the hall feel shaded. Sia slid pocket cards onto door frames as they went. **This room rests people. No paper service.** Plain language. Places loved plain. When you spoke like a manual, doors behaved. When you spoke like a poem, doors got creative. Kaelan had taught them that and then apologized for liking poems.

A guy in a ball cap stood half-in, half-out of an office door with a form upside down. He looked at the corner of the ceiling like it had emailed him. "Bathroom's that way," Mia said, pointing with the calm of someone who knows where the sinks are. He didn't move. Sia touched the jamb with two fingers.

"This door hosts names," Sia said, warm and clear. "No riding."

The guy blinked like someone slapped sleep out of him, laughed at himself without shame, and went to find a sink. Small wins counted and they counted early.

They passed the reading room mouth. The green lamps made quiet pools on wood. Eric's cones sat stacked by the door like orange tulips waiting for a parade. The smell changed as they moved deeper. Dust and paper gave way to that pre-storm ozone that meant the building was shuffling weight around under the floors. The hum climbed half a step, like a machine turning on in a room you couldn't see yet. Mia placed her palm on the wall to feel if it was lying. It felt like paint and good intentions. That almost made it worse.

The Hotel should have sloughed thin rides at the doors like jackets at the coat check. It wasn't. The House wasn't expelling. That meant a switch was off or a rule was stuck or a steward was out of reach. Mia didn't say any of that out loud. Saying problems like that made rooms heavier. She filed the fact and kept working.

At the corridor corner, a little boy sat cross-legged with his backpack on, staring at a vending machine through the glass like it owed him rent. His hands were open on his knees and his mouth had the soft slack of a catnap sitting up. No ride there. Just too much morning for a nine-year-old.

"Want a map," Mia asked him, too cheerful on purpose.

He nodded so hard his hair separated into parties. She handed him one and pointed at a path that led safely to the big fish tank with the fake river. "Find that," she said. "Blue line all the way. It's a mission."

His eyes focused. He stood. He had a mission now. Off he went with the intensity of a person who just got hired by a spy agency.

"Good choice," Sia murmured.

"I contain multitudes," Mia said, then snorted at herself because that was a Kaelan sentence and she shouldn't borrow it.

They hit the south bend. The lights were normal. That made the warm-headache feeling worse. Mia let the tone fall into floorboards, something a foot could keep even if a brain forgot. Sia pasted a card at eye level, then a twin at knee height for people who didn't like looking up.

"Nap spaces next," Sia said. "If anyone tries to land paper there, I want the wood to be proud of being a bench."

"Copy," Mia said. She believed in proud benches. Proud benches saved lives.

Tommy's voice drifted from behind them, practicing. "If you feel floaty, there's a bench right here." He'd added a little hand flourish that made the bench seem like a game show prize.

Visitors smiled and sat and then realized sitting had been the right move. Good job, Tommy.

They moved past the little education alcove where an intern had lined up magnifying glasses like a science party. Two teenagers were filming each other with whisper-shouts about dinosaurs. Their whisper-shouts were normal. Mia cataloged normal on purpose so her head didn't turn every sound into a threat.

Truth padded into view with her ears tipped forward, nose barely off the floor, tail level in that medium-ready line that meant a job had arrived and it was her favorite. She sniffed the baseboard, sneezed like it was rude, then gave Mia a look that translated to found it and I'm mad at it. Her paws made silent decisions toward the stacks.

"Stacks," Mia said.

"Stacks," Sia echoed.

Eric swung around the corner from the other side as if summoned. He had a roll of tape looped on his wrist and a cone tucked under his arm like it was a fancy briefcase. He kneeled to lay a strip on the tile that turned the wrong hallway into staff only without saying staff only. People read tape faster than complicated signs. The calm on his face had weight. Rooms bought it.

"Noise in there," he said, chin pointing toward shelves. "Cough that doesn't belong to lungs."

"Thanks," Sia said, and pressed a pocket card into his palm to plant two doors down. "Post nap space copies too."

"On it," he said, and already was.

The sour undernote got louder. Not stink. Not rot. Just that drywall breath buildings get when they feel sorry for themselves. Mia's hum went lower, a bass thread only her chest cared about. She wanted the hallway to feel like shade under a porch. She didn't want people to feel managed. That was the underside of this job. Rules without shame. Order without control.

They hadn't even reached the stacks and the day had shifted in those small ways that tell you you're going to remember it later. A museum mom stood with a kid who wore a hat with shark teeth stitched to the brim. The kid bared her fake teeth at Mia and hissed. Mia hissed back, then winked. The kid broke and giggled so hard her hat fell over her eyes. The mom mouthed thank you. Mia nodded. She would take every easy moment the day offered and put it in her pocket.

Mia's hum skimmed the floor and settled in the lines between tiles. Sia's cards built a ladder for the room to climb. Eric's cones edited the space without starting a fight with anyone's pride. The volunteer stationed near the reading room mouthed her lanyard line like a prayer. "Paper reads in names at desks during posted hours. No service at benches, seats, or stairs." She practiced the cadence until her mouth owned it.

"Say it to me," Mia said, passing.

The volunteer looked up, surprised, then proud. "Paper reads in names at desks during posted hours," she said, clean and steady. "No service at benches, seats, or stairs."

"Perfect," Mia said. "Thanks for saying it out loud."

The girl beamed like she had just unlocked a new level in a game that mattered. It did.

The hum under the building climbed another half step. Not louder. Closer. The kind of closer that makes your body look for exits even when your head knows this is the right hallway. Mia put her palm to the wall again because skin is a better meter than eyes when rooms decide to be coy. Paint. Good intentions. Patience wearing a suit.

A janitor cart squeaked by. The squeak had the pitch of a complaint. The complainant was a wheel with a grudge. Mia stepped aside and smiled at the person pushing it. "Can I fix your wheel for you," she asked.

The custodian laughed like she'd heard that ten times this week. "Please do," she said. "With your mind."

"On it," Mia said. She hummed a single high note at the wheel in a joke voice, then stopped, then watched in delight when it actually quieted. The custodian blinked. Mia blinked. Sia hid a smile under a card.

"Magic," the custodian said, amused, and pushed on. Maybe it had just needed attention. Sometimes wheels are like that.

They were almost to the stacks when a thin line of cooler air slipped across their ankles like somebody had opened a freezer drawer in the wrong place. Not big. Just a little draft that didn't have a door attached.

Mia looked at Sia.

"I felt it," Sia said, low.

"Not the vents," Mia said.

"Not the vents," Sia agreed.

Truth's nose dipped harder. She stopped, bristled in a way that didn't include teeth, then looked back at Mia with the seriousness of a dog who had thoughts about jurisprudence. Her tail ticked once and pointed left.

"Hold a second," Mia told the hall like it could hear her. She rubbed her thumb and forefinger together to reset her own pulse. She wasn't scared. She was awake. Those are different.

She adjusted the tone by a fraction so it felt like the kind of quiet you get after a summer thunderstorm when the heat breaks and you can think again. Sia tapped the corner of a door frame and posted one more card at knee level for latecomers who couldn't read eye level today.

A boy wandered out of the small theater with a headset looped around his neck and the look of someone who had just had feelings about a documentary. He blinked at Mia's face, looked like he might ask a question about dolphins, then decided against it because the tone under the air told him to save it for later. He walked toward the lobby without bumping anyone. Mia marked that as another tiny win.

A dad in a baseball jacket stepped into the corridor, froze, then frowned in that subtle way guys do when they can't remember whether they locked the car. He patted his pockets. He wasn't ridden. He was overwhelmed by the number of signs in his day. Mia pointed him at the T. rex and his face eased because monsters with bones are easier to understand than bills.

They reached the stacks entrance and stopped on purpose.

Stopping on purpose changed rooms. If you pause like you meant to, rooms will wait for you. Sia set her palm on the frame.

"Ready," Mia asked.

"Ready," Sia said.

Mia took one breath and let her shoulders lower that one centimeter that tells your body you belong in your own skin. The tone settled on the threshold like a cloth. She didn't go in yet. She listened. Paper smell, dust, the sour note she hated, the memory of showers from field trip mornings clinging to kids' hair. Under that, something like sleep sugar stuck to a shape that didn't deserve sweets.

From behind them, the board bell chimed a single polite ping that meant someone had read posted hours and wanted to negotiate with them. Mia almost laughed from muscle memory. Negotiating with posted hours was a hobby in this building. She let Tommy handle it.

"Okay," Mia said, voice steady. "We're going to keep this floor gentle. We seat people, we cool the rides, we don't shame anybody. Then we see what this hallway thinks it is."

Sia nodded and lifted the marker stone like someone about to knock on a neighbor's door. Truth took one slow step forward and lowered her head.

From the corridor behind them, Eric's tape made a single soft rip. It sounded like a page turning. A volunteer read her lanyard line under her breath like grace. A kid somewhere asked if the shark jaws were real and someone told him some of the teeth were and the rest were honest plastic so the shape made sense.

Normal sat next to not-normal and they got along for one more minute.

Mia thought about Ella and Tobias without trying to. She imagined them somewhere else in the building feeling their own version of this and writing their own small rules against it. She let the thought go before it got teeth. It wasn't a prayer. It was a promise to meet in the middle with work done.

"Staff wing," she said again, softer, because words help you aim.

Truth's ears tipped like little sails catching wind.

They stepped across the threshold and into the shelves. Mia kept the hum at the edge of hearing so it felt like shade and not control. She didn't push the room. She offered it a better idea. That was the whole trick. Offer better ideas until bad ones have nowhere to sit.

The day leaned. She could feel it. They would hold this level until help hit the stairs or the stairs needed them. Either way, the next move lived ahead.

THE STACKS HELD COOL air and the sweet-dust smell of paper. Shelves ran in tight lanes, spines like teeth. The sour note under it had grown from hint to taste. It coated the back of Mia's tongue like cheap mints.

"Keep it quiet," Sia said, low.

Mia let her note sink to floor level so it brushed ankles and knees. Shade, not sleep. The kind of quiet that helps people find themselves.

Marcus stood three aisles in with a short shelf angled between him and a shape that didn't like being noticed. It shivered at the edges like heat on asphalt. Gray where the light should have made color. It kept changing the idea of where its elbows belonged. Marcus had a chair leg in both hands, not up for a swing, set like a lever.

"On your left," he said without looking away. "It wants angles."

"Lane rule," Sia told the floor. She touched the tile with her card and spoke plain. "This line is a lane. Anything not invited slides out."

Mia spread pressure through the air like a weighted blanket. Not force. Just enough to make motion cost. The thing hissed, a thin kettle sound, and tried to wobble Marcus's sightline again. He didn't let it. He nudged with the chair leg at the exact angle of Sia's line, guiding, not jamming. The rule did the rest. The thing slid like a bug on a clean plate and flattened against the lower shelf.

"Hold," Sia said to the lane. "No crossing."

The line held. The shelf took the pin for Marcus so he didn't have to. You could feel the room agreeing with itself.

"Appreciate the jar," Marcus said, stepping back a half shoe.

"Anytime," Mia said. She kept the tone steady and felt her ribs relax. Work like this made the day make sense.

Two visitors wandered out of a side reading nook. A man in a city hoodie and a woman in a parka too warm for the month. Their hands were fists. Their steps matched like they had a metronome between them.

"Hey," Mia said, soft. "You both look like you could use a sit. Bench is right there."

She pointed at a small bench under a fire map. They didn't look at her. They looked through her. She drew her note into a lazy lullaby rhythm and angled it at breath. "In on four. Out on six." She spoke the numbers once. The woman's shoulders followed. The man's fists loosened finger by finger. They sat. She watched their throats. Swallow. Blink. Blink. Good.

The sour undernote thinned a little. Not gone. Just less proud.

"Hotel still isn't pushing them out," Mia said under her breath.

"No," Sia said. "We post and keep people safe. Whatever's stuck, it's not on this floor."

That landed hard and true. They couldn't flip the switch from here. They could hold, though. Holding mattered.

Eric appeared in the mouth of the aisle like a magician making cones from nowhere. Tape looped his wrist. He put a strip at knee height on the stacks entrance so the wrong turn would feel like storage. He set an orange cone where even a distracted person would choose the nicer path.

"Guests keep drifting to the reading chairs and getting that glassy look," he said. "So I turned two chairs to face each other and put the magnifiers on top. Now it looks like a science station. People sit and talk instead of staring. You're welcome."

"Love the brain," Mia said.

He grinned and pointed with his chin toward the far end. "You've got a cough that belongs in a drain, not a person. Back row, third cutout."

Truth tracked ahead, nose to baseboard, paws quiet. She hit the back row, sniffed the gap behind a book cart, and gave it a single disgusted snort like she'd found a sandwich in a locker in June.

"Show me," Mia said.

The cough came again. It had the wrong rhythm. A human cough has a break in it. This didn't. It was a loop trying to pass for breath. Sia angled her card to the floor and tapped twice.

"This corner hosts silence," she said. "No hiding in the room's echo."

The wrong sound stopped like someone had yanked a cord out of a speaker. Something gray and elbow-confused peeled off the baseboard and tried to rise. Marcus slid a hand truck in front of the cart and set his foot on the axle. He didn't hit the thing. He let the room's rules catch it. It pressed against an idea that refused to make space for it and finally puddled back into flat.

"Good," Sia said. "Tag the spot."

Eric slapped a small paper dot on the baseboard with the kind of precision that made docents love him. "Found you," he said to the wall, cheerful.

A whisper of motion in Mia's peripheral made her turn. Not

the gray. People. A pair of teens shadow-boxed in the reading aisle like they were pretending to be bored. Their steps had sync they didn't earn. Rides like to borrow rhythm.

Mia didn't sing at them. She stepped into their space just enough to be undeniable and lowered her voice a notch.

"You two look like you need an errand," she said. "Can you take this to the front desk and tell them we need more map copies and two sharpies."

"What is it," the boy asked, hand already out.

"A very important pencil," Mia said, and deadpanned it until they laughed. She placed a dull pencil in his palm like a treasure. The girl smiled despite herself. They took off at a jog that wasn't quite running. The rhythm snapped. Good.

"You weaponized errands," Eric said.

"Grandma training," Mia said. "You give teenagers a job or they pick the bad kind."

They swept the next aisle. The gray smear of a coin lay half tucked under a shelf bracket near the floor. It shone too bright for the light. Mia hated how coins got that smug face even when they were pretending to be innocent.

"Don't touch," she said fast.

Eric crouched, snapped a photo on his phone for the board, then stuck a jar over it. He slid a cardstock under the mouth like a spider rescue. He didn't lift it.

"Leave it caged," Sia said. "We'll file it in names when we have a desk and time."

Marcus leaned an inch to check the bracket. "No second one.

They like to pair."

"Thanks," Mia said. She made a mental note to sweep every bench leg later. Coins loved legs.

A grandfather in a flat cap wandered in from the corridor, blinking like a person who walked through too many smells. He paused at the aisle, looked at the sign for fossils, then at the one for birds. He wasn't ridden. He was tired of choosing.

"Sir," Mia said friendly. "Birds today. Fossils next time. That way."

He blinked at her in gratitude like she had pulled gravel out of his shoe. "Birds," he said. "Yes. Good."

He shuffled on. The day was kind to some people if you told it how. She liked being that kind for a minute.

The pinned gray shape near the hand truck twitched, testing the line. The floor refused the idea of crossing. Sia tapped the tile once more so the rule would feel heard.

"Thank you," she told the lane.

A volunteer slid into the aisle with a lanyard card in her fingers. She was one of the college crew. Pink hair at the tips. Wide eyes that were not panicked, just full. "I have three on a bench who say they're dizzy," she said. "I told them what the card says. They're drinking water. Do I do more?"

"You're perfect," Mia said. "If anyone tries to hand you paper, point to the Desk Only card and say it out loud. No one signs anything but the desk."

"Okay," the volunteer said. She breathed like the word desk was a dock. "Desk only. Got it."

She left with purpose and pink hair that looked like a flag.

"More in the back," Eric said. He had the tape in his hand again. "I'm going to make the wrong alcove look like storage."

"Bless you," Mia said.

They cleared the last run of shelves and came out into the open stripe before the library doors. The green lamps glowed like little planets. The study carrels lined up like ships. A kid slept with a book face down on his chest. His shoes were off, toes touching. The sign above him said please do not sleep in the reading room. This was not the day to enforce that. Sia looked at the sign, shrugged, and set a small card on the carrel.

This seat rests people. No paper service.

"Better," she said.

Marcus checked the corners. He had a way of moving that made rooms tell him the truth without effort. He lifted a hand. "Clear."

"Alright," Mia said. She planted a cooling chord in the center of the library. It felt like stepping into shade after a parking lot in July. Not cold. A reminder. Anyone riding would hate it. Anyone tired would love it. The sleepers' breaths evened without dropping too deep.

Eric turned two tables on a bias so the wide path to the door was obvious. He didn't block anything. He made the easy thing easier. He taped one strip low on the doorframe. A kid with the shark hat peered in, saw the tape, and decided the fish tank was cooler. Great. Fish always beat rules if you let them.

"Volunteers?" Sia called soft toward the desk.

"Two on water," a teen answered from behind a stack of pamphlets. "One on maps. I told them floaty bench is a thing."

Mia smiled. Floaty had stuck. Good.

She walked the three sleepers. Girl on the carpet with the hoodie rolled under her head. Boy on the bench with his hand still around a pencil he never used. A grandmother who had fallen asleep upright like a pro. Mia slipped paper wristbands onto their wrists and wrote times. She added a small circle next to the boy who had been breathing too fast before. She tucked the blunt pencil back into his hand so he wouldn't wake and think he lost something important.

"Up here stays gentle," Sia said to the room and to herself. "No one wakes too fast."

"Copy," Mia said. She could feel the building's hum shift higher again, a half-step up. Not louder. Closer. Like a machine behind a door that someone just decided to feed.

Truth circled the threshold and sat, ears angled at the hallway. She made a sound that wasn't a growl. It was a count. Three, then two, then still, like paws on tile down the corridor that she didn't trust yet.

"Radio on," Eric said, touching the clip on the board so it would hiss if anyone called.

The hiss came. A single pop. Then Tobias's voice, steady even with steps under it.

"Library. Now. Our fight is below."

Mia didn't ask a single question. She didn't need to. The words had weight. Sia looked at her. Marcus had already turned toward the staff stair. Eric set the tape roll on the desk with the safety cutter tucked under it. Truth stood.

"Volunteers," Sia said to the teen at the desk, warm and firm, "you stay on lanyard lines. Offer water. Keep people where they are. If paper shows up anywhere but the desk, point to the card and say Desk Only. Do not touch it."

"Yes," the teen said, yes like a promise.

Mia gave her a quick smile that meant you've got this. She walked to the edge of the room and set one low tone in the doorway that would sit after she left. It wasn't a leash. It was a porch.

"Ready?" Sia asked.

"Ready," Mia said.

Marcus took the point, hands empty, shoulders loose. Eric slid behind to kill glare. Sia fell in at Mia's right with the marker stone in her hand. Truth trotted ahead and put her paws on the top stair as if to count for them.

Mia checked the band times one more time, left two paper cups of water on the desk, and nodded to the volunteer. The girl nodded back and mouthed the lanyard line once more. Desk only. Names. Posted hours.

They stepped through the door. The shade-chord kept the room comfortable behind them. The hum under the floor pressed a little harder against Mia's ribs, not mean, just honest. The stair waited with the old concrete truth she liked.

"Breathe," she said for herself and anyone listening. "In on four. Out on six."

They went to meet the fight where it lived.

THE LIBRARY BREATHED LIKE it remembered how. Shade-sound settled where Mia left it, the kind of cool that helps brains come back online. A girl slept under a table with her hoodie rolled as a pillow. A boy on the bench clutched a pencil he never used. A grandmother dozed upright like it was a sport. The volunteer at the desk kept one hand on the stack of paper cups like they mattered, which today they did.

Sia taped a fresh card at the frame and pressed the corners flat. **Desk only. Paper reads in names at desks during posted hours. Nap spaces host rest. No service.** The tape didn't lift. Good sign.

Mia did a fast pass of the room. Study nooks clear. Corners clear. Green lamps where they belonged. She thinned the cooling chord until it was memory, not weight. Calm without numb. Better for waking.

Eric slipped a cone to the side of the door so it didn't look like a barricade. He turned two tables a hair to make the path out clean and obvious. Marcus rolled one shoulder, then the other, setting his center like a runner at blocks. Truth circled the threshold twice, nose low, then sat, tail line steady. She glanced down the hall like a dog who had a schedule.

The radio hissed. One sharp pop. Tobias's voice came

through steady with steps under it.

"Library. Now."

He hit the doorway three heartbeats later, sweat at his temple, eyes doing the fast math he only did when rooms started lying. Ella slid in behind him, hand out without looking. Tobias tossed her the sword. She caught it clean, set her grip, and didn't waste a second checking the blade like a mirror. It fit her hand the way a tool fits after a summer of work.

"Our fight is below," Tobias said. "The Hotel won't work until we save Charles."

That was the line Mia had been holding space for without knowing it. The day snapped into clear shapes.

"What do you need," she asked. Keep it short, make it easy for him to say yes.

"Team on me," he said. "Rail side, not wall. Hands on rails so the stairs tell you the truth. If a seam opens, we use height and angles. Ignore clipboards. Call coins."

"Copy," Eric said. He already had tape around his wrist.

Sia didn't ask for the rest. It would waste time. She went straight to assignments. "Ella and Tobias front. Marcus anchors and breaks anything that tries to pull a body out of shape. Eric makes the easy path louder, blocks wrong turns without shouting. I'll post lanes and doors. Mia stays midline, holds breath and tone. Truth runs corners and warns on seams."

Truth thumped her tail once at her name and stepped to the edge of the first stair like she was about to count.

The volunteer at the desk swallowed and lifted her chin.

"What do I do?"

"You're our dock," Mia said. "Stay on your lanyard lines. Offer water. Keep people seated. If paper shows up anywhere but the desk, point to the card and say Desk Only. Don't touch it. If someone wakes up confused, read the nap card out loud. You've got this."

"I've got this," the volunteer repeated. It landed like a promise.

Mia slipped two paper wristbands into Sia's pocket and kept two for herself. She tagged the sleepers with times in blunt pencil so the next hands would know who to check first. The boy on the bench twitched in his sleep like he was late for something. She tucked the pencil tighter into his grip so he'd wake with purpose instead of panic.

Ella tested one short pass with the blade. It sang in that way only she seemed to hear. "Ready," she said, and it wasn't bravado. It was lunch-break plain.

A teen pair from earlier jogged up with a box of maps and two sharpies because Mia had weaponized errands. Eric pointed them to the desk with a thanks. The rhythm break in their steps held. Good. She didn't want any more borrowed beats in this room.

Tobias gave the library a fast once-over, the kind of look that counts exits, corners, and how many people are breathing without being told. He met Mia's eyes a half second, enough for yes. He wasn't going to debrief. He'd already done the only briefing she needed: below.

Mia took one breath and set a single low tone in the doorway. It would sit after she left and make the exit feel like a good idea for anyone who woke. She cut it so the room would own it, not her.

"Volunteers," Sia said to the desk, warm and firm, "if a guest wants to help, give them a job that keeps them up here. Maps, water, directions. No one goes downstairs."

"Yes," the volunteer said. "Maps, water, directions. Desk only."

Marcus shifted to point. Eric slipped behind to kill glare on the glass wall by the staff hall. Sia fell in on Mia's right with the marker stone in her palm. Ella set to Tobias's left, not a step ahead, not a step behind. Truth trotted to the top stair and placed her paws like a dog counting one, two.

Mia looked once at the sleepers. The girl under the table sighed and rolled to her other side. The grandmother's mouth opened, then closed. The boy clutched his pencil like it was a banner. Two cups of water waited on the desk for whoever woke first.

"Alright," Mia said, mostly to herself. "We leave this floor gentle and breathing."

Sia nodded. "We fight where we can change the board."

They crossed the threshold. The hum under the floor shifted half a note higher, the kind of change you feel in your ribs. The stair gave them old concrete honesty. Tobias took them down steady, not rushed. You don't run unless you want the building to run with you.

At the first landing, where that name-first clipboard had once hung, the hook was empty and the screw heads were new. Eric palmed the plate. No heat. No buzz. He flicked his fingers once. Clear.

"Rail side," Tobias said, quiet. "If a seam opens on the wall, don't give it a shoulder."

"Copy," Ella said.

They took the next flight. The air cooled, then picked up a thread of ozone. The Flux sat ahead behind a door that wore its paint like a badge. Even from the stair, Mia could feel the building moving stress around under the public floors so they wouldn't crack. She loved it for that. She hated that thieves could hide inside patience.

Truth's ears tipped forward. Her tail line rose a notch that meant a seam was thinking about telling a lie. She bumped Sia's leg with her shoulder. Sia touched the panel seam and spoke plain so the joint would hear.

"This line is a seam," she said. "It keeps its shape. No exits here."

Metal cooled under her fingers. Mia felt a little pressure drop in her teeth. One small door closed.

They hit the service hall. Lights hummed like aquarium lids. Pipes ran with dust that looked right for an old building. Tobias kept his shoulder a hand's width off the walls that moved when they wanted to. Marcus hovered a step behind him, clean anchor. Eric drifted the edges, making bad turns boring with tape and small shifts.

At the door to the prison level, Tobias paused just long enough to check positions, then pushed. The hinge answered without a squeal. Air with no dust and no smell sat inside. Rules lived in rooms like this.

The gallery laid itself out: rail, tempered panes, fine filament lattice, the demon from weeks ago crouched in its cube like a bad idea waiting for oxygen. The rider sat with his head tipped back, breathing, tethered to a knot of light that kept its distance from skin. The manual board on the wall held calm little lights. Calm lights lie.

Mia held midline and let her voice sit at foot level. She didn't want to blanket anyone. She wanted to make panic cost extra. Sia set her palm on the rail to tell the room a person who cared had arrived.

Seam noise crawled up the far wall. Not loud. Precise. Like someone lifting wallpaper with a razor. Truth's ears locked on it. Marcus lined his hips with the nearest post. Ella stepped forward without getting greedy. Tobias raised his hands the way you do when you plan to move a body without giving it anything to grab.

The seam lifted a clean strip. A hand came through, long fingers, wrong knuckles. A shoulder followed. Two more bodies pressed behind. The air tasted like nap sugar on something that didn't deserve sweets. They looked for rails and levers, not faces. They'd rehearsed the room.

Mia didn't sing at them. She sank the tone one notch until the floor felt like shade on a hot sidewalk. It would make the wrong steps feel like extra work. Not a command. A suggestion the room liked better.

The first flicked a bone chip at the toggle box. Ella smacked it down with the flat of her blade. It pinged off the guard and skittered under grating. The second snapped a strip of shadow at knee height. Marcus hopped it, planted a foot on the rail, and killed the angle. He grinned without humor. Physics was on their side if they kept their heads.

"Don't chase," Tobias said. "Make them spend legs."

Sia set a lane line with the marker stone. "This row moves toward the rail. No crossing." The floor took it. Mia felt the path harden. The second tried to cut across and hit a surface that refused to understand the move. It slid, hissed, reset.

The seam hiccuped. A fourth hand tested it. Truth gave a small sound that wasn't a growl. It was a count going up. Ella pressed the lead with short, mean taps from the flat. Marcus shoved the third into Sia's line like you push a grocery cart into a curb. The rule did the rest. Eric slapped a paper dot on the baseboard below the seam so the wall would remember it had misbehaved.

Mia kept the chord under her sternum steady and watched her own team for the wrong signs: glassy eyes, stutter steps, lips moving with someone else's rhythm. Nothing yet. The cards upstairs were starving the dream route. Good.

Inside the nearest cell, a hand hit glass. Charles. His mouth moved, but the pane made words thin. He didn't look scared. He looked stuck and busy.

"Board's dead to him from inside," Tobias said, almost to himself. He didn't step toward the door. He kept the fight from caring about the board at all.

The lead swung for the toggles again. Ella batted it aside with a teacher's ruler slap. Marcus pinned the third against Sia's lane. It bucked and failed and bucked again until it got bored of losing. The fourth tested the seam and found a wall that had decided to be a wall. It slid down and rethought its life choices.

"Push to the corner post," Tobias said. "Make the gallery small."

They did. Sia laid a second line to fuse with the first. The two rules made a V. The only comfortable direction was out. The demons don't like choices made for them. They moved anyway because options were gone.

Mia felt the room lean her way for a second. She took it. She let the chord lift and drop once to make time sticky. The seam thinned. Hands withdrew. The lead tried a last swipe at the board and smacked a guard so hard the sound made the boy on the library bench flinch two floors up. Ella tapped its knuckles with the pommel. It let go like it had touched a hot pan.

"Enough," Tobias said. He didn't yell.

They shifted two steps back from the rail. Not retreat. Space to react. Sia slid to the cell door and pressed two fingers to the seam. She didn't force it. She told it what it was.

"This door hosts a steward," she said, low. "It opens in names when asked by hands that can ask." She wasn't opening it. She was filing a truth the House could use later.

The lock listened. It didn't change. That was fine. Charles stayed where he was. The board stayed out of his reach. That was the problem they'd fix next chapter, not now.

Tobias took one last look at the seam. It stayed flat. He nodded once. "We're done trying to be interesting up here," he said. Then, to the team, "We move. Below."

Mia cut the tone. Her throat felt raw in the good way work does. She tightened the band on her wrist so the time wouldn't smear and took a breath.

"Volunteers are good?" she asked Sia as they backed toward the door in formation.

"Good," Sia said. "Water, maps, Desk Only. They'll keep it gentle."

Eric killed a glare with the back of his hand as they reached the service hall. Marcus glanced once at the stair and rolled his neck. Ella checked the sword hilt and let her shoulders drop a hair. Truth trotted ahead, paws soft, ears forward, ready to count again.

Mia spared one thought for the sleepers upstairs. Cups on the desk. The card on the glass. The kid with the shark hat probably telling a stranger about the fish tank like he built it. Normal living next to not-normal and not getting in a fight about it. That was what she wanted to go back to.

Tobias led them out of the gallery and into the hall that pointed deeper. The hum under the building nudged them in the ribs like a coach at the bend.

"Breathe," Mia said. "In on four. Out on six."

No one joked. No one postured. They just did it. Then they went to meet the fight where it lived, and Charles stayed locked, the board out of reach, the Hotel waiting for someone to flip the right switch in the right room.

CHAPTER 18

Basement with Teeth

SIA

And now I demand that you do what the ignorant might feel is the easier thing. You must refrain from dying in battle. Revenge is not redress. Revenge is a wheel, and it turns backwards. The dead are not your masters.

Terry Pratchett, Monstrous Regiment

SIA STAYED IN THE middle because the middle kept the line from wobbling. Tobias and Ella led at an easy, steady pace. Marcus watched the rear, checking side halls without drifting. Eric walked the edges and moved small things out of the way. Mia kept to Sia's right with a low hum in her throat that made it easier to breathe without thinking about it.

The staff stair still smelled like paint and old concrete. Sia kept her left hand on the rail. She liked the way metal told the truth. The rail buzzed under her palm with a steady note. The Window upstairs was shut, and that mattered. Fewer bodies could come through now. But that pressure had to go somewhere, and it felt like the building carried it in its bones.

They crossed the line Sia set only after everyone said their name in order. Just as they had practiced on the farm and used to find each other in that battle that felt like years ago, yet it had been but weeks. Tobias, Ella, Sia, Mia, Marcus, Eric. It felt silly for half a second. Then the air on the other side grabbed for their balance and she was glad the room had a rule to hold.

"Match each other's pace," Tobias said. "No gaps."

"Got it," Ella said.

Sia kept the umbrella low and a step off center. The corridor looked clean and straight. That was suspicious by itself. Rail on the right. Glass on the left. Polished tile in front. A small access door every ten yards, each one marked with a number that meant nothing to her.

The first problem came simple. A utility face that had been flat a second ago puffed like a bubble. It pushed out three hand-sized shapes that skated across the tile in a shallow V to split the group.

"Lane," Sia said, and drew a short line with the chalky stone in front of her shoes. "This is a lane. No crossing."

Mia tightened her tone until Sia felt the sound in her

knees. Tobias shouldered the first shape without stopping. Ella slapped the second with the flat of her blade and made it change direction. The third hit Sia's umbrella, bowed the canopy, then bounced back like someone tossed a tennis ball into a trampoline. Marcus slid a half step and posted it against the rail. Eric pulled a cone from the wall, latin whispers escaped his lips and set it two feet into the bad angle. The shapes thinned and smeared into the panel that had tried to spit them out.

"Don't chase," Tobias said.

"No one's chasing," Ella said, eyes on elbows, knees, and rail points.

They moved again. The ceiling tried a drop-in with a soft thump, the way a cheap vent spits dust. Sia touched the grid. "Ceiling's closed. No drop-ins." The thump turned into regular air and kept going.

Something scratched across the tile like a nail. Coins again. Painted to match the floor, tucked behind a hinge so the ping would be clean if a heel hit it. Eric spotted the setup and put a plastic cup over the worst stack without touching it. "Keep them off your flesh. Else we'll start talking backwards and need all sorts of priests."

"No paper service on this run," Sia said, seemingly into a void, but her audience was the Basement. "Travel only."

The paint lost its little shine. The seam settled. In the glass on their left a reflection shifted out of sync with their steps. It made Sia feel like she was walking by a long window full of people who were a hair slower than the real group. The feeling was disgusting. It wanted her to stutter.

Sia piped up another direct order, "No unauthorized reflections in the gallery."

The reflection snapped into sync and stayed there. Nothing dramatic. It just stopped trying to confuse her. A thin seam along the baseboard fluttered. Sia looked at it long enough to make sure it was a seam and not a mouth. "Baseboards stay sealed. No openings at foot level." The flutter quit.

They reached the first long corner. Two demons waited with hands on the rail again. They were bigger than the ones upstairs. Their shoulders looked like they had been built to carry other people's weight, and their palms pressed the metal in a slow rhythm like they were listening to the rail remember its weak spots.

"Gate," Tobias said. "Two. Same deal."

Sia set a V underfoot so her body knew where edges were. "This pushes toward storage. No waiting in the walk."

Mia dropped her pitch and made forward movement feel like sand for the demons, the air about them wavered as they slowed. Ella went low and used the blade flat as a bar. She didn't cut. She pushed wrists off metal and kept moving. Tobias took the second one by the elbow, turned its shoulder into the rail, and let that be the wall it deserved, his blade cut in quickly to dismiss the Demon's presence from the hall. Marcus stepped in, used the weight of his hip, and checked it into the same corner Sia had defined. Eric nudged a rolling bin into place with a touch of spellword and turned a broken sign face-in so the space read storage. The demon then had to read the word several times as the sign slammed repeatedly into it's face until it stopped moving. With a puff of smoke it eased into the seam of the walls.

They kept walking. A door to a side gallery shook like someone was kicking it from the far side. Sia did not want to think about what counted as far in a place like this. "Door holds function," she said. "No exits from the wrong side." The door stopped shaking and went quiet. If anyone had been watching, they made as if they had gotten bored.

A voice swam through the glass, not words, just the feeling of a voice. It tried to be the kind of sound that makes you turn your head before you know why. Mia cut it off with a bright, clean note that reminded Sia of a school bell at the end of a test.

"Nice," Eric said.

Another utility face twitched. This one spat darts no bigger than dry beans. They came in a curved arc for the level where necks and eyes live. Ella brought the blade up vertical and let them hit the flat. Tobias knocked two out of the air with the bracers on his forearms. One dipped almost like it had a brain of its own and aimed for Mia. She bumped her note higher by half a step. The air in front of her wavered and the dart hit sound and fell like a bird discovering a closed window.

"Everyone good?" Tobias asked.

They each signalled they were okay.

"All Good," Mia said, calmer than Sia felt.

They passed the first bank of glass cells. The lattice hummed. The sound made Sia want to swallow without reason. In the second cell, the rider stood with his hands clasped behind his back, head tipped just enough to be smug. The lattice made his mouth shapes worthless. She looked away. She couldn't afford to be the person who stared at a problem she couldn't fix yet.

As they continued, the building itself seemed to go for a new strategy against them. The floor lost a little friction. Not slick like ice, just off. As though a sudden streak of grease had found its way across the floor. Shoes wanted to slip. Panicked people fall when that happens. People holding a line do not.

"Floor stays grippy," Sia said. "No slip." It was not a pretty sentence, bu it worked. The rubber under her soles came back.

"Thank you," Mia said, and meant it.

A thin fan of shadow spread across the tile ahead like the cheap kind of movie effect. It made fingers instead of straight lines and tried to convince feet to step wrong. Sia didn't give it the scene.

"Floor hosts feet. No tricks," she said.

The fan broke into normal shadow. They walked through it.

"Halfway through," Tobias said. "That window still closed?"

"Feels like it," Ella said. "Same faces, different angles. I think they don't have any backup coming thanks to Sia"

"Good," Sia said. "I like repeat tricks. They get easy to memorize."

Sia stepped to the line where the run met the open space before the panes and planted the umbrella tip on it. "This threshold waits for names. No entry by hurry. No exit by panic." She said it the same way she had before and felt it sit. She laid her palm on the rail. The metal hummed like it had been waiting for her to say it again. It was working, her use of the Dreamer's authority over the place was holding and through no shortage of irony, she had the demons to thank for making the connection to the Dreaming so clear to her here.

Mia tuned her tone down to a slow, even pulse that sat in Sia's teeth and made it easy to breathe. Ella rested the blade against her thigh like a swimmer resting a hand on the lane line. Marcus set his feet so he could catch a shove from behind without moving Sia. Eric put small tape marks where each of them stood so the room would remember the picture if it tried to shuffle people around.

Having arrived at the entrance to the Jail, they could see across the glass. The rider watched like a man in an airport who thinks he is better than the chair he's sitting in. In the far pane, something taller turned its head the way a person tests their neck after sleeping wrong. None of them mattered yet. The board might as well have been on the moon.

"Status," Tobias said.

"Front's set," Ella said.

"Anchor set," Marcus said.

"Edges set," Eric said.

"Pulse steady," Mia said.

"Midline set," Sia said.

The corridor tried one last thing. The floor pulled a soft drag that wants to make people rush. Sia spoke to it without looking down. "Floor stays floor. No stick." It let go.

They held the line for a full slow count until the room stopped trying to test them. No one talked in that count. It wasn't silent. The building still made building noises. But nobody needed to fill the quiet.

Tobias nodded once. "We own the approach. Door next."

Sia adjusted her grip on the umbrella. She didn't look at Charles because she would want to fix him first if she did. She looked at the threshold, the rail, the posts, the glass, and the rest of her team. They were here. They were ready. The board stayed out of reach. Charles stayed locked. That was the truth, and it was the right place to stop for now.

"On your call," Sia said.

"On mine," Tobias said. He lifted his chin toward the panes without stepping forward. The room listened. They had time for one more breath before they moved.

THE GALLERY WASN'T QUIET anymore. It breathed like a gym before a fight, then skipped the countdown and swung. Two gray shapes came low at Tobias's knees. He slid one step left, clipped the first with his forearm, and used the second to push the first into the glass. Ella met the third with the flat of her blade and shoved it into a rail post hard enough to rattle the metal.

"Keep pace," Tobias said. No shout, just the tone that makes your feet listen.

Sia kept center. The umbrella rode low in her hands, steady as a bar. She could feel the place trying stupid tricks along the edges, small pulls on shoes, stray breaths from vents, but none of it mattered next to the things with hands and teeth in front of them. Mia's tone sat under everything, steady and clean. It kept Sia's breath on count even when her brain wanted to run.

A tall demon unwrapped from a seam ahead of Ella like it was stepping out of a curtain. It had a man's outline and a head that didn't decide on a shape. It moved like it had trained in close quarters. It went for Ella's wrists. She turned her blade flat and met it like a bar fight, wrist to wrist, shoulder to shoulder. Tobias slid past on her left and took the second hit, steering a smaller demon into the post with a shoulder and knee.

"Left," Marcus said.

Sia saw it. A crawler came out of the floor with fingers that bent backward. It grabbed for Mia's ankle. Marcus got there first. He hooked it with his boot, lifted, and kicked it off the line. It skidded across tile and folded under a rail like trash someone would sweep later.

Eric snapped a sigil with his off hand. It looked like he flicked a match into air. The mark stuck to a demon's chest and flashed a ring of light tight around its elbows. The thing slowed down like jelly cooling. Ella hit it once with the pommel and used the pause to pass.

"Door on the right," Tobias said. "That's our turn."

The security door sat in the glass run like a bad idea. It looked sealed and meant it. The handle had no play. The panel had no gap. The wall around it had been patched a dozen times and sanded flat. Behind the glass, two cubes glowed at half power. In the closer one the rider stood with hands behind his back. In the next one the demon from their first week crouched like it was waiting for a whistle.

Sia didn't let her eyes hang there. The door mattered. The line mattered. She let the umbrella tap the threshold once and set a rule so the room would calm itself. "Frame stays frame. No fake openings." She didn't need to say more.

"Eric," Tobias said.

"On it," Eric said. He set his palm to the panel and drew a quick circle with two straight cuts through it. The sigil didn't glow so much as decide to exist. The light climbed the frame and then sank. The latch gave a small clunk like a throat clearing.

Two demons leaned out of the seam above the door, trying to make the frame a mouth. Marcus grabbed the first by its shoulders and used the door itself to smash it back into the seam. Tobias hit the second with his forearm and stepped aside so Ella could slam the pommel into its cheek. It didn't have bones to break, but it reacted like it did.

"Move," Tobias said.

He took the hinge side. Ella took the handle and pulled. The door swung inward an inch, then stuck like it had opinions. Sia stepped into the gap and shoved the umbrella ferrule against the drag point. She didn't push the house. She told the hinge what to do. "Hinge swings. Latch clears." The metal gave. Ella pulled. The door opened on a corridor that smelled like hot dust and old copper.

The sound hit before the sight. Wards buzzing, then choking. Low alarms clicking on and off like a smoke detector with a dying battery. A grind, deep and wide, like something heavy thinking about moving.

They stepped through.

The corridor was all angles and glass and rails. The panes had that soft green tint you get from thick safety glass. The rail posts had fine lattice between them. Most of the lights were on. A handful blinked. The air was warm and dry and tasted like a coin pressed to your tongue.

Three demons were already in the corridor. One hung from a ceiling bracket, peeling a ward sigil up with two fingers like scotch tape. One knelt at a base panel with a line of coins set out in a neat little row. One stood in the open and waited like a bouncer who'd picked the wrong club.

"Take the bracket," Tobias said.

"Got it," Ella said.

She went high and fast. The demon on the bracket tore the sigil free and reached for her face. She ducked under its grab, drove her shoulder into its hips, and slammed it into the rail lattice. The ward between panes flashed like someone smashed a camera. The thing's hands sparked. Ella didn't watch it fall. She moved to the next one.

Marcus took the bouncer. The bouncer took Marcus and didn't like what it got. Marcus drove forward, checked it with his shoulder, and used the rail to pin it without giving it leverage.

Eric threw a sigil like a playing card at the coins. The circle splashed across the row and snapped shut. The coins jumped like popcorn, popped out of line, and went dead.

Sia aimed for the ward panel on the right. The same warm pencil mark she had seen in the halls ran along the seam. It wasn't a seam. It was the edge of a ward path trying to fail. She tasted metal again and didn't love it.

"Can you hold it," Mia asked.

"Trying," Sia said.

She set the umbrella ferrule to the seam and kept her words tight. "Line stays locked. No drift." The buzz steadied for a breath. The panel kicked back, hard enough to sting her hand. She rode the hit and planted her feet.

A demon lunged from the left with a fist full of nails. Tobias shifted into it and took the hit on his forearm guard. Ella stepped past him and slapped the hand down with the flat. The nails pinged across tile. One hit Sia's boot and bounced. She felt the ring through the sole and hated it.

The bracket demon came back with a twist at Ella's hair. Ella turned her head, let the fingers slide, and cracked it again with the pommel. It left a dent this time. The thing hissed and showed too many teeth. She ignored the mouth and hit the wrist.

"Mia, louder," Tobias said.

Mia did not sing louder in volume. She thickened the tone. It sat in Sia's ribs and made her shoulders feel like they remembered sleep. The next hit that came at Sia felt like it arrived through a wet towel. She had a second to think, which was everything.

"Right cell," Eric said. "The rider's ward is bleeding out."

Sia risked one glance. He was right. The lattice around the rider's cube flickered like a bad fluorescent bulb in a school hallway. The demon from their first week pressed both palms to the glass of its cube and watched them without blinking.

"Keep them off the panels," Tobias said. "We do not let those doors finish."

They fought small. That's what made it work. No giant swings. No speeches. Quick choices that helped the person next to you. Marcus blocked with forearms and shoulders and knees, then let the body slide to where it wasn't a problem. Ella used the flat to ruin grips and the pommel to ruin timing. Tobias watched the lane and called targets so nobody took a surprise from the side. Eric threw binding sigils and short flash shields that gave people half a second to get their hands back. Mia kept the tone under all of it and, when a dart flicked at Sia's eyes, snapped a bright dissonant note that knocked it off course without breaking the beat.

Sia focused on the ward seams. She wasn't a glass worker or a rail person. She was the voice that told places how to behave, and the prison level was a place that needed firm jobs. She kept it simple every time. "Glass holds." "Posts keep shape." "Panel stays latched." When she got fancy, the room argued. When she kept it plain, it helped.

A demon the size of a high school forward shouldered into Marcus and took him three steps back. It had a metal scrap hooked through its skin like a badge. He hooked it under the armpit, lifted, and turned his hip like a wrestler. It hit the tile on its shoulder and slid into a rail post. Sia felt the metal hum from the contact and told it not to flex. "Rails rail." It listened.

"Left panel," Eric said. "They're cutting the ward."

Sia saw it. A set of gray fingers curled through the lattice and pinched a glowing thread on the ward plate like they were snuffing a candle wick. She took two steps and stabbed the umbrella ferrule at the seam. "Ward holds. Hands off."

The fingers sizzled. The smell turned the back of her throat sour. The hand jerked and vanished. The thread brightened. The plate buzzed like a bug light and then settled.

The corridor pushed back harder. Three demons came together. Not a perfect line, more like the shove you get on a subway platform when the crowd decides to move at once. Tobias planted and let the first hit him like a door. Ella took the second and moved its hands to the wrong place. Marcus stepped into the third and used his whole back to carry it sideways into a pocket next to a post. Eric snapped a circle at their feet that flashed white like a camera and made the trio lose a step.

"Good hit," Mia said. Her voice sounded like a teacher talking you through a panic attack in a nurse's office. Calm. Efficient. Almost kind.

"Right," Tobias said.

They moved as one. The door mechanisms on the two cubes

made a sick grinding sound. Sia felt it in her teeth. The sound of systems failing slowly is worse than a clean break. It tells you the thing is thinking about betraying you.

"Eric," Tobias said. "Can you stall it."

"Trying," Eric said. He drew a half circle in the air and pressed it to the rider's lattice. The light crawled across like a spider and then broke. "Wards are keyed. My binds won't stick to that glass."

"Then buy time in front," Tobias said. "Marcus, help him hold the lane."

"On it," Marcus said.

They stacked the bodies side by side to make the smallest wall a line can be. Ella stood forward and low. Tobias set his shoulders beside her. Marcus stood half a step back and off to the left so he could steal a hit meant for Sia or Mia. Eric took the right, hand up, two fingers ready to cut small sigils out of air. Sia set the umbrella like a baton and felt the weight of the room push at her wrists.

The rider turned his head and watched her over his shoulder, not in a creepy way, just like he knew the problem and wondered if she did. She looked away, because looking didn't help.

Something big moved behind the panes. Footfalls. A drag. A sound like a metal desk being pulled across tile. The first cube's lattice flared too bright, then went dark at one corner like a tooth missing a filling. The air changed. It thinned. It made Sia want to take a breath that wouldn't fill. Mia's tone went lower and wider until it sat in Sia's stomach like food.

"Pressure," Ella said.

"Hold," Tobias said.

They did. A demon with too many elbows came at Ella with its arms up like it knew boxing. She did not box it. She ruined its balance by popping the inside of its wrist and then stepped on the top of its foot without looking at her shoes. Tobias took the follow-up on his forearm and pushed it into Marcus, who tilted it away from Sia with his hip. Eric cut a quick circle at its ankles. The mark flashed. The demon stumbled enough for Ella to put it down with a shoulder and the rail.

"Left side," Marcus said. "Two more."

"Block," Tobias said.

Sia didn't get fancy. She kept the umbrella where it could push small things back and speak to the room when the room forgot its job. Another seam tried to open at the base of the rider's cube. She tapped the edge with the ferrule and said, "Seam stays shut," like she was talking to a door that liked to drift open in a wind. It wasn't big magic. It didn't look like anything. The feeling changed. That was enough.

The walls themselves shuddered. The second glass cube, the one with their first demon, shivered like it had goosebumps. The hum in the lattice rose and rose until it stung Sia's ears. White light ran along the edge of a glyph, climbed, and died. The lock bar inside the door clicked halfway up, stuck, then rose the rest of the distance with a sound that made Sia's stomach drop.

"No," Sia said.

Her mouth had said it before her brain could tell it not to. She set the umbrella to the door seam and tried to tell it to stop, but the ward wasn't listening to her. It was listening to something bigger and older and probably stupid. She bit the inside of her cheek until she tasted blood and let go of the urge to beg.

"Mia," Tobias said.

Mia didn't raise her voice. She shifted to a pattern that made Sia think of seatbelts and handrails. You will not fall. You will not. Sia's hands steadied. The door did not care.

The first demon stepped out of the cube like it had always lived there and had finally gotten bored. It was taller than Marcus and wider in the shoulders than Tobias. It had a chest like a drum and a face that looked halfway human until you saw the edges. It smiled the way bad people smile when they think they're charming. Sia felt her skin crawl and then felt silly for letting a smile get to her when the thing in front of her had hands.

"Line," Tobias said. "Keep it here."

The demon hit them like a linebacker who'd had a bad day. Tobias took the center of it and held. Ella stepped to the right and chopped the inside of its elbow with the flat, then backed off so it wouldn't grab her blade. Marcus hooked his forearm across its collarbone and pulled. It didn't love any of that. It shoved and tried to split them. Eric drew a quick square in the air and slapped it to the demon's chest. The square flashed and tightened like a belt. The thing slowed a fraction. It was enough. They didn't try to slam it back into the cube. They just didn't let it through.

"Second door," Eric said.

The rider's door clicked in slow, jagged beats. The lattice along the edge broke like ice thawing and refreezing. Sia saw the fail walking toward her, step by step, like a line of dominos where each one took ten seconds to tilt.

"Keep them off me," she said. She didn't know she was going to say it until she did.

"Do your job," Tobias said.

She moved left, kept the umbrella down, and pressed the ferrule to the crack where the rider's door was failing. She didn't touch the ward. She spoke to the building around it. "Frame stays frame. Seal stays sealed. No shortcuts." Her words hit the seam and slid. She could feel it. The rule bounced because someone had set a different rule here a long time ago. She wasn't going to win a law fight by repeating herself.

A hand shot for her face from the right. Marcus saw it before she did and took the arm at the wrist with both hands. He twisted, stepped, and used the move to throw the demon into the wall. It left a smear and came up hungry. Ella clipped it with the pommel without looking.

"Thanks," Sia said.

"I've got you," Marcus said, breath level, eyes on the next hit.

The first demon pressed again. Tobias grunted and set his feet deeper. Eric cut another square and slapped it on the demon's thigh. The belt tightened. The thing slid an inch. It was still coming. Mia's song sat in Sia's bones like rebar.

The rider's door gave a final unhappy clack and unlocked. It swung open two inches like a mouth working up a line. Sia didn't waste time telling it to stop. She drove the umbrella ferrule into the gap and shoved. "Door closes." It did. For a breath. Then it shuddered and pushed back like a strong hand.

A shadow slid through the gap and became the rider's foot. He stepped into the corridor like a teacher walking into a classroom. He didn't look at her. He looked at the board across the room, like he had a to-do list, and this was the first checkmark.

"Eyes," Tobias said.

"On me," Ella said.

She popped the first demon's wrist and cut the angle so Tobias could breathe. Marcus shouldered the next body into a post so Eric could slap a circle at its ankles. Mia lifted the tone a hair and sang a wordless, three-note shape that made Sia's fingers stop shaking.

The rider turned his head and finally looked at them. He wore a smile like the other one, but his meant something. He raised two fingers in a lazy salute and then flexed his hand like he was about to crack his knuckles.

"Not your room," Sia said. She didn't expect him to listen. She said it because the room needed to hear it.

The rider tilted his head like he agreed and then ignored her. He stepped to the side without hurry, taking the lane that led to the master board. He didn't sprint. He didn't need to. The line in front of him was about to break because the first demon shoved again and the next three swarmed behind it.

"Tight," Tobias said. "Keep it tight."

They did. The push hit and they bent but didn't snap. Sia felt the press like a wave up her arms. Her shoulders burned. Her hands hurt. She wanted to sit down. She didn't. She pushed where she could and kept the umbrella between her face and anything dumb enough to reach for it.

The corridor decided to make it worse. The lights flickered once. The alarms died and came back in a new rhythm. Somewhere below them a door slammed with the sound of a vault. The floor seemed to settle lower, not by inches, just the feeling you get when an elevator stops too smooth and your stomach expects more.

"Hold," Tobias said. He said it like the word had weight.

"Hold," Ella said.

"Hold," Marcus said.

"Hold," Mia said, and the word became part of the song.

"Hold," Sia said, and meant it for the glass and the rail and the posts and every stupid seam that wanted to look important today.

The first demon leaned in to grin at her like a creep in a hallway. She didn't give her face to it. She shoved the ferrule into its collarbone like a doorjamb and told the post behind it to keep shape. It did.

The rider slid along the wall. Eric stepped to cut him off. The rider didn't hit Eric. He smiled, flicked a hand, and three loose coins from some pocket rolled toward Eric's feet in a neat line. Eric hopped them and cut a binding square in the air. The rider slid under it without getting smug. He did not stop moving toward the board.

"Tobias," Eric said, not shouting.

"I see him," Tobias said. "We can't break the line here. We'd lose the whole room."

"Copy," Eric said. He didn't swear. He didn't look angry. He adjusted his grip and kept the right side from turning into a mess.

Sia felt the choice like a knot in her teeth. They could chase the rider and let the first demon tear them in half, or keep the line and let the rider get closer to the board. Both were bad. One was worse right now. She kept her spot.

The first demon laughed again. Mia stepped closer to Sia and bumped her shoulder into Sia's on purpose. She didn't say it out loud. The touch said it. I'm here.

The glass two panes down ticked as a lock bar tried to rise. Eric threw a sigil at the wall rune that powered it. The mark flared, popped, and threw sparks. The bar settled with a sulk. Marcus reached back, grabbed the body trying to climb Ella's back, and pulled it off like you pull a heavy bag out of a trunk. He dumped it into the pocket between two posts and stepped on its shoulder until it dissolved.

The rider reached the end of the wall and turned into the final lane that led to the master board. He wasn't running. He was about to arrive. Sia's stomach dropped and then steadied on Mia's beat. She shoved the umbrella into the first demon's chest one more time. She didn't get fancy. She made space.

"Locks," someone said.

Sia didn't know who said it. Maybe the room said it in her head. The locks failed in a short, final rush. The rider's door swung fully open behind him like a body finally giving up. The first demon finished a shove that slid Tobias half a foot. It stepped out of the old cube and stood tall, free, and pleased with itself.

The corridor breathed in like a throat that was about to shout. The sound from the room below rose up through the floor. The hair on Sia's arms lifted under her sleeves.

Tobias set his feet.

Ella lifted her blade.

Marcus pulled the next body off Mia without looking at its face.

Eric cut three sigils so fast the lines blurred.

Mia's song dropped to a single low note and held.

Sia felt the umbrella's weight in her hands and the hitch in the building's breath, and knew exactly where they were in the story. The doors had failed. The rider and the first demon were free. The line held for one more second.

"Ready," Tobias said.

"Ready," they said.

The throat finished its breath. The room shouted. The fight became the fight, and there was no more time to admire anything.

THE CORRIDOR BROKE OPEN into the prison room like a mouth. Glass cubes lined the right and far walls. The master board sat behind a waist-high rail, lit and smug, just out of reach. Charles stood locked in the nearest cell on the left, hands spread against the pane, jaw tight. In the center space, the rider and the first demon were already moving with a pack of elites sliding out of seams to join them. The air stung like hot pennies. Somewhere under the floor something big kept grinding.

Crowley stepped into view in front of Charles's cell. He looked like a man who dresses better than he should and never pays the bill. He smiled like he'd rehearsed it in mirrors. The room seemed happy to have him.

"I warned you about coins and vents," he said, voice too casual. "The Window was a nice touch. Shame about the dreams."

Ella didn't answer. She put two fingers to her sternum, breathed, and let the breath out slow. When she lifted her head her eyes had that clear heat Sia had seen once before. It wasn't a costume. Uriel was there with her, clean and precise, a blade without rust.

"Stay on her lane," Tobias said. "Nothing gets past to clip her."

The first demon came at them hard, shoulders first. Tobias met it like a wall with legs. Ella stepped half a shoe left and brought the flat across its wrist, then drove the pommel into the socket where its arm met its chest. Marcus took the next hit coming at Mia without even looking. He hooked it by the collar and dragged it sideways like a heavy duffel toward the corner where the rail posts made a pocket.

Eric's hands were already moving. Quick cuts, two fingers drawing lines that hung in the air for a breath, then snapped to where they belonged. A binding flared around a demon's knees. It took a one step stumble and that was all Ella needed to smash it off the lane. Eric threw a second sigil at a wall rune that had started to bleed light. The leak stopped.

Mia sang under it all. She didn't try to be loud. She made a tone that sat in everyone's ribs and told muscles to do their job. When a spray of bone flakes flicked toward Sia's face, Mia snapped a short bright note that cracked the arc and let the pieces fall safe.

Crowley tilted his head at Uriel. "Do we do speeches first or skip to the part where you swing and I enjoy the attention."

Uriel stepped forward with Ella's feet. "You talk too much," she said.

She moved. Crowley moved to meet her. Light hit shadow and made the space between them hurt to look at. Uriel's cut turned Crowley's coat to smoke. His counter made a crack in the air like someone snapped a thick board. The room flinched. Charles didn't.

"Hold the lane," Tobias said, sharper.

Two elites tried to flank to the right. Tobias walked into the first and knocked it backward with his forearm. Marcus took the second and bounced it off a rail post like he was closing the door on a gust of wind. Eric tagged a twist point on the post with a small sticker rune and the metal kept its shape.

The rider slipped the edge of the fight and went for the board with the kind of walk that cuts lines. Sia stepped into his path and hit him with the umbrella ferrule like a baton. He took the blow on his forearm, smiled like the world was his, and kept moving. Not running. Sliding.

"Eric, stall," Sia said.

"On it," Eric said. He threw a fast square that thumped the rider's shin and made him pause just enough for Ella to cut across the line and force him back with the flat.

Crowley laughed without looking at them. He didn't need to. He fought Uriel like a man marking time, as if every exchange counted toward some math only he liked. "Strike me down and I go home," he said to the room. "Home sends me back fresh. You get tired. I don't."

"Then stop coming here," Ella said, or Uriel said through her. It didn't matter. The voice had weight.

The first demon tried to bull Tobias again. Tobias let it commit, stepped half a shoe to the side, and bounced it off his hip into Marcus, who folded it into the pocket. The move looked simple and hurt like a moral. Marcus held a second until Eric could slap a circle on the floor that made the demon feel heavy.

Sia threw two clean blasts with the umbrella focus and knocked a pair of crawlers off the ward plates. The umbrella shivered up her arms with each hit. It wasn't a whip or a wand. It was a lever that told the room where pressure belonged. The ferrule went hot in her hands. She gritted her teeth and moved again.

More elites slid out of seams like knives coming out of paper. The Window upstairs was closed. You could feel that truth in the room. They weren't endless. They were enough.

"Left flank," Marcus said.

"I've got it," Tobias said.

He didn't step big. He adjusted the angle of his shoulders and used his weight the way a coach teaches, not the way a movie pretends. Two came in. One met his forearm and regretted it. The other tried to go under and got Ella's knee for its trouble.

Mia's song shifted to a shape that made Sia think of a seatbelt clicking. She felt it cross her ribs and lock. The next impact didn't knock her breath loose. She could think. That was everything.

Eric's voice cut through, quick and plain. "Rider is probing the board route. I can't lock him down without blowing a ward."

"Don't blow a ward," Tobias said.

"I'm aware," Eric said, and flicked a needle-thin line of light that snapped across the rider's ankle like a rubber band. It wasn't much. It made the rider misstep into Ella's range. She took the gift and used the flat to treat him like a rude guest in a museum. Not pretty. Effective.

Crowley let an ugly pressure roll off one hand. It wasn't a

blast. It was a weight that made knees want to bend. The nearest panes ticked, the lattice brightened, and the room took a drink of fear like it had paid for it. Uriel flared brighter in Ella's body and cut that weight in half just by being there.

"You can't stop return," Crowley said. "You can only delay. That's my point. You get it, don't you, little rule-keeper."

He meant Sia. He didn't need to look at her to say it.

Sia kept the umbrella up and the rules short. Panels hold. Posts keep shape. Floor stays floor. Every time she went long, the room argued. Every time she kept it short, the room helped.

Two elites tried to set the rail up as a whip. Eric stickered the twist joints fast. "Joints hold," Sia said. The hum under her palm kept its note. The wave didn't travel.

"Uriel," Tobias said, "he's baiting you into a chase."

"I'm not chasing," Ella said, and she wasn't. She stayed present, blade flat when she needed control, edge only when breaking a grab. She didn't show off. She made space for the team and took it back when Crowley tried to steal it.

The rider cut right again, low and fast. Sia stepped into him. He looked amused that she tried. She hit him across the shins with the umbrella and said, "Not your path." He slid back a step. He still looked amused. His eyes were wrong in a way that made Sia want to look away.

Marcus blocked an elite with both arms and threw it sideways into the pocket. It hit the post and hissed. He didn't follow. He held his ground at Sia's back and checked on Mia without turning his head. "You with me."

"I've got you," Mia said, and lifted her tone a hair. It smoothed the flutter in Sia's hands.

The first demon laughed again. It had a human laugh. Sia hated that more than the teeth. It feinted at Tobias, kicked at Marcus, then reached for Sia like a man reaching across a diner table. Sia popped the umbrella up and cracked its fingers. They bent and then reset like gum. She swallowed bile and kept moving.

Crowley let Uriel press him toward Charles's glass. He didn't care. He looked past her at Sia. "You're clever. This place likes you. It will listen when you're calm. But you can't rewrite me. I'm an ecosystem, dear."

Ella cut him there. Enough talk. Steel met a body that didn't play by normal rules and still had to do physics. The floor rang. The sound ran through glass and metal. Charles winced once and didn't step back. He was watching Sia now. He'd been watching the whole time. It wasn't pressure. It felt like faith he hadn't told her he had.

Sia blasted another crawler off a ward plate. She could do it all night. Her arms would shake. They would eventually slip. Eric's binds would fail. Marcus would get tired and that's when the hurt starts. Mia's voice would crack. Tobias would still be standing, but he'd be standing in front of broken people. And Crowley would still be smiling because even if they broke him here, he'd just go home and come back.

Return. The word fit in her head like a puzzle piece. Not numbers. Not clever. His trick was that dying didn't matter.

She thought of thresholds and keys, of how places keep lists. She thought of the Garden and its chalk paths and the way Thanatos set a scythe down on a border and made a world listen. She thought of her own signs hung in the hotel above and how the words had started to feel like law in the halls.

She knocked a lunger away with the umbrella and said it out loud, short and plain. "Cover me."

"No," Marcus said on instinct.

"Yes," Tobias said on purpose. "Box her."

They moved as if they had practiced it. Tobias stepped into the pocket in front of Sia and widened his stance. Ella shifted half a step to lock Uriel's fight to Crowley and not let it bleed across Sia's space. Marcus backed into Sia's left shoulder and made a wall. Eric snapped a tight circle on the floor around their feet and set three quick anchors at the edges. The circle wasn't a cage. It was a stencil for the room. Mia rolled her tone down to a hum that felt like a cushion.

"Three breaths," Tobias said.

"Take five," Marcus said.

"Don't get cute," Eric said, already looking for the next threat before it had a body.

Sia set the umbrella tip against the floor inside the circle. She didn't sit. She didn't need to lie down. She let her eyes half close and let the song ride her down the way a hand guides a tired head to a pillow. The fight didn't go away. It slid back one layer. The chalk smell of the Garden came in like a breeze. Green on water. Prints of her own shoes on the path. Thanatos near in that quiet way of his, scythe leaning against the gate, not a threat, just the idea that borders are real.

Crowley's voice kept talking on the other side of the glass. "You can't make a house that strong without paying for it with time," he said, sounding pleased with himself. "I have time."

Sia believed him. That was the problem. He had time because death didn't end his access. The hotel had never been told to stop inviting his kind back. It had never been told how to treat demon death different from a broken pipe or a guest checkout.

"Two more," Tobias said, blade-flat calm.

"I've got you," Marcus said, muscles tight across Sia's back.

"Breath in," Mia said, low.

Sia stepped all the way into the Garden and let the room at her back hold. She could hear the clash of Uriel's light. She could hear Eric's sigils pop and Tobias's boots slide on glass grit and Marcus's breath. She let herself be a person in the middle of a circle she trusted.

Thanatos didn't smile. He didn't need to. He pointed with his chin at the border stones Sia had set in earlier talks and said, in a voice like simple math, "Name who comes in."

Sia nodded. "I will."

She opened her eyes. The circle around their feet was still there. The fight was still the fight. Uriel and Crowley were locked, blade to hand, light to pressure. The rider slipped for the board again. The first demon pushed like a bad tide. But Sia had the word in her mouth now. Not a speech. A rule. Short. Clear. The kind that floors and doors and rails understand and repeat.

"Hold three more," Sia said.

"Copy," Tobias said.

Eric's circle threw a quick pulse as a body hit the edge and fell off. Mia's tone pressed against Sia's spine like a friend. Marcus laughed once without humor as he dragged a screamer out of the lane and kept it from touching Sia. Ella's eyes never left Crowley.

Sia breathed in on four and out on six. She tasted the metal air, felt the heat of the umbrella in her hands, and walked the chalk in her head.

Then she dropped the last inch into daydream on purpose. The Garden took her weight. The rule waited on her tongue. And in the room, her friends covered her like a wall while Crowley kept talking, not yet understanding that in this house, rules are what matter.

CHAPTER 19

Posting the Rules

Sia

It is not wise to violate the rules until you know
how to observe them.

T.S. Elliot

SIA FELT THE CIRCLE first. Warmth at her heels, a soft press at
her calves, the weight of friends standing shoulder to shoulder
around her. The sound of the fight thinned the way a storm
sounds through a shut window. It was still there, just one room
away.

The Garden took the rest of her weight. Chalk dust. River air.
Green that smelled like shade. She did not fall. She stood where
the gravel path widened near the gate stones. Her umbrella felt

lighter in her hands, not because it had changed, but because the place did not try to pull it away. The scythe leaned on the gate post, tall and simple, metal as dull as rainwater.

Thanatos was already there. He did not loom. He waited the way a doorman waits for a name. No push. No test. Attention like a coat hung ready for a guest.

"You came standing," he said.

"I do not have time to lie down," Sia said. It came out a little sharp. She swallowed and tried again. "We are getting pushed. Crowley is in the room. The rider is loose. The first demon is loose. If they die down there, he comes back. I can hit bodies. Hitting bodies does not fix this."

"Then do not name bodies," he said. "Name the door."

Sia looked at the gate stones. They were the size of her thigh and the color of old paper. She had set them here in small, dumb ways over the last few nights without thinking much of it. One held a fingerprint where she had touched it when she was too tired to walk straight. The print had dried into the stone like it wanted to keep her company.

"Rules work when they are simple," Thanatos said. "They work when the place knows who speaks them. They work when the cost is clear. If you lie about the cost, the rule breaks the person or the place. Sometimes both."

"What is the cost," Sia asked. She did not want to flinch. She did anyway.

"You will be the one who cleans this house after you speak," he said. "When you say no, you must stay to keep saying it until the walls learn to say it for you. That is not a weekend. It is a season."

Sia thought of her friends upstairs. She thought of the hotel halls that had started to listen when she asked. She thought of the way the town outside felt new and tired at the same time. A season sounded fair.

"Okay," she said.

"Do not make a speech," he said. "Make a lock. A lock has a shape. It has edges. It tells a door what a key is. Do not write poetry. Write a job description."

"Yeah," Sia said. "I have been practicing that part."

The river moved slow along the far edge of the lawn. The water did not show her a special reflection. It showed trees and sky and a duck that looked like it did not care about rules. Fine. She did not need a vision. She needed a sentence.

She walked the path once, umbrella tip scraping a line in the gravel because her hands needed a job. She said words as she tried them on.

"No demons here," she said. "Too short."

"Demons are not welcome here," she said. "Better. Not done."

She pointed the umbrella at the left border stone. "No crossing," she said. "No riding. No anchoring. No staying. No returning by death."

"That is a list," Thanatos said. "Lists can be fine. Lists can also drift. Why would the house accept your list."

"Because I am the steward," she said before she could doubt

it.

"Say that out loud," he said.

Sia faced the threshold and felt her neck get hot for no good reason. Saying it felt like telling a room full of adults she had decided to sit at the head of the table. She did not want to feel small in her own Garden.

"I am the steward," she said. The words did not echo. They sat in the grass like a tool on a workbench.

"Who told you," Thanatos asked.

"The house did," she said, and then corrected herself. "The work did. It keeps listening. It keeps testing me. It keeps remembering what I say. That is what a place does when it wants someone in charge."

He nodded once, which counted as a lot from him. "Then write the job in your own words."

Sia rolled her shoulders to shake out the feeling of being sixteen and not old enough for anything. If she waited for older, people would keep getting hurt. She took a breath on Mia's count. In for four. Out for six. The beat came through the Garden faint and steady. She let it time her mouth.

"By the steward of this House," she said to the stones, "demons are not welcome here."

"Good start," Thanatos said.

Sia kept going because stopping would make her second-guess herself. "No demon may cross, dwell, ride, anchor, or return on these grounds."

"That names the door and what it refuses," he said. "Return

is the spine. Keep it."

Sia nodded. She pictured the prison room. She pictured the gallery. She pictured the lobby, the front steps, the roof line, the loading bay, the boiler stairs, the old conference room where the carpet still had cigarette burns. She made the word grounds include all of it.

"Do you want your rule to travel," Thanatos asked. "This house has long arms."

Sia thought about the town. She thought about Kaelan and Mariah upstairs, about Truth holding a hall like a sad-eyed bouncer, about guests who did not deserve to wake up with broken windows and missing hours. "Let it spread on its own," she said. "Let it spread like a scent. I am not asking the cornfields to behave yet."

"That is wise," he said. "What else."

"Movement," Sia said. "Demons use seams. They ride people. They jump planes. Crowley tries to make death into a door. I want that door shut and locked. Not jammed." She did not like jammed. Jammed meant stuck under pressure. Locked meant chosen.

She spoke the clause slow so she could feel it lock into the first sentence. "All interplanar travel on these grounds is paused until the House is safe."

"Define safe," he said.

Sia almost said when we are not fighting. That was wishful. The House would always be holding something at bay. "Safe means the prison level is under control, there are no active breaches, and the staff can sleep for a night without taking shifts," she said. "Safe means the House is not carrying more pressure than it can recycle."

Thanatos tipped his chin as if to say, that will do. "Who enforces it."

"The House does," Sia said. She looked at the gate stones the way you look at a friend and ask them to come with you. "Not me pushing people. The House knows who is a guest and who is not. It knows what a demon is in the same way it knows what a fire alarm is."

"And consent," he said, not because he doubted her, but because it mattered.

"Consent applies to people," Sia said. "This target is not a person. I am not ordering a stranger to raise a hand or change a memory. I am telling a building who is not allowed inside it and how to handle a category of risk. If a demon comes in, the House will treat it like a live wire. It will not ask the wire if it wants to calm down. It will shut the breaker until the wire is gone."

"Plain," he said. "Keep going."

Sia glanced at the scythe. She did not want it. She respected it. It said border without a speech. She did not need to pick it up to mean the same thing.

"What about names," she asked. "Do I have to list them."

"No," Thanatos said. "You do not want a rule that fails when a new face arrives. Species is enough. If you must, you can include the old words for them, but the House understands demon better than catalogs. The House has kept ledgers longer than you have been alive. Trust it to sort."

Sia let that be a relief. She did not want to write a phone book.

"Do I need to say where the rule starts," she asked.

"You already did," he said. "You said grounds. Say House if you want the bones. Say Hotel if you want the mind. You can also say Sanctuary if you want both the bones and the mind to remember why."

Sia liked that. She pictured the sign Eric had mocked up in pencil as a joke the first week. She pictured the better one they had hung after. She pictured a sign made of metal, the kind you bolt to a wall and polish once a month. The words were clean and not bitter.

"By the steward of this House," she said again, slower, tasting each piece. "Demons are not welcome here. No demon may cross, dwell, ride, anchor, or return on these grounds. All inter-planar travel here is paused until the House is safe. The House will enforce this rule."

"Add the ownership line," Thanatos said.

Sia set her shoulders. She did not want to sound grand. She wanted to sound like a person who would still be here tomor-row. "The House recognizes Sia as steward for this rule," she said. "While it stands, it stands through me."

"That line is a hinge," he said. "It tells the door whose hand is on it. If you leave, the door will ask for a new hand. That is how you keep a place alive longer than you are."

"Good," Sia said. Her throat felt thick. She did not cry. She did not have time.

Thanatos watched her face the way a parent watches a child who is picking the right hard thing. "Say what happens to a demon who is already inside," he said. "Name the exit in plain words."

Sia thought of Crowley's smile cracking. She thought of elites stuck in loops. She thought of guests upstairs who had something riding them and did not know it. "Demons already inside will be caged or expelled by the House," she said. "They will not be allowed to hide in people. They will not be allowed to linger as smoke. They will not be allowed to leave by dying and come back from Hell."

"Good," he said. "Leave holes small enough you can fill them later. Do not try to solve every type of clever. Most clever is noise. Place law hates noise."

Sia nodded. "I am not locking angels out," she said, glancing at him and then away. "I am not locking gods out. I am not locking friends out. This is about demons."

"Then say demons," he said. "You did."

She looked at the river one more time. It flowed easy and did not care about Crowley or coins or vents. It would still be a river when she was old. That thought helped.

"What about the freeze," she asked. "I do not want to trap our own people when we need to move them. Ella will need to travel soon. Longwang invited her to train. If I say freeze, do I block that forever."

"You said until the House is safe," he said. "You also carry the hinge. You can lift the pause and put it back. Say that out loud when you wake if you want the building to log that you are using the switch."

"Okay," she said. "Okay."

She walked the length of the gate one more time and let her shoes crunch on gravel so she would remember how this felt later. She stood between the stones and spoke the whole rule in one go. Not loud. Clear.

"By the steward of this House," she said, "demons are not welcome here. No demon may cross, dwell, ride, anchor, or return on these grounds. All interplanar travel here is paused until the House is safe. The House enforces this rule. The House recognizes Sia as steward for this rule while it stands. Demons already inside will be caged or expelled by the House. They cannot hide in people. They cannot linger as smoke. They cannot leave by dying and return from Hell."

The wind moved through the Garden and did not change course. The scythe did not ring. The stones did not glow. None of that would have helped. Sia felt the thing that mattered. The sentence locked in her mouth like a key in a door that had been waiting for the right hand. It did not feel heavy. It felt correct.

"Say it again in the room," Thanatos said. "Say it like a person turning a switch. Do not shout. Shouting is for people. You are talking to a building."

Sia swallowed. "There is always a cost," she said, because she wanted to be the one to say it, not wait for someone to throw it at her later.

"There is," he said. "You will have to clean your own law. It will make messes. You will have to stand when you want to lie down. You will have to listen when you want to hide. The House will love you for it. It will also be terrible sometimes. That is true for every family."

She almost laughed at that, and then did laugh once because the sound of it felt like not dying. "I can do seasons," she said. "I can do terrible sometimes."

He looked past her toward the place where the circle sat in the other room. His not-eyes tracked Uriel's light and Crowley's pressure and the slow, patient threat of return that held the whole fight under its thumb. "Go say your lock," he said.

Sia turned from the gate and took two steps on the chalk path, then stopped. "If I mess it up," she said, "will you tell me."

"I have been," he said.

She nodded. That counted as a promise.

The Garden did not throw her out. It loosened its hand. The chalk smell thinned into hot metal air. Mia's hum came back full and close. Eric's sigils popped like flashbulbs. Tobias grunted once. Marcus laughed without humor. Ella's voice carried Uriel's heat. Crowley's words slid along the wall like grease. Glass ticked. Rails hummed. Sia's body finished the breath she had started and opened her eyes.

The circle was still around her. The fight was still the fight. The rule was ready on her tongue, plain and sharp. She did not need to build courage. She needed to speak.

"Cover me for three more," she said.

"We've got you," Tobias answered.

Sia stepped forward inside the circle, lifted the umbrella tip off the tile, and faced the room that had tried to learn her voice for weeks. The Garden held steady at her back like a hand on a shoulder. She set her breath with Mia's count and drew in a clean four.

She was ready to turn the key.

Sia opened her eyes into heat and noise. The circle still held around her. Tobias stood in front with his stance wide. Marcus pressed along her left shoulder like a wall that breathed. Eric's anchors glowed at the floor in three tight points. Mia's tone hummed steady. Ella and Crowley were locked ten yards ahead, light against pressure, steel against a hand that turned air heavy.

The rider had made it to the last lane. He was a step from the master board. The first demon crowded Tobias and laughed like it knew the joke. Elites slid along seams and looked for a gap.

Sia lifted the umbrella tip off the tile and breathed with Mia's count. Four in. Six out. The rule sat ready in her mouth.

"By the steward of this House," she said. She did not shout. She said it like a person turning a switch. "Demons are not welcome here. No demon may cross, dwell, ride, anchor, or return on these grounds. All interplanar travel here is paused until the House is safe. The House enforces this rule. The House recognizes Sia as steward for this rule while it stands. Demons already inside will be caged or expelled by the House. They cannot hide in people. They cannot linger as smoke. They cannot leave by dying and return from Hell."

The room listened.

Rails straightened like they remembered their job. Posts stopped flexing. Lines of light traced along thresholds she had named in the gallery and down the corridor. The floor took on clean weight under Sia's shoes. Wards stood up like soldiers who had been sitting too long.

Every demon in the room flinched at the same time. Not from force. From policy. You could see the rider feel it first. He staggered mid-step as if someone pulled a leash you could not see. The first demon choked on its grin. The elites flickered and tried to sink into seams that no longer opened for them.

Crowley felt it last. His eyes cut to Sia and his face slipped for half a second. He looked wrong in a way that made Sia's stomach go cold. Not teeth or claws. Real fear. The kind a person has when a trick stops being a trick.

"What did you do," he said. The easy tone was gone.

"Set the rule," Sia said.

He thrust his hand toward the lattice and tried to tear it open like a curtain. The lattice did not tear. The glass hummed and refused. Uriel pressed him hard and he gave ground without meaning to.

"Hold the lane," Tobias said.

"On it," Marcus said.

The rider lunged for the board on reflex. Sia tapped the floor in front of him with the umbrella ferrule and said, "No crossing." He hit an invisible line and stopped cold. He looked down like a man who has walked into a glass door. Eric snapped a binding square over his ankles and it held this time. The edges of the square went from white to iron gray as the House wrote the rule into the floor under it.

The first demon drove at Tobias with both hands. Tobias let it commit, took the hit on his blade, and rolled it into Marcus. Marcus grabbed a fistful of whatever passed for collar and dragged it off the ward plate. He dropped it in the pocket between two posts and stepped on its chest. The post hummed. The demon tried to slide into a seam and found no seam to use.

Mia's song shifted to a steady rise that made Sia think of a hand lifting you off the floor when your legs give out. The note wrapped the team and made everything feel possible. It was not pretty. It was useful.

Elites clawed at rails and got nothing. One tried to sprint across a lane and tripped over a rule that was not visible until it mattered. It skidded on tile and hit a post. The post did not bend. Eric tagged it with a small rune and the metal carried the tag like a brand.

Crowley tried the oldest path a demon has. He threw his arms wide and called death like it was home. Nothing opened. Nothing pulled. Sia watched his understanding arrive. If he died here, he would not go home. He would stay. The House would not let him leave by dying.

He glanced at Sia with a look that was almost respect and almost hate. "That is not fair," he said.

"It is a rule," Sia said.

Uriel did not argue with him. She took the step he gave her. Her blade cut a clean line across his chest. Smoke should have poured from the wound. A door should have tried to form. Neither happened. Crowley made a sound that was too human and stumbled.

"Finish it," Tobias said.

Crowley threw a heavy pressure at Uriel's knees. The lattice ticked as if glass felt the weight. Uriel burned it away by being present. She slid to his right and cut again. It was clean work. No speech. No drama. He tried to fall into a seam and the seam refused him. His eyes showed the math. He had nowhere to go.

He feinted toward Sia out of habit. Tobias stepped into that lane and put his body in the way. Crowley had to flinch. Uriel did not. She slices through the air and his neck as though it carried no more resistance than what surrounded it. Crowley's mouth made a shape like a joke he could not finish. He failed to turn to smoke. He failed to fall into a crack. He went down on the tile like a person who has lost. He saw his own body slump to the other side in the final moments of mortal experience. The floor did not allow him to exit by dying.

The air changed. The hot metal taste started to thin.

"Crowley's down," Tobias said. He did not celebrate. He checked left and right and then looked at Sia for the next job.

"Hold the freeze," Sia said. "We keep the travel pause until the House is safe."

"Logged," Eric said. He could hear it the way she could. The House marked her words like a switch on a board.

The first demon twisted under Marcus's boot. It tried to push a hand through the rail like a knife. The rail kept shape. Marcus leaned his weight in and gave it the kind of tired shove that says stop. It did not stop. It no longer had a way to escape, and that made it angry without purpose.

The rider tested the square at his ankles and met a rule again. He looked at Sia with steady eyes. He did not beg. He did not boast. He stood still because there was nothing else to do.

"Bind them," Tobias said. "We are done being their stage crew."

Eric cut a chain of symbols across the floor. They linked and tightened like a set of zip ties. Two elites went to their knees and stayed there. The House took hold of the chain and made it stronger. Mia kept the rise in her voice until Sia felt the rule hum in her teeth.

A last surge tried to form at the far seam. Three elites pushed at the same time. Ella turned, eyes still bright with Uriel, and lifted the flat of her blade. She did not swing hard. She set the blade across the lane like a bar. The surge broke on it and scattered.

"Clear left," Marcus said.

"Right is quiet," Eric said.

"Front is contained," Ella said.

The rider stared at the master board like a man looking

through the glass of a bakery case. Sia set the umbrella tip on the tile and told the lane, "No approach." The floor took that job and held it.

Charles had not moved from his cell. He had watched everything with that focused annoyance he wore like a uniform. He put his palm to the glass and waited. He did not need to ask. They knew the order. Crowley was down. The room was settled. Now they could get him out.

"Hold two more," Tobias said. "Then we cut Charles free."

Sia checked the edges. Rules held. Wards stood. The House breathed in a way that felt like it had remembered how. Heat still hung in the air. The metallic taste had faded enough that she could swallow without thinking of pennies.

She let the umbrella tip rest and felt the new framework sit inside the old like a brace. The hotel had chosen to listen. That did not mean it would always be easy. It meant she would not be alone when she spoke.

"Travel freeze stays up," Sia said again, so the building would log it twice. "We lift it after the prison level is under control and the staff can sleep."

"Logged," Eric said, and tapped the floor with his knuckles.

Elites that were not bound began to dull around the edges like food going out of focus. The House decided whether to cage or expel. One vanished with a soft pop, the way a candle goes out. Another slumped and melted into a hard glassy crust that the floor lifted like thin ice and slid toward a drain. The first demon did not escape. It kept trying to push. It simply had fewer places to push to.

Uriel stepped back from Crowley's body. Ella's face showed through the light for a second, pale and steady. She nodded once to Sia like a worker clocking a finished task. Sia nodded back.

"Now," Tobias said.

They moved as a group to Charles's cell. Tobias took the manual release housing. Eric checked the rune locks. Marcus posted to catch anything coming from the side. Ella stood ready with the flat to block a reflex strike from anything that still had opinions. Mia let her song fall to a low, even cadence that sat in everyone's spine like a reminder to breathe.

Sia laid her palm on the pane. "This cell opens for allies," she said. She set the umbrella ferrule to the seam and spoke to the frame. "Frame moves. Seal releases."

Eric traced a short pattern over the lock. "Ready."

"On three," Tobias said. "One. Two. Three."

The release turned. The bar inside the door dropped. The seal let go with a tired sigh. Charles stepped out like a man who had been trapped at a desk and finally stood up. He did not stumble. He did not smile. He took the Key from the chain at his neck and touched Sia's shoulder once with his free hand.

"Thank you," he said. He sounded like a person in the middle of a workday who had no time for speeches.

He crossed to the master board. The House had stopped pretending nothing was wrong. Lights showed red where work waited, amber where work had been done, clean green where rules held. Charles pressed the Key to the board and turned his wrist. Lines lit that Sia had not seen lit before. The building shifted under her feet like a ship that had found the right current.

"Hotel sweep," Charles said. "Apply new law. Expel or cage by species. Release riders from guests. Send them to bed."

The board hummed. The sound went up through the panes, up through the rails, up through the floor into the halls above. Sia felt it like a wind that did not move air. The fight upstairs went quiet in pieces and then all at once. The building shook itself once and settled.

Mia stopped singing for the first time in what felt like an hour and took one raw breath. "Did it work."

Charles looked at the board and nodded. "Possessions cut. Guests falling asleep where they stand. Demons above trapped or expelled. Travel pause is active. Good."

The rider stood very still, bound at the ankles, eyes steady on Sia. The first demon lay under Marcus's boot with its hands open and empty. Elites sat dazed inside new cages that had formed where seams used to be. Crowley's body was just a body.

Sia kept the umbrella in her hands until the shake left her fingers. She said the freeze line one more time and felt the House mark it as active. The rails hummed a normal hum. The glass went clear.

"Quick checks," Tobias said. "Hands. Eyes. Blood."

"Good," Ella said.

"Good," Marcus said.

"Good," Eric said, and then added, "I hate the taste of pennies."

"Same," Mia said. She wiped tears she had not noticed. They were not dramatic. They were chemical.

Sia rolled her shoulders and let herself feel tired for one breath. The rule held. The House held. They had kept the room and the people in it. They had a night to earn upstairs. She could lift the freeze later. Not yet.

She looked at Charles. "I can keep the pause until we clean the lower floors. Then I can lift it and put it back if we need to move people."

"Do that," Charles said. He touched the Key to the board again and nodded once, like a conductor checking tempo. He looked past Sia toward the corridor and smiled the smallest, meanest smile she had ever seen him make. "Crowley hated being ordinary," he said. "He can practice."

That was the only joke anyone made. It was enough.

Sia leaned on the umbrella for a second because she could. The rails hummed steady. The panes stayed clear. Above them, alarms had stopped. The House felt like a place again.

CHAPTER 20

After The Storm

KAELAN

"Perhaps home is not a place but simply an irrevocable condition."

James Baldwin, Giovanni's Room

KAELAN HAD BEEN AWAKE long enough that coffee felt like a hobby she used to have. The lobby lights were dimmed to the overnight setting, that warm hotel glow that pretends the world is kinder at three in the morning. It was not three in the morning anymore. It was the gray before sunrise, when the big cutout letters on the museum's donation box looked like a shadow you could pick up and carry.

Truth leaned against her calf, all fluff and seriousness, eyes

454

tracking the room like a guard in a little bear suit. When a guest stirred on a couch, Truth's ear twitched first. When a blanket slipped, Truth nosed it back up and gave Kaelan a look that said, hello, I am doing my job, keep up.

"I see you," Kaelan whispered, scratching the soft place behind Truth's ear. "Promotion has not gone to your head at all."

Truth accepted the praise with a huff and moved to the edge of a hallway, sitting with her back straight and her tail wrapped around her paws. Temple Dog, first day. She was very busy.

Guests were everywhere. Not in a chaotic way. More like a sleepover that got out of hand and then became the point. Two teens in merch hoodies were curled on a bench under the mastodon poster. A pair of tourists in matching hiking pants had slid down the wall beneath the map of the Western Territories, heads leaning together like a love story. A bus driver in a jacket that had seen cities slept in a chair with his hat over his face. A family of four lay in a tidy row on the big woven rug, shoes lined up at the edge like they had been taught. The museum had never looked more like a church than it did with everyone quiet and breathing.

Mariah and Mia kept the air level. They worked soft, not performance soft, but kitchen soft, the way music sits in a room when someone hums without thinking. Mariah leaned on the welcome desk and sent a simple line of tone down the hallways, the kind of sound that makes your shoulders drop and your jaw unclench. Mia sat on the edge of the fountain ledge with a water bottle in her hands like a microphone she did not need. Her voice braided under her mother's and filled in the places where worry wanted to sprout.

Eric had claimed the far corner near the brochures and set up a triage table with a legal pad, a Sharpie, and a stack of those tiny bottled waters that make you thirsty by existing. He wrote names the way he cast spells, fast and neat. He had labeled columns with NORMAL QUESTIONS, LOST ITEMS, and ACTUAL PROBLEMS. Under ACTUAL PROBLEMS he had written in smaller letters, breathing, blood, dizzy, missing person, door that refuses to be a door. He had already crossed off door that refuses to be a door.

Marcus moved furniture like the furniture had wronged him and he wanted to give it a chance to apologize. He did not slam anything. He lifted, turned, and set pieces down where the flow made sense. He checked doorframes with the side of his hand and looked at hinges the way you look at a person's knees to see if they are going to buckle. When he passed Truth, he gave her a solemn nod. Truth gave one back. Colleagues.

Kaelan walked the loop. Lobby, rotunda, gift shop doors, ticketing desk, back to lobby. She had walked shrines like this a thousand times, feet learning a building so well that you could find the good nail with your eyes closed. The House felt different under her. Not louder. Not brighter. It had a new bass note, the kind of steady that makes other sounds find a place to sit. Sia's rule lived in the bones now. Kaelan did not need to see a sign to know it. She felt it in the way coins stayed put on counters, in the way a draft failed to gather itself at a seam. The bad tricks had gone quiet. The House had good manners.

Her phone buzzed once in her pocket. Charles. Short text, because he was who he was.

sweep underway. you have the floor.

She texted back.

copy. lobby steady. coffee?

No reply. She smiled. If Charles needed coffee he would arrest a coffee and wring it into a cup.

A man on the couch near the coat check snorted awake and flailed for a second before freezing. Truth stood and wagged once, very polite. Kaelan got there before panic remembered its name.

"Hey," she said, soft. "You're okay. You fell asleep during a late night drill. We kept everyone down here to make it easy. You're at the museum. Do you want water."

The man blinked at her, then at Truth, then at the water bottle she had already held out. "What time is it."

"Early," she said. "Sun's almost up. We'll be serving coffee and a very impressive buffet of granola bars when folks are ready."

He took the bottle and swallowed like it owed him money. "I had a weird dream," he said. He looked embarrassed, like he wanted to apologize to the room for admitting it.

"Everyone did," Kaelan said. "We're going to blame the vintage HVAC and the fact that the fossils have strong opinions about bedtime."

He laughed in a startled little way. "Fossils."

"They demand warm socks and quiet," she said deadpan. "They're tyrants."

He smiled for real and relaxed back into the couch. He looked past her at Truth. "Is that your dog."

"She is her own dog," Kaelan said. "But we're coworkers."

Truth tucked her chin, pleased.

Mariah drifted over and eased a light blanket over the man's legs with the kind of touch that makes people remember they are allowed to be cared for. "Sip," she said, and moved on like a breeze.

At the welcome desk, Mia's song pressed a last little cough of fear out of the air. Eric had moved three names from ACTUAL PROBLEMS to NORMAL QUESTIONS with satisfyingly firm lines. Marcus stood up after sliding the big bench a foot to the left and checked the front doors one more time. He did not touch them. He put his palm near the seam and felt for that old magnetic pull that made the hair on your arm misbehave. Nothing. The doors sat like doors.

Kaelan stepped up beside him and looked through the glass. It was still gray out. The empty street had the kind of hush you only get when a city holds its breath and decides to be kind for five minutes. A bus rolled past without blasting its engine. The streetlamps ticked off in a neat row like polite soldiers. Someone outside dropped a coin. It pinged on the step and did not roll toward a crack. It simply lay where it landed, like a child waiting for a parent to pick it up.

"You feel that," Marcus asked without looking at her.

"Like the House learned please and thank you overnight," she said. "Yes."

He nodded once and scanned the sidewalks the way other people check headlines. "Sia did that."

"She did," Kaelan said. Pride and worry braided in her chest and then let each other sit. "She is probably asleep standing up right now."

"Tell her she owes me a new back," he said. It looked like a joke. It sounded like a promise.

"You plan on telling her yourself," Kaelan asked, because habits die hard and she liked hearing him say yes out loud when the room was quiet enough to hear it.

Marcus looked like he was about to answer. Eric called his name, and he turned and went, moving with that controlled energy that says I can keep going until someone smarter than me says stop. She watched him until he reached the desk, then let herself breathe out slow.

Guests began to stir in clusters. Air mattresses were not a thing they had, but people made do with stackable chairs and backpacks as pillows. Kaelan passed out bottled water and slid baskets of bars to every cluster with a joke about supply lines and the dramatic power of oats. She had a calm voice for strangers. She grew it in temples, using it on wedding days and wet spring funerals and those times when someone needed to sit on cool stone and sob without being alone. It worked here. People took their cues from the way she stood, the way she smiled with the corners of her mouth and not much else, the way she kept hands visible and let the silence stand where it needed to.

A teenage girl in a band tee blinked awake and then sat up fast like she had missed a test. Truth trotted over and put her chin on the girl's knee. The girl touched fluff and made a noise like a hiccup that turned into a laugh.

"What happened," she asked, looking at Kaelan because Truth had already answered most of the question she needed.

"Short version," Kaelan said. "We had a late night systems test. It was boring. We brought everyone down here to rest so we could reset. You were never in danger. You might feel like you ran a mile in your sleep. That is normal. Drink water and sit up slow."

The girl nodded. "I dreamed about the dinosaur bones singing."

"They rehearse," Kaelan said, like this was a well known museum fact. "Tone deaf, but committed."

That got a smile from two couches over. The smile bounced to the next cluster and woke a dad who looked like he had been a linebacker twenty years ago and still remembered how to stand up without rocking. He rubbed his face and nodded to her like a coach noticing another coach. She nodded back.

Eric met Kaelan in the middle with updates.

"I have six lost items that are not really lost and three people who insist they left their car keys in a vent," he said, flipping his pad closed with the satisfaction of a completed side quest. "Two actual medicals, both headaches and nausea. I gave them water and the lobby floor gave them the idea to nap sitting up.

It worked. No one is concussed. One kid is convinced he had the best dream in history. He is telling it to a fossil."

"Let him," Kaelan said. "The fossil will keep his secret."

Eric grinned and then grew serious in the way he does without changing his face much. "You feel the rule under us."

"Every step," she said. "Coins behave. Doors are boring. I could cry with gratitude."

"Same," he said. "I never want to see another coin trap for the rest of my life."

"Write it on a plaque," she said. "We'll mount it under the fire extinguisher."

He saluted with his Sharpie and went to intercept a man who was trying to open a staff door with a look that said, I am helpful, let me make work for you.

Mariah slid onto the stool at the welcome desk and looked like a poster for Calm Person You Trust. Mia stopped singing long enough to sip water and make a face like a human. When she set the bottle down, the room asked for her voice again without words. She gave it without being told.

"Break in twenty," Kaelan said to both of them. "We'll switch to recorded birds and pretend it is an art exhibit."

Mariah smiled. "I will sing until we are done. Then I will eat half a pantry."

"Fair," Kaelan said. "I owe you pancakes."

Truth circled back and leaned into Kaelan's leg again. Her fur smelled like dust and a little like something clean that does not come in a bottle. Kaelan crouched and pressed her forehead to the top of Truth's head. "Thank you for helping me keep the hall," she said. "You were perfect."

Truth wagged once, very dignified, and trotted off to investigate a granola wrapper with the posture of a tiny professional.

Kaelan checked the front doors again. Morning had arrived in a measured way. The sky went pale and the street woke up but did not argue. She opened the doors a crack to feel the air and watched the line between inside and outside the way shrines teach. The House's manners had started to bleed past the threshold. It was not dramatic. It was in the little things. The air held still for a beat before moving, like it asked permission. A single plastic bag that would normally go on a neighborhood tour hit the sidewalk, hesitated, and laid itself neatly under a bench like it had remembered how to behave. A cyclist rolled past without clipping the curb. The curb looked proud of itself.

"Kaelan," Marcus said from behind her.

She turned. He had a stack of folded museum blankets in his arms and a look that made her think of a rock in a river. Not moving. Carrying what the water gave him.

"How many more," she asked, reaching to take the top two.

"Four in the back hallway and three in the gift shop door," he said. He balanced the rest in a clean pile and set them on the bench that Mia had declared a lost and found with a gesture and a piece of tape.

"You should sit for five," she said.

"I will after the next round," he said. "Charles says the sweep is almost done. The board likes our new rules."

"Good," Kaelan said.

He hesitated like he had a second sentence he had not decided to say. Eric called his name again, because of course he did, and Marcus exhaled with a tiny laugh like he had been rescued from himself. He went, already moving in a straight line toward the next problem.

Kaelan turned back to the doors and watched a couple in matching jackets take a selfie with the museum in the background. They framed it so the building's name and the banners looked heroic. The woman's hand shook a little. The man put his hand over hers on the phone to steady it. The picture they took would not show why they were tired. It would show a morning that was calm enough to remember.

"Five minutes," Mia said, voice rough from the work and still more beautiful than any speaker could buy. "Then I am switching to a playlist before I blow a gasket."

"You earned one," Kaelan said. "Make it birds and rain. Everyone will decide we planned it."

"Always," Mia said, and sent one more soft line of sound down the hallway. A child sleeping on two chairs in the corner rolled to his other side and settled deeper.

Kaelan checked the little pile of paper meal vouchers Charles had printed. They looked like something a hotel would give you when they mess up your reservation. She liked the normalcy of it. She had stamped each with a tiny sun. Not magical. Cute. People liked tiny suns.

A woman in a business suit stood carefully and came over

with her purse tucked under her arm like a shield. "Excuse me," she said. "I think I slept in your lobby."

"You did," Kaelan said. "We brought everyone down for a safety drill. I'm sorry for the confusion. We have water, granola bars, and as soon as the cafe opens, real breakfast. This is a voucher to cover it. You can use it here or at the corner bakery across the street if you need to get moving."

The woman took it and blinked twice like she was surprised to find herself not angry. "Thank you."

"No problem," Kaelan said. "If you feel like you ran a race in your sleep, that is normal. Take it slow."

"I dreamed about my grandmother's kitchen," the woman said, a little startled to have said it out loud.

"Good kitchens borrow each other," Kaelan said. "It means you needed it."

The woman closed her eyes for a second and nodded. "Okay."

When she walked away, Truth followed her for three steps to make sure she did not tip over, then returned to her post, pleased with herself again.

Kaelan's phone buzzed. New text from Charles.

lower floors clear. coming up.

She answered with a thumbs up and an image of a pancake that had more blueberries than pancake. She did not know if he would recognize the emotion behind it. He did not need to. He would recognize the shape of work done.

She did one more loop and let the building show off. Doors held. Posters hung straight. The skeleton in the rotunda looked less like an omen and more like a grandparent showing you a trick with their teeth. The air did not taste like pennies, which was her new benchmark for heaven.

At the welcome desk, Mariah shifted to a lower hum and gave Kaelan a look that said, break. Kaelan nodded and took it like a gift you should not argue with. She walked behind the desk, opened the little fridge that made more noise than it had a right to, and pulled out two cold waters. She handed one to Mia.

"Drink," she said.

Mia took it and leaned her shoulder against Kaelan's for a second like a sister. "You good."

"I am pretending to be," Kaelan said. "It is working."

Mia smiled and returned to the fountain ledge. Mariah changed the key without being asked, and the room followed like water taking the shape of a bowl.

Truth trotted over and bumped Kaelan's knee with her head. When Kaelan looked down, Truth gave her a look that said, the front step would like to report that it is behaving. Also, please pet me or I will die.

Kaelan crouched and put both hands in Truth's ruff. "Tell the step thank you," she said. "Tell the street it is invited to be reasonable."

Truth wagged like a diplomat.

The first real sun hit the lobby through the tall windows and made the dust look like glitter no one would regret later. People woke and stretched and laughed the way you do when you realize you are still here. The House held its new shape like it had always meant to. Kaelan stood up straight, rolled her shoulders, and let herself believe that this time, the morning really was on their side.

By the time Charles came up from the lower levels, the lobby had shifted from sleepover to morning-after. People were upright, hair was trying its best, and granola wrappers had formed a small civilization near the recycling bin. Mariah kept the room level with that soft, steady tone people call mothering when they mean professional kindness. Mia leaned on the fountain ledge and harmonized in a way that made breath come back on command. Eric handed out vouchers like a magician producing cards from thin air. Marcus had already repaired two stanchions, reset a rope, and made friends with the mop bucket.

Charles did not sweep in. He simply arrived, as if the building had walked him to the right square. He carried a long, flat package wrapped in brown paper and taped like a person who respects corners. Sia walked beside him with her umbrella and the kind of tired that lives under your eyes and still makes room for a smile. Truth spotted them first and trotted over, tail high, posture very important. She stopped before Sia and sat like a statue.

"Morning, temple dog," Sia said, and scratched under Truth's chin. Truth had planned to be dignified about the new title. She failed for three seconds and then recovered.

Charles turned the package and set it on the welcome desk. "Ready for the posting," he asked. He sounded like a man who had said this twice already in other centuries.

Kaelan glanced at the crowd. Enough guests were awake and upright to make this feel less like housekeeping and more like the kind of moment a place remembers. She nodded. "Here is good," she said. "Center of the wall, eye level."

Eric cleared the display space below the museum map with fast hands. He took down the faded poster asking DO YOU KNOW WHERE YOUR MEMBERSHIP CARD IS and leaned it against a crate that was pretending to be a table. Mia stopped singing long enough to press two pieces of painter's tape flat. Mariah called, "Eyes front," to no one in particular, which made a handful of people look up and smile without being told why.

Charles peeled the paper back. The metal caught the lobby light and held it without showing off. The plaque had weight. The letters were cut deep and blackened, not painted. Sia touched the bottom corner like someone shaking hands.

THE DREAMER'S ACCORDS

By the steward of this House

Demons are not welcome here.

No demon may cross, dwell, ride, anchor, or return on these grounds.

All interplanar travel here is paused until the House is safe.

The House enforces this rule.

The House recognizes Sia as steward for this rule while it stands.

Demons already inside will be caged or expelled by the House.

They cannot hide in people.

They cannot linger as smoke.

They cannot leave by dying and return from Hell.

GUEST RULES

Be kind. Ask before entering staff areas.

No coins on hinges. No doors made into games.

Respect the quiet. Report strange drafts, sounds, or lights.

If you are afraid, tell the desk. Fear is data. We listen.

Kaelan read the lines with her whole body. The metal did not hum, but the space around it settled the way a room does when someone finally says the thing everyone had been waiting to hear. It was not dramatic. It was correct.

"Good height," she said to Eric.

"Good type," Eric said to Charles, which was his way of saying he approved. He passed Charles a driver. Charles used two bolts that looked like they trusted gravity. The plaque seated against the wall with a small sound that made the hair on Kaelan's arms lift.

Sia stood close and quiet. She did not try to look important. She didn't have to. The House leaned in when she breathed.

Kaelan watched the air like a priest watches a flame. The bass note she had felt in Scene 1 steadied under the floor. The corners of the lobby stopped trying to collect drafts. Someone outside dropped a coin again. It hit the step and stayed where it fell as if it had learned manners. Truth heard it and decided not to investigate. That was new.

Charles stepped back and let Sia take center without announcing it. Sia's tired smile turned into a work face. She set the umbrella tip to the tile and rested one hand on the rail to her right like a person greeting a coworker.

Kaelan felt the shift before Sia spoke, the way shrine grounds feel when someone with the right authority says the right word. This was the part that mattered. The plaque was an announcement. The House would remember the voice.

Sia kept her tone plain. "House," she said, just loud enough to carry. "Lift the travel pause. Keep the demon ban."

The building did not flare or ring. The change was a clean click all through the bones. The lobby air took a breath without the heavy at the bottom. Somewhere in the vents, the sound of moving space settled into an easy, straight run. The floor under Kaelan's shoes felt like it had put its shoulders down.

Mia blew out a breath she did not know she had been holding. Mariah smiled without looking away from the room. Eric pulled a sticky note off his pad, wrote TRAVEL OPEN and DEMONS STILL NOT WELCOME, and stuck it on his water bottle like a label he meant to keep. Marcus rolled his shoulders once, like a jacket had fit again.

A few guests clapped. It started as an awkward sprinkle, then gathered into a small, honest sound. They didn't know what had changed. They knew the room felt safe. Truth stood under the plaque and did a very serious sit no one had taught her. The seriousness lasted five seconds before she wagged at a toddler who pointed and whispered, "Dog."

Kaelan stepped to Sia's side and lowered her voice. "Feel it."

Sia nodded. "Lighter," she said. "Not empty. Just not trying to fight itself."

"That is what a shrine feels like when it remembers its job," Kaelan said. "You gave this place a job. It likes having one."

Sia glanced up at the lines under GUEST RULES and snorted softly at Fear is data. "Eric's?"

"Absolutely," Kaelan said. "I added the no games line."

"Good call," Sia said. She tapped the plaque once with her fingertip. "It will hold?"

"It will hold," Kaelan said. "The House will repeat it until it wears grooves in the day. That is what we want." She tipped her chin toward the front doors. "Come outside for a second. I want you to feel something."

They had to step carefully between sleeping bags and backpacks. Truth padded ahead like a parade marshal and stopped at the threshold. Sia touched the frame as if it were a living thing. It felt that way to Kaelan too. The wood was old. The polish was new. The air between inside and outside held a visible line that had not been visible yesterday.

They stepped out onto the top stair. Morning had arrived

properly. The street did its usual, cars and shoes and a bus groan three blocks over, but everything was a touch more polite. The difference was almost nothing if you looked for big signs. If you were a shrine maiden who had lived her life feeling edges, it was everything.

"Here," Kaelan said, and tilted her head toward the nearest lamp post. The metal had that thin hum you get from city power, but beneath it ran the House's new bass. Not loud. Steady. "It is using the posts and frames. Anything that repeats in lines. It is offering its manners to the town."

Sia squinted at the lamp like she was trying to see sound. "Is that what I'm feeling in my teeth."

"Yes," Kaelan said. "Thresholds are contagious when they are taught, not forced."

Across the street, the bakery sign flicked from closed to open. The door cracked, and warm air spilled out heavy with cinnamon. A man stepped out with a broom, swept once, and stopped to look at the museum without knowing why. He nodded to no one and went back in. The nod felt like the first stitch of a seam.

Sia's shoulders dropped a little. "I was worried the rule would make us a hard shell."

"It could, if you tried to carry it like a wall," Kaelan said. "You wrote it as manners. Manners spread. People copy them. Metal listens to them. By the end of the week, the town will feel like a place that expects good behavior from its doors. Demons will stay confused at the edge. That confusion is a blessing."

Truth sniffed the top step like a supervisor doing an inspection. She looked up at Sia with a face that said the stairs report compliance.

"Thank you, inspector," Sia told her, and rubbed the top of her head.

Footsteps scuffed behind them. Eric came out with two coffees that looked like they had done a tour of duty to get here. He handed one to Sia and one to Kaelan. "I signed for these with a voucher that said we inconvenienced you with a metaphysical policy upgrade," he said.

"Perfect phrasing," Kaelan said. She tasted the coffee and felt the world slot into its right places one by one. "Did you put the smaller staff rules behind the desk."

"Printed and laminated," Eric said. "No senior discounts on metaphysics. If it squeaks or drafts weird, call Sia or me. If you're afraid, tell once, then twice, then push the blue button. No coin art. I put it in a frame because I want people to believe it is old."

"It will be old in a week," Kaelan said.

Sia drank, then watched a leaf tumble along the curb. It hit a storm drain grate and did not try to wriggle through. It rested against the bar as if it accepted the idea of edges. She smiled at nothing and everything.

"Charles will want a small note about travel," Kaelan said. "Do you want to say it now."

Sia nodded. She stepped back inside to the plaque and spoke clearly for the House. "Travel is open for guests and staff. The demon ban stands."

The room accepted the update with another of those quiet clicks. In the far wing a door that had been patient through the night opened like it had been waiting for permission. Mariah raised a hand and the door settled into a polite swing instead of a rush.

A kid near the gift shop asked in a loud whisper, "Is this a ceremony."

Kaelan smiled at him. "It is a posting. Ceremonies have cake. We will get cake later."

Sia leaned on the rail for a moment and let the coffee be a coffee instead of survival. Close up, the tired in her face showed all the miles they had walked in a day. She still looked like a person who would answer a radio at three in the morning and laugh once before doing the hard thing. Kaelan felt a private rush of pride, then set it down where it would not get in the way.

Truth sat under the plaque again, eyes bright, chest out. A guest snapped a photo and whispered, "Temple dog," to his partner like he had spotted a celebrity. Truth took the compliment like a professional.

Marcus joined them at the wall and read the whole plaque with a slow nod, lips pressing into a line at Fear is data. "Yeah," he said. "That tracks."

He glanced at Sia, then at the doors, then back at Sia. The look wasn't a question yet. It was the shape of one. Kaelan filed it and let it pass for now.

Charles reappeared beside the desk, already working three

things at once without looking busy. "The board is clean," he said. "We'll keep pairs on the lower levels today and cycle staff off for real rest. Kaelan, how are the guests."

"Safe and obedient," Kaelan said. "We are using the full power of snacks."

"Excellent," Charles said. He looked up at the plaque and let the corners of his mouth lift a fraction. "It reads well."

"It does more than read," Kaelan said.

He met Sia's eyes. "Thank you," he said simply.

Sia nodded, drank the last of her coffee, and set the cup under the desk. "We still have to live with it," she said. "So does the town."

"We will," Charles said. "That is what towns are for." He checked his watch like a man checking the tide. "We'll make a short announcement in twenty minutes. Housekeeping story, breakfast notes, apologies, and vouchers. Keep it boring."

"Boring is my art," Eric said from his corner.

"Good," Charles said, and moved on to the next task, the way rivers move around stones, certain and patient.

Kaelan stood with Sia a breath longer and watched the plaque, the doors, the people who had shared a strange night. The House felt steady in her bones. Outside, a city bus idled at the corner and did not rattle the windows the way it used to. A woman dropped a coin. It bounced once and stayed. A teenager held the door for a stranger without being told to. None of that would make a headline. All of it counted.

"You did well," Kaelan said, low, so it belonged to Sia and no one else.

Sia's smile was small and tired and happy. "We did," she said.

Truth huffed agreement and leaned into both of their legs at once. The plaque sat on the wall like it had always been there. The lobby remembered how to be a lobby. The House remembered how to be a House. And outside, the town began to learn the manners of a sanctuary.

LATE MORNING PUT A soft shine on the rotunda marble. The banner for the Ice Age exhibit hung straight for the first time in weeks, like even fabric had decided to behave. Guests drifted between benches and display cases with that cautious politeness people use after a weird night. Coffee cups, water bottles, granola wrappers. It looked like normal life had walked back in and set its bag by the door.

Tobias stood under the balcony with his duffel at his feet and a printed itinerary in his hand. If you squinted, he could be any coach packing up after a tournament. Ella checked the gear straps on the same bag, then checked them again. She wore the sword sheathed and quiet. Uriel stayed quiet too. That was a relief.

"Flight times are set," Tobias said, tapping the paper. "Church routing will skip every place that asks too many questions. We'll land, meet the contact in Shanghai, and catch the high-speed to Nanjing. From there, Longwang's people hand us to the local side. We keep our heads down, do the training, and bring the good manners home."

"Good manners are contagious," Kaelan said. "So are bad ones. Don't pick any up."

"I'll bring you a souvenir," he said. "Something tacky."

"Bring me a clean schedule," Charles said, appearing like he had been there the whole time. He looked better with sunlight on his face. He looked like a man who believed in lists again. "Travel is open, remember. But we still file movement reports."

"Already sent," Tobias said, and handed him a copy because he knew his audience.

Ella rolled her shoulders. The motion was small and told the truth. "We'll go once the next sweep is done and the lobby is fully back to boring. Two days, three if anything twitches."

"You don't need my permission," Charles said. "You have it anyway."

Ella smiled, real and quick. "Thanks."

Mia came with a grocery bag of snacks for the road because of course she did. "This is everything I wanted someone to hand me after the worst day of my life," she said. "Yogurt, fruit, a sandwich that might be half mustard by the time you eat it, and a bag of gummy bears because sugar solves a percentage of problems."

"Scientific," Tobias said, taking the bag. "Thank you."

Eric handed Ella a slim folder. "Phones prepped. Contacts printed. Two burner numbers with codes. If anything moves weird on your end, call me. If I don't pick up, call Sia. If neither of us pick up, find the nearest shrine or police station and ask the desk for a landline. Say the phrase on page two. Someone will make a phone ring in my pocket."

"That sounds like a good story," Ella said. "I'll ask you about it when we get back."

"Please do," Eric said. "I never get to tell my stories."

Truth chose that moment to patrol past like a small, very serious parade. She stopped by Tobias, sniffed the duffel, and sat. Tobias scratched her head. "Keep the lobby safe, officer."

Truth accepted the rank and trotted on. Guests were watching her, which she took as her due.

Kaelan stayed close to Sia without hovering. Sia looked wrung out in the exact way that means someone did the job and was paying the bill in muscle and sleep. The plaque on the wall had turned the lobby into a room with a spine. It made Sia look more like herself.

Marcus crossed the floor with a coil of tape and a repaired stanchion rope. He set the rope, tested the post, then stood as if his body had just remembered how to be still. He looked at the doors, then at Sia, then at Tobias. His jaw set. It wasn't nothing.

"We'll hold the place," Eric said, glancing between Sia and Marcus like he could grease a hinge with words. "Mia and I have the systems. Kaelan knows borders better than any of us. Charles has the board. Truth has a badge now."

"And me," Marcus said, but it sounded like he was trying it on. He looked at Sia again. It was a full look that stayed on her face and didn't pretend to be about the room.

Kaelan heard the quiet beat in her own chest that means leave this alone. She stepped half a pace back and let the lobby be loud for them.

Sia moved to Marcus and touched his elbow. "Walk with me," she said.

They went to the side hallway where the light fell thin through the museum windows. Truth started to follow, realized this was not her job, and went back to her patrol. Kaelan didn't watch them go. She traded three granola vouchers for two grateful smiles and made a note in her head to find better snacks for next time. She didn't listen for words. She let their privacy be a real thing, not a polite performance.

Tobias slung his duffel. Ella checked the strap again because she is Ella. "We'll be back before the town forgets how to behave," Tobias said.

"The town won't forget," Kaelan said. She could feel the field out past the doors now, touching porch frames, bus stops, the bakery's brass handle. It ticked along street lamps and settled in doorways like a polite cat. "The House is teaching it."

Ella took that in and relaxed a fraction. "Good," she said. "I don't like leaving when the ink is still drying."

"It's dry enough," Charles said. "Go learn the next thing. Bring it back."

Mia hugged Ella hard. "No hero stuff," she said. "Just the training."

"No guarantees," Ella said, but her smile said she heard the point.

Eric offered Tobias a fist bump. Tobias returned it without irony. "Page two," Eric said, tapping the folder. "I mean it."

"Page two," Tobias said. "Yes, sir."

From the hallway came the sound of a quiet laugh that sounded like Sia's, and then Marcus's answer, low and simple. They returned a minute later. Marcus's face hadn't changed much, but the set of his shoulders had. He looked lighter and heavier at the same time, which is how decisions sit.

"We're good," Sia said to the group, and to Kaelan, and to herself.

Marcus didn't make an announcement. He stood beside Sia like it was the most natural place to stand, nodded to Tobias, and said, "Go do it. We've got home."

Kaelan let herself breathe out. That was the answer that mattered.

Charles checked his watch and made a small face at time, like time had said something rude. "We'll do the announcement now," he said. "Short. Routine. We apologize for the drill. We thank them for patience. We give out breakfast. Then we go back to work."

He walked to the welcome desk, pressed the small mic button, and used the voice that makes people take comfort in lines and clipboards. "Good morning," he said. "Thank you for your patience during last night's safety drill. We're clearing the upper floors in stages. Please enjoy complimentary breakfast in the cafe or with your voucher at the corner bakery. If you feel unwell or have questions, see the desk. We are here to help."

People clapped again. It wasn't a cheer. It was release. The kind that comes when someone tells you yes, this is the story, and the story is boring in a way you can hold.

Ella turned to Sia. "One more thing," she said. "Longwang asked to meet me at the water's edge near Nanjing. He offered to train me in things I need. I'm going because I want to be better when I stand next to you."

Sia's answer was small and honest. "I want you safe when you stand next to me."

"Both," Ella said. "We'll make both true."

They hugged the way people do when they remember other rooms where it was harder. Tobias nodded to everyone, including Truth. Truth wagged exactly twice in professional acknowledgment.

"Get out of here," Eric said. "Before I start another speech about checklists."

"Please don't," Tobias said, and left with Ella at his side. The doors opened with good manners and closed the same way. The room didn't deflate. It set its shoulders and got on with the day.

Sia watched the doors for one breath, then turned to Kaelan. "I'm posting the staff card now," she said. "If we have to be the adults, we might as well look like it."

They went behind the desk together. Sia pulled a smaller plaque from a folder, the size of a menu. It was plain and clear.

STAFF PRACTICALS

- If it squeaks or drafts weird, log it and call Sia or Eric.

> - No coin art. No door games.
> - Ask before shaping. Listen before naming.
> - If you're afraid, tell once, then twice, then push the blue button.
> - Rest is work. Take your breaks.

Kaelan held the frame while Sia set two screws. The metal clicked into place with that same correct little sound. The sign didn't need a blessing. It had one anyway.

"You want the last line," Sia asked.

Kaelan smiled. "I already have it."

She looked across the lobby. Mariah pulled a tray of muffins from nowhere and convinced a bus driver to sit down for five minutes. Eric walked a kid to the lost and found and reunited him with a sneaker like it was a trophy. Mia sat on the fountain ledge and ate a yogurt like it was a sacrament. Marcus stood by the doors and watched the street with a guard's eyes and a man's heart. Truth leaned against the base of the Dreamer's Accords and accepted a scratch from a shy child with a patience that made the child's mother cry a little for no reason she would admit.

Charles returned from speaking to a staffer and checked the board on his phone. He lifted his chin a fraction, which was how he smiled when life made sense. The building held a low hum like a choir before a hymn.

Kaelan walked to the doors and pushed them open with two fingers. The Sanctuary field reached across the street now. It wrapped porch frames in quiet and traced the edge of the bakery window like a neat hand. A delivery truck slowed before it needed to. A boy on a skateboard paused at the curb and looked both ways without his mother telling him to. The town wasn't a fortress. It was a place with expectations that made bad ideas trip.

Sia came to stand beside her. "You feel it too," she said.

"Everywhere," Kaelan said. "By the end of the week, it'll touch the river. After that, we see who we are inside it."

They stood there for a breath. The new plaque gleamed behind them. The staff card sat under the desk where it would be read twice a day until it became muscle memory. The lobby sounded like conversations and plastic lids and apology laughs. Real life, not the kind that pretends.

"Welcome to our base," Kaelan said.

"Our home," Sia said, and it didn't feel like a big word said too soon. It felt like a key turning.

Truth nosed their hands, then trotted out to the top step and sat like a statue. People took pictures. A little girl waved and said, very seriously, "Good morning, temple dog."

Truth wagged once. The banner above them hung straight. The doors behaved. The town learned the manners of a sanctuary, one frame and one porch at a time.

The Green Envelope

Sia

Late sun slanted through the museum doors and turned the lobby's dust into glitter that didn't feel cheap. The Dreamer's Accords plaque caught the light and held it, black letters steady as breath. Guests drifted out with coffee and vouchers, laughing in that quiet way people laugh after a scare they don't remember well. The banner in the rotunda hung straight. The doors behaved. The House had that new bass note under everything, the one that meant rules had settled in the bones.

Sia stood at the welcome desk with her umbrella leaned against her leg and tried on the idea that this was normal. She could get used to normal if it looked like this. Eric was arguing about muffin flavors with a bus driver and losing on purpose. Mia had started a polite playlist so Mariah could rest her voice. Truth patrolled like a tiny professional, tail tucked in a serious

"

curve, eyes doing a loop of the room every ten seconds. When Truth passed the plaque she sat for a heartbeat, then continued, as if checking that the words were still there.

Kaelan came out of the office with a flat, pastel green envelope pinched between two fingers. Vellum, not paper, twisted from fallen leaves. The seal was opaque leaf green wax stamped with a sigil that made Sia's skin tingle before her brain caught up. It wasn't the Summer Lady's mark. The crown points were different, the leaves deeper cut. The Summer Queen.

"You've got mail," Kaelan said, like this was a normal sentence and not the opening to a life pivot.

Sia wiped her palm on her jeans and took the envelope. It had weight. She broke the wax with her thumbnail, careful not to tear the crest, and slid the letter free.

The handwriting had the neat precision of a person who'd been writing the same way for a thousand years. The language rode right on the line between old and simple. She could hear Kaelan in the back of her head, reminding her to read every word and stop on the ones that matter.

To the Dreamer who keeps House at the Sanctuary,

We recognize your establishment and the law you have spoken.

Present yourself at our Court for acknowledgment before both Seasons.

Do so by the next cross-quarter day.

Enter with an escort we name as welcome, bring a guest-gift,

> *and declare three small boons you will trade in courtesy.*
> *Summer guarantees safe passage from the Border to our*
> *hall.*
>
> *We will not take your law. We will hear it.*

The signature wasn't a name so much as a style of pressure. When she traced it with her eyes, the wax seal warmed like a coin found in sunlight.

Sia read it twice, then a third time. The words didn't change. Good. She didn't want them to.

"Summer Queen," she said. "Not the Lady."

Kaelan nodded, mouth curved in that careful way she had when the sacred and the practical shook hands. "This is formal. It's not flattery. Recognition means your rules touched the Border. The Courts don't like to pretend they don't notice the weather."

Sia held the letter so the late sun turned the vellum softer. "Cross-quarter is in three weeks," she said. "We can't show up before we're sure the House won't fall on its face the second I turn my back."

"It won't," Charles said, appearing like the House had rolled him to the right spot. He looked better in daylight. He always did. "You leave when we're ready, not when a letter tells you to sprint. But we should hit their window. It's rude not to."

Sia folded the letter and slid it back into the envelope. "Terms are easy enough. Escort named by Summer, a guest-gift, three small boons for courtesy." She looked at Kaelan. "I'm not going alone."

"You're not," Kaelan said. "I'll escort you. Summer knows my name and I know theirs. I'll walk you in and out and cut any strings you don't see." She said it like directions, not drama. "We'll do etiquette on the walk over so you don't have to pretend you learned it in a dream."

"What do I bring as a gift," Sia asked. "A baked good that won't go stale in a different air pressure."

"Summer respects food and art," Kaelan said. "Bring something that says who you are. A small frame with your map of the Garden would work. Or a song, but only if you want to sing it. Also a physical thing they can hold so the gesture doesn't float."

"I'll do the map," Sia said, relief unclenching something under her ribs. "And the boons. Three. Small. Useful but not binding."

Kaelan ticked them off on her fingers. "You can offer a day of hospitality for an envoy who behaves. You can offer clear passage from our border to the front steps for one ceremony day a year. You can offer to hear a complaint and relay it to me and Charles without promising judgment. Say them plainly. Summer likes plain when it smells like confidence."

Sia grinned despite herself. "You should have been a lawyer."

"I am," Kaelan said. "Just the kind that uses shrines."

Charles had a hand on his phone, likely reading the board through it, and another on the desk like he was checking the pulse of the building itself. "We'll handle the House," he said. "Eric and Mia hold systems and calm. Mariah sets music hours. Truth keeps halls. I'll be on the board. We'll rotate sleep like adults."

Truth, hearing her name, trotted over and touched Sia's knee with her nose. Sia scratched her under the chin. "You're promoted again," she said. "Senior Temple Dog."

Truth looked as if she would accept the title for a small fee of treats. Kaelan made a note with her face. Treats would happen.

Sia stepped to the plaque and set her palm under the line that said The House enforces this rule. The metal felt cool and ordinary. She didn't need ceremonial words. She needed the building to log the change.

"House," she said. "Sanctuary holds under the Accords while I'm away. The demon ban stands. Travel stays open for guests and staff."

The room changed in that quiet click she'd come to trust. Charles nodded, eyes distant for a second, then focused on her again. "Logged," he said. "We'll be fine."

Guests moved through the lobby in polite lines. A woman stopped to thank Sia for "making the lobby feel like Sunday morning." Sia managed to say, "That's the goal," without turning red. It landed harder than a medal would have.

Marcus crossed the floor with a stack of clean towels and a face that didn't hide much. He set the towels on the bench, glanced at the envelope in Sia's hand, then at the front doors. He didn't speak in front of everyone. He didn't have to. Kaelan saw the question sit between his shoulders.

Sia stepped close and touched his elbow. "Walk with me," she said.

They took the side hall that led toward the education rooms, where the light fell thin and the air smelled like dust and markers. Truth started to follow, then read the moment and stayed put, sitting on her patch of sunlight like a good boss. Kaelan turned away and checked the desk log even though she didn't need to. Privacy was a real thing or it was nothing.

The talk didn't carry, which was the point. Sia came back first, envelope tucked into her jacket, eyes steadier. Marcus followed a breath later, jaw set in a way that didn't mean anger. It meant he'd picked an answer. He didn't announce it. He stood beside Sia like he'd always stood there and gave Kaelan a look that said, don't worry about me. She wasn't going to, but it helped.

"Okay," Sia said to the room, and also to herself. "We'll do this without making it a parade."

"Parades are for politicians," Eric said, sliding by to restock the brochure rack with a new card that said PLEASE DO NOT FEED THE DOORS. He held it up for approval. Sia snorted. Mia gave him a thumbs up. Mariah laughed out loud and then coughed because her throat finally remembered it was a throat.

Charles checked his watch. "You should go see the steps," he said. "The Border is paying attention. It's polite to nod back."

Sia and Kaelan walked to the doors. The wood of the frame felt warm from the sun and from the House's low hum. The threshold had a visible line now if you knew how to look sideways. Outside, the street was itself. Cars. Shoes. A child in a superhero cape who had very strong opinions about the science gift shop. But the edges had changed. The Sanctuary field wrapped porch frames in quiet. It ticked along the lampposts and settled into shop doors without asking permission because the doors liked it.

Kaelan pushed the door open with two fingers. Air rolled in, soft and green under the city smell, clover and warm stone. The hair on Sia's arms lifted and then calmed. She could taste clean heat on the back of her tongue, the way air tastes near a river.

Across the street, when she let her gaze slide off-center, a thin seam showed a road that wasn't asphalt. It ran in a gentle curve between trees that hadn't been planted by anyone she knew. Nothing came through. It waited. The wax seal in her pocket warmed again without burning.

Kaelan stood close enough that their sleeves brushed. "Protocol," she said, voice low. "You don't offer your name twice. You don't eat anything until it's offered to all. You don't promise what you don't want to lose. If a bargain starts to smell like a trap, we step back and call it a story for another day. Summer respects clear lines."

Sia nodded. "Guest-gift is the map," she said. "Boons are small and clean. Escort is you."

"And me," Kaelan said. "If they send a herald, we accept the banner for the road and make sure it doesn't try to stay when we come back."

Sia took one breath on Mia's count even though Mia was across the room. Four in. Six out. The House felt like it would stand without her for a week. Charles had the board. Eric had the checklists. Mariah had the songs. Mia had the calm. Kaelan had the edges. Truth had the halls. Marcus had the... Marcus would do what Marcus did. She didn't need to make a speech about it.

She turned back to the lobby for a second and lifted her voice enough to carry without bouncing. "Travel stays open. Demon ban stands. Sanctuary holds. If you need me, call the blue button. If I don't pick up, call Eric. If neither of us pick up, tell Charles and stand on the plaque line. The House will hold you."

Eric saluted with his Sharpie. Mia gave her a thumbs up with a yogurt spoon. Mariah pressed her hand to her heart. Charles nodded once as if someone had set a clock correctly. Marcus didn't smile. He didn't need to. Truth trotted over, sat at Sia's feet, and looked up with eyes that said, I approve this mission but also please return.

Sia rubbed the top of Truth's head. "Keep the lobby safe," she said.

Truth wagged once, very solemn, and stayed.

Guests watched without knowing they were watching. A little boy whispered, "Are you going on an adventure," in the stage whisper of small children everywhere.

"Work trip," Sia said, and that got a grin from his mom.

Kaelan touched the door frame the way a person touches a forehead in blessing. "Ready," she asked.

"Yeah," Sia said. She lifted her umbrella, not like a weapon, like a walking stick that belonged to her hand. The wax seal warmed one more time. The green seam across the street held steady. The House behind her hummed the bass note of a promise it had made to itself.

"Demons remain not welcome," she told the building, clear and simple. "Travel stands open under the Accords."

The lobby answered with that quiet click. She felt it in her shoes. She felt it in the rail under her palm.

"Let's go meet a Queen," Kaelan said.

They stepped onto the top stair. Sun lit the plaque inside. The small staff card under the desk caught a gleam of light and looked old already, which was exactly what Eric wanted. The air on the steps tasted like clover. A faint shimmer hung across the street if you looked wrong on purpose. It was an invitation, not a trap.

Sia took the first step. Truth sat like a statue and wagged once, then twice, blessing the road with dog approval. The door behind them stayed open just enough to be friendly, then closed with good manners as they reached the sidewalk.

The Sanctuary held. The town learned. The road waited. Sia kept walking.

www.ingramcontent.com/pod-product-compliance
Lightning Source LLC
Chambersburg PA
CBHW020514110726
47899CB00004B/1117